To Mjoey
Stanton

Sword of the Wild Rose

Blessings
Ruth C. Glynn

Sword of the Wild Rose

Ruth Carmichael Ellinger

AMBASSADOR INTERNATIONAL
GREENVILLE, SOUTH CAROLINA & BELFAST, NORTHERN IRELAND

Sword of the Wild Rose

© 2010 Ruth Carmichael Ellinger
All rights reserved

Printed in the United States of America

ISBN: 978-1-935507-15-4

Cover Design & Page Layout by David Siglin of A&E Media
Cover Art by Debra Bryant

AMBASSADOR INTERNATIONAL
Emerald House
427 Wade Hampton Blvd.
Greenville, SC 29609, USA
www.ambassador-international.com

AMBASSADOR BOOKS
The Mount
2 Woodstock Link
Belfast, BT6 8DD, Northern Ireland, UK
www.ambassador-international.com

The colophon is a trademark of Ambassador

Dedication

To my son, James Ellinger
Who travels the path of our colorful ancestors
And to my brothers, Art and James Carmichael
Of whom it is said
The spirit of the wild rose rests upon them

Acknowledgements

Weaving a tale of fiction around actual historic fact is, for any storyteller, an arduous undertaking. I began this project almost two years ago after my readers suggested that I write Derick's story, a tale based on my own patriot ancestry. Without the help and encouragement of the following people, I might still be stuck on the battlefield at Bushy Run, my first research trip for the opening scenes of *Sword of the Wild Rose*.

At every turn of events, I was challenged by my two male protagonists who did not think or react as I did, especially in matters of military significance and in matters of the heart. To clear my mind of those lurking feminine responses, I camped out on Mars where the Alpha males residing there adjusted my thinking.

Those who offered valuable input were: J. David Knepper, who offered his military expertise and Dave Chagnon, (Clan Davidson's Sennachie, USA) the man who keeps me straight on all things Scottish, and finally, to my son, James, I owe thanks for his enthusiastic support of this project.

I express my appreciation to the staff at the beautifully restored Handley Library in Winchester VA. They offered invaluable resources and supplied information on the life of Daniel Morgan, the colorful hero of Frederick County VA. Since my desire was to portray the General in his authentic setting, George Schember, Winchester's distinguished historian and president of the Winchester/Frederick County Historical Society, volunteered his time to review this work of fiction based on historic fact. George and his lovely wife, Jeanne, invited me to their beautiful home in Winchester, the same historic home where Daniel Morgan passed away in 1802. What a treasure!

Once again, my editor, Adele Brinkley, waded through my manuscript with dogged determination despite the liberal use of Gaelic language phrases and Colonial speech. When I became lost in story, Adele brought me back to the nuts and bolts of the King's English.

Many thanks to my publisher, Ambassador International, and to Tim Lowry, who offered continual support during this writing project. Over the years, I have come to value our friendship and to appreciate the common goals we share as writer and publisher. The *Wildrose* series has been a faith-journey with many unexpected surprises along the way.

Lastly, I thank my best friend, Wright—husband, pastor, and soul mate, the one who offers me his constant encouragement and does not complain about the many sandwich suppers when I am writing.

Numerous thanks and God bless all of you; *Go dtuga dIa ecch dutt as an tobar nach dtrann.*

(May God give you a drink from the well that never runs dry)

Note to the Reader

Sword of the Wild Rose is a prequel to the two previous novels in this series, *The Wild Rose of Lancaster,* and *Wild Rose of Promise*. Due to the many requests for this prequel, I have endeavored to weave Derick Davidson's story into the events leading up to the American Revolution and my patriot ancestors' involvement during those turbulent times when revolution was a radical idea.

The founding fathers of the United Stares of America believed that only a virtuous people grounded in faith in God could ever hope to remain free. Only a moral nation can abide by the United States Constitution, a document dreamed of by those who understood oppression, fashioned by those who honored God, and upheld by those who valued freedom more than life itself. *This is their story.*

Unfortunately, there was little information on which to base Derick's story. I have only a patchwork image of his actual life, which I gleaned from the scanty details of my own personal research. He left no personal journals, no letters, and only a small amount of recorded history. This story, therefore, is a work of fiction pieced together into what I feel is a believable tale of the Scot-Irish involvement in the events preceding the War for Independence.

I do know that several times during the course of those unsettling years, the paths of my patriot ancestors crossed and re-crossed during the Battle of Point Pleasant, Bunker Hill, Ticonderoga, and Saratoga.

Isaac Zane, known as *The White Eagle* by the Wyandot Indians who captured him, *is not the same* Isaac Zane who served as Justice of Frederick County, 1772, and the Virginia House of Burgesses in 1775, and who established the Marlboro Iron Works. The two Isaacs were first cousins.

Isaac Zane in my story is the same Zane in the historical novels written by author, Zane Grey, and was brother to Ebenezer, Silas, and Jonathan, men who blazed a trail known as "Zane's Trace," into the Ohio wilderness. This Isaac Zane was indeed captured by the Wyandots at the age of nine. He later married Tarhe's daughter, Myeerah. This is a well-documented love story, dear to the heart of every Ohioan and well worth researching. Isaac and Myeerah lived and died in Logan County Ohio near the town of Zanesfield.

In the generations following the War for Independence, descendants of two Scottish clans, the Carmichaels and Davidsons, united to produce my father's generation. The "Bear Hunter," John Cutright, was my maternal patriot ancestor whose descendants married into the Carmichael-Davidson lineage to further an ongoing legacy to their name. The incredible life of the *Bear Hunter*... well, that's another story for another time.

My portrayal of General Daniel Morgan, the Revolutionary War Rifleman and hero of Saratoga, is as accurate as the records I have researched, which is to say, that historic accounts may vary, but I have endeavored to be true to Morgan's unique character. The life of Daniel and Abigail Morgan is a human saga in Colonial life: a couple dedicated to American independence and to each other despite their human foibles. Morgan's rough yet honest character intrigued me so I included him in this tale.

Note to the Reader

Any discrepancy in historical fact is the author's fallibility and no reflection on the historian. As I began my research on military engagements in early American history, I chose to leave such arduous detailed writing to experts in that field, to those who understand the methods and intricacies of warfare. I'll write my tale between the cracks of the rifle and the booms of the cannon. As always, I count on my readers to be forgiving.

In writing this historical series, my purpose is to show God's Sovereignty in our lives and in the lives of our ancestors, those generations who participated in the national and world events that have at times, altered the course of history. Despite the undeniable oppression caused by sinful man, God remains faithful, waiting for a lost world to turn to Him. God's love story has been divinely recorded in a wee book called the Bible, but I am the storyteller who holds a different pen.

—The Author, *Ruth Carmichael Ellinger*

Legacy of the Scots

"The Scottish people have always been independent, individualistic, awkward if you like- and have long memories. Their land is sufficiently dramatic in itself. There is scarcely a yard of the country without its story to tell, of heroism and treachery, of warfare or worship, of flourish or folly or heartbreak - for the Scots never did anything by half."
—*Nigel Tranter*, 1909 – 2000, Author of Scottish Historical novels

For that is the mark of the Scots of all classes: that he stands in an attitude towards the past unthinkable to Englishmen, and remembers and cherishes the memory of his forebears, good or bad; and there burns alive in him a sense of identity with the dead even to the twentieth generation.
—*Robert Louis Stevenson*, 1850 – 1894

Prologue

*They longed for a better country, that is, a heavenly one.
That is why God is not ashamed to be called their God. Heb 11:16*

SCOTLAND — 1772

Derick stood on the wind-swept moor above the village, his tartan plaid whipping around him, enveloping him like a great green shroud. He could see the ships in the distance, their white sails settling in Moray Firth like immense white gulls bobbing on the surface of the blue water. Various ships of commerce, royal ships of war, and smaller privateers were willing to be hired if the price was right.

He turned to see Doran hurrying down the footpath toward him, her dark hair flying loose in the wind, a tiny bundle tucked under one arm.

"Derick," she cried breathlessly, "I thought I would find ye here. I have been searching for ye. They are ready, waiting for ye to meet them at the point. They will take ye to the ship from there." She paused and turned away, her eyes filling with sudden tears. When the bundle moved slightly, she relaxed her confining grip on the wee babe cradled in her arm.

"I know, lass," he answered looking across the moor, not wanting to meet her eyes. "I must go. It's a great weight on me heart, to be sure, a terrible sadness to bear. I was just a lookin' over the green moorland, watchin' the rolling of the sea, listening for the whistle of the stag...tryin' to remember...to keep her in me mind. Like as not, I'll not see her resting place again, nor the likes of bonny Scotland—not in this life."

"No, Derick, don't say it! Ye will come back to Scotland someday. This terrible disposition can't last forever. The King has promised us lands along the southern coast, on the western shore. Ye *can* return to Scotland, Derick. It's not too late to change your mind—even now. The ship can wait."

"Lands along the western coast? Can we graze our sheep there, our cattle? Can we till the rocks? Can we arm ourselves, protect our homes? Nay, we cannot. That coast is not a habitation, Doran. It's a prison! We have been driven from our good lands and I, for one, will not abide it. I want more for me sons, more for ye, Doran. I will find a new homeland, and God willing, it will be ours forever. No one will take it from us, so help me God!"

Seeing her distress, Derick softened. "There now, Doran, don't be so grieved, lass. I will send for ye and the bairns by and by." He looked at his twin sister with great sadness, his piercing blue eyes searching her grief-stricken face now streaming unashamedly with tears. He wrapped his comforting arms around her, and for the first time since the death of his wife, he allowed the tears to come. They came in great shuddering gasps, his powerful body racked with the fierceness of his emotion. Doran wept with him, and the wee babe wept too, as if sensing their despair.

"It's late, lass. I must not keep them waiting." Derick lifted the babe from her arms and removed the cloth from around the tiny face. Blue eyes stared back at him and a tiny fist reached from beneath the blanket to hold tightly to Derick's finger as though to keep him there.

Doran wept as Derick kissed his babe with a gentleness odd to a man of such great size and strength. He stared long at the rounded features of the babe, looking into the clear eyes staring back with curious boldness. A slight smile curved the corners of Derick's mouth.

"Aye, laddie, remember, ye are a Davidson and a Scotsman. One day, we shall raise our fist to the arrogant King George in one final glorious battle for freedom. But until that day, laddie, remember Scotland, remember your father, and that ye are a free man—a Davidson."

He kissed Doran and placed the babe in her arms. "Be careful of the bairns, lass. I know ye will. Duncan and Margaret will help ye. He has promised. He is doing all he can to secure his own lands." He looked away over the rolling sea.

"If I do not return by and by, or if some mischief befalls me, remember me to wee William. Tell him for me..." he paused, drawing a shuddering breath. "Tell him that I loved his mother, aye, loved all me bairns."

He turned away, not looking back, his plaid billowing in the chill misty wind while his claymore slapped lightly at his side. He followed the worn footpath to the sea and to the ship waiting in the cove.

Chapter 1

Bushy Run

He who keeps not his arms in time of peace
Will have none in time of war

From the dense undergrowth in the forest, the screams of a captured Royal American soldier rose above the whoops of Chief Pontiac's warriors, piercing the summer night with an unearthly chill. "Oh God," prayed Colonel Henry Bouquet in angry protest, "let him die quickly."

He eased himself onto the hard, uneven ground and leaned wearily against an oak tree for support. Fifty of his men were missing or dead. His troops had retreated to this raised clearing while the murderous Indians searched through the thick tangle of underbrush for injured survivors. Wild yelps of triumph erupted from the dark cover of the forest as another wounded soldier was discovered. The ambush had been an overall surprise.

The Colonel pulled pen and paper from his military field satchel and began to compose a letter, his last message to his commanding officer, General Jeffery Amherst. As he wrote, he glanced up repeatedly, scanning the lines of battle, barely visible in the waning light at the edge of the forest. His dark eyes strained to see through the gathering mist of the muggy August evening. On the top upper right hand corner of his missive, he wrote the date and place: *August 5, 1763, Bushy Run Station.* He wrote in a steady hand, hastily penning his thoughts, unwelcome thoughts, skirting on the edge of unreality.

He called to his aide who stood nearby holding a shaded lantern. "Schmidt, find Major Campbell if you can, and if you cannot find him, bring Sergeant MacWilliam, Robert Kirkwood—any of the Highland officers you can find. Bring them here at once." The aide saluted mechanically. He was exhausted, and his shoulders sagged from strain and fatigue. Holding the lantern before him, he moved quietly into the starlit night, his heavy musket cradled in the crook of his free arm.

Resting against the oak, Colonel Bouquet sighed deeply. His muscles ached with weariness, while his mind raced on tirelessly, rehearsing the events of this horrific day over and over again. How could he have brought his troops into this terrible trap? When the army reached Bedford, he had signed on thirty additional veteran frontiersmen, certain the experienced scouts would alert his military relief party to a possible ambush. He had expected harassment from the Indians at Turtle Creek, but not this soon and not by so many.

He should have guessed what was coming. He shook his head in consternation. No! He should have known that the recently allied tribes of 500 Indians would devise a plan to cut off the rear guard, trapping his army between two contingents of hostiles. During the seven hours of intense battle, he had spotted Ottawa, Huron, Delaware, Mingo, and Shawnee in company with smaller groups from other tribes.

Now, Bouquet and his men were between Indians besieging Fort Pitt to the west and the confederated forces of Chief Pontiac to the east. Pontiac was the fierce and influential Ottawa Chieftain who had united the Indians in a vicious campaign against the frontier settlers. There was no escape. Dawn would bring certain death or worse—hideous torture at the hands of the merciless natives. The Colonial army faced an adversary that operated covertly, using existing terrain to every advantage, and intimidating their enemies with ostensible savagery.

All day long, Bouquet's combined army of 400 Royal American soldiers, grizzled frontiersmen, and Scottish Highlanders had continuously repulsed the hordes of incensed and screaming Indians. Surrounded on a raised clearing called Edge Hill, the army's position was at a dismal disadvantage, surrounded by thick forests with no room for a battle strategy.

Although the army was on a slightly higher elevation, they had little or no cover from sniper fire, a small amount of food, and no fresh water to slake their thirst. The extreme heat of the sweltering August day had sapped the army's strength and they were exhausted and weary to the bone. They were visibly losing heart.

This catastrophic situation would cost Bouquet's men their lives. For the hundredth time that day, Bouquet felt a tragic sense of disappointment in his inability to command this critical mission and an acute grief for the men he had come to know and respect. The sudden and unexpected attack that had overtaken his army along the Forbes road as they journeyed westward to relieve Fort Pitt, not only meant certain death for his own troops but also jeopardized the lives of those who waited expectantly at the fort. The besieged settlers had fled to the fort for protection and were counting on the army to rescue them from the marauding Indians.

Although his men never saw a flicker of regret in his dark eyes, his remorse was palpable, like a sharp stabbing pain gnawing at his chest. The ambush at Bushy Run was too much like Braddock's defeat all over again; only this time, it was his turn to taste the bitter gall of failure. Not far away from Bushy Run, the bones of Braddock's army lay bleaching in the summer sun, dug from their shallow graves by the wild beasts of the forest. Braddock himself was buried along the road of retreat, not far from the disastrous battle.

This current military debacle would read as *Bouquet's Defeat* in the annuals of history, Bouquet thought sardonically, but he had no time to dwell on the events of the past ten hours. He must focus on the present. He continued to write his missive, dismissing all but the present situation and considering any resolution that came to mind for this present predicament.

From his location at one end of the clearing, Bouquet could see the faint outline of the flour-bag barricade at the far side of the gentle slope. His troops had hastily assembled the makeshift fortification using provisions from the wagon convoy. The food supplies were designated for the refugees at Fort Pitt in addition to his own troops, but now the flour bags were in use as a redoubt around the natural hollow on top of the clearing. This afforded some protection, but the morning would bring a renewed round of attacks and would surely break through the improvised fortification and penetrate the army's position. His troops could not withstand another day of such fierce fighting without adequate provisions. There appeared to be no way of escape for the army, now hemmed in on all sides by the Indians.

As Bouquet wrote his final letter, he expressed this conviction to General Amherst, explaining that neither he nor his men would survive the battle that would commence at first light. He ended the communication with his regret over the insurmountable difficulties he and his troops faced and with his fond expression of admiration for his officers and men. He praised their cool and steady behavior under such deplorable conditions. Placing the communication into his field satchel, Bouquet hoped his scouts would successfully slip through the lines before daybreak with his last message for General Amherst.

Sniper fire erupted from the forest, jerking Bouquet back to the present, tormenting his mind with troubled thoughts, and reminding him of the great responsibility that lay like a lead weight on his shoulders. He shook himself, ignoring the deep ache of loneliness, the tragedy of his predicament, and the solemn charge of his office. Such reflection was too terrible to consider at such a time. He must maintain a clear and rational mind. His men looked to him as their leader, and with assistance from the Almighty God; he would not fail them now. He would rally them to face the battle, to face death if necessary, and he would fight with courage and honor until the end.

At forty-four, Bouquet was at the height of his military career. A Swiss-born professional military officer from a military family, he had entered the armed forces at age seventeen. Fluent in English, German, and French, he was offered a commission in the British army, a commission taking him to the American Colonies to maintain the victory over the French and to control the Indian uprisings on the northwest frontier. Until this present moment, he had been highly successful in this venture. He had learned Indian warfare by carefully observing the skilled frontiersmen and the native-born bordermen who understood the ways of the various Indian tribes.

Bouquet became skilled at woodland survival and in the art of wilderness warfare. His manner was natural and unaffected. He was a handsome man, well built and aristocratic in bearing. The young colonel was admired and respected by his colleagues as courageous and honorable, yet he fit naturally into the genteel society of the elite of New York and Philadelphia.

Watching cautiously from his position beneath the oak tree, Bouquet caught sight of four figures gliding smoothly along the faint outline of the flour-bag barricades at the far end of the clearing. They were momentarily silhouetted against the dimly lit night sky. The shadowy figures ran lightly over the rough terrain toward the tree where Bouquet rested in the faint moonlight.

Major Campbell and his men came into view, their dark tartan kilts distinguishing them as Scots from the 77th Regiment of Foot, the Scottish Highlanders. Two of the men were from the 42nd Regiment of Foot, the Black Watch. Veterans of wilderness warfare, the 77th had been with General John Forbes during the capture of Fort Duquesne, renamed Fort Pitt by the British, and strategically located on the forks of the Ohio River at the point where the Allegheny and Monongahela Rivers met to form the mighty Ohio River. Whoever controlled this great waterway bordering the Ohio country controlled further movement into the Northwest Territories and the rich and fertile Ohio Valley.

Colonel Henry Bouquet rose to his feet as the Highlanders approached. When the men saluted their leader, Bouquet returned their salutes. The acknowledgement of respect and submission seemed frivolous at such a time, but it was the expression of years of training and discipline. He understood their adherence to regulations and appreciated the Highlanders for their strict observance of protocol, even under great duress and difficulty.

"Major Campbell," Bouquet asked matter-of-factly, "how many men have you lost?"

Campbell was a large brawny man with piercing black eyes and a closely cropped black beard. He was an able leader, fearless and bold in battle, and Bouquet knew he would dispatch countless Indians to the happy hunting ground before the next day had ended. The Major smelled of sweat and blood and the Colonel noticed a flesh wound oozing blood along the calf of his right leg. However, the Major seemed unaware of his wound.

"Four be dead and two missing," answered the Major. "Me lads did their best to find Graham and MacKay, Colonel, but they are somewhere in the forest, and God knows we can't help them now, poor lads." Sergeant MacWilliam and Lieutenant Davidson looked toward the forest where intermittent gunfire continued to harass the army. Private Robert Kirkwood of the 42nd Highland Regiment of the Black Watch and the MacWilliam lads had been with the Forbes expedition in '58. Colonel Bouquet knew he could count on their instincts in such extreme situations, and wanted to hear from the Highlanders before he summoned the rest of his officers from the Royal Americans and the recently recruited frontiersmen. Robert Kirkwood had been captured by the Indians at Fort Duquesne and after his escape, he proved to be an able interpreter of Indian activities.

"At your ease, men," said the Colonel. He was always amazed at the arsenal the Highlanders carried on their bodies and in such a relaxed fashion. Armed to the teeth, as was their customary habit, they carried an army issue Brown Bess musket and bayonet, a razor-sharp dirk, a vicious battleaxe, and a highland pistol strapped to their belts. A claymore broadsword hung across their backs. The claymore was preferred to the bayonet for close encounters or hand-to-hand fighting.

The Highlanders were skilled with the use of this brutal and formidable weapon, the pride and terror of their native land. In battle, these men of the Black Watch were fierce and wild, perhaps more so than the Indians they were fighting. Unafraid and with centuries of experience in guerilla warfare bred into their race, they would rise to the occasion, do whatever Bouquet commanded, and fight with every ounce of courage and strength to the very end. Of this, Colonel Bouquet was confident.

"You understand the seriousness of our predicament, Major Campbell?"

"Aye, I do."

"Do you have any suggestions?" the Colonel queried.

After a few moments, Major Campbell rubbed his beard and spoke. "Have ye a map, Colonel?"

Bouquet pulled a map from his field satchel and the men squatted on the ground while the Colonel spread the map and his aide held the lamp above them.

"We are here," the Colonel said, pointing to a barely visible area on the primitive map, "about a mile from Bushy Run Station. As you can see, we are surrounded by forest on all sides with no clear avenue of retreat. The Indians have blocked off the only road. We will have to make a stand."

Unconsciously, Bouquet sighed. "I want you to prepare your men for the battle that will commence at first light." He paused and looked into the faces of men who had fought beside him, loyal soldiers who had served him without complaint. The Highlanders did not blink an eye and accepted this order as normal procedure. "You understand," continued the Colonel with a steady voice, "we will probably lose this battle. We are outmatched and outmaneuvered with no water or food. This unforeseen attack has left us in an unfortunate position with no clear way of retreat. We cannot maneuver or attempt a battle formation among such dense forest and brush."

Thinking of possible alternatives to this grim prophecy, the Highlanders looked at one another. After a few moments, Lieutenant Donald Davidson spoke. "With all due respect, sir," said the Lieutenant with a lift to his broad shoulders, "we can gie the reddies the Hielan charge. Aye, twill be a wee bit irregular, to be certain, but satisfying indeed if it's to be our last fight."

Major Campbell smiled wryly, showing even white teeth. "Aye, sir, the lad is right," agreed the Major. "Me lads can give those devils a wee dram of their own medicine—if ye will permit that is." Major Campbell took out his dirk and drew some sketches in the dust. "Allow me to show ye what me lads can do in this situation," he said pointing to his drawing.

Colonel Bouquet looked at the Highlanders for a long moment and then at the crudely drawn battle plan Major Campbell had sketched in the dirt. Bouquet turned his map over and began to draw another sketch of their present position. An idea was forming in his mind, a plan that might give them some hope for escape. With the help of the Almighty, it might work, and the Highlanders would play a significant role in the success or failure of this battle strategy.

All through the stifling August night, Bouquet consulted with his officers, walking about the camp and preparing his troops for the coming battle. Resting in shifts, the men took turns at the watch, cleaning and polishing their weapons, waiting for dawn. The 77th Highlanders and remnants of the 42nd were in constant communication as they prepared for the impending conflict, going over the battle plan until every soldier knew exactly what to do. The timing for their part in the encounter was crucial, and courage and control was absolutely essential if they were to carry out the plan Bouquet had perfected into a well ordered military maneuver. They had one chance to get it right. They must not fail.

Major Campbell returned from giving last minute instructions to his lads and then sat on a fallen log where Lieutenant Davidson was sharpening his sword. "So ye volunteered for the first surge at daybreak, Lieutenant Davidson?"

"Aye, that I did."

Major Campbell paused, waiting, but the Lieutenant said no more. "It'll be a bloody battle, that's certain," the Major added. "Will ye leave a word with the militia scouts? They'll be a slippin' out before daybreak, and if God be with them, they'll get back to General Amherst."

Lieutenant Davidson continued to sharpen his sword with smooth, vigorous strokes. "Nay, I think not, Major." Donald Davidson tested the edge of his sword with the tips of his fingers. He seemed satisfied with the result. "If I be a missin' in the log books of the 42nd, by and by, they'll tell me family in Cromarty. The clan knows me purpose here. I'll not burden the scouts with takin' me last farewell. You can tell 'em for me, Major. If I fall in the battle, tell 'em me last thoughts were of me home and of me brother's lads, the ones I left behind. Tell 'em not to forget me, nor Culloden Moor, and the Davidsons who died there—all me clansmen."

A dark cloud passed over the Major's countenance as he shook his head at the irony of their present predicament. "Well, Lieutenant, I may not be around meself to recollect those sentiments, but if I survive, I'll tell 'em for ye." Campbell looked up at the celestial canopy of stars watching the goings on of the human race in a ceaseless vigil high above the earth.

"What made ye join up with His Majesty's troops, Davidson?" queried the Major. Somehow, speaking of the deeply personal motives bringing both men to this fateful night seemed oddly significant. "To save your lands perchance?"

"Aye, among other things," the Lieutenant answered. "Let's just say I was *pressed* into service by His Majesty's timely persuasion, and, aye, to save me lands," he said with a sidelong glance at the Major. "I once loved a bonny lass, but she could never be mine, so I joined the Black Watch with others of our clan. Of course," he added with a short laugh, "I wanted to keep me claymore."

Major Campbell's eyes crinkled at the corners and he laughed softly, his great shoulders shaking with understanding. "Aye, a Highlander without a claymore is like a man without eyes." He paused, unsheathed his own dirk and stone, and considered the Lieutenant who appeared undisturbed over their dire predicament and the coming battle.

Lieutenant Davidson had volunteered for the first significant phase of the battle plan, the most dangerous and deadly stage of the conflict. The sharp shooting riflemen would try to cover the Highlanders rush with their long barreled rifles, a firearm far more accurate than the Brown Bess muskets carried by the regular army. The frontiersmen and riflemen used their own grooved rifles and brought their own bullet molds with them on the march.

"Between ye and me," Major Campbell said to Lieutenant Davidson, "if I live through this battle, I will go home when me time is up." His own words sounded sweet to his ears, bringing to mind images of Loch Fynne along the westerns shores of Argyll, the lands of his fathers, land that he loved. He could almost smell the salt air and see Inveraray Castle where it stood shrouded in the morning mist. Yes, if he lived through this battle, he would go home to Argyll and his family.

"Sounds like a sweet dream to me, Major. I will have no home to go to if I leave His Majesty's service," Davidson replied, "but if I stay with the Highlanders and swear allegiance to King and country, me brother and three nephews, Duncan, Daniel, and Derick, will be secure, and our lands will be spared, or should I say, 'improved and restored', so says the King. This is much to hope for, aye? It is for the lads, I fight. Brave lads they be, like their Da'."

"And you believe the King will keep his word?" grunted the Major.

"I must believe in something," Davidson said looking toward the heavens and the canopy of stars shedding a pale light in the night sky. "Freedom is costly, aye, and difficult to obtain, as we Scots know so well. It is very precious. The blood of men is the price we pay for freedom, and war is the means of purchase, Major. There is no other way. It has always been so, like a penance for Adam's sin, aye, it seems so. There is never an end."

Davidson brought out his dirk and slid the edge of the blade along the sharpening iron. "I have no wife, no bairns, and if I die, few will mourn me, but if I live to see the hinner end of this war, I will stay here with the American Patriots. Like meself, they seek freedom." He pointed his dirk toward the rough and bearded men crouching around a fire several yards away. "I will live as do the longhunters."

The Major chuckled softly at his remark, noting the group of buckskin-clad frontiersmen who were molding bullets over a low fire. "Will be a lonely life, that," Campbell said, nodding in the direction of the frontiersmen. "The longhunters are an extraordinary breed of men, not like the common settler, aye? They roam about, hunting, exploring, and fighting Indians."

"Well, I be a lonely man, Major, a displaced warrior, just like the Indians, a strange man with no place to call home." Davidson looked at the older man and smiled. "Solitude and freedom go hand in hand. I will be free as the longhunters and explore this great land until I find a home, a place where me weary soul can rest, where I can hear the song of the Highlands in me heart and the voice of God blowing in the wind. That will be me home. Nay, Major Campbell," he said shaking his head, "I will not return to Scotland."

The MacWilliam lads arrived, slipping silently among the troops with final orders from Colonel Bouquet. Taking their positions, the Highlanders made ready for the signal that would determine the outcome of this deadly drama. A faint light spread a thin, gray line across the eastern horizon, announcing the approach of dawn. In the forest, war like shrieks and the sporadic firing of guns became more frequent as the Indian camp rallied itself in preparation for what they believed would be the final slaughter of the Colonial army.

"I'll see ye at the back o' three," Major Campbell said to his Lieutenant.

Donald Davidson saluted his superior and said, "Aye, Major, at the back o' three."

Despite objections from his officers to stay clear of the main lines of conflict, Colonel Bouquet took his position at the battlefront along with the 60th Regiment of Light Infantry. He ordered the drums, the pipes, and the standards brought to the top of the rise where all could hear and see the position of the final encounter with Pontiac's warriors. His men were ready, deathly calm and determined, knowing this engagement would be skin for skin. Several of the scouts had slipped away before dawn, hoping to make it through the enemy lines at some stage of the conflict.

As first light began to illuminate the theatre of action, the frontiersmen, eager for the battle, clenched their knives between their teeth, their rifles ready. Scalp locks swung from their belts as a show of pride and victory over their dreaded enemies. The Indians danced and whooped just outside of musket range, but when one from the war party edged closer to mock the soldiers, a rifleman picked off the painted warrior with a long shot, sending his messenger of hot lead into the midst of the Indian camp. Then the firing of muskets began in earnest. The riflemen remained resolute and unyielding. Barricaded behind the flour-bag redoubt, riflemen fired into the hordes of painted Indians who were creeping closer, edging up the rise, and running from tree to tree while screaming in maniacal frenzy.

Major Campbell and his company of the 77th Highlander Grenadiers formed an extended line, keeping up a heavy fire as troops from the 60th, Royal Americans, and the 42nd Highlanders of the Black Watch took up flanking positions. Volleys from the 77th fired relentlessly, creating a path in the enemy lines but still, the Indians came on, sheltered behind the trees.

The Highlanders who had volunteered for the first surge of the battle, rose from their positions and charged down the hill toward the advancing Indian contingents. The British forces and veteran riflemen scrambled to reload their guns to cover the ongoing charge. Screaming their own Gaelic war cries above those of their savage foes, the Scottish forces rushed toward the advancing Indians, their war cries piercing the morning air.

Highly offended with this clearly futile attempt by the small party of Highlanders to stop their advance, and encouraged by their fellow Indians in the forest who ran to join in the fight, the Indians threw down their muskets and eagerly pressed forward. Seeing only a small troop of Highlanders, they pressed the advantage and continued up the wooded rise. Tomahawks flashed in the sunlight, and knives glimmered as the Highlanders screamed their battle cries and ran down the slope to meet the enemy, dodging trees and leaping over brush and rocks.

The volley of gunfire from the riflemen was intense, filling the air with a thick, smoky haze. Men fell on both sides, their screams rising above the clash of tomahawks and swords. The British troops began to retreat from the field in a somewhat disorderly fashion. Once they were over the crest of the rise, they hid themselves from the battle scene in progress on the slope of Edge Hill.

When the Highlanders began to fall back, the Indians were immediately emboldened by the sight of the Scottish troops in retreat. The Royal Americans and the remainder of the Highland companies were also withdrawing from the fray. Certain now of a swift and immediate victory, the wildly screaming Indians ran in hot pursuit of the retreating army. They called to their comrades who broke cover behind the trees and underbrush to overtake and destroy the remainder of the British force.

When the army had retreated over the rise of Edge Hill, the legendary Highlanders of the Black Watch turned toward the advancing Indians and rushed to the front, while the lines of the 60th and 77th rose from their hiding places, and surrounded the Indians in a deadly trap. Colonel Bouquet watched in amazement as the small troop of Highlanders faced the Indian forces head-on.

Perplexed and surprised, the Indians hesitated, finding themselves surrounded, flanked on all sides by Bouquet's army whom they had assumed fled the field. They now faced a foe more vicious and more deadly than themselves—*warriors of the Black Watch*.

The Highlanders fell upon the allied Indians with great strength and pandemonium broke out among the ranks of bewildered Indians. From the right and left flanks, troops from the 42nd, 60th and 77th sent a concentrated volley of fire into the midst of the throng of Indian warriors now surrounded by Bouquet's army and the charging Highlanders bearing down on them with their deadly claymores and dirks.

When another volley of fire from the flanks dropped scores of Indians, the remaining attackers, confused and not certain how to get out of the ambush, began to break apart. Many had thrown down their muskets after seeing the army retreating and now held only their tomahawks, war clubs, and knives.

Disorganized and bewildered, they fell back, retreating down the slope and away from the deadly fire of the riflemen. Bouquet had deceived the Indian alliance with a well-orchestrated and timely ruse determining the final defeat of Pontiac's rebellion.

The Highlanders continued their pursuit, their wildly swinging claymores cutting down the retreating warriors, leaving them flailing and screaming on the ground. With their tomahawks and knives raised high, the frontiersmen joined in the bloody fray. At the insistence of his officers, Colonel Bouquet had changed from his red military jacket to a buckskin hunting shirt in order to be less visible to the enemy. From his flanking position with the 60th, he watched the ongoing battle on the slope of Edge Hill. He would never forget what he witnessed that August day in 1763.

The Indians fled the field, running in confusion and bewilderment. *What had happened? What had gone wrong?* Their perplexity seemed to slow their progress down the slope and they glanced repeatedly over their shoulders, still disbelieving they had fallen into a snare. The Highlanders swiftly overtook the stragglers and beheaded them with one swift swing of their razor-sharp claymores.

Bouquet shuddered with dread as he recognized the familiar war cries of the Highlanders rising over the noisy clamor of battle. The Highlanders pounced on the enemy with a fierce fury, crying, *"Beware of MacDonell! Beware of his wrath! He knoweth no bounds to his love or his hate!"* Some of the Highlanders of the Black Watch called out in Gaelic, *"Claidheamh-mor, Claidheamh-mor,"* the great sword, the great sword!

As Lieutenant Davidson charged down the slope of Edge Hill, his claymore was knocked from his grasp by a flying tomahawk belonging to a large swarthy Indian who ran toward him screaming his native war cry. Drawing the pistol from his belt, Davidson took quick aim, leveling the gun at the warrior's midsection. He fired. The Indian dropped to the ground, groaned and rolled over, and lay still.

Breathing heavily, Davidson watched the Indian for a moment, and then turned to retrieve his sword. As he leaned over to pick it up, the same dead Indian leapt on him from the rear, closing a sinewy arm around Davidson's throat in a deathlike grip. Struggling desperately to free himself from the Indian's clutches, Davidson fell to the ground, but the warrior fell with him, never loosening his stranglehold on the Highlander's throat.

The two combatants rolled over and over, down the slope until they crashed into a poplar tree. Davidson managed to reach the dirk in his belt just as a veil of blackness gathered before his eyes and threatened to overtake him. With a last valiant effort, he twisted his body and plunged the dirk into his opponent's stomach. He felt the Indian's grip grow slack, his body jerking with pain and shock. Rolling over on top of the warrior, Davidson gasped for air, holding the dirk above his head, ready to plunge it into the heart of his adversary. Steely black eyes stared back at him while the lifeblood poured from his belly.

Clutching his wound, the warrior spoke in English. "Long Knife...no good...shot." Then he smiled faintly before a spasm of convulsions racked his body and his eyes glazed over in death.

A lanky woodsman scout ran to assist in the skirmish, but seeing the Indian had died during the struggle, he drew his knife and lifted the scalp lock in his hand, ready to cut off the tuft of black hair. He knew the Highlanders rarely took an Indian scalp for their war trophies, but the frontiersmen often took scalps without compunction. The Highlanders' idea of booty was weapons, clothing, food, and money.

"Nay, lad," Lieutenant Davidson said extending his hand above the Indian. "This one be mine." The scout nodded and moved on to help a fellow woodsman who was scalping the dead warriors lying on the field of battle. Most of the hostile Indians had fled into the forest, and the drums and pipes of Colonel Bouquet's army were sounding the victory salute.

In the distance, the last of Pontiac's warriors retreated into the shelter of the forest. The allied Indian forces were beaten, crushed by trickery and a timely ruse executed by an unlikely and improbable battle plan that amazingly carried the day for the British army of Colonel Henry Bouquet. Providence had been with his army, and there was no question, the Black Watch and the 77th

Regiment of Foot of the Scottish Highlanders had played a major role in obtaining this astonishing victory. This reign of terror and destruction from Chief Pontiac and his allied Indian tribes would be the Ottawa Chief's final attempt to conquer the white settlers. The rebellion was over.

Kneeling above the dead Indian, Lieutenant Donald Davidson looked around to survey the bloody battlefield for any hostile enemy. Seeing none in close proximity, he shut the Indian's eyes still staring at him, even in death. The last valiant effort of the brave young warrior was to kill with his bare hands. His weapons gone, courage and determination were all that was left to him, but even those had not been enough.

"Forgive me, but it was you or me," Donald Davidson said to the dead Indian. "You were brave, but I am *Feros ferio*. I am fierce with those who are fierce." He left the field, returning to the flour-bag fort to locate the rest of his company and to reconnoiter with the lads of the 42nd and the 77th Regiment of Foot, the strong and mighty arm of his beloved homeland.

Chapter 2

Sword of Honor

Neither draw me without cause,
Nor return me without honor

It was early evening when the ship dropped anchor in the narrow cove north of Boston Harbor. Rain-drenched men, cold and silent, rowed toward the rocky shore in small, unwieldy boats laden with a variety of living cargo: animals, people, and sailors alike, wretched companions in their shared misery. On shore, they stood in the deepening gloom of the November evening, not certain where to go. Gradually, they dispersed into the shadows; some finding companions to accompany them in their desperate journey and some choosing a solitary path, heading inland, away from the sea and the slapping sounds of endless surf.

Turning south, Derick Davidson walked unsteadily until his legs adjusted to the unyielding surface of rocky landscape. During the long sea voyage, he had continued a vigorous regimen of exercise in an effort to maintain his physical strength, but despite this habitual routine, the constant movement of the sea seemed to have unsettled his usual momentum. It was November of 1773, and during the waning months of the year, the seas were often turbulent.

Alone now, Derick threw his pack over his shoulder and followed the well-worn path along the coastline. Raindrops fell intermittently from a gray, gloomy sky and beaded on his plaid, but the cold rain did not penetrate the thickly woven wool. He would find some place to stay, out of the rain and cold. He was certain the uppermost part of Boston Harbor was not far. There he would find taverns, hot food, and a warm bed.

At length, Derick arrived at a cluster of dingy weathered buildings perched high above the sea and away from the eroding effects of the tides. Light from the nearest tavern spilled through an ancient rain-drenched doorway, lighting the muddy roadway as he approached the ramshackle wooden structure. Derick ducked through the low opening and into a large room crowded with a diversity of strangely attired men. Some wore the redcoats of the British soldier; others were clad in native buckskin, fringed, and well worn. Rough and bearded men, they gazed at him with guarded curiosity.

Along one side of the crowded room was a long bar where men stood drinking ale and spirits. Other patrons sat at wooden tables, eating their supper of meat and potatoes while tavern servers brought pewter mugs of cider and hot coffee. Derick approached the tall, thin, cadaverous looking man behind the bar.

"Do ye have rooms?" inquired Derick.

"Yep, if you have money to pay," answered the man eyeing him with obvious suspicion.

"I have money," Derick said matter-of-factly. He pulled some silver coins from his pocket and laid them on the bar. "This be enough?"

The man's eyebrows rose over the narrow slits of his eyes when he saw the coins.

"Yep," he said looking considerately more pleasant. He swept up the money in one smooth motion. "Supper?"

"Aye."

"Have a seat. I'll see to your meal."

Derick found an empty table and chairs near the far end of the room and took a seat, turning his back to the wall and facing the door. He stashed his pack under the table and surveyed the motley assortment of men before him. His blue eyes swept over the crowded room, assessing each person with an experienced eye. He noted every door, every exit, keenly aware of the contemptuous stares of the red-jacketed soldiers lounging at the bar, their swarthy faces mocking. They gesticulated boisterously while their red-rimmed eyes burned from strong whiskey. Even in their half-drunken state, they were taking stock of him and seeking to devise some mischief. Derick would be ready.

Another man clad in worn buckskin breeches and a faded hunting shirt turned slowly from the bar to face the smoke-filled room. His sharp gray-blue eyes swept over the patrons, hoping to discover what was so intriguing to the British soldiers.

He was a large man, heavily muscled, with a distinct scar running from cheek to lip. Despite the disfiguring scar, he was a striking figure, masculine, commanding, and erect in bearing. The man caught Derick's eye and nodded slightly. A crooked smile revealed a gap where several teeth were missing. After a few moments of keen observation, the man moved from the bar and advanced toward Derick with a loose careless stride, his quick eyes noting the heavy woolen plaid across Derick's shoulder. Instantly, Derick was on the alert, his hand resting lightly on his dirk.

"Easy, friend," said the newcomer as he approached the table where Derick sat at attention. "No need to pull your knife—not yet, anyway." Uninvited, he pulled out a chair, scraping it across the wooden floor. He chose a seat on Derick's left and from this vantage point, he too was able to observe the room of patrons.

"Just come across, did ya?" the stranger asked.

"Aye, early evening, just above the harbor. Been walking some. Would this be Boston?"

"Yep, the outskirts. You might find better accommodations further in. This place will do, but not the best by a long shot. Food's good though. Whiskey's cheap enough. Buy you a drink?"

"Nay—thanks. It addles me wits, and I've a feeling I might need them tonight."

For a moment, the man looked incredulous, and then he threw back his head and laughed loudly, the scar wrinkling along his cheek. Leaning back in his chair, he studied Derick with amused candor and thrust forth a beefy hand. "Well, whadda ya know," he said with amusement in his voice, "a Scotsman who refuses a drink! Well, that's a bloody wonder, I'd say. My name's Daniel Morgan—from Virginia." Derick returned the smile and shook the large brawny hand of the stranger.

"Derick Davidson." The Highlander felt genuine warmth from the friendly overture of the frontiersman. "Davidson, Of Ross-shire, in the north of Scotland." Derick knew he must be wary of all men, but something in the face of this man inspired a cautious measure of trust. "Morgan, did ye say? Aye, I've known some Morgans in me time. Be Welshmen, aye?"

"Yes, I be a Welshman, by blood, but an American by birth and by choice," Morgan added with a grin. He pointed to the plaid across Derick's shoulder. "And you're a Scot running from King George." Derick colored slightly and shifted in his chair as though to rise.

"Settle yourself, man. I know what it is to be under King George's royal thumb," Morgan said. "Don't blame ya one bit. I'm finished with that bunch of soul stealing tyrants. I've tried to be agreeable with old King George, indeed I have. Even joined his troops for a spell during the French and Indian War, but alas and alack, we just didn't hit it off, so I joined the Americans! After all, it's what I am, by gum." Derick nodded, his eyes studying the scar-faced man.

"I know a man who goes by the name of Davidson. Fought with the 42nd regiment for the British at the Battle of Bushy Run—if my memory serves me correctly. I've known him for years, not well though. He is with the longhunters most of the time. Stops by on his way to town in the spring. I see him about once a year, when he brings furs to Winchester to trade."

"That be all ye know about him?" Derick inquired.

"Yep, that's about it. Lots of hunters come through in the spring with their winter catch. He's a quiet man. I don't remember his given name. He lives on Cedar Creek in the summertime. Would he be your kin?" Derick shrugged.

"Hard to know. A number of Davidsons crossed the water after the last war—Culloden. Me uncle fought in the Indian Wars. All we heard from his company was that he was missing. I have a strong feeling he is yet alive. Want to look for him—among other things."

"Well, Davidson, I hope ya find him," Morgan said. Derick nodded his appreciation. He appraised the group of incongruous and animated men gathered in the tavern. They were talking in low earnest tones, keeping a clear eye on the soldiers lounging at the bar.

"What's going on here, Morgan?" Derick asked.

Morgan lowered his voice confidentially and inclined his head toward the British soldiers. "The Colonials are tryin' to give those whiskey-sodden redcoats a royal send off back to their mother land. After the massacre in Boston in '70, relations with the redcoats and old King George haven't been exactly cordial. Last May, Parliament invented a plan to make it look like we supported taxation without representation. They lowered the cost of tea and gave the East India Company a monopoly on the import of tea, so we had to buy from them. Some want to pay the tax rather than do without their tea. Others say it is a trick. If we pay tax on the tea, we acknowledge taxation by Parliament. It is a scam, Davidson, a ruse of King George and those parliamentary pig-heads. Now, since you're a newcomer to this land, let me give you some free advice. That's about the only free thing around these parts."

Morgan paused when a tavern server approached the table and placed a plate of steaming meat and potatoes in front of Derick. "What to drink?" the server asked.

"Hot coffee, if ye have some," Derick answered. The servant nodded and disappeared into the room behind the bar. The steaming plate of food caused Derick's mouth to water. It had been long months since he had eaten a good hot meal. The roasted pork cooked with onions and garlic was succulent and the potatoes were lightly browned and crisp around the edges. A generous portion of beets, carrots, and cabbage rounded out the meal.

As Derick ate his supper, he noted the clamorous conduct of the redcoats still lounging against the bar. The two British soldiers were growing more raucous and pointing in Derick's direction. The stockier of the two soldiers left the bar and walked somewhat unsteadily toward the table where Derick and Morgan sat, waving his sword with obvious pleasure. The second soldier followed, clasping his mug of ale with an air of indifference.

"Well, well," the redcoat said with undisguised disdain. He laid one hand on the table and leaned forward as though to inspect the two men. "What do we have here? A bonny lad, in tartan plaid?" He threw back his head and laughed uproariously at his own clever wordplay and then looked contemptuously around the room at the other patrons.

"Gentlemen, gentlemen," the soldier said, swinging his sword in a broad sweep encompassing the entire assembly. "You will note the Scotsman is not dressed in the King's Royal Highlander's uniform. I believe we might have a dissenter or even a defector in our midst, don't you think, laddies?" The redcoat laughed drunkenly and turned to stare at Derick.

Knowing his words would only incite the inebriated soldiers, Derick did not answer. The soldier was spoiling for a fight, stirring the pot, eager for trouble, but Derick did not wish to initiate a confrontation. Morgan moved his chair back, balancing it expertly on two legs and said in a voice filled with bored nonchalance. "I don't recall inviting company to our table, soldier. Perhaps you didn't notice, but this is a private party, so if you'll put your sword away and return to your—ah—place at the bar, this gentleman and I can continue our discourse."

"Gentleman—bah!" sneered the stocky redcoat. "He's a traitor Scotsman to His Royal Highness if I ever saw one. Tell me now, man," he said leaning close to Derick, "did you swear allegiance to King George, or did you come by way of those skulking privateers who take silver in exchange for passage?" Still, Derick said nothing. "In the name of King George of England, stand on your feet and answer me at once, man!"

Derick's steely blue eyes blazed with indignation and insult, but his face betrayed no show of fear. He slowly rose to his feet as though to acknowledge the drunken soldier's request. He stood rooted to the spot, like a towering nemesis. Only his eyes moved as he appraised the situation before him with his keen and calculating mind.

Derick Davidson was six feet and four inches tall, and his powerful frame was well hidden beneath the cloak of his woolen plaid. Black waving hair and thick dark brows contrasted with the piercing blue of his eyes. A claymore war sword rested unobserved beneath his long tartan cloak, and two dirks were in easy access, one on his leather belt and one in his boot. He carried no gun.

Rising quietly from the table, Morgan stepped back a few paces as stealthily as a cat. His shrewd eyes swept over the scene, considering what possible actions he could expect if there were an altercation. His mind raced ahead to consider his role in this imminent drama. Morgan was no stranger to tavern brawls. His youth had been spent in a variety of such confrontations, and he possessed an uncanny ability to come out of these scrapes unscathed, or at least, with only minor injuries.

The old thrill of battle rose in Morgan's breast like a newly kindled fire on a cold hearth. He savored the moment, experiencing the rush of heat in his veins and the tingling sensation of energy coursing through every fiber and muscle of his body. He was up for the challenge, ready for action. What would the young Scotsman do?

On his first day in the American Colonies, Derick Davidson did not appear to be getting off to a favorable start. Morgan knew better than to interfere with this newcomer's inherent sense of judgment for the situation. Many years of such experience with other frontiersmen had taught Morgan some fundamental wisdom, and with this painfully acquired wilderness wisdom, he had also gained a generous amount of shrewdness and sagacity. He possessed the necessary patience to allow the big Scotsman to set the parameters in his own way.

Morgan knew instinctively that Davidson would choose to handle the mouthy redcoat, and he would attend to the other ale-sodden soldier. Should be easy enough. *Blast the English anyway!* They were always in a foul mood, insisting on throwing their weight around and looking for trouble while drinking their wages away in Boston's many taverns.

Smiling slightly, Derick nodded to the waiting soldier as though to acquiesce to the insulting demands of the sword-wielding redcoat. He rested his hands on his hips in a casual, non-threatening manner, but in the next instant, with one swift unanticipated motion, he employed the claymore broadsword. The steel blade gleamed, catching the dim light of the tavern on the razor sharp tip of the cutting edge. Quick as a panther, Derick stepped sideways, brought the sword down quickly, and cut a clean slice down the front of the soldier's red jacket. Brass buttons clattered noisily to the floor, rolling away and scattering in all directions. The soldier looked down in amazement as his red jacket gaped open to expose his none too clean linen shirt.

In the next instant, Derick touched the tip of his sword to the neck of the redcoat, close to the pulsing juggler, causing a thin trickle of blood to ooze down onto the collar of the soldier's fine jacket. Derick said nothing, but kept his blue eyes trained on the soldier.

Noting with pleasure the apparent surprise and consternation of the two soldiers, Daniel Morgan, try though he might to contain himself, could not stop his broad shoulders from shaking with obvious amusement. The surprise for the two English soldiers, who for the moment stood in stunned silence, was complete. They looked around at the tavern patrons for some show of support, but the men watching the confrontation parted like the Red Sea, some joining in with Morgan's delight at the astonishment of the soldiers while others distanced themselves from any possible controversy with the King's men.

Derick withdrew his sword tip from the neck of the redcoat, resting it casually at his side. The soldier still grasped his own sword in his hand, but he knew the Highlander standing before him with his cool demeanor and casual air of indifference, outmatched him.

"You stinking Scot," the soldier said with all the arrogance he could muster. He removed a dirty handkerchief from his pocket and wiped the blood trickling down his neck. "How dare you defy the King's men? Who do you think you are? Where did you come from?" Without waiting for an answer, he bellowed. "I'll see you hanged as a traitor, Scot!" He then proceeded to curse long and loud.

"Well," Derick answered, shrugging his shoulders indifferently, "you'll need to be alive to witness the scene."

Catching the subtle threat in Derick's words, the soldier snarled and then spat on the floor. He knew he was facing a man of superior size and strength, a skilled swordsman who would not be bullied or intimidated. Here was a man whose movements were not slowed by excessive drink, a man whose head was unclouded and keen.

The redcoat had wanted a fight, but now, thinking better of his boastful demands, he hesitated. He fought only men he knew he could beat, those he could bully and humiliate. He especially liked to harass those who showed cowardice or weakness, but this big Scotsman stood erect, sword in hand, legs apart, waiting for him to make the next move. This man was not going to back down. If he had any sense at all, the Scotsman would fear the repercussion that would surely follow his deliberate assault on a soldier of the Crown.

"I'm marking you, Scot. Do you hear me?" snarled the soldier peevishly. "If I see you again, you'll be sorry you ever set foot in the King's Colonies, I can promise you that."

"Promise me? Well, now," Derick said coolly, "I'm familiar with the King's promises, so I won't be a holding me breath." Another round of laughter filled the smoky room and the soldier's face turned bright red.

Looking around the room at the rough patrons feigning indifference to the altercation, the soldier hoped to find some collaboration. Seeming to find none, he turned to Derrick and gave him a look of intense disgust and hatred. Then he motioned to his drunken companion. He waved a hand in the direction of the door, and he and his compatriot moved toward the exit of the tavern.

Quickly, Derick gathered up the brass buttons from where they had fallen on the rough plank floor and called to the departing duo. "Wait a wee moment, gentlemen." They halted, and he strode toward them with a light easy step. Stretching out his hand, he offered the soldier the brass buttons he had sliced from his jacket. The soldier scowled his derision and refused to take the proffered buttons. He looked down at his gaping jacket and then turned away. The two inebriated soldiers slipped through the door into the damp drizzling night. The confrontation was over.

Derick pocketed the buttons and returned to the table to finish his meal. Morgan followed, seated himself next to the big Scotsman, and considered the newcomer with genuine respect. Derick ate in silence with his back to the wall, keeping a cautions eye on the men gathered around the bar and those who were sitting in small groups, talking and drinking ale.

"Well, well," Morgan said nonchalantly, "you have taken your first trophy, Davidson—brass buttons! A shame it weren't their bloomin' heads."

"Aye, would have been considerably more satisfying, to be sure," Derick answered with a grin, "but I didn't come all the way from me mother land to fight, and I dinna want to spill blood me first night here. Aye, the soldier will be laying for me, that's certain."

"Appears so, Davidson, but as I was saying before we were so rudely interrupted, there are some things you need to understand if you want to keep your head on your shoulders. I admire your style, indeed I do. Actually, I'm downright impressed. You have a cool head and a quick mind, but you'll be hangin' from a tree before the week is out if you don't learn how things work around here."

Derick looked up from his plate and pointed a fork at Morgan. "And how's that, Mr. Morgan? What do I need to know to keep from swinging on a tree?"

"First of all, get rid of that plaid and stop sayin' *I be*, and *ye*, and *aye*. You need to start talkin' American English, or at least, frontier English."

Now it was Derick's turn to smile. He threw back his head and laughed heartily, his blue eyes sparkling with mirth. "Can a leopard change his spots, Morgan? Can a Scotsman learn the King's English? I guess *I be* a dead man, then. I canna change, nor do I want to. I be what I am—a Scotsman."

"Listen, Davidson, I understand to a certain extent, but if you crossed the ocean to the American Colonies just to get yourself hanged, then you're a bigger fool than I imagined. You could have gotten hanged in Scotland just as well and saved yourself a sack of money and the trouble of a sea voyage." Morgan's countenance registered mild irritation.

"This is America, Davidson," Morgan continued, "and if you have come here for any other reason than to be an American and a Patriot, then you took the wrong boat. This country is on the brink of a revolution. I mean all out war with the bloody English and old King George. It's inevitable. You need to know that. The lines are being drawn even as we speak, and you will be making some hard decisions if you decide to stay here atop this powder keg." Morgan nodded toward the door through which the soldiers had disappeared and settled back into his chair. "I know you hate the English, so I'm thinkin' you'll take your position with the Colonials, and I want to help you stay alive to do it."

Derick shoved his empty plate away and met the blue-gray eyes of his new friend. "Mr. Morgan, I take no position in this coming revolution ye speak of. Aye, I understand the Colonies are about to explode, but I came to this new land for another reason and fighting was not in me plans. I came here to find freedom—freedom to follow me own dreams, to build a new life, a life excluding the tyrannical English. Why would I want to fight them again when I already know the outcome of such a conflict?"

Derick leaned close to Morgan's ear and said in a confidential tone. "Aye, I realize war may come, Morgan. I've heard the talk, the endless debates. I say, let it come! As for me, I did not come here to fight the English. Nay, I did not. If I ever raise me claymore in battle again, I will fight with the Americans—*if* me life depends on it, but I will fight as a Scotsman, Morgan, 'tis what I am." He smiled at Morgan, a rare and whimsical smile, his eyes softening.

"I know how ye feel, Morgan. I understand the fire burning in your heart, the passion for freedom. I have felt it too, but I will not fight the King's army again, not unless I be forced. However," he said leaning back in his chair, "I will consider what ye say. I will do me best to keep me head on me shoulders—*that* I can promise. I want to live, indeed I do. I want to live long enough to see the British pulled down from their lofty pinnacle of power. The oppressing tyranny over men, breaking their spirits, aye, it must be stopped. The British are devouring the world like a devilish, man-eating canker."

"This time, Davidson, we will stop them," Morgan said with confidence. "And if you truly want to see them pulled down from their 'pinnacle of power', *then fight with us!* The Patriots will bring an end to tyranny, and you are the kind of man who can help us. How do you expect the British to be defeated if you, and others like you, refuse to fight?"

Derick shrugged his shoulders and Morgan sighed. "I understand your doubts, Davidson, but this time, it will be different. This time we will win."

"Are you saying the Americans will beat them?" Derick asked skeptically. His eyes hardened, and he spoke with bitterness in his voice. "For centuries, the blood of me own countrymen soaked the battlefields of Scotland while fighting for freedom, but the English—they always come back, and when they do, it is to crush 'the rebel opposition' as they term it. God Himself has witnessed the suffering of me countrymen, the proud and ancient clans of Scotland. Aye, Morgan, the blood of me ancestors cries out from the moors and glens of bonny Scotland as did Abel's blood, and it is but a voice in the misty wind. We lose in the end."

"This time it will be more than a voice in the wind, Davidson. This time we will win, we *will* conquer the English," Morgan said confidentially. "There is an entire ocean between King George and the Colonials, and the frontier presents an entirely different battleground—one the English don't understand." Morgan noticed a group of men not far from their table, watching them with interest. He lowered his voice.

"There are spies about, ready to inform the redcoats of any insurrection talk. We must be careful. I have said too much already, and you have definitely compromised your own safety. Stay with me tonight. You'll be safe enough, but you'll need to move on tomorrow. Those soldiers won't forget how you humiliated them. They'll be the devil to pay on the morrow for sure, and mark my words, Davidson; they'll be lookin' for you at first light."

"And in the morning, where would ye suggest I go to escape their wrath?"

"Come with me to Virginny for a spell. I'll show you around the Colonies, teach you the ropes, learn you to talk American." Morgan smiled, his lips stretching across the dark gap to reveal his missing teeth. "Why, I'll show you how to be an American—a real Patriot. You're here now, pilgrim, so you might as well learn our ways. Some things might not be to your liking, but you're bound to like some of 'em, like hustlin' the redcoats back to England, for one."

Derick's only answer was a slight nod. He was beginning to like this Daniel Morgan, this self-proclaimed Colonial Patriot. Morgan had offered Derick friendship, and he was badly in need of a friend. Davidson could see that Daniel Morgan was rough and possessed no formal education, but was zealous and radiated an honesty and candor that attracted him.

Derick and Morgan left the dining room of the tavern and climbed the narrow stairs to the sleeping rooms located on the second story of the old building. At the top of the wooden stairs, a common room with two rows of crude cots accommodated up to ten men. Off this room and to the left of the common room, three private rooms, complete with doors and locks, were available for the more affluent traveler who valued privacy. Daniel Morgan took out a key and opened the last door. He motioned for Derick to enter and then followed him into the room.

"Nothin' fancy, but clean and private," Morgan said.

Derick glanced at the sparse furnishings. The room had two beds, a washstand with pitcher and bowl, a small bureau with a cracked mirror hanging above it, and a chamber pot under one of the high beds.

"Has a window, opens onto the porch roof and the stable at the rear of the tavern. Checked it out myself, just in case I need a quick escape," explained Morgan with a crooked grin. "You never know, and I like to be prepared for a hasty exit. I don't suppose you have a horse?"

"Nay, not yet, but I have silver enough to buy a good steady mount," answered Derick.

"Let me go down and see what I can do," suggested Morgan. "You'll need a good horse. There's a man downstairs, trades in horses. Give me what you can afford. I'll see if I can do business."

Derick studied Morgan for a long moment, wondering if he could truly trust this complete stranger. He was cautious of all men and had not dared to hope for a friend this soon. This unexpected meeting with Morgan was more than he had bargained for. He was alone in a strange country with not a single contact or acquaintance and Morgan had befriended him at once.

One thought ran through his mind—he was convinced that Morgan would have come to his aid had there been an altercation with the soldiers. On this premise alone, he opened his pack and counted out the silver coins.

"I know what you're a thinkin'," Morgan said taking the money. "If I don't come back, take my pack, take all I have in the room. Take my horse, too. Third stall on the left, the big sorrel gelding." Derick felt chagrined. He must learn to hide his thoughts.

"It's been me way of life, Morgan, for a long time now. Don't fault me for it."

"I don't," Morgan answered seriously. "A fella can't be too careful, but I can assure you—I'm a friend."

Daniel Morgan left Derick alone in the room and locked the door behind him. Removing his sword and outer garments, Derick poured the tepid water into the wash basin. He folded his plaid and placed it in his pack, grateful for the opportunity to bathe. Then he lay down on the bed and waited for Morgan's return.

Even though he felt exhausted, Derick could not sleep. His thoughts were as scattered as the evening stars on a Highland night. He wondered if he had been too hasty, if he had made a mistake in trusting Morgan. What if he came back with a troop of English soldiers? What if he were a spy or a traitor himself? He knew nothing of the man other than what he had learned at supper. What had he been thinking?

Derick's mind returned to one primary thought: no matter what else Daniel Morgan was, he was a Patriot. Of this, Derick felt certain. Morgan could not hide his burning passion for his country and for freedom. If he were any judge of character, he felt certain he could trust Morgan. His actions during the confrontation with the soldiers confirmed this opinion.

After what seemed like hours, Derick heard quick footfalls coming down the hall. The key turned in the lock and Morgan, breathless and impatient, entered the room.

"Get your pack together, Davidson, and strap on your sword," he panted. "There's a company of redcoats heading this direction, and they don't look too friendly. Most likely, they're comin' for you, so hurry. We'll go through the window before we're discovered. I've a horse for you in the stable. Follow me." Without further explanation, Morgan locked the door from the inside, gathered up his trappings, and opened the window. He climbed onto the roof, looked carefully around, and then signaled for Derick to follow. They crept stealthily along the rooftop and dropped to the ground at the back of the tavern.

Entering the stable, Morgan led Derick to a buckskin horse with a black mane, saddled and ready to go. "This *be* your horse," said Morgan with his crooked grin. "Now, let's get out of here."

There was no time to evaluate the purchase. Derick followed Morgan to the back entrance of the stable that led into a narrow alleyway. They walked the horses down the alley until they were a hundred yards from the tavern, then mounted their steeds and rode swiftly into the damp chilly night.

Turning in the saddle, Morgan signaled Derick, pointing to the tavern in the distance. Light spilled from the doorway onto the silhouettes of a troop of British soldiers entering the tavern. It would not be long until Morgan's duplicity was discovered and the soldiers came looking for them.

Derick sighed wearily as they rode through the damp November night. He had only been in this new country a short time, not even one day, and already he was a hunted man. He shook his head in consternation. Pulling his horse abreast of Morgan, he asked. "Where are ye going?"

"Home," was the simple reply.

"Where might that be?"

"Virginny, remember? I told you I live in Virginny. I'm thinkin' I just might get married, Davidson. This little adventure has made up my mind, by gum! Gee haw, Samson!" With the command to his horse, Morgan sped away into the night with Derick close on his heels. After several miles, Morgan turned onto a side road and traveled in a southerly direction for several more miles. The road was a mere wagon trail and not well traveled. The horses picked their way through a tangle of brush and brambles growing across the road in an unkempt fashion and skirted around several boggy marshes until they came to a wagon road that appeared to be considerably more durable. At last, Daniel Morgan reined in his mount and turned to Derick.

"We should be safe now," he said, rubbing his chin. "I know this country. Those soldiers are a bunch of sissies when it comes to real frontier trackin'. If they can't bring a whole regiment down the pike, they won't come. You get 'em one on one, and it's not even a contest. We'll go easy and find some place to hole up for a rest. You ride well, Davidson."

"Aye, 'tis the way of the Scottish clans. The mountains are rugged and steep, and the moors are a trackless sea. Our horses know the way of the highlands. They are warriors in their own right. Many be the mount who has saved me life, true enough." He reached down to pat the neck of his newly acquired mount. "I believe he knows me plight, Morgan. What be his name?"

Morgan paused, his perceptive gaze meeting the ice blue eyes of the big Highlander. "His name is Warrior. Suit you?"

Derick offered a reserved smile. "Should have known it. He has the spirit of a warrior. Thank ye, Morgan. Ye did me a kindness, to be sure. A good mount by your side is as necessary as a good man. Do I owe ye?"

"Nope. The man owed me a favor, and I got far more for your money than you could have yourself, that's for sure."

"Then I'm twice obliged, Morgan. I'll sing for ye at your wedding."

Morgan threw back his head and laughed, then nudged his horse toward the south. Derick followed, urging Warrior on with the steady pressure of his knees, testing the strength and mettle of his mount. As he rode abreast of Morgan, Derick felt warmth radiating from the steaming body of his horse and smelled the sharp, tangy vapor rising in the cool mist of the November night.

The animal odor of the sweating horse was not unpleasant to his senses, but rather comforting after the long sea voyage of smelling nothing but salt air, unwashed bodies, and the odor of bitter vomit from the passengers' continual bouts with seasickness. It was good to smell the scent of a horse.

As they journeyed southward, Derick Davidson, son of Scotland and of the blood-soaked land of his nativity, wondered where he was going with this self-proclaimed American Patriot, this Daniel Morgan of Virginia, and where he would find himself in the ensuing drama when the Colonials faced the inevitability of war with England. He knew one thing: he was in pursuit of freedom, and he would continue his quest until he obtained his purpose. Of this, he was certain.

Reaching into the pocket of his woolen jacket, Derick searched for the gold locket that once belonged to Meagan, his wife. When he felt the tiny oval keepsake, his heart wrenched with renewed grief. The unremitting longing for his bonny lass who lay in a silent grave in faraway Scotland never seemed to wane, never seemed to fade with the passing days. Now, he must go forward and make a new life in this strange wild land. He could not bring Meagan back, nor could he return to Scotland.

Chapter 3

Trail to Virginia

Truth is often hard to tell

Derick followed Morgan along the crude wagon road leading south. On either side, the trail was banked by trees so thick that light could not penetrate the interior of the virgin forest. A slow continual drizzle left the roadway slippery with mud, and the way became more difficult to navigate. Decaying leaves clung tenaciously to the tree branches, and the scent of evergreen boughs perfumed the atmosphere with a clean, heady aroma.

Slowing his pace, Morgan picked his way carefully through the deepening shadows of the November night. The soft brush of winged night creatures flew from low hanging branches at the edge of the forest where they waited for some unwary prey. It was growing too dark to travel. They needed to stop and make camp for the night.

Dense woodland gave way to an open field where a burned out log cabin stood silhouetted against the night sky. The acrid smell of charred wood and wet ashes permeated the air. Morgan reigned in his horse and retrieved his hunting jacket from his pack. The chill damp air began to soak through the outer layers of his clothing. He turned in the saddle to face Derick.

"There's a spring close by," he said matter-of-factly. "I saw this place on the way up to Boston and spent a night in the lean-to behind the cabin. It will serve to shelter us some."

Still keeping his sword at the ready, Derick retrieved his woolen plaid from his pack and wrapped the heavy cloak expertly around him. Urging his horse up the gentle rise to the cabin, he passed the scorched remains of logs and stone and wondered at the cause for the abandoned ruin. As far as he could tell, no one was about. Following the trail to a three-sided shelter standing about fifty yards down the opposite side of the slope, he waited for Morgan who lingered on the trail to study the ground. In minutes, he appeared at the lean-to sitting astride his mount.

"Well, here we are, Davidson, our excellent accommodations for the night," Morgan said with a chuckle. Derick surveyed the rough shelter and noted that Morgan was canvassing the edge of the forest beyond the clearing with an appraising eye.

"Are ye thinking the redcoats will follow this far?" asked Derick. He noted Morgan's keen attention to the southern side of the woodland now shrouded in dark shadows. His quick eye swept over the tree line, and seeming satisfied, he relaxed his vigilance.

"Nope," Morgan answered and dismounted his horse. He began to gather up small pieces of the damp wood he found stacked in the lean-to. "I told you before, if they can't bring an entire platoon, they won't come. Besides, this road is not on the beaten trail, so the British won't find us here. The only thing we need to worry about is prowling Indians pillaging for whatever they can find. I haven't seen any Indian sign, so I think we're safe enough for the night. We're still close enough to Boston to make it a trifle uncomfortable for the Indians to pick a fight." Morgan smiled and stacked the wood next to some dry kindling in front of the lean-to. He made a circle of stones for a small campfire.

Derick looked toward the desolate cabin. On the tiresome and tedious trip across the stormy Atlantic, he had heard tales of the savage Indians and their brutal raids on the frontier settlers. His shipmates had spent untold hours recounting stories of the red-skinned inhabitants of the eastern woodlands and the horrible atrocities awaiting anyone who fell captive to them. Derick had come to the American Colonies to find peace and freedom, and he certainly didn't want to tangle with any hostile Indians driven by bitter revenge. He had tasted the same stinging bitterness himself and understood how land disputes could stir up the spirit of murder in a man's heart.

Morgan retrieved a tinderbox from his pack and chose a small piece of char cloth, which he had made himself, and folded it several times. Then he laid the char cloth across a nest of tinder and dry kindling and reached for the flint and steel. Holding the flint in one hand, he struck the flint in a downward motion with a small file of steel. Sparks flew in all directions and sizzled on the damp wood.

As Morgan continued to strike the flint, several sparks landed on the char cloth and began to burn and eat away at the cloth. Morgan picked up the cloth and kindling, folded them together, and blew softly on the nest. Flames burst from the cloth, and soon a hot fire burned in the circle of stones.

While Morgan made the fire, Derick watered the horses at a spring not far from the cabin and refilled their canteens. He tethered the horses close to the crude shelter for the night, ready for a quick escape if necessary. Derick Davidson knew horses and was a master at handling them. The handsome mount that Morgan had purchased for him was much to his liking.

Attempting to befriend the noble steed, Derick ran his hands along the muscled flanks of the stallion, feeling the strength of his thick neck draped by the bristly black mane. He held the horse's head with both hands, and looked into the liquid brown eyes of his stallion, eyes shifting away from his gaze, not quite trusting this stranger.

"Nay, laddie, nay," Derick said softly, "Ye needn't be a pointing your ears at your new master. You're a warrior, aye, that ye are. Be true to your name, and I'll be true to mine, 'tis all I ask. We'll be friends, aye, before the sun rises over the treetops."

"Are you talkin' to yer horse, Davidson?" Morgan asked as he dipped into his pack for some venison. He brought out a bag of parched corn and some freshly dried trail jerky and handed some of each to Derick. The strong aroma of coffee boiling in a small tin over the fire was comforting to the weary travelers.

"Well," answered Derick with a grin, "a horse be good company for a solitary man like meself, Morgan, and I'm obliged to ye for getting me such a fine animal. He's larger than me Highland lads, but he doesn't need to climb so sharply among the glens and mountains. Aye, he'll be me friend and maybe even me savior by the way I'm beginning me journey in this strange new land."

Daniel Morgan snorted. "You're starting off with a walloping bang, that's for sure. I hope you're ready for whatever follows, and I seriously hope bad luck isn't following you along this trail." He shook his head with incredulity at his friend and then settled down to eat, his back to the shelter, his eyes constantly sweeping the clearing, his rifle by his side.

The hot coffee warmed the two men considerably, and when Morgan finished the meager but tasty supper, he pulled a flask from his pack and held it out to Derick. "An after dinner drink, my friend?"

"Nay, thank ye. I told you before, Morgan, drink dulls me senses, and I'm for leaving it alone."

"Suit yourself. I'm not of the same persuasion, however, but I know what you mean. Too much drink can destroy a man if he allows it."

Morgan took another long drink and returned the flask to his pack. "I've done a lot of drinkin' in my day, Davidson," he continued, "some hard drinkin', too, especially in my younger days, but I could always stop when I'd a mind to. Some men aren't so lucky, or maybe not so iron-willed."

Derick looked thoughtful, raising his eyebrows as he considered the words of his fellow traveler. "Aye, I've seen it take many a strong man down, Morgan, even those with iron in their bones."

"So have I, so have I," Morgan said, spitting into the fire. Leaning back on one elbow, he stretched his long legs toward the fire. He drew a plug of tobacco from his pack and stuffed a wad into the recesses of the scarred cheek. "When I was a young buck, I enlisted in the British army to fight the French and Indians. I learned many hard lessons in my youthful days, Davidson. Far more than I ever intended. Learned to fight, to speak French, to use the long rifle, and learned the art of ranging from a man named Robert Rogers. At his own expense, he raised and commanded a troop of riflemen during the war. They were the best the British army had to offer. Mostly Scot and Irish, they were, and familiar with that type of unusual warfare Rogers preferred."

"Unusual? How's so?" Derick asked.

"Well, Rogers called his men *Rangers*. They fought in irregular and un-British like ways. The Rangers could creep up on the enemy, quiet as a cat, penetrate their territory unobserved, lay an ambush, and surprise the encampment before they knew what was going on. Sometimes the Rangers attacked at night, and in their confusion, the French and Indians shot each other. Rogers' ranging methods were so successful the French tried to use the same strategies on the Rangers, but Rogers could smell an enemy trap, vanish without detection, and be home in time for supper." Morgan spat a stream of tobacco juice into the fire before continuing his story.

"The Rangers were well trained and skilled riflemen who could hit the head of a nail at a hundred yards. Their unique reloading system kept up a constant fire raining down on the enemy camp. They hid in trees, brush, streams, behind rocks and were clad in buckskin and leather to blend with the natural countryside."

"Aye, I understand," Derick said. "That's me own brand of combat. I ne'r understood King George's methods of fighting, although his battle preparations made a bonny show, if ye lived to tell about it. Ever since Culloden Moor in '46, the Highlanders have been scouting the glens and moors, secretly, of course. If the Scots were caught, they were executed or hanged as traitors to the King and country. Some were exiled, their lands confiscated, or sent to prison. Me Da' was wounded on the battlefield at Culloden and me Ma was raped by Cumberland's men and run through with a sword as were the women and children who followed the battle." Derick paused to draw in a ragged breath.

"I'm sorry, Davidson," Morgan said with genuine empathy. "War's a bloody business, and everyone loses something or someone."

Derick shrugged his shoulders and shoved the bitter memories back into the recesses of his mind. "I don't remember me mother and have only heard of the battle, but I have seen the results in the lives of me countrymen. I was only a wee bairn then, in the care of me aunt and uncle. To care for his own bairns was too much for me own father. His wounds were too dreadful and he never regained his health. It was a fiendish slaughter, they tell me."

"Two of me brothers and me wee sister hid in the brush until the slaughter ended and the soldiers went away. Me mother and brothers were following the camp to care for the young lads, the men. It was the last Highland charge, the last one our lads ever made. We were beaten, completely routed."

Morgan spat another stream of tobacco juice into the flames.

"After losing the battle," Derick said, "severe penalties were leveled against the Scots and especially on the Highlanders, unless we swore allegiance to the crown, to King George. Many a lowlander swore allegiance, some Highlanders too, landowners and such, and some of us just danced around the King's fires. How could I swear allegiance to an unjust cause, Morgan?"

Morgan eyed Derick with a considerable measure of sympathy and respect. He understood brutality, and he instinctively knew this particular man, a man who seemed to possess an unusual sense of honor, would never swear allegiance to a corrupt cause, especially a cause he did not sanction. Morgan tried to imagine what it would be like to meet Derick Davidson in an altercation of swords. He was a rifleman, not a swordsman, and he knew he would be cut down in short order if he were matched against this Highlander.

"Nope," Morgan answered simply, "I don't think you could swear allegiance to the King, not after such treachery."

Derick threw a stick into the fire. "I was suspected of being attached to the numerous secret raids on the British garrisons stationed about the highlands. King George's men were hot on me trail, but they could never prove anything on me. The English law said we could not bear arms so we carried no visible weapons. We hid our claymores and dirks, and when the way was clear, we practiced with our swords by the hour. The Scots are excellent secret swordsmen."

"I can believe your report," Morgan said ruefully. "An impressive demonstration of swordsmanship back at the tavern. I'll be the first to admit, I rather enjoyed watching the show."

The flames of the fire danced against the night sky and Derick dropped his eyes and said with a note of hesitation. "Me and me brothers roamed the glens and discovered the places where the British were camped. We knew every rock and stone in the glens, every burn, and every ben. When we had a chance, we laid a few of King George's men to rest." He looked directly at Morgan. "Aye, I know about stealthy fighting. I was but a wee bairn when I began me blood feud against the King's men and the Crown. Now I'm weary of it, sick of it, Morgan."

"Blood feud?"

"Aye, blood for blood." Derick paused, and sighing heavily, gazed into the semi darkness beyond the fire. "Well, Morgan, I came across the water to get away from it all—to forget. I want peace and quiet and freedom. I'll do no more secret fighting, no more avenging. I'm tired of killing and hating. I want a better life, a peaceful life." An ancient query rose to his eyes. "There has to be more than the never ending conflicts between men and countries, aye?"

A deep rumble rose in Morgan's chest, and erupted in a low growl of laughter. "I hate to disappoint you, Davidson, but you came to the wrong country, *and* you came at the wrong time. The Colonies are ready to explode, and there are the constant Indian uprisings to add to the present uncertainty. Peace and quiet? I think not! Freedom? Maybe, if you will fight for it, maybe even die for it. If you're in no mood to fight, you're in the wrong place at the wrong time."

With a wave of his large hand, Derick dismissed Morgan's gloomy perspective. "Enough of me own troubles. Tell me more about Rogers. Where is he now?"

"Well, Rogers had one appalling habit," Morgan said throwing another log on the fire. "He drank." He looked at Derick for a reaction, but the Highlander's face was a mask. "Some men can hold their liquor, but Rogers couldn't seem to stop. His drinking ways got a 'holt of him, and he couldn't shake loose. He had a pretty little wife," Morgan said shaking his head, "but she couldn't stand the drinkin'. She finally got tired of hopin' he'd change and left him, so he drank even more."

Hearing Morgan's dismal commentary caused Derick to shake his head in disbelief. Morgan jabbed at the fire with a stick and continued.

"Before he began drinkin', he commanded the Rangers with respect and honor. He wrote an instructional field manual he titled *Rogers Rules of Ranging*. It's one of the best and most complete field manuals on ranging ever written, and we use it today. I studied the book myself, hoping one day to join the Rangers. Well, after the war with the French and the Indians, the Rangers disbanded, and Rogers became a warrior without a war." He shook his head at the irony of this idea and then glanced at Derick who remained in thoughtful silence.

"He simply loved the predatory life," Morgan said, biting off another wad of tobacco and chewing the dried leaves appreciatively. "Ranging with his special forces was all he knew, all he wanted to do.

Out of sheer boredom and restlessness, he drifted from one place to the next, and the drinking became an obsession, something he couldn't live without." Morgan shook his head at the recollection.

"So where is he now?" Derick asked.

"He went to England, made some powerful friends, and King George made him governor in the Michigan area. Rogers had some enemies too, General Gage for one," Morgan said stretching his long arms. "Gage wanted to ruin him, so he hatched up a plot to put Rogers in the poke for insubordination. Just about five years ago. Rogers was eventually acquitted, but he came out of his trouble bitter as gall and set sail for England. He is still there, last I heard, trying to get old King George to pay his debts and grant him some compensation for all his ill treatment."

Derick lifted his shoulders and shook his head in wonder at the tale. "They'll be building snow castles in the desert before that ever happens," Derick said. Morgan grunted his agreement. The prospect of King George actually granting such a request was quite remote.

"Well, despite all his personal trouble and his drinkin' ways," continued Morgan, "Rogers was a rare leader, a natural frontiersman, and a brilliant Ranger."

"Aye, even so, no skilled and intelligent man can remain a leader when he himself is plagued by the love for spirits. It will take him down," Derick paused, "sooner or later, as sure as I'm sitting here with ye."

Morgan appeared somewhat uncomfortable with the conversation. "What you're a sayin' is so, Davidson. That's why I'm careful about my drinkin'. Besides, Abigail hates it." He smiled whimsically at the mention of Abigail, his eyes lighting up with considerable meaning. "We have to keep our little women happy, don't we?"

Not wanting Morgan to read his thoughts, Derick turned his head away, his eyes filling with pain. He could not think about his former life, the life he had left behind. He stretched his great arms above his head and yawned, signaling Morgan the conversation was over. Then he settled himself deeper into the shelter and pulled his cloak around him.

The night grew darker. Thick, ominous clouds shrouded the November sky, obscuring the stars. A fine mist bathed the thick barren branches of the trees until the gathering moisture fell in great droplets to the earth below. Steam rose from the flames as the damp wood sizzled and hissed in the circle of stones.

"I'll take first watch," Morgan said, noting Derick's weariness. Throwing more wood on the fire, he settled back into the shelter and leaned against the wooden frame. "I know you're dog tired and need to sleep. Get some shut eye, and I'll wake you in a few hours."

"Aye, Morgan, I be obliged. I'm close to a dead man." Derick made a pillow with one end of his woolen cloak and lay down against the damp earth. Although his body was weary, his mind seemed alive with a cacophony of disturbing thoughts. The earth, solid and unyielding beneath him, seemed unusually firm after the constant movement of the ship during the long sea voyage.

He had not allowed himself to think of his home in the highlands of Scotland, his beloved homeland where the heather covered mountains called to him, and where a green-eyed lass had stolen his heart on a misty summer night. Nor could he think of the blue-eyed babe who had clutched his finger with such curious boldness, such desperation, as though he knew his father would never return. And what of the wee lads who stood on the shore watching his departure, tears streaming down their cheeks?

Shutting his eyes tightly against the vivid picture creeping uninvited into his mind, Derick thrust the painful memory of his recent exile from his tormented thoughts and silently prayed for sleep, a sleep deep enough to obliterate the gnawing ache in his chest. He would think about his troubles another day, when the burning hurt of the memory was not so keen, when the wound had healed over and only scars remained. Someday, perhaps his former life would fade into a bearable memory, but now, he must try to forget. Now he must sleep.

At two in the morning, Derick took his turn at the watch and Morgan took over again just prior to dawn. An iron-like pressure on his arm roused Derick to wakefulness just as the first light of day penetrated the darkness. Morgan was crouching beside him, the horses' bridles in his hands and his rifle by his side. He put his hand to his lips and then whispered to Derick while his eyes darted around the clearing.

"Indians," he hissed. "About five of them, a raiding party. Don't look too friendly to me. War paint and scalps hanging on their belts. Best get out of here."

Throwing his cloak across his horse, Derick was on his feet in an instant, tying his pack behind the saddle while Morgan held the reins. The horse whinnied loudly as Derick mounted, jerking his head at their hasty departure.

From the trees surrounding the clearing, the unearthly scream of the war party burst upon the clearing. Derick dug his heels into the horse's flanks and drew his sword at the same time. He saw Morgan take aim with his rifle as the Indian closest to him raised his tomahawk. The rifle belched fire, and the Indian crumpled to the ground, a small round hole in his forehead. Derick wheeled around on his horse, slashing at an Indian who was grabbing at the bridle, a knife ready to plunge into Derick's thigh. The sword came down across the Indian's shoulder, causing the knife to fly through the air. The Indian screamed in agony as the edge of the sword connected with flesh and bone.

Two of the Indians ran toward Morgan who was trying to mount his horse. Just as the first Indian reached him, Morgan drew his knife. The two engaged in a hand-to-hand struggle with tomahawk and knife while the other Indian yelped and screamed around them.

Derick dismounted as the third remaining Indian aimed his tomahawk in his direction. He moved aside quickly, and the weapon flew by his head, shaving off some hair just above his ear. Plunging into the battle, he tried desperately to employ his broadsword. The Indian drew his knife, and the two circled each other, the Indian keeping well away from the sword.

"Long knife, long knife," chanted the Indian in English, and for a moment, Derick saw amusement cross his opponent's features. The brave drew his arm back to throw his weapon, but before he could get the thrust in motion, Derick rushed forward and plunged his sword into the chest of the young brave. The Indian stopped, a look of surprise on his face, the knife still held in position above his head. Then his eyes glazed over, and he crumpled to the earth, his knife falling by his side. He made one last feeble effort to grasp the knife, but his strength failed and he lay still.

The larger of the two remaining Indians was locked in mortal combat with Morgan. The smaller Indian danced and yelped and darted around the two combatants, trying to distract Morgan, waiting for an opportunity to strike a fatal blow. The wild screaming and garishly painted bodies of the Indians made a maniacal scene in the clearing. Derick rushed toward the fray, swinging the heavy claymore in a wide circle. He struck down the unsuspecting Indian with one smooth swing of the broadsword.

Morgan and the last Indian rolled across the rain-drenched clearing, knives held aloft, each waiting for the other to weaken enough to press his advantage. Derick tried to find an opening to aid Morgan, but he knew it was too dangerous to plunge into the midst of the undulating bodies of the two men.

Suddenly, Morgan's knife sailed through the air. He quickly grabbed the Indian's wrist with both his hands, holding the warrior's knife well away from his body. Again, Derick moved in to assist Morgan, but he could not find the eye of the needle to relieve Morgan.

The two combatants wrestled for position and with another turn, the Indian's knife dropped from his hands as Morgan snapped his wrist. When the warrior disengaged, Morgan pummeled the Indian with his fists until the brave went limp and lay senseless on the ground. Morgan rolled away and slowly raised from the fight, heaving and sweating with sheer exhaustion, his clothes a muddy ruin.

For a few moments, Morgan stood over the Indian, sucking in air, saying nothing, and wiping sweat from his face. He glanced at Derick and nodded. Looking around the clearing at the unbelievable carnage, Morgan retrieved his knife from where it had fallen into the mud. Still breathing heavily, he located his rifle where it lay in the tall grass, picked it up, and reloaded it without a word, all the while looking around at the slaughter in the clearing. Morgan himself appeared to be unscathed.

Neither man said a word, but the scene in the clearing spoke volumes. Derick rounded up the horses and brought the canteens of water from their packs. He drank his fill and handed Morgan his canteen. Morgan accepted the canteen, took a long drink of the cool, refreshing water, and then poured the remainder over his head.

"Welcome to the Colonies, Davidson," Morgan finally gasped, "the refuge of all the homeless exiles, the peaceful sanctuary you are longing for." He threw back his head and managed a rasping laugh. "I told you, this is the wrong country for peace and quiet!"

When the Indian that Morgan had knocked insensible showed signs of returning to consciousness, Derick looked in his direction. "He is coming around, Morgan," Derick said, jerking his head toward the prostrate warrior. "He's your man."

Morgan glanced indifferently in the direction of the young brave. "Terrible waste of good lead. Would you mind doing me the honor?" Morgan asked, pointing to Derick's sword.

"Nay, I will not. The wounded are left on the field after the battle. I will not kill the wounded. That is murder. I fight to live, Morgan, *not* to kill. It is a matter of honor." Morgan gave Derick an incredulous look and then grunted his annoyance.

"Aren't you the one who just relieved that Indian of his head?" Morgan asked, pointing to an Indian who lay decapitated in the clearing. "And didn't you tell me about you and your brothers deliberately hunting down the British?" With a measure of disgust, Morgan shook his head in wonder at the lifeless form of the headless warrior. "I can assure you of one thing, Davidson, that headless hero would kill you before you draw your next breath if he could. And that one over there," Morgan said jabbing a long finger toward the prostrate man, "just give him one opportunity, and his tomahawk will split your skull wide open. You're a dead man if you turn your back on him, mark my words," Morgan said and nodded toward the rousing Indian.

Morgan spat on the ground. Still shaking his head in bewilderment, he moved toward the fallen Indian who was holding his wrist and groaning with pain. Derick followed, and the two men stood over the young brave who lay moaning on the ground, his eyes closed. Morgan knelt beside him on the grass, assessing the symbolic figures and strange markings drawn on his body.

The Indian blinked several times and then opened his eyes to see Derick and Morgan leaning over him, their weapons raised. Folding his arms across his chest, the young warrior waited wordlessly for the deathblow, his eyes holding respect and honor for Morgan, the one who had bested him in battle. For a long moment, Morgan stared back at the burning black eyes and then jerked the Indian to a sitting position by his scalp lock. Noting the Huron war paint, he spoke to the Indian in French.

"Who are you, and why did you attack us? We have not molested you or your tribe."

"I am Red Fox," faltered the young brave, "a warrior of the Huron of the lakes. We follow two men, thieves and murderers of my people. They go to the village of Boston. We travel many days."

"We are not your men," Morgan said with obvious impatience. "We are traveling to Virginia. This man has just come over the big water, and I come from Boston." Morgan motioned toward Derick who pointed his sword at the Indian's chest. "We are not your men, understand? I would prefer you inquire before throwing tomahawks at innocent travelers." The Indian made no reply, obviously skeptical of Morgan's explanation.

"I would kill you now," Morgan said in French, "just as dead as your dead brothers over there, but my friend says—*no kill,* to let you go. Remember this, Red Fox of the Huron Nation, if I ever see you again in this life, I will not be so merciful. Now go, leave before I change my mind. Go!"

Morgan yanked the Indian to his feet and pointed to the forest. The young warrior, who called himself Red Fox, studied the big man standing beside Morgan as though to memorize the Scotsman's rugged features, his dark eyes locking with the intense blue eyes of his savior. He stood unsteadily on his feet and looked around at his fallen companions scattered about the clearing. Without another word and holding his broken wrist, he limped painfully toward the forest. He did not look back.

"Well," Morgan said, his old humor returning as he watched the warrior disappear into the trees, "perhaps he'll die of shame and disgrace before he reaches his village. It's a possibility." He turned to Derick with a grin. "C'mon, Davidson, let's get out of this devilish place."

Chapter 4

The Colonials

The warp in the old wood
Is hardest to remove

The road to Virginia was long and rough. Morgan seemed in no particular hurry to reach his farm near Winchester. His passionate discussions with many of Boston's zealous revolutionaries left Morgan preoccupied and deeply concerned over the recent unrest in Boston. As he related his upsetting encounters with the leading Colonials, Derick paid close attention to all Morgan had heard and witnessed in Boston. He considered every detail of the argument for independence and sovereignty for the American Colonies.

As they journeyed to Virginia, Derick examined every aspect frontier life and was eager to discover what made the American Patriots so impatient for war. For Clan Davidson and the Scots, the dream of independence from England had died on the bloody battlefield at Culloden Moor, and Derick Davidson was not eager to take up the banner again. He had had his fill of war and revenge.

Except for the occasional rain shower, the remainder of the trip was uneventful and highly invigorating for Derick, especially after his long confinement on the ship for numerous weeks. The weather grew unseasonably milder, making the way tolerable for camping in the wilderness. Following the tomahawk-blazed trails toward Virginia, Morgan carefully combed the trail for Indian signs, inspecting their campsites with the eye of a skilled woodsman. Whenever possible, they spent the nights in a small frontier settlement or under the shelter of a settler's barn.

They exchanged news with the Colonials while they sat by the fireside and shared meals on rough log tables. On these occasions, Derick remained quiet, listening intently to the conversation and endeavoring to grasp the heartbeat of this vast new country. The talk invariably turned to war and taxes and the tyrannical impositions of the British government. The inevitability of an imminent conflict was a favorite topic of conversation. Since the Stamp Act in 1765 and the Townsend Act in 1767, angry Colonists vowed to end the unfair taxation, even if their decision resulted in civil disobedience to King George and his monarchial rule over the American Colonies.

The rawboned settlers of the frontier were American in their sentiment and opinion. They had carved their existence from the virgin forests and wilderness lands. This resourceful group of Colonials consisted of planters and farmers, hunters and trappers, business owners and tradesmen, and they saw their King as an avaricious tyrant who wanted only to expand his holdings in America and carry on commerce in an endeavor to exact more taxes and money from his subjects.

Among this number of American born Colonials was a smattering of wealthy Bostonians such as John Hancock, a Massachusetts merchant and American Patriot, and Samuel and John Adams, political leaders and Patriots whose resistance to English authority fueled the fires of revolution. The King himself had no real interest in the new world except for what he could gain from exploiting those who lived and worked there.

On the other hand, the Loyalists, the aristocracy and upper class of England, those in sympathy with the King and the British government, lived primarily in the larger eastern cities and maintained a life of relative affluence and prosperity. Landowners, judges, lawyers, and statesmen, men of influence and power, were the liaisons of Great Britain and were friends of the King. Some were speculators, wealthy planters and merchants, and military officers who received commissions and payment for their efforts in keeping order and for civilizing the people of the frontier.

To uphold order and maintain lands recently wrestled from the French, British officers were given commissions to establish fortifications along the ever-expanding westward frontier. The settlers on the western borders, revolutionaries at heart, were dependant upon the British garrisons for protection from Indian uprisings, yet they could not come to terms with the domination of English rule. Caught betwixt the two, their position rested in a precarious balance. With the country fairly writhing in the boiling tides of insurrection, it was only a matter of time before a conflict would erupt along the eastern seaboard. With the increasing hostilities, a war with England seemed unavoidable.

It was the middle of December when the two weary travelers arrived in Virginia. The skies had turned a leaden gray and the low hanging clouds foretold of an approaching snowstorm. Morgan led the way through the rolling countryside until he reached his own 255 acres, the prime farmland of Frederick County. It felt good to be home again.

From a distance, a Negro servant saw the pair riding up the gentle rise to the house and hurried to meet them, a broad smile on his old face. Daniel Morgan pulled his long rifle from the leather scabbard and fired his gun into the air.

"Well, praise de Lawd, if'n it isn't Marse Morgan his own self," said the servant in a burst of high spirits. "We was hopin' you'd git home befo' the winter storms sweep yon valley."

"Hullo yourself, Saul," Morgan said dismounting his horse and slapping his hired man on the back. "Here you go, Saul. I know you missed your old friend, Samson. Look after my friend's horse as well." Morgan handed over the reins and closed his eyes. He breathed deeply, savoring the pleasure of standing on his own land and feeling the joy of homecoming. "My, but it's good to be home again after so many days on the trail," he said.

He exchanged small talk with his stableman and then turned to Derick. "Well, here we are, Davidson, my humble abode."

Derick surveyed the modest wooden structure with an appraising eye. It was a pleasant appearing home, well kept and inviting. The frontier homes were so unlike the ancient stone dwellings in the Scottish highlands, but he liked the way the frontier people built their homes in the open, as if to make a statement to their enemies. If they needed to flee their homes, they could refugee to the nearby forts; otherwise, they must stand their ground.

"Aye, it's always good to come home," Derick said wistfully, "but ye Americans build your dwellings with no defense in mind. A few fire arrows could burn ye out. Will take getting used to, but I like the boldness of it."

"Well, someday, I'll build a proper home for Abigail, maybe stone or brick," Morgan stated awkwardly. He placed his hands on his hips and surveyed the simple dwelling. "I want to have a nice place for visitors and for Abigail."

"Appears to be very adequate for the country," Derick replied. "The homes here on the frontier hold a simple charm. I find them most welcoming. In Scotland, we live in stone houses, virtual fortresses, and a constant reminder of our vulnerability. But then, they are not easily burned or invaded as are your frontier dwellings made from wood and logs."

Green shutters framed the windows of the two-story house and several steps led to a small porch sheltering the main entrance. A woman's presence in the home was marked by the feminine touch of soft lace curtains hanging in the widows.

Smoke curled from the tall chimneys spanning opposite sides of the house and the pungent smells of burning wood and cooking meat filled the air. Within minutes, the front door flew open and two little girls of about six and eight ran from the house, their blonde braids flying behind them.

"Papa, Papa!" they called in a joyous chorus." The two girls flung themselves into the brawny arms of their father and Daniel Morgan scooped them up together in a huge bear hug, kissing their plump little cheeks with obvious affection.

Setting them down again, he said, "Little gals, this is my new friend, Mr. Derick Davidson, and these," Morgan said laying a hand on each child's head, "are my two little gals, my daughters, Nancy and Betsy." Morgan beamed, his expression radiating pride.

Stepping back a few paces, Morgan made room for Derick to greet the little girls he had introduced as his own daughters. Surprise and astonishment raced though Derick's mind, but he maintained his usual composure, not allowing this unexpected revelation to register on his countenance. On the long road to Winchester, Morgan had not mentioned having children or a family.

Perhaps, Derick thought, his wife had died, and the marriage for which he was returning to Virginia was a marriage of convenience to a woman who would care for his two motherless daughters. Perhaps Morgan had not spoken of his upcoming nuptials with his future wife simply because he did not truly love the woman. Such arrangements were common enough on the frontier, and given time, love would come.

Derick knelt on the ground beside Morgan's daughters and extended his large hand, which the girls took in turn. "I bid ye good day, and I be pleased to meet such bonny lassies." He kissed their little hands in a chivalrous gesture. Feeling uncertain about the greeting, the girls smiled shyly, glancing sideways at their father for approval.

"Mr. Davidson means he is all-fired glad to meet my pretty little gals," Morgan said in way of explanation. "In his country across the ocean, they call a little gal a lassie, and they kiss a lady's hand when they meet." Morgan cleared his throat. "Of course, Mr. Davidson can see my little gals are genuine frontier ladies, so naturally, kissin' your little paws is quite fittin'."

"Oh," Nancy said brightly. "I like being a lady, Mr. Davidson." Morgan laughed heartily, and they all joined in.

The door opened again and a beautiful young woman in her late twenties ran into Morgan's arms, tears of joy and relief running down her cheeks. She was a tiny woman, more like a young girl than a wife and mother. Thick honey-colored hair hung down her back in waves, and her eyes were the color of the ocean, green and blue at the same time.

"Oh, Daniel, Daniel! I thought you would never come back, that you had—" She suddenly caught sight of Derick standing a few paces away and broke off in her greeting. Derick hung back, not wanting to intrude on the homecoming. "—had changed your mind about...about..." she stammered. Her voice trailed into silence and then she brightened. She looked at Morgan with obvious affection. "How thankful I am to see you home again, safe and sound." Morgan lifted the young woman into his arms, swung her around in a circle, and kissed her soundly.

"Well, Abby," Morgan said after a moment, "you drive a hard bargain, but how could I stay away from you and my little gals? Now I'm home and ready to git hitched proper like, with a piece of paper statin' it's so, and with words said over us by the preacher, just like you want. He can tie the knot a little tighter if it makes you happy. I'll carry out my part of this infernal sham. Send for the preacher right now, Abby, and let's get this marriage legalized before nightfall."

Suddenly, Derick understood. For whatever reason, Daniel Morgan's marriage was not a legally binding union, and Morgan had retuned to Virginia to meet the terms of Abigail's request and to take the necessary steps to legalize their ten-year commitment. Derick could only guess at Morgan's reluctance, for he seemed to genuinely love the woman he was holding in his arms. The children definitely belonged to Daniel Morgan. The resemblance to him was unmistakable.

"Oh, Daniel," Abigail laughed, "we can't send for the preacher this late in the day, but we'll send first thing in the morning. Then I'll have time to get things ready and send for the neighbors. They can stand as witnesses." Daniel Morgan rolled his eyes and sighed in resignation. Then he remembered Derick who was patiently waiting for this little scene to play out.

"Abigail, meet my friend who I met in Boston. No doubt, he saved my hide along the trail to Virginy. He's just arrived from Scotland. Davidson, this is my...err...uh..."

Abigail blushed profusely and stepped forward and extended her hand, not waiting for Morgan to extricate himself from the blundering introduction. "Pleased to meet you, Mr. Davidson, and if you have saved Daniel's life, I am truly grateful." Abigail smiled warmly. "I hope you will stay with us for a while and learn the way of the frontier folks."

Derick took her hand in his, immediately liking this lovely young woman. He wondered how the rough ex-soldier, wagoner, and frontiersman had managed to capture the heart of this tender-eyed lass.

"A pleasure to acquaint meself with ye, madam," Derick said bending over her hand and kissing the top of her slender fingers. "I believe Mr. Morgan saved me own neck from bein' wrung by the likes of King George's men, so we naturally formed an unusual friendship."

Daniel Morgan raised his eyebrows at the gallant way in which Derick greeted Abigail. He grinned and winked at his little girls who were watching the proceedings, wide-eyed and conscious of something unusual in the way this stranger had greeted their mother. Morgan was not in the least offended by the gracious gesture and understood that Derick Davidson was not the ordinary coarse and unrefined frontiersman like most of the men he knew.

Derick Davidson was not only an excellent swordsman who could easily survive in an untamed wilderness, but Morgan was convinced he could also hold his own among the genteel of Boston society. Somewhere in his past, Derick Davidson had been educated as a gentlemen of culture and refinement, and despite his warring ways, his stately manner clung to his nature as did the claymore to his side.

Something in Davidson's bearing set him apart from ordinary men, but Morgan could not put a name to it. He possessed some quality of character, some strength of mind and spirit from deep inside him. Exactly what this was, Morgan was not certain, but he instinctively liked the big Scotsman and hoped he would remain in Winchester for the duration of the winter. He wanted to learn more about him and discover what made this man different from most Colonials he knew.

After a hearty frontier supper of roast venison, potatoes, fried squash, hot bread, and pumpkin pie directly from the oven, Abigail asked Morgan to show Derick to the bunkhouse attached to the stables and said he might spend the night there himself. After the marriage ceremony on the morrow, she whispered with an engaging smile, she would arrange a room for Derick in the house and Daniel could return to the room he shared with her. Morgan was obviously annoyed and outraged with this arrangement, but rather than make a scene on his first night home, he grudgingly acquiesced.

The large bunkhouse-like room was next to the stable. A stone hearth with a small fireplace stood on the outside wall. This accommodation, although somewhat crude by city standards, was snug and serviceable for the many travelers who passed by and was used primarily for this purpose. An entire family could spend several days or weeks in this room before moving to their next destination.

Abigail had furnished the room with four beds, a table and chairs, and one chest of drawers. Hooks for hanging clothing, travel packs, and horse tack extended along the walls, and bright rag rugs were scattered about the floor. Colorful calico curtains hung at the windows, adding a cheerful atmosphere to the cozy setting. The distinct touch of a woman's hand had arranged this homey guest quarters.

When the door to the room closed behind the two men, Derick threw his pack on an empty bed and sat on another facing Morgan, his face splitting into a grin, and his blue eyes twinkling with unrestrained mirth. It was the very first time Morgan recalled seeing such an indisputable display of humor in the Scotsman.

On the long trek from Boston to Virginia, the man had been sober, cautious, pleasant enough, but constantly on the alert. Now he was grinning from ear to ear like a Cheshire cat. Relaxing his vigilant attitude, he gazed at Morgan in a comfortable manner. His foolish-looking grin irritated Morgan. He guessed at the cause for Davidson's uncharacteristic show of humor, but he did not want to confront the source of his amusement. Finally, Morgan could take this display of unexpected humor no longer.

"What is so all-fired funny, and why are you grinning like some ignorant fool?" Morgan stormed. He threw his pack none too gently to the floor and looked around at the room with obvious distaste. He placed his hands on his hips while Derick continued to grin. Finding no help for his unbridled delight over Morgan's discomfiture, Derick broke into a genuine laughter, shaking the bed in his amusement. He held his sides as he laughed and bellowed in his deep bass voice.

"I don't see what you find so amusing," Morgan complained with evident disgust. "I didn't realize you possessed a funny bone in that big body." Morgan kicked viciously at the pack he had thrown to the floor, sat on the nearest bed, and angrily pulled off his boots.

"Shut up, Davidson," Morgan warned. He removed his boots then pulled off his jacket and his hunting shirt. He looked long into the mirror hanging over the bureau. "Can't say as I blame her, though," Morgan said thoughtfully as he viewed himself for the first time in weeks.

The laughter from the other bed ended abruptly. Derick gazed in disbelief at Morgan's bare back, now fully exposed to view from the pale light of the lantern. Along the trail to Winchester, Morgan had undressed only a few times, just to wash himself in the semi-darkness of the campfire. He always kept his back turned away.

After Morgan removed his shirt, Derick could see the incredible mass of vivid raised scars spanning the entire length of Morgan's back. Unconsciously, he sucked in his breath at the appalling sight. There was not a space where the whip had not cut into the flesh, not a smooth place over the shoulder muscles or along the ribs or over the waist. Every inch of flesh was scared over, leaving a lumpy accumulation of misshapen tissue across his bare back. Derick's face sobered and he turned his eyes away. He felt anger rising in his bosom, a natural urge to vindicate such brutality to his friend.

Morgan understood why the laughter had suddenly ceased. He sat on the bed opposite Davidson, trying to decide where to begin. He knew this moment would come eventually and he wanted to share his story with the Scotsman.

"I was a wagoner at the onset of the French and Indian war," Morgan began in way of explanation. "I owned my own team and wagons and that's how I made my living, Davidson. I hired out as a civilian in those days, to haul supplies for the English army. The job paid well, and I saved my money and eventually bought this place." He paused, idly studying the rag rug beneath his feet.

"I was eighteen, young and ambitious," Morgan continued. "Major General Edward Braddock hired me to haul supplies for his expedition to Fort Duquesne. The expedition itself was a military fiasco, but I was paid plenty for my trouble. During that military disaster, I ended up hauling dead bodies away from the battle. It turned my stomach and I have a strong stomach."

"I've heard of that military defeat, even in Scotland," Derick remarked.

"Well," Morgan continued, "I hauled cargo for the British and in the spring of 1756, while hauling supplies to Fort Chiswell, a British officer and I had words over my methods as a wagoner. During our conversation, I spoke a little too disrespectful for the Lieutenant's liking and he struck me with the flat edge of his sword."

Derick listened in silence, his mind racing ahead. He could guess the outcome of the confrontation.

"Well, I wasn't used to being struck for no good reason, simply because I didn't share his uneducated opinion. I've never been bested by a fool, and especially by an English officer who knows nothin' about wagoning. Well, Davidson, I figured I could whip him good since I always make it a practice not to corner anyone meaner than me. Well, I drew back my fist and knocked that arrogant Lieutenant out cold, just like a dead man, with one well-aimed punch to his ugly mug."

A slow smile spread across Derick's face as he pictured Morgan's account of the altercation. He admired Daniel Morgan's tenacity, his freedom-loving attitude, and his loyalty to the American way of life. It was true, his ways were rough and crude, but they were also honest and candid, and his courage in the face of great odds was admirable. Morgan's keen insight and his enthusiastic sense of justice made up for his lack of a formal education. Derick understood how the insult from the British Lieutenant would have incensed the young wagoner.

Shifting on the bed, Morgan reached for his pack and pulled a plug of tobacco from the recesses of the leather bag.

"The next thing I knew, I was in the clink facing a court martial for insubordination," Morgan said as he wadded the leaves into a tight ball. "I was sentenced to be flogged by an old military judge who had a lot of practice and looked to be meaner than a snake. Meanness don't just happen overnight, you know. It takes some practice, some real effort to cultivate, and that spiteful old devil of a judge appeared to have plenty practice."

Morgan stuffed the wad of tobacco into the hollow of his scarred cheek, and then continued. "They tied me to a post and counted the lashes to the beat of a drum." He paused, an ironic twinkle in his eye. "I counted too, trying to keep my mind off the pain. I didn't want to faint in front of those British soldiers. Every stripe was extreme torture once there was no more skin to break."

Most men wouldn't have lived through such a beating, but Daniel Morgan was from tough Welsh stock. He would live to tell this gruesome tale to his grandchildren. Derick shuddered at the thought of such cruelty. For as far back as he could remember, something rose in his breast in defense of the helpless. It was one thing to fight in battle, a fair fight, but to beat a defenseless and helpless man was an act of pure cowardice in his estimation.

"The man who was a whippin' me stopped when I passed out, so the British still owe me one," laughed Morgan sardonically. He stood to his feet and gazed out the window into the gathering darkness. "Two years later, I joined a local company of Rangers serving the British here in Winchester." He paused again, noting the look of amazement on his companion's face.

"Plum crazy, huh? Well, I liked the military style of the Rangers, so I put up with the rest. I applied for a commission and was granted a position as Ensign. My partner and I were carrying a dispatch from Fort Edward to Winchester when Indians waiting in the brush near Hanging Rock, ambushed us." Morgan shook his head.

"My partner was killed outright and I had to leave him there. Hated like the devil to do it too. Those Indians will mutilate a body. Well, Davidson, I was blessed to have a good steady mount under my backside that day. Me and my horse outran those red devils. Escaped by a gnat's eyelash. Just as I was riding out of range, thinkin' I'd made it with my scalp still attached, I took a bullet from behind, a lucky shot for an Indian, and was spitting my teeth out and riding for the settlement like one possessed. The bullet tore up my cheek."

Morgan pointed to the scar on the left side of his face. "I was bleeding like a stuck pig and could hardly sit a saddle when I reached safety."

"I wondered about the scar," Derick said. "Left ye pretty well marked, Morgan." He retrieved his own pack from the bed and brought out a clean linen shirt, the last clean shirt he had.

"That's a fact," Morgan agreed. "When I recovered from the incident, I went to wagoning again. I gambled, drank, and brawled my way to manhood, I mean *real manhood*." He smiled ruefully. "A rough way to grow up, I'll admit. I wouldn't advise it."

Derick smiled wryly. "Aye, nor would I, me friend," he agreed.

"Despite my brawling ways," Morgan continued as he washed from a basin of water placed on the washstand, "I was still Welsh enough to save my money, and in '59, I had saved enough to get me a house in Winchester."

"The Welsh are known for their frugal ways, as are the Scots," Derick alleged.

"Then," Morgan said softening, "I found Abigail." His eyes sparkled as he pulled on the clean nightshirt Abigail had given him. He smelled deeply of the fresh scent. "Ah," he breathed appreciatively, "domestic life has its simple pleasures." Derick nodded agreement, knowing how difficult it was to stay clean on the ship, not to mention along the trail from Boston to Virginia.

"Abigail was all fire and spit and beauty," Morgan offered, "and she tore at my heart like no other gal ever had. I was twenty-six, and she was barely sixteen." He smiled at this confession.

"I knew she was the one I wanted to spend my life with, so I set out to court her proper like. At first, she wouldn't pay me no mind so I bought some fine clothes and slicked up a bit and eventually, she came around. We set up housekeeping together in Winchester." He waited for a reaction from Derick, feeling certain he would have something to say about this arrangement, but Derick only nodded.

"She is a lovely lass, Morgan. I wouldn't have believed..." He left off speaking, not knowing how to put his thoughts into words.

"I know what you're a thinkin'," Morgan said brusquely, "you can't believed Abigail would hook up with the likes of me."

"You put those words in me mouth, Morgan. I was going to say how amazing that a lass so young could understand the worth of a good man. I know people, and you can never tell about a person on the outside. Some you might think are rough, crude, and not so bonny, but they are often the most honest, most loving, and true to ye. Sometimes the bonny ones will fool ye and cut your heart to pieces."

"True, very true," Morgan agreed. "Well, Abby saw something in me she liked, and I know…" he paused in his narrative, a look of infinite tenderness crossing his features. "I know she loves me, Davidson. That means somethin'. Abby wasn't just another woman…ya know?"

"Aye, I know." Derick's voice mellowed to almost a whisper. "It's the sweetest thing life has to offer ye, Morgan, the tender love of a bonny lass." Derick looked away, an uncomfortable lump rising in his throat. He was happy for his friend and he didn't want Morgan to see his grief, not on the eve of his wedding.

Daniel Morgan was an observant and perceptive man, and during the long journey from Boston to Winchester, he had sensed the deep sorrow springing from the soul of the Scotsman. This silent suffering seemed to overwhelm Davidson at times and Morgan knew from experience how grief could weaken the strongest of men. Morgan was not a man to pry into the private lives of his comrades, and Derick Davidson respected and valued Morgan's privacy as well. Morgan felt the Scotsman would reveal the details of his trouble in his own time. He pretended not to notice the dark shadow falling over their conversation.

"At any rate, Abby was always frettin' over not sayin' our vows in front of a preacher, with papers and all," Morgan said, changing the subject. "After the little gals came along, she fretted even more. I told her we were just as joined by God as anyone could be, but she wouldn't be satisfied." He shook his head as if he could not comprehend this fact.

"About a year ago, she went to some church meetings and came home with religion. Said she got saved and was going to live the Christian life. I was mad as a hornet and went off on a month-long hunt thinkin' it would all blow over by the time I came home."

"I'm guessing ye were wrong?" Derick queried.

"You can bet your prize horse on it! Was the dumbest, most foolhardy stunts I ever pulled. My stayin' away only encouraged her to become more involved in the church. So, I drank and brawled and made life miserable for her. I thought if she saw how religion was making me worse, then she'd give it up. Fact is, I was the one who was miserable."

Derick smiled. "I guess that battle strategy didn't work very well with Abby. Sounds like it worked in reverse."

"You're right about that, my friend. All I got for my trouble was a walloping hangover and a sick headache with Abby nursing me through it." He softened again. "Naturally, I love my little gals more than I can say, and Abby is the joy of my life, so how could I live without 'em? Then one day I came home and Abigail had moved me into the spare room! Said if we didn't get married proper like, she couldn't be my wife, like...sleep with me, you know?"

Derick nodded. "That episode must have provided the inspiration for your trip to Boston," Derick surmised.

Morgan looked chagrined. "You bet your sweet life, it did. Abigail said when I made up my mind to let the preacher marry us proper, she would welcome me back to *our* room. I got so mad I could spit nails, so I headed for Boston, determined to wait her out." He rolled his eyes and looked heavenward.

"What else could I do? I couldn't stay away, Davidson. Besides, I didn't even know why I was being so mule headed about gettin' hitched by the preacher. No good reason I could think of. I was just mad about being turned out of my own bedroom and in my own house to boot. I'm not a religious man myself, but I decided it wouldn't hurt anything if Abby and the little gals became God-fearing Christians if that's what they wanted, so I made up my mind to get married by the town preacher, and Davidson, you know the rest of this ridiculous story."

"Actually, me friend, I like the tale. Beats anything I ever heard," Derick said smiling. He stood, turned down the blankets, and yawned.

"Well, glad you appreciate my suffering and find this account so entertaining."

"Well, at least," Derick added with a note of whimsy, "the tale will have a guid end to it. Remember, *Is maith an scáthán súil carad.*"

"What the devil are you a sayin'? I told you—*speak American.*"

"It means, a friend's eye is a good mirror. I see good things ahead for ye. I think ye are doing the honorable thing by granting Abby's request. Ye won't regret it."

Daniel Morgan punched up the feather pillow on his bed with a needless vigor. "I'm turning in for the night," he growled and then blew out the flame burning low in the lantern. The two men lay on their beds in the darkness, thinking of their own peculiar circumstance.

In a short time, they fell sound asleep, weary of the trail and the continual uneasiness of the journey. Caution fell by the wayside, and the men slept like babes. During the night, snow fell across the valley, covering the world with white and blotting out the unsightly blemishes of the earth.

The following day dawned cold and clear. The storm clouds had moved on to blanket the Potomac Valley and beyond. Servants rose early and set out on horseback to fetch the preacher and invite the neighbors to attend the overdue nuptials of Abigail Curry and Daniel Morgan.

A frontier feast was prepared for the occasion, and neighbors gathered to witness the legalizing of the marriage union. In the frontier settlements, a permanent preacher was not always available, and couples either waited until spring when the traveling preachers rode through the area or simply took up housekeeping as man and wife until a preacher was available. This practice was tolerated as a matter of convenience among the Colonials, and only the extremely legalistic minds shunned those who said their own vows. Daniel Morgan, however, had seen many preachers come and go over the years.

The preacher arrived early in the day, and soon afterwards, friends and neighbors crowded into the main room of the house, quite eager for the proceedings to begin. Abigail was radiate, dressed in a deep green silk trimmed with heavy black lace. She had saved this frock for this special day of "setting in order." Daniel Morgan wore a white linen shirt with full sleeves trimmed in lace and a butternut colored woolen coat with matching breeches. He looked quite miserable in his dress clothes, and Derick smiled his sympathy for his friend.

For special occasions, Derick wore a tartan sash over a white shirt made of the finest linen, and brought from Scotland. His close fitting breeches were a gift from Daniel Morgan who was determined to Americanize the newcomer. Abigail's house servant, Zadie, had worked all morning to alter the breeches to fit the Scotsman's large frame.

Derick stood by Morgan's side as the unenthusiastic bridegroom welcomed his guests. He introduced Derick to his fellow Colonials, explaining Derick's recent arrival from Scotland and that he would be spending the winter at the Morgan farm.

Curious neighbors whispered behind their hands and speculated about Daniel Morgan's surprising friendship with the newcomer. Derick stationed himself by the fireplace while Morgan brought his best wine from the cellar.

The last of the company arrived, stamping snow from their boots and joining in the general merriment of this impromptu wedding party. From the last group of late arrivals, a young woman removed her fur-trimmed bonnet and shook ice crystals from her thick dark curls, laughing merrily as she did so. She kissed Abigail and hugged Daniel Morgan fondly, wrapping her arms around his waist while the latter planted a kiss on her rosy cheek.

When she waved to her friends across the room, she noticed a tall stranger standing by the fireplace, a green tartan sash across one shoulder. He was a striking figure, and his noticeable presence seemed to dominate the space where he stood watching the ongoing proceedings with keen interest. Then he looked her way and the deep brown eyes of Kearan Mackenzie met the inquisitive blue eyes of Derick Davidson.

Chapter 5

Kearan

*Green is the grass
Of the least trodden field*

Kearan Mackenzie could not recall ever seeing the stranger before. *Maybe in my dreams,* she thought laughing softly to herself. The unfamiliar guest was leaning against the hand-carved wooden column of the fireplace with an air of indifference, a self-imposed detachment setting him apart from the other men in the room. Kearan thought he seemed unusually tall, strongly built, and uncommonly handsome. Their eyes had met for one brief moment, but before he had shifted his eyes away, Kearan had caught a momentary spark of interest in the clear blue eyes of the stranger.

Daniel Morgan was busy directing his guests and arranging the parlor for the long awaited wedding ceremony to be celebrated with the only woman he had ever truly loved, Abigail Curry. The neighbors in the county had tolerated the common-law marriage arrangement, viewed for the most part, as a justifiable inconvenience in the lives of many of the frontier folk, especially when a preacher was not available. To Abigail Curry, however, Daniel Morgan had put off the exchanging of vows long enough. The ultimatum had been delivered after Abigail's conversion to the faith. Daniel Morgan had no excuse. Winchester had a permanent preacher who would gladly legalize their common law vows.

Morgan's close friends and neighbors had shared the news of Abigail's confession to the faith with a mixture of best wishes and trepidation over what might occur. His subsequent flight from his home upon hearing the startling and unwelcome news of Abigail's conversion gave the frontier settlement no little concern. Fearful of the outcome and knowing Morgan's temper and his obvious displeasure over Abigail's religious awakening, the entire community had waited nervously for Morgan's return.

They were pleasantly surprised and quite happy to hear the couple would say their vows before the preacher and the entire neighborhood was hastily summoned to celebrate the joyous occasion. Morgan's nearest neighbor and close friend, Silas Mackenzie was particularly happy when he heard Daniel had returned home safely and was ready to tie the matrimonial knot with Abigail.

"Well, Dan'l," Silas Mackenzie said pounding him on the back, "looks like Abby won this round." He guffawed loudly and several of the neighbors joined in. "What's the use of kickin' up a fuss when you and Abby have no plans on callin' it quits? Should'a done it long ago."

"Yep, you're right, Silas," Morgan agreed grudgingly. "I just hate losin' a battle, that's all. Just doesn't seem fittin' for the women folk to get their way. Well, what does it matter, by gum?"

"Whadda ya mean, get their way? Why, Dan'l Morgan, you've had your way for quite a spell now, so just call it even. Now it's Abby's turn. Besides, it's best for your little gals, ya know. That's what matters. You gotta think of them gals too. They're a growin' up fast, and things need to be fixed up respectable lookin' for their sakes, I say." Daniel sighed and nodded in agreement.

"True enough, Silas, true enough," Morgan acknowledged. Silas surveyed the room full of guests and looked toward the tall man standing a little apart from the rest of the guests.

"Who might the stranger be standing agin the fireplace mantel, Dan'l? I don't recollect seeing him before."

"You haven't seen him before. His name's Derick Davidson, and he just got off the boat from Scotland. I met him in Boston several weeks ago. We had a little confrontation with some redcoats who were just itchin' to hang him just for fun, so I brought him to Virginny with me. Come on over and give him a neighborly howdy."

Several other men in the company of guests were summoned and after Morgan offered introductions, warm handshakes and greetings were exchanged. Invitations to visit the neighboring farms were extended and the men of the county welcomed the newcomer with honest frontier hospitality. Derick was warmed by their willingness to include a stranger.

The Scottish clan system with its rivalries, suspicions, and prejudices, seemed nonexistent in this frontier settlement. Derick was glad of this. He knew what it was like for neighbors to quarrel. It was prevalent among the Scottish clans, and he was weary of clan disputes and the endless internal strife that ultimately led to bloodshed.

"Come now, Mr. Davidson, meet my family," Silas Mackenzie said with enthusiasm. With one long arm, he extracted Kearan from a gaggle of young girls and turned her to face Derick. Kearan blushed profusely as her father dragged her forward. "This here is my baby daughter, Kearan, and yonder there," he pointed to his wife, "yonder talking to Abby, that's Lily Jayne, my wife. My oldest daughter, Mattie, is married and lives t'other side of Winchester.

Our son, Alfred, is away deer huntin'. Morgan sprang this weddin' business on us with no warnin' whatsoever, or Alfred would be here, to be sure. He thinks a lot of Dan'l and Abigail. Dan'l is Captain of our local militia, and Alfred is one of his sharpshooters."

Kearan extended her hand toward Derick, not quite certain how to acknowledge her father's rudimentary introduction. Derick took the proffered hand in his, and bending over it, he kissed the top of her delicate white fingers. "A pleasure to meet you, lass," Derick said looking into a pair of dark brown eyes flashing with indignation and confusion. Kearan looked quite perplexed and quickly drew her hand away, hiding it in her skirt. The group of young friends Kearan had been conversing with before her father had claimed her, smiled knowingly, nodding their approval at the courteous greeting from the stranger. This was the mark of a true gentleman.

"Don't mind these silly young gals, Mr. Davidson," Silas said when he saw Kearan's friends making a to-do over Derick's unaccustomed greeting. "They aren't much used to bein' kissed on the hand by a young gentleman. They are more likely to get a good slap on the back in way of a *hello*." Silas laughed heartily at his own joke. "The frontier ways are quite uncommon, to be sure, but you'll get used to our simple ways. Isn't that right, Kearan gal?"

"Oh Papa, how can you talk so?" Kearan said reproachfully. "My apologies, Mr. Davidson. Papa is just so out of touch with modern society and the ways of genteel folk." She cast her father a withering glance.

"I meant no offense, Mr. Mackenzie, nor to ye, lass," Derick said apologetically. "It is the way of me clan, of our people. Forgive me if I have offended ye. I am unaware of your custom in greeting a lady. Mr. Morgan has yet to teach me."

"No offense taken, Mr. Davidson," Kearan assured him, "and actually, I think it is very..." she paused, searching for words, "very refreshing to be greeted as a lady, even though we do live on the rough frontier. It is a very gallant custom indeed, and one our frontier boys would do well to imitate." Silas Mackenzie laughed again, slapping his knee with pure enjoyment. He was a Scot by name and blood, but an American frontiersman by birth. His speech held no trace of the Scottish burr of his ancestors.

"Now, that's my Kearan, Mr. Davidson," Silas said. "Thinks she's all growed up for all her seventeen years. Tellin' folks just how things oughtta be. She'll keep us all in line, and that's a fact." Kearan blushed again, this time glaring daggers at her father.

"Oh, Papa, you are so—so hopelessly crude."

Kearan's discomfiture was evident and Derick felt empathy for the brown-eyed lass who seemed to be the delight of her father's jokes.

She excused herself and rejoined the wedding party now forming before the makeshift altar before her father could cause her any further embarrassment.

A long harvest table covered with a white linen cloth and topped with lace stood at one end of the parlor. The last of the colorful fall foliage had been hastily gathered for the occasion, and one of the guests had added bittersweet berries and holly to the arrangement. The effect was quite festive.

The preacher, now a permanent resident of Winchester, took his place behind the table while Abigail and Daniel stood to face him. In a matter of five minutes, thirty guests had joyfully witnessed the exchanging of wedding vows, and Daniel Morgan and Abigail Curry were legally bound together as husband and wife until death should part them.

The fiddle was tuned and the feasting began. Platters of roast venison, pork, sweet potatoes, carrots, turnips, cornbread, and a variety of fruit pies were served to all the guests. The servants had worked tirelessly all morning, scrambling frantically to prepare a proper wedding feast on extremely short notice.

The feasting and merry making lasted until late afternoon when the well-wishers said their farewells and gathered their families together for the journey home. The Mackenzie family lingered, their farm being only a short distance from Daniel Morgan's homestead. The two families were close friends, and for many years, they had weathered the hardships of frontier life together.

A bright fire crackled on the stone hearth, casting a soft glow on Abigail Curry Morgan, now legally bound to Daniel Morgan. Abigail felt content and put her little girls to bed with a happy heart. The two couples sipped mugs of hot tea and talked over the events of the past several weeks when Daniel was away. Morgan spoke of his journey to Boston and his subsequent meeting with Derick Davidson.

Kearan sat in a rocking chair near the fire, twisting a dark curl around her finger and gazing absentmindedly into the flames as she listened to the conversation.

Outside, the skies had cleared and a full moon was rising to shed a soft mellow light on the inch of snow covering the barren ground. In the stable, Derick fed and groomed his horse, talking conversationally to Warrior as he brushed the steed's tail and mane. As he combed out the knotted tangles, the stable door opened with a low creaking noise and Kearan Mackenzie peered inside the dimly lit interior. A lantern hung on a hook against the wall, lighting the stall where Derick worked. Seeing him there, Kearan hesitated for a moment and then opened the door wide.

Derick could see her womanly form silhouetted in the moonlight, her long dark hair flowing softly around her shoulders. Her face was in the shadows, but he knew she was undeniably beautiful, painfully young and innocent, a true frontier lass with the blood of the Scots flowing in her veins.

"Hello, Mr. Davidson. I...I thought you had gone to your room," she ventured in a reticent voice. She came closer. "I was coming for the horses...to saddle them for the ride home."

Derick stopped brushing Warrior and peered at her over the back of the horse. Indeed, she was undeniably beautiful.

"Did ye now?" he asked straightening to his full height. His manner was terse, though not unkind. "Won't Mr. Morgan's servants saddle the beasts for ye?"

"I am sure they would be happy to, but I prefer preparing my own mount," Kearan said with a lift of her chin. Her voice had taken on a defensive tone, but she was not sure how to proceed in a conversation with this man. The Scotsman intrigued her, and all day she had secretly watched him mingling among the other guests. He had moved among the gathering of neighbors and friends with an easy gracious manner. He spoke little, but he listened with interest to the general conversation of the men, which eventually turned to war and how best to obtain independence from British rule.

The Scotsman was different than most of the frontiersmen Kearan knew. He seemed mysterious, inexplicable, unapproachable, yet he had mixed with the wedding guests with ease and impressed them with his quiet way and amicable nature. Derick Davidson had not sought out the company of the single young women, so perhaps he was married. Surely, a man would not leave his homeland and all he knew to come to a strange country without his wife. Daniel

Morgan didn't seem to know much about the private life of his guest, but she would make it her business to find out.

Derick noticed her hesitation and said, "I believe your horses are stabled at the end of the corridor, the last two stalls," he said pointing to the dim recesses at the rear of the building.

"Yes, thank you. I know where the horses are." He must think her a complete dolt, she thought, standing there as though her feet were stuck to the ground.

"Would ye like for me to assist ye?" he asked. His lips curved slightly at the corners as though she amused him. "If ye prefer, lass, I can saddle the beasts for ye."

"No, thank you," Kearan said and slipped past him to the far end of the stable. Derick shook his head and shrugged his shoulders. This young woman was definitely high-spirited and perhaps a wee bit independent. Not many women would refuse an offer to help saddle a horse. He continued grooming Warrior, and in ten minutes, Kearan returned, leading the horses. When she drew near him, she paused, wondering if he would speak to her, perhaps bid her goodnight.

Derick looked up from his work and seeing her standing quietly in the corridor as though waiting for something, he said, "I see ye have managed quite well on your own."

"Of course," she replied confidently, "I am used to caring for the horses. My brother is away hunting quite often, so I tend the horses while he is away. I don't mind, though," she added with a little laugh. "I find caring for the horses quite soothing to my spirit. They are such beautiful and noble creatures."

"Aye, that they are," Derick agreed. He said no more and dropping his blue eyes, he returned to grooming his horse.

Kearan felt somewhat rebuffed. *He certainly isn't one for conversation,* she thought dismally. She was hoping the Scotsman would engage her in some lighthearted conversation about the afternoon wedding, or perhaps some thoughts on his life in Scotland, or even some details of his recent ocean crossing, but he had remained silent as the tomb. Well, she could initiate a conversation herself.

"May I ask you a question, Mr. Davidson?"

Derick stopped in mid stroke of the brush, a look of unease crossing his features. He nodded his head slightly. "Aye, lass. Say on."

"Are you…are you a married man? I mean, did you leave a wife in Scotland?" Kearan was not prepared for the look of pain that rose in his blue eyes. He looked away as if seeing something in the distance and then turned to her again.

"Nay, lass, I am not married—not anymore. My wife is—she is dead." His words were edged with pain and sadness. He offered no explanation. Looking away, he picked up his brushes and laid them on the shelf above the stall.

Kearan was immediately regretful of her decision to engage the newcomer in conversation. She inwardly chided herself for her obvious boldness and for prying into this man's personal life. It was none of her business after all. Why had she been so audacious? She had just met him that very afternoon! Living on the frontier made one careless and insensitive to propriety, she reasoned. She must be more careful of her manners.

Kearan cleared her throat and said with some misgiving. "I am sorry, Mr. Davidson. I have gone beyond good manners in asking such a personal question. I see how it grieves you. Please forgive me."

He looked at her then, his blue eyes studying her as he spoke. "I take no offense, lass. It is natural for ye to wonder about a stranger, someone who is different from others ye have known. I know that I am different in many ways." He paused again and looked away, his eyes thoughtful. Then he looked directly into her brown eyes and his gaze was penetrating. "It's *not* your question that pains me, lass. It's the telling of me story that brings me grief and it cannot be shared with a stranger."

As he continued to search her face, his blue eyes held something akin to sympathy, or perhaps it was simple kindness, but the look in his eyes stirred Kearan's heart. She felt something pass between them, like the gentle beginning of something quite extraordinary.

"You are young, a mere lass," Derick suggested seeing her faltering emotion, "and the young are often inquisitive—impulsive."

His words stung and Kearan blushed, feeling the heat rise to her cheeks. She felt extremely foolish and immature. This man could see right through her! Yes, she was young and quite used to speaking her mind to the men in her life. But there was something different about this man, a masculine reserve that did not invite familiarity. This quality was not present in the young men of the frontier who frequently sought her attention. Her mind went to young Thomas Aubrey, an enterprising young rifleman waiting patiently for her to return his obvious interest.

Suddenly, Kearan felt overwhelmed with shame and embarrassment. His words were kind enough, but he had correctly guessed her motive, causing her further humiliation. Prying into the marital status of the stranger had been indelicate, a breach of deportment and good manners. She knew better, of course, but she had persisted in seeking an answer. Somehow, she thought he would overlook her boldness, but he had named it correctly—*youth and impulsiveness*. She must escape from this man's presence before she died on the spot of pure humiliation. She quickly turned to leave.

"I bid you good evening, Mr. Davidson," Kearan said as she opened the stable door. She endeavored with a mighty effort to gather the rags of her dignity into a semblance of calm control for her exit from the stable. "And I do hope, Mr. Davidson, that you find your stay in our county most pleasant."

"Thank ye, lass, and good evening to ye and safe journey homeward."

Kearan hurried past him through the door and into the wintry evening. As she passed by him, she caught a whiff of his musky masculine odor, a pleasant mixture of horse, spicy herbs, and aged leather. Outside, the frigid air helped to cool her burning cheeks. If only she could forget everything she had said to the Scotsman, if she could wipe every trace of her utter stupidity from her memory, but she could not.

She dropped the horses' reins and spun around in the snow in a fit of profound mortification over her presumptuous questions. Perhaps she could spin until the memory spilled from her head. Suddenly, the stable door opened in the middle of a spin but Kearan heard nothing.

Derick Davidson halted in the doorway as he caught sight of the young girl turning circles in the moonlight, her dark hair flying about her face in a wild disarray, her hands reaching toward the heavens in a beseeching gesture. He stood still, watching the strange frontier ritual with amused curiosity. What on earth was she doing?

Kearan stopped short in mid spin when she heard the creak of the wooden door as it swung on the hinge. Seeing the stranger standing there watching her with that curious look on his face, brought hot tears of frustration to her eyes. Now he would think her quite mad—spinning around in the snow like a woman possessed. She stammered an explanation, blinking back her tears.

"I was just...just...," Kearan faltered, and words failed her. She simply stared at him, not knowing what to say. Even the truth would seem ridiculous, so why try to explain at all. She felt utterly wretched. The horses neighed impatiently, tossing their heads as if to add their own equestrian frustration with the whole affair.

"Is this some manner of Colonial ritual," he asked with an amused tone in his voice. He crossed his arms over his chest, legs apart, and when she said nothing, he suggested, "Perhaps ye are just—practicing the minuet?"

Kearan could hear the unmistakable amusement in his voice and knew he was mocking her. She lifted her chin and a burning fire rose in her bosom. "Yes, exactly so, Mr. Davidson. I am practicing the minuet," she said coolly. Picking up the horses reins, Kearan Mackenzie walked briskly toward the house, not daring to look back. She would leave this man's company immediately before she said or did one more idiotic thing. He was mocking her, and she would be hanged if she would stand there providing a subject for his obvious amusement.

In the distance, the sound of hoof beats reverberated in the winter night, pounding the frozen earth with a rapidity that could only mean trouble. A rider was approaching on the road from Winchester at an alarming pace.

Derick shut the door to the stable and moved silently toward Kearan who had paused on the path to the house, watching with apprehension as the rider thundered into the dooryard. Derick joined Kearan on the path, standing next to her in a protective gesture, one hand on the sword at his side, his eyes alert, wary.

His sheltering presence and his quiet move to stand beside her touched Kearan with a true sense of his person. He was strong, unyielding, and ready to defend her from this unforeseen danger. She decided right then to forgive him for laughing at her. He was wordlessly offering his protection and assistance should she need it. Feeling the quiet strength of Derick Davidson as he stood next to her in the moonlight, Kearan marveled. She looked up at him, an unspoken question in her dark troubled eyes. He looked down at her and understanding passed between them.

A surge of regret swept over Derick when he glimpsed the trembling young Kearan Mackenzie standing beside him, the anguish and embarrassment of their earlier exchange still written on her face. He had not meant to shame her. The curious questions she had so boldly presented disturbed him, dredging up memories he wished to forget. But the lass could not have known. She was innocent, guileless in her frontier simplicity, but she had touched a chord he thought was long dead.

"Steady, lass," Derick said comfortingly. "There's naught to fear."

Kearan unconsciously moved closer to him.

"Ho, the house," shouted the rider as he reined in his weary mount. Almost immediately, the door of the house opened, and Silas Mackenzie and Daniel Morgan appeared in the lighted doorway, their rifles in their hands, ready for whatever came down the pike. The rider slid from the saddle, tied his horse to the rail, nodded to Derick and Kearan, and walked straight toward Morgan. Tying her horses next to the rider's mount, Kearan and Derick followed the man to the house.

"Why, John Cooper!" Daniel exclaimed in surprise. "What on earth brings you from Winchester this cold evening? Are the Indians a chasin' ya? Must be some kinda trouble brewin' somewhere."

Morgan motioned for Derick and Kearan to join them and he ushered John Cooper into the warm country kitchen where Abigail and Lily Jayne were enjoying a cup of tea.

After they had settled comfortably around the table, Morgan explained to Derick that John Cooper was a Colonial representative from Winchester and known by everyone in the county. There was an odd space between Cooper's two front teeth, and when he spoke, a peculiar hissing and whistling noise escaped through the gap.

"Well, Dan'l," John said breathing heavily and whistling through his teeth, "there's a heap of trouble comin' down the pike for all of us. The Patriots in Boston had them a right proper tea party."

"What?" Morgan asked incredulously. "What in the devil are you a talkin' about, John?"

The group around the table waited eagerly for the visitor to continue. Abigail and Lily Jayne brought mugs of steaming hot tea and leftover pie and cornbread. John took a generous slice of cornbread, slathered it with butter, and then sipped his mug of hot tea appreciatively.

"Well, it's like this," John began sinking his teeth into the cornbread. "The East India Company sent ships filled with tea to Philadelphia and New York, but they weren't allowed to dock 'em because of the tax levied on the cargo. In Charleston, the ships docked all right, but the tea was confiscated and put aside in a warehouse. Three more ships sailed into Boston harbor and docked with all the tea on board. An uproar like you ain't never heard commenced at once, and seven thousand Colonials and

Patriots got so mad, well, by gum, they started stormin' the wharfs and declared they'd burn up the ships." Cooper slapped the table for emphasis, hissing and clucking his disapproval.

"Next thing you know," Cooper continued, "Sam Adams and others of his persuasion held a secret meetin' at the old south meetin' hall to see what was to be done with the ships. Such a squawkin' and a wranglin' you ain't ever heard before in your life!" John paused as though reliving the scene all over while Morgan and Mackenzie waited with some annoyance for Cooper to continue his tale.

"Well, John," Silas said, "it was bound to happen sooner or later. The English are tryin' to pull the wool over our eyes by lowering the price of tea and then taxing the tea so we'll be tempted to accept the terms of the taxation, but the Patriots can see what they're a doin' and won't stand for it, nope, even if they lose their tea."

"What happened next, John?" Morgan asked impatiently. "Spit it out, man!"

Cooper sipped his tea slowly, the irony of imbibing the disreputable drink causing him to point dubiously at his mug of English brew.

"Well, friends," Cooper said hissing vociferously, "the committee was a tryin' to be agreeable like, so they decided to allow the ships to leave the harbor unharmed, but so happened, the customs collector wouldn't let the ships leave again, not without their payin' duty. Back to the meetin' hall, they all go, and this time, it was a real hullabaloo—worse'n the first. Everyone was mad at someone else, and words, *which I daren't repeat in the presence of ladies*, flew thick and fast, I mean it wasn't fit for ears to hear. The same evening, about 200 American Patriots dressed up like a passel of painted Indians, boarded the three ships, broke open the tea chests, and dumped all the tea into the bottom of Boston Harbor! Yep, it's so!"

"Oh, no!" Abigail wailed. "All the tea?"

"Yep," Cooper confirmed, "every last bit of it. Why, they even paddled out in boats at first light next morning to beat down the tea a bobbin' an' floatin' on top of the water."

At this piece of information, Daniel Morgan threw back his head and laughed until he cried. Silas Mackenzie stared at him, a worried look crossing his angular features.

"What the devil did the people do when they saw what happened to the tea?" Silas asked.

"Well, some just laughed until the tears ran down their cheeks," Cooper said, "just like old Dan'l here, but some just sat down on their stoops and cried their hearts out for sheer want of a good cup of tea!" Emphasizing every word, Cooper clucked and hissed through every pause in his story. "Happened just days ago, Morgan, sixteen of December, in this here year of our blessed Lord, 1773. I reckon a full account will be printed in the Winchester paper next time it comes out. This is history, Dan'l, history!" John stretched his arms and cracked his bony knuckles loudly.

"I came out tonight because the Patriots are beginning to feel anxious about English retribution," Cooper said with some concern. "Sam Adams is formulatin' his group of Colonists he calls the "Sons of Liberty," although some folks was a callin' them somethin' else which doesn't bear repeatin'."

Abigail cleared her throat and Lily Jayne rolled her eyes.

"They want you to alert the Fredrick County militia, Dan'l," Cooper continued. "There's bound to be trouble over this when King George and the Parliament hear about it. There'll be the devil to pay and that's a fact. The Patriots want to be ready. This could mean war, sure as shootin'."

"Our militia is still under British authority, John," Morgan said. "There's no way we can train a local militia until we officially part ways with the British, and it ain't happened—not yet. If I were to train a militia for the cause of independence, I'd be arrested for sedition and hanged as a traitor."

"Well, just train 'em, and don't say what for," suggested Cooper.

"I'll think on it, John and see what's to be done. The British pretty much know who is sympathetic for the Patriot cause, but I've fought for the Brits before, so I might work some kinda arrangement."

"Good enough, Dan'l. We'll be a waitin' to hear from ya," Cooper said agreeably.

Derick had said nothing during the conversation, but now he shook his head in bewilderment. "Another war with the English?" he said wearily.

"It's been a brewin' for years now, Davidson," Morgan said, "and it's finally coming to a head. This is no surprise. The Patriots are ready to take on old King George and his fat old parliament."

"Don't be so hasty, gentlemen," Derick cautioned. "No matter how passionate ye are for freedom from the crown, the English will eventually win. They always do. They'll wear ye down until ye are naked and starving. It's their way. They'll hire mercenaries by the thousands. There are always too many, always more."

"No, Davidson, not this time," Daniel Morgan shot back fiercely. We will win this time. "Oh, yes, I understand how you think, how disheartened you are by the English conquest of your country, but

I agree with the Patriots—it is time to fight! We already have a trained militia, right here in Virginny. We have enough frontiersmen right here in this very county to train as sharpshooters, scouts, and rangers. If war does come, we will be ready, but we must train under the backing of the Brits until independence is declared." Morgan leaned back in his chair, resolution furrowing his brow.

Derick shook his head. "The talk of war is sweet to those who love freedom, but the paying is bitter, Morgan, and the British will make ye pay."

"No," Morgan said emphatically, we will make them pay this time."

"But Daniel," Abigail said in a voice filled with apprehension, "what about the women and children? Not only would we be vulnerable without our men to protect us, but the King could take our lands and our homes—if there is a rebellion and the English win. We will lose everything. We will have nothing."

Morgan reached over and took Abigail's hand in his. "Now, Abby, it won't happen, not while I have breath in my body."

Derick lifted his eyebrows at Morgan's bold statement and slowly rose from the table, his chair scraping against the polished plank floor.

"Don't be so sure, Morgan. Ye can't underestimate the strength of the English forces. They have a powerful navy with ships enough to block and control every harbor on the coast. They have a regular army of trained soldiers with an endless supply of weapons. The King will hire cruel mercenaries and make allies of the Indians here in the Colonies. Are the Patriots really ready for this?" He rested his hands on his hips, waiting for a reply.

The three men at the table looked serious. Their own expectations and that of America's future rested like a heavy weight on their minds.

The outcome of this ambitious mission was frightfully uncertain, riddled with doubt and uncertainty for those sitting around the table, with the exception of one—*Daniel Morgan*.

Morgan stood leisurely to his feet and John Cooper and Silas Mackenzie followed suit. "I will answer for myself, Davidson," Morgan said facing his tall friend. His face held a look of purpose and determination. "You saw the scars on my back and you, of all men on this continent, know what waits for us at the end of tyranny—loss of our fundamental and God-given rights, freedom to choose our own path, and eventually—exile or death." He paused, looking meaningfully at the little group in the kitchen, his passion rising like a burning fire.

"I do respect what you say, Derick, but we Patriots have this one chance, this one opportunity to win liberty and freedom. It is now, *right now*, or forever submit to a life controlled by socialistic and tyrannical powers. If war comes, I pledge to fight for liberty with all the strength I possess. If we ever lose our will and desire to fight for what we believe, for what is right, we lose our freedom. It's just that simple."

A slow smile spread across Derick Davidson's face. "Aye, my friend," he said laying one hand on Morgan's shoulder, "I know ye can fight, and doubtless will, but," he paused, looking at the men around him, "can ye win? Aye, any man can fight, and most men will fight for such a cause, even though they be wasted in the effort. When I fight again, gentlemen, I will fight to win the war, not just a battle."

"Well, the way I look at it," Silas Mackenzie offered, "independence from old King George will be worth the fight, worth the cost."

"Aye, those who love liberty must pay a price, and men who love freedom will pay it, too," agreed Derick. "The principle of liberty is fed by the blood of Patriots and tyrants. I admire your zeal, me friends, but I will not fight, not in another war with England. I know their ways, and they be hard and cruel. Perhaps the Patriots will find a way to gain freedom and discover how it must be done. But should ye lose the battle, remember this: the crushing hand of tyranny will not cease until every Patriot is made to surrender and comply, or be hanged."

"We will find a way, Mr. Davidson," Kearan said fervently, "and we will not be beaten." Suddenly, Kearan realized she had spoken without thinking. All eyes turned to her and she dropped her gaze to stare at her shoes. Now what had she done? Who was she to be speaking, and what did she know about war? Derick's eyes sought hers, and then he smiled, the rising light in his blue eyes holding some intimate secret. Kearan met his gaze unwaveringly, feeling he must be picturing her turning circles in the snow.

"I believe ye will, lass." Derick said with conviction. He looked around the room, at his new friends, nodded politely, and said, "I thank ye all for your kind hospitality and your warm welcome to a stranger in an unfamiliar land. Guid fortune and much happiness to me host, Mr. Morgan, and to the charming Mrs. Morgan. I will bid ye all goodnight." Without further comment, Derick bowed slightly to the ladies and left the house to return to his quarters at the end of the stable.

When Derick closed the door behind him, John Cooper said with a whistling hiss through the gap in his teeth, "Whew! That Davidson is a curious man. He speaks like one of those Philadelphia politicians from up yonder. By George, and I do mean by *King George*, he speaks quite pessimistic about us Patriots takin' on the redcoats, wouldn't you say so, Dan'l?"

"Or perhaps he's just a coward," suggested Silas Mackenzie with a measure of doubt. "I rather liked the fella' at first meeting. Didn't strike me as a man who was a'feared of anything. Seemed like an honest sort."

"He's not a coward," Daniel Morgan offered in defense of his friend. "Not by any stretch of the imagination. I was with Davidson when he stood up to a couple of redcoats in Boston, and believe me, it was only God's mercy that he didn't cut 'em down right then and there. You never saw a sword flash any quicker in all your born days. The blade was at the throat of that drunken redcoat before he took a second breath." Morgan rubbed the scar along his cheek.

"Another time, on the way back to Virginy, Davidson defended me against a party of marauding Indians. Could a ridden off to safety and left me to fight it out alone, but he jumped off his horse and into the middle of that bloody fight. No, by thunder, Davidson may be a lot a things," Morgan said chuckling, *"but he's no coward."*

"Why's he so down on a war with his own ancient enemies then?" Cooper asked.

"Has reason to be bitter, I suppose, but in time, when he sees the English paradin' and swaggerin' around the Colonies like peacocks a spreadin' their tails, I'd wager he'll get his belly full and join the Americans. He's just feelin' his way now, and we want him on our side." Morgan glanced toward the door through which Derick had disappeared.

Morgan continued, "He's grievin' over some kind of personal trouble, and tryin' to forget what he left behind, tryin' to grab a toehold in a land ready to boil over itself, so I suggest you gentlemen give him some leg room. He is a fearsome man, intelligent and powerful. I think he comes from some 'higher up folks' over in Scotland. You can see it in his ways. And he brought a considerable amount of money with him, more money than the average crofter would possess. In time, he'll forget his sorrow and whatever drove him from home."

Morgan's comments met with nods of agreement on the subject in question. Moments later, the party in Morgan's kitchen gathered their belongings and prepared to make the journey home. It had been an eventful day.

John Cooper mounted his horse and headed for the next homestead where he would spend the night. Silas, Lily Jayne, and Kearan, mounted there horses and traveled along the wagon road to their home a quarter mile away. As Kearan rode her horse through the moonlit night, she listened to her parents speaking in low tones as they rode side by side through the winter evening. Kearan's thoughts turned to what Morgan had revealed about Derick Davidson. He was grieving, and Kearan understood why. A girl he had desperately loved, his own wife, lay in a silent grave somewhere in Scotland. Could a man ever truly get over such a sorrow she wondered? Could he simply put away his grief as Morgan suggested? Could a person forget the one love he had cherished in life?

Kearan remembered his clear blue eyes and the pain she had read in their depths. She wondered if he were from the *higher up folks*. She dare not ask him any more questions about his life. Just the very thought of his candid response to her query as they talked in the stable brought a fresh flush to her cheeks. No, she would not ask him any more questions.

The Scotsman was apparently uninterested in pursing a friendship although she had felt some strange connection pass between them as they waited on the snowy path for John Cooper to arrive. Well, he was quite old. Morgan said he was twenty-eight or so, far too old for a young frontier lass. She shook her head as though to rid herself of the troublesome thoughts. Spurring her horse forward, she cantered toward the distant light and the comfort and safety of her own home.

Abigail and Daniel sat before the dying embers of the fire, weary from the activities of the day. A smile lit up Abigail's face and she paused in her rocking to look at Daniel Morgan, the man she had loved for many years.

"Well?" Daniel said with pretended gruffness, "What are you smiling about, woman? You can't put me out anymore, Abby girl. This whole charade is officially over, so I hope you are happy."

"It's not a sham, Daniel, and I am pleased you have come back to me. You made this day so very special. Saying our vows has meant so much to me. I was wondering, Daniel, since you didn't carry me into our house the first time, I wonder if perhaps you could…could you…?" She paused, blushing slightly.

When he understood her request, Daniel Morgan shook his head with incredulity, wondering what made a woman so ridiculously sentimental. He would never figure it out, so might as well go along with the game.

"Okay, Abby, girl," Daniel said with a grin. "Whatever makes you happy. I aim to please." He rose from his chair by the fire and scooping her up in his arms, he carried his officially pledged wife to the front door, opened it wide, turned around, and carried her across the threshold of their home, closing the door none too gently with a backward kick of his boot.

Chapter 6

Women Warriors

The essence of a game is at its end

The winter of 1774 was filled with a flurry of activity, fueled by the fires of the ever-increasing animosity between the American Patriots and the Loyalists. Captain Daniel Morgan called together his militia of riflemen to carry out a series of training maneuvers during the long winter months of inactivity on the farm. Morgan's riflemen, as they came to be known, trained on his farm, using the existing terrain and wooded landscape for this exercise. Morgan expected obedient and immediate submission to orders from his troops who were well-disciplined men, cut from the hardy frontier stock of robust woodsmen.

In turn, the men of the Virginia militia loved and respected Daniel Morgan, often referring to him warmly as "the old wagoner." Morgan's skill as a military riflemen, ranger, and scout won the admiration of his men and the combined forces of Virginia militia who emulated Morgan's fearless attitude.

If Morgan felt any of his men were lacking in courage, he lifted his hunting shirt to display his scarred and mutilated back, leaving his men with no excuse for weakness or cowardice. He also expected the militia to be neat and clean and appear in all ways like the professional soldier. This was a tall order for men who took more pride in appearing unkempt and rugged—the identification mark of a true frontiersman.

The friendship between Daniel Morgan and Derick Davidson strengthened in mutual respect and esteem. The unlikely pair had bonded in some inexplicable way. A rare and unusual loyalty had formed between them and although Derick did not share Morgan's enthusiasm for the Patriot cause, he dutifully trained with the riflemen during the long winter months, volunteering his expertise in using the sword in close combat.

Morgan was able to secure a Pennsylvania long rifle for Derick, which was made by German gunsmiths in Lancaster County, skilled craftsmen, who built firearms of the finest quality. Derick soon mastered the technique and skill of the sharp-shooting rifleman. He competed with the rest of the militia and could soon hit the center of a target at a hundred plus yards. His eye was good and his hand was steady.

The long hours of target practice with Morgan at his side cemented this unusual friendship. The man, Daniel Morgan, was a rough frontiersman, often crude, with only a rudimentary education, and much of this he owed to Abigail. However, he was a skilled rifleman and woodsman, a plucky man with natural leadership ability. Derick Davidson exhibited many of the same qualities, but with the grace and manners of his Edinburgh University education. At the same time, he demonstrated the fearless courage and war-like demeanor of his chieftain ancestry. His skill with the sword was remarkable, and he spent hours with the militia, training and teaching the techniques of hand-to-hand combat with sword, dirk, and battleaxe.

Abigail had urged Derick to take a room in the house, but he had declined, preferring rather to stay in the room at the end of the stable, a quiet and comfortable refuge for the weary warrior. "He needs his space," Abigail had said, and so Morgan left him to his own devices, not intruding into his private life nor asking further questions about his flight from Scotland.

Morgan sensed that some great misfortune had driven Derick Davidson from his homeland to the American Colonies, and in the course of time, perhaps the Scotsman would move beyond his trouble, just as all men must. Morgan knew from experience that moving beyond tragedy was not always easy.

He remembered too well his own youth—how he had walked away from his own home, never to look back. Time was the only healer for the heartaches of life, and it took some men longer than others to move forward again. Morgan saw himself in the young Scotsman and desired for his new friend to succeed in his quest, just as he wished to be successful himself.

The Mackenzies were regular visitors to the Morgan farm, and when the men were training during the winter months, Kearan and Lily Jayne took their dinner and spent the day with Abigail and the girls, either sewing baskets by the fireside or baking and cooking for the men. Kearan often found herself across the table from Derick at supper, but she never again asked him questions concerning his personal life. Gradually, their relationship became more comfortable.

Although Derick remained somewhat reclusive, Kearan made a point of drawing him out, hoping to ease the pain she saw in his eyes. She chatted about extraneous things: her frontier friends, the latest gossip in Winchester, and her love for horses. He listened patiently, sometimes not seeing her at all, looking through her to some distant place, but other times, his eyes were kind, politely commenting on what she had to say.

On milder days, Kearan sat on the stone fence along the training field to watch the militia train. Derick was always there, teaching the men who carried swords how to use the weapon more effectively in close encounters. She marveled at his skill, his perfect timing, his finesse and agility with the blade. Secretly, she longed to learn how to use the sword herself, but she feared to ask him to give her lessons. He would laugh at her, think her foolish, but she seriously wanted to learn.

On an unusually clear afternoon in February when the riflemen were practicing defensive maneuvers, Abigail sent Kearan to see if the militia had finished for the day. When Kearan reached the dooryard gate, Derick was walking alone across the field, returning from a training session. He made no sound, and in his hands, he carried his arsenal of training weapons: several rifles, swords, a battleaxe, a pistol, and a dirk.

To Kearan, this seemed the perfect opportunity to broach the subject of sword lessons. If he laughed at her, no one was about to hear. As he approached the stable, Derick saw her standing near the fence, the place she often occupied while watching the men go through their training maneuvers. He nodded his head and proceeded toward his room. Before he entered, Kearan hurried to catch him. Once he closed the door, she would not have the courage to knock.

"Wait, Mr. Davidson, please wait a moment," Kearan called.

He paused, leaning his weapons against the wall, one hand on the door latch.

"You are coming in early?" she queried somewhat breathlessly.

"Aye, lass, Mr. Morgan moved into yon woods, training with the sharpshooters. The sword drills be over for the day, so I thought t'would be a guid afternoon to take me horse for a ride through the glens—the valley." He was endeavoring to talk American as Daniel Morgan had suggested. He might be capable of changing his grammar and his use of unfamiliar words, but there was no help for his Scottish brogue.

"Before you go for your ride Mr. Davidson," Kearan began, "I was wondering if you would consider teaching me to use the sword?" There! She had said it. She might as well be out and open about her desire to use a sword. All he could say was...no.

Derick furrowed his brow, not quite certain he had heard correctly. "Did ye say," he paused, a question in his eyes, "did ye say that ye wanted to learn to sword fight?"

Derick could not help noticing that her lips quivered a little and an odd excitement shone in her brown eyes. In the brief time he had known Kearan Mackenzie, it was apparent that she was not the average frontier lass. She waved away the attentions of the local young men who vied for her favor and chose rather to listen to the men while they talked around the fireside of war and politics and the coming conflict. While she appeared quite adept at the womanly arts of needlework and homemaking, it was apparent that she preferred the more stimulating conversation of the men.

"Yes, you heard correctly, sir, and please," she took a deep breath, "for once, take me seriously and don't tease me," Kearan warned. "I am dead serious. My father does not use a sword, nor does my brother. They like using the rifle, of course, but I am so intrigued with the beauty and majesty of sword fighting, not to mention, I'm sure a sword would be far better protection for a woman as opposed to a rifle. You have one shot with a rifle and then what? Yes, I would like very much to learn."

For a long moment, Derick measured the young woman standing before him as though her question posed some strenuous mental consideration. His expression was one of astonishment and wonder.

Kearan brushed away a strand of hair blowing across her eyes and said, "Well, don't just stand there staring at me like I am a complete idiot. Go ahead—tell me I am the most foolish and ridiculous woman you have ever met and be done with it!" To Kearan's surprise, Derick Davidson burst into laughter. Without another word, she turned on her heels and walked briskly toward the house.

"Wait, lass," Derick called after her as he stifled a laugh. "Be not grieved at me. I'm not laughing at ye."

Kearan paused in mid stride, turned around, and retraced her steps to stand next to him, daring him to laugh again.

"Well..." she said drawing out the word, "if you're not laughing at me, then who?"

"If only ye could see the expression on your face, lass. It gave me a wee bit o' mirth, that's all. I feel fortunate ye didn't have a sword in your hand just then." Derick took his hand from the door latch and crossed his arms over his chest, legs apart, and a light danced in the depths of his blue eyes, a light Kearan had not seen before.

"You will teach me then?" Kearan asked hopefully.

"Aye, I will teach ye," he said observing her slight figure and wondering if she could manage to grasp a heavy sword, "if your Da' permits, but not with me claymore. This sword be too heavy for a mere lass. Ye must have a lighter, smaller sword if ye wish to learn."

"I have a sword at home, but I don't know if it will be right. It belonged to my grandfather Mackenzie."

"Bring it then, next time ye come, and we will have a look. If ye wish to train for close combat encounters, ye will need the proper sword." He turned toward the door as though to end the conversation.

"Mr. Davidson?" He turned to her again.

"Aye?"

"Do you think I am quite foolish for wanting to handle a sword? None of my friends have ever expressed even a fleeting desire, so maybe I am a little daft." Kearan looked down at the ground as though fearing to hear his response. Silence fell between them for a moment and then Derick finally spoke in a gentler tone.

"Nay, lass, I do not think ye be," he broke off as though searching for the right word. "That ye be outrageous. It be in your blood. Aye, simple as that. Dinna fash yourself for thinking so. There be many a lass who could use a sword with skill and bravery. *Women warriors*. My own sister, Doran, can wield a sword and has bested me more than once."

"Really? I am so glad to know I am not…well, not so strange." She smiled up at him, her relief visible. "You have a sister?"

"Aye, my twin, and two brothers."

Kearan waited, hoping he would say more, but he did not. She wanted to ask about his family, but she saw a veil descend over his countenance and decided against further questioning. She was just glad he had consented to teach her to use a sword. This was a major step for the reclusive Scotsman who would barely enter into a conversation with her.

The following week and with her father's consent, Kearan brought the sword belonging to her grandfather to Morgan's house. Silas and Daniel were sitting around the fire after a hearty supper, conversing with their wives about the rising tide of Indian attacks along the frontier borders.

"Well, now," Silas Mackenzie said changing this tiresome subject, "what do you think of my own baby gal taking up sword fightin'? It may not be a bad idea with all the scrappin' and squawkin' we're facing today. Indians on the west, British on the east, and us peaceable frontier folk, smack dab in the middle of the ruckus." He shook his head in bewilderment.

"No one respects the treaties, never have," Morgan complained. He stuffed some top grade Virginia tobacco into the bowl of his pipe. "The British make treaties with the Indians and break them when they get greedy for land. It won't be long until the Indians are pushed beyond the Ohio River. It's bound to happen." He held a straw over the fire until it ignited and lit his pipe. "Our own governor is a staunch Loyalist, land hungry, and self-serving. Mark my words, Silas Mackenzie, he'll come up with some lame excuse for breakin' another treaty." Daniel Morgan leaned back in his chair, a grim expression on his face.

"Well, that Stanwix Treaty with the Iroquois was never signed by the Shawnees, Mingo, and Delaware, so they don't see any reason to honor it," Silas stated. "Besides, opens the door for the British to bargain for another treaty, with more land, of course. We can expect trouble down the road, Dan'l. The Indians won't stand for much more trickery."

"Papa," Kearan said after listening to the conversation for quite some time, "I'm waiting for all of you to finish your war talk so Mr. Davidson can look at my sword."

Her father laughed and nodded his head. "Go on then, gal. Bring out your granddaddy's sword so Mr. Davidson can have a look." Silas looked thoughtful. "My granddaddy carried this sword from Scotland when he was a young man, and my own Pa was killed in a frontier uprising with the Indians when I was just a tad, so I never learned much about our people or about this sword. I kept it for our son, but Alfred, well, he isn't much interested in using a sword. He's a rifleman, and a good one, too." He nodded toward Kearan. "I reckon Kearan might have the sword since she's of a mind to learn." Kearan handed the sword to Derick who was sitting next to Morgan.

"What do you think, Mr. Davidson?" Kearan asked hopefully. Derick stood and slid the long shining blade from the decrepit looking leather scabbard. He ran his fingers along the blade edge turning it over several times. With his large hands, he gripped the hilt, swinging it around, testing the weight. Kearan waited, her eyes shining with eagerness.

"There's a saying in me homeland that fits this piece," Derick said smiling. "A good sword has often been in a poor scabbard. This is a good sword, especially for a student and a lass of your wee size. I think ye can handle this one."

Derick looked at Silas Mackenzie and said, "In Scotland, Clan Mackenzie was close neighbors to me own people." Then he smiled wryly. "Well, as close as neighbors are in Scotland. Our families fought together, hunted together, and I was often at Castle Leod, the seat of the clan."

"Well, my granddaddy was brother to a chief, I know that much," offered Silas, "but he left his old country and it's ways long before I was born. Since my Pa died young, I never learned much about my Scottish relatives. No matter anyhow. We been Americans now for a long time."

"Do you see the inscription written across the crossbar, Mr. Davidson?" Kearan asked pointing to a script written in a language she could not understand. Intricate knot work was etched along the silver grip.

"Aye, 'tis written in Gaelic, the language of the ancient Scots. This is a very bonny sword indeed, well crafted, but not often used in battle. It was possibly used as an officer's sword, a military dress sword."

"Can you read the Gaelic inscription?" Kearan asked.

Morgan laughed, his bushy eyebrows rising with the question. "Of course, he can read Gaelic, Kearan gal," Morgan said, "but we have been tryin' our best to make him forget it! He is constantly spouting off Gaelic comments we can't understand, probably on purpose, no doubt."

Derick turned to Morgan, touching the sword tip to his chest. "Some things die hard, Morgan."

They all laughed, and Derick lowered the sword. He turned to Kearan. "Aye, lass, I can read Gaelic. The inscription says, *Cha bhi suaimhneas aig eucoir, no seasamh aig droch-bheairt.*" He smiled and continued to inspect the sword, his eyes sparkling with surreptitious amusement.

"And do *ye* think *ye* could possibly translate the inscription into American English, kind sir?" Kearan rolled her eyes heavenward. This man was truly exasperating. He knew very well she wished to know the English translation.

"Aye, I can translate the Gaelic for ye, too. In *Anglish* it reads, '*Wrong cannot rest, nor ill deed stand*'." Derick handed the sword back to Kearan and returned to his seat next to Morgan.

"It is a fine sword, lass, a sword ye can be proud of." Derick's eyes swept over the group gathered around the fire. "In ancient times," he explained, "many women warriors fought in battles, next to their clansmen. They were light and quick and could fight as well as many in the clan. One such lass was named Maid Lilliard."

"Oh, tell us, please tell us her story, Mr. Davidson," Kearan begged. Derick's lips curved into a rare smile, and he began to speak.

"Maid Lilliard was an uncommon beauty, admired throughout the Highlands for her bonny ways," Derick began. "Lily, as everyone called her, was brave in her spirit and honest of heart. She was betrothed to a brave lad who was to become her husband after the battle of Ancrum. They were very much in love and Maid Lilliard could not stay home to wait for him to return from the battle, so she accompanied the camp followers to the battleground."

"How very touching," Morgan mocked. He drew his handkerchief from his pocket and wiped a pretend tear from his eye.

"Stop it, Daniel," Abigail said. "Go on with the story, Derick. Daniel is a hopeless unromantic and could not possibly comprehend such tender devotion. Pay no mind to him, Derick."

"Now, wait just a minute, Abigail Morgan," said the accused. "Who recently undertook a perilous journey just to marry the gal he loved? Well, I'd say that was pretty romantic," Morgan said with a lopsided grin that wrinkled the scar on his face. "Go on with it, Davidson."

Derick clasped his hands together and continued. "Alas, for young Maid Lilliard, for her lover was killed during the battle and she sprang on the English infantry with a passion. She killed many men before she was mortally wounded herself. Her grave is honored as a memorial to women warriors in our country," Derick concluded.

"Oh, *not* a good ending to the story," Kearan said in a disappointed tone. She looked at her sword, a trace of melancholy shadowing her countenance.

"No, perhaps not a good ending for some," Derick said, "but it is often the way of things."

"The inscription on the sword," queried Silas, "what would you say about the meanin' of such words, Derick?" With the exception of Kearan, the group gathered around the fire used Derick's given name as a gesture of their acceptance and friendship.

"*Wrong cannot rest, nor ill deed stand* is frequently inscribed on swords," Derick explained. "If the sword could speak, it would say, *by the strength of this blade, give wrong no rest, neither allow evil to triumph in the land.*"

"Nor in our lives," Abigail added with enthusiasm. "If evil does not triumph in our lives, then we won't have to worry about war. When the people of our land trust God and serve Him, evil will be conquered in our hearts, and war will cease to exist."

Daniel Morgan removed the pipe from his mouth and shook his head. "You can preach all you want to, Abby, but it ain't gonna happen. Men are bound to fight as sure as the sparks fly upward. Been goin' on since the beginnin' of time. I sure hope Davidson don't have those words written on his sword because he's sure givin' *wrong a rest*, especially since he won't join the militia."

Derick rubbed his chin thoughtfully. "Nice try, me friend, but I'm not rising to the bait. Abby's right, though, and so are ye." He turned to Kearan. "I'll meet ye by the training field tomorrow, Miss Mackenzie."

Chapter 7

Return of the Longhunter

Though separation be hard,
Two never met but had to part

The next morning, Kearan rose early in anticipation of her sword lesson. She dressed quickly and rode her horse past the training field, her grandfather's sword and scabbard tied securely to her mount.

From a little distance, Derick watched her coming, riding as though she were being pursued by hostile Indians. When she arrived at the gate, she slid from the saddle without assistance and stood truiumphantly before him, her face beaming with eagerness.

"Here I am," Kearan exclaimed, "ready for my first sword lesson!"

"I can see that," Derick answered with an amused grin. He motioned for her to follow him. "I'm thinking ye can train right here next to the keep for now. I don't want to get in the way of the milita and ye need to be taught some basic principles before ye take sword in hand."

"I do? What keep? Where is a keep?" She looked around quizzically.

"The house," Derick replied, "although I'm thinking it wouldn't keep anything safe for very long."

Kearan looked confused.

"Never ye mind, lass. 'Tis a strong dwelling, a safe keeping place. Nothing to do with sword fighting. Now, if ye will put your horse in the stable, we'll commence with the lesson."

Kearan stabled her horse, as was her habit, and Derick set about drawing a wide circle in the skiff of fresh snow covering the ground. The day was brilliant, frosty, and clear. He glanced up as Kearan walked from the stable. He could not help admiring this beautiful young woman. She was full of life and enthusiasm, innocent and trusting. A curious sense of protectiveness swept over him, the same fatherly feeling he had for his own children. Kearan was a child after all, barely seventeen, and had not yet experienced the harsh realities of life. The thought saddened him, and he pushed it from his mind.

Kearan had strapped her grandfather's sword to her side, and Derick studied it critically. "Before we begin," he said pointing to the scabbard, "ye must lower your weapon so ye can manage to unsheath the sword before ye are killed."

She blanched, nodded, and then repositioned the belt holding the scabbard. "Is this good?" she asked.

Derick studied her again, wondering if this slight girl standing before him could manage to weild a heavy sword effectively. Knowing her eagerness to learn and her determination to try, he decided to say nothing more to dampen her enthusiasm. She was dressed in a snug fitting blue jacket over a white bouse with full sleeves and a skirt with enough room to maneuver her body, but not so full as to get the sword tangled up in the folds.

"Is there something wrong with my clothing?" Kearan asked when she noticed him studying her closely. "I tried to find something suitable, nothing that would slow my movements."

"Nay, lass, I think ye be right proper," Derick said, "for today."

"Why do you always call me *lass*? I have a name, Mr. Davidson."

"Aye, lass, this I be knowin'. Now—the first thing ye must be aware of is..." he said ignoring her question and plunging into the lesson, "that ye must understand the difference in swords and that there are many kinds of swords and many ways of sword fighting."

Derick drew out his own sword, a heavy double edged blade. "Me own sword is a broadsword and it serves one primary purpose— to kill and destroy an enemy." He slashed the air with his blade, beheading his invisible enemy. "This particular sword is a slashing instrument, meant for battle. It is not for dueling or gaming. It is for killing."

Kearan's face suddenly grew pale. His words seemed cold, calculating, without emotion or feeling, and he spoke them so easily, like he was accustomed to killing.

Derick continued with his explanation of the physical aspects of the weapon. "The straight, two-edged blade can be swung in all directions while running or riding a horse. The weight of the claymore broadsword can penetrate armour, cut to the bone, slash two or three men at once if swung in a circle, and can easily knock a musket or weapon from an enemy's hand. The curved sword is used by the calvary for the most part, but the straight sword can be used on horseback or on the ground in close combat."

Kearan felt her stomach lurch. She had wanted only to defend herself and learn the art of sword fighting, not to hear a running commentary on how to maim and kill.

Seeing her face grow pale, Derick paused and lowered his sword. "Are ye unwell, lass?" He had not expected this reaction, not from Kearan Mackenzie, the independent and enchanting young thinker of Frederick County. She certainly must be ill.

"Actually, Mr. Davidson, I wasn't really interested in maiming and killing," she replied a bit sarcastically. "I was thinking more of self defense. You know what I mean? More the artistic form and techniques of handling the sword."

Derick stared at his young pupil, not certain he understood her meaning. He thought for a long moment. "An artistic form? Aye, it can be that, but will ye have no opponent, then?" he queried. "Do ye just want to slash the air or simply thrust your sword at a ghostly enemy?"

Kearan felt her face grow warm. "Of course not! Certainly not! It's just...well, you describe sword fighting with such lack of emotion, such total disregard for your opponent, rather like you have ice water running in your veins."

He paused at her words and then smiled sardonically. "Aye, lass, and perhaps I have, but remember this—one of the first things ye must possess when crossing swords with an opponent is—" his face grew stern, "is lack of emotion."

Kearan stared at him, a mixture of hurt and unbelief on her face. She felt he could read her face like an open book, as though the thoughts of her heart were written on her countenance for all the world to see.

"Perhaps," he said more gently, "perhaps me lack of feeling is what ye are hearing from me." He looked toward the training field, searching for a way to help her understand. "If I allow emotion or feeling to take control during an encounter, I will lose my concentration, my momentum. Staying focused and keeping your emotions in submission is a very necessary part of training. I can assure ye, lass, I do have feelings, but they be a curse to me," he said fiercely.

His words had startled her, but she was determined to go forward, despite his callousness. After a moment, Kearan said, "I can understand some of what you say." She paused, contemplating her sword, then continued.

"Actually, I have not considered that aspect of sword fighting at all. I don't expect to use what I learn on real live people—unless I am defending myself and my life, of course, but I'm sure you are right, Mr. Davidson."

She placed one hand on her hip and looked up at him, hoping her comments were sufficient enough to end this discussion. "So what comes after stifling all your natural, God-given emotions?"

Derick answered her question with a patient smile. He couldn't help it. She was so naïve, so innocent, and so very charming.

"Next," Derick said, resuming his attitude as the teacher, "ye must have no fear of your opponent, Miss Mackenzie. Fear no enemy and regard no emotion except for the passion to win. If you allow fear to take your concentration, you will surely lose the day."

"And how do you turn off your fear of pain and death when your adversary is ready to cut you open?" Kearan asked.

Derick considered the young girl standing before him and wondered if he had spoken too soon in offering to teach her the art of sword fighting. Perhaps he had been unwise. Instead of answering her direct query, he changed the subject.

"Do ye wish to reconsider, then? I will not fault ye for doing so. Pain and death are always a possibility when crossing swords, and I understand your reluctance. Not many women are able to withstand the strenuous training. It takes nerves of iron. Your life hangs in the balance when your opponent wishes to cut ye to pieces."

Kearan's chin tilted upward at his words, and her brown eyes filled with sudden fire. The look on her face was clear enough; she was up for the challenge, and his comments only served to strengthen her resolve.

"I have no thought of reconsidering," Kearan said. "I will sort this *fear of death* thought out for myself. And," she added emphatically, "I do not need to be reminded that it takes a strong will and steady nerves to handle a sword. I believe I have both, Mr. Davidson, so stop talking about the weaker sex and let's get on with the lesson."

"Very well," Derick said somewhat amused, "but remember, it takes more than mere strength and determination to handle the sword skillfully, lass. You must possess the courage to kill your opponent if necessary, to drive the blade into another fellow being. This will be the most difficult part for a gentle lass to perform."

Picturing herself slaying another living person, Kearan swallowed hard. She set her jaw and looked into Derick's eyes.

"I'm ready, Mr. Davidson. I have named my sword *Liberty*, and liberty is my objective."

As the sun climbed higher in the morning sky, the chill air grew milder, melting the thin layer of snow covering the barren ground and bathing the two figures in the dooryard in warm sunshine. Gunfire erupted in the woods beyond, reminding Derick and Kearan that Morgan and his men were performing their drills in preparation for the Patriot cause.

Removing his outer jacket, Derick assumed the *on guard* position: one foot forward, body turned to one side, sword pointing toward his opponent. All morning they practiced the combat position until Kearan could draw her sword quickly and assume the defensive and offensive positions without hesitation. She was a quick learner and Derick was pleased with her progress.

"Enough for the present," Derick said and sheathed his sword.

"That's all you're going to teach me today?" Kearan asked. "I already have the combat positions mastered."

"Ye think so now, but ye need to practice until drawing your sword is as natural as breathing. Ye must draw your blade before ye actually think about it. Not until ye have mastered this spontaneous motion are ye ready to cross blades."

Kearan sighed and returned her sword to its sheath. "I was hoping to learn a little more than drawing my sword and standing properly," she said peevishly. She looked toward the house and then back to Derick. "Shall we go to the house for some hot tea and dinner? I'm starving."

"Aye, that would be guid. One more thing ye must remember. When ye have *Miss Liberty* sheathed to your side, practice thinking ye are going to use your weapon. Mentally prepare to draw your sword. When ye do draw your sword, keep it pointed toward your opponent and don't point it away from him for any reason. Always keep the blade up and ready. Can ye start thinking like a warrior?" He picked up his jacket and threw it across his shoulder.

"Is that the way you think?" Kearan asked. She took a few steps toward the house, and hesitated, noticing that Derick was not following. He was standing at attention, listening carefully, and ignoring her question. Morgan and his men were in the field and would not return until evening. What was he hearing? Suddenly,

Kearan heard the sound of hoof beats, faint but steady, coming down the road toward the house.

"Several horses on the road," Derick said. "Are the Morgans expecting visitors today, do ye know?"

"Not that I know of," Kearan answered, "but folks do drop in unexpectedly, especially in the country. Should we be alarmed?" Kearan smiled impishly. "Don't worry, Mr. Davidson," she said grasping the hilt of her sword, "I and Miss Liberty will take care of ye! Wrong cannot rest, nor ill deed stand, not while I'm here beside ye."

Derick could not help smiling at the small waiflike figure as she assumed an *on guard* position, one slender hand on the hilt of her sword. Kearan Mackenzie was a delightful lass with a whimsical sense of humor. For all her unconventional ways, Derick Davidson was enamored by her youthful candor. Some day soon, one of the frontier lads would beg Silas Mackenzie for her hand in marriage, but first, the lad must wrestle her small hand from the hilt of her sword. The thought made him smile.

A horse and rider came into view from around the bend in the road a quarter mile away. As they advanced, Derick could see two additional horses tethered to a rope and following behind the rider, their weary heads bending low as they pulled their burden. Both packhorses seemed overloaded with goods and appeared ready to drop in their tracks.

"Oh," Kearan said as she watched the approaching figure, "it looks like one of the longhunters coming from his winter trapping. I don't think it's anything to be alarmed about, Mr. Davidson. They often stop at our place or Mr. Morgan's on their way to Winchester to trade their furs. The horses do look rather weary, don't they?"

Derick moved toward Kearan's side and waited, his muscles tensing, his mind alert. His natural reaction to any stranger was to be ready for anything that might occur, ready to defend if necessary. Kearan remembered his recent admonition to always be ready. She felt stirred at the nearness of Derick Davidson. He stood in a protective posture, the same posture he had assumed the night John Cooper arrived with news of the Boston Tea Party.

Derick's chest rose and fell as if preparing for a conflict or an altercation. How strange and careful his habits were, Kearan thought. He must have come from a brutal and bloody land, a place where every man was a possible enemy. What had prompted such caution, such vigilance, to suppose that every man who came down the road might be an adversary? Someday, when he knew her better and trusted her more, she would ask him about his life in Scotland before he came to the Colonies.

In Kearan's young and naive eyes, Derick Davidson was strange and wonderful, daring and dreadful at the same time. He possessed an aura of unfathomable mystery, and she was drawn to him as to no other man she had ever known. She admired his strength, his noble bearing, his kindness, and his patience with her, and yes, she was even intrigued with his strangeness and longed to know what was in his heart, what brought the fire to his eyes and the tenderness to his voice. Her mother would call it infatuation, and Kearan thought she was probably right.

The rider waved a greeting when he saw the two figures standing by the fence. He continued down the road toward them, halting just outside the dooryard gate. He glanced around the parameter of the house, his keen eyes sweeping across the open space as if searching for an invisible foe. "Is Cap'n Morgan about?" the stranger asked.

A winter's growth of beard covered the rider's face, and his long silver-streaked hair was pulled back and tied with a strip of rawhide. Some indistinct animal fur was fashioned into a cap that nearly covered his head. His eyes, deep blue, piercing, penetrating, were all that was visible. The low rumble of a Scottish burr was in the stranger's voice, the ancient and familiar sound pleasant to Derick's ears. The stranger dismounted and stood waiting by the gate.

"Captain Morgan is in the field at this present moment," Kearan said. "He is training with the riflemen, sir, but Mrs. Morgan and the servants are at home. Do you need to see Mr. Morgan? If so, I am sure one of us could take you there."

"Not necessary, lass. I was hoping to stay the night before going on to Winchester to trade me furs. I've a good winter catch and me horses be loaded down with animal hides and meat."

The man pointed to his horses. An amazing amount of wild animal pelts was loaded on their backs. "Come a far piece today and thinking I'd make Winchester by nightfall, but me beasts are too weary for any more traveling today." He glanced at his packhorses as though he wished to ease their burden.

"I know Cap'n Morgan," said the stranger, "known him since the seven years war. If I be traveling this way, I stay a night or so when I come from a hunt. Came in early this year." His blue eyes twinkled as he gazed appreciatively at the house. "Calls this place, Soldier's Rest. I understand why. I be an old soldier meself, like Cap'n Morgan."

The words of the hunter seemed too much for him and he left off speaking for several moments. His only conversation for many months was the words he spoke to his horse. "I'm sorry to bother you, lass. You must be Cap'n Morgan's daughter all growed up."

"No, sir, Mr. Morgan's daughters are a few years younger than me," Kearan answered, "but I'm rather like a daughter to Captain Morgan and Abigail. My name is Kearan, and I'm a neighbor and close friend of the Morgans. Since you are a friend of the Morgans, I know Abigail will be happy to see you again and get you settled in for the night."

"Are ye the young Mackenzie lass?" queried the Longhunter. "I remember ye now. Why, the last time I laid eyes on ye, ye weren't more'n a bairnie on your papa's knee. Here ye are now, all bonny an' grown up."

Kearan blushed. "We do grow up fast on the frontier, don't we? I'm sorry I don't remember you personally, but all the longhunters look alike to me. Please come to the house and we'll see if someone can fetch Captain Morgan from the field."

"Aye," Derick offered, "if ye are a friend to Daniel Morgan, I'm sure he'll be wanting to see ye. I can fetch him for ye."

For the first time since his arrival, the hunter gave an appraising look at the tall man standing next to Kearan Mackenzie. Sweeping over Derick's large frame, his eyes narrowed, inspecting him from head to foot in a suspicious manner. Such intense and shameless scrutiny made Derick feel uncomfortable, and he unconsciously rested his hand on the dirk sheathed to his belt.

The Longhunter's eyes followed his movement, and he smiled slightly beneath his beard, understanding the thoughts of this fellow Scotsman. His eyes crinkling at the corners, he spoke directly to Derick.

"Are ye not from the land of mist and tears?" asked the stranger with a husky note to his voice. "No need for ye to answer me, lad, I can hear it in your speech, as clear as the sound of the pipes in the glen and the call of the curlew along the seashore."

Derick paused, weighing his response to this tall stranger who stood straight as an oak tree in the noonday sun. The man facing him was his equal in size, broad shouldered with large sinewy hands holding lightly to the reins of his horse, a distinctive contrast noted by Derick.

The stranger ran his hand fondly over the long nose of his mount, patting the velvety muzzle with obvious affection. The odor of horse, smoke, and drying venison clung to his deerskin clothing. Behind his rough outward appearance, a sense of dignity graced his being, like a rare treasure wrapped in coarse cloth.

Derick guessed the hunter to be in the mid forties, but only his graying beard and hair were any indication of his age. His deep blue eyes were bright and keenly observant.

"Aye, that I am," Derick finally answered. "I come from the land of mist and tears as ye so aptly name me homeland, and for me, it was chiefly tears."

A sound like a muffled groan escaped from deep in the Longhunter's chest, and he moved toward Derick with a sudden motion, a strange light burning in his eyes.

Derick backed away a few paces, keeping an eye on Kearan. He felt no instinctive fear of the man, only a strange sense of curiosity. Had it been any other man, he would have drawn his dirk, but the Longhunter was a Scotsman, a fellow countryman, a man who understood the pain of leaving home and family to make a life in the new world. This was his countryman, a man like himself whose ancestors had bled the glens red with blood for freedom's cause, and still they had lost.

The stranger moved forward again, grabbing Derick's forearm, but before he could complete the action, a sword slipped between the two men, coming to rest on the throat of the Longhunter.

"Turn loose of his arm at once," Kearan said in a calm, cool voice. "Turn him loose or you will understand how clean this blade can cut."

Immediately, the hunter backed away, astonished at the young girl holding the sword and looking for all the world like she meant to use it.

"I intended no harm, lass," the stranger said with amazement. "I was only meaning to greet a fellow countryman, to discover what part of me homeland his clan abides."

Casting a dubious look at Derick, Kearan looked for confirmation of the Longhunter's statement. For a brief moment, Derick hesitated: then, taking into consideration the words of the stranger, he nodded an affirmation. Kearan withdrew her sword and sheathed it with a noticeable flourish in the scabbard at her side.

A slight smile tugged at the corners of Derick's mouth. "Aye, it is so, lass," Derick explained to his young pupil. "When clansmen meet, they sometimes grasp forearms and embrace. Of course, ye are unaware of this custom, but 'tis the way of it, the way of the clan."

Kearan looked somewhat chagrined and crossed her arms over her chest, a disgusted look on her face. She tossed her head and dark curls escaped from beneath her bonnet while her brown eyes smoldered with embarrassment. The Longhunter exchanged amused glances with Derick and, stifling a grin, cast his eyes on the ground.

"However, ye did remarkably well with your sword, lass. Aye, indeed, ye did quite well," Derick offered. "In truth, ye might have saved me life had this man been a true enemy."

"Thank you, sir, for your kind words," Kearan said to Derick in a mocking tone. She held a hand to her brow and cleared her throat. "Actually, it would have been rather exciting to think I saved you from imminent danger, but since I haven't done anything but make a fool of myself, I offer my apologies for rushing to judgment—for my mistake," she concluded. "I am quite impulsive at times, as you have so often pointed out. This is due to my youth and lack of experience as you mentioned early in our acquaintance. It certainly appeared as though the hunter was going to attack you—so sudden like was his motion, and coupled with that odd and peculiar noise, you know."

"Dinna fash yourself, lass," said the hunter. "T'was an honest mistake and meant for good. The frontier folk clasp right hands but we Scots clasp the forearm and embrace and bow to the lasses and ladies, of course. 'Tis the way of me people, me clan."

Nodding slightly, Kearan wished she could creep away and escape from this awkward situation.

The stranger turned his attention back to Derick, a question in his clear eyes. "Ye have the look of me brother who was wounded at Culloden Moor. Aye, lad, his face is ever before me, ever in me mind. I was fighting the French and Indians for the Crown when he was trying to aid Bonnie Prince Charlie." Sudden tears pooled in the eyes of the stranger.

"Memories of the last highland charge, the final battle for freedom, memories of me kin stir me heart always. And ye...ye bring remembrance of me own people, sharp and sweet, they be. Surely," said the Longhunter with visible emotion, "ye must be one of me clansmen, perhaps me kin."

A yearning for the ancient and familiar ways was evident in the tone of the stranger, and in his voice was the tragedy of every countryman and the loss of all the hunter had known and loved. He spoke softly, quietly, as not to awaken memories too painful or even too endearing to recall.

The hunter recalled days gone by, when in his youth, he and his brothers had hunted the highland glens beneath the undulating shadow of Ben Wyvis. Even now, he could smell the odors of the Alpine bearberry on the slopes of the bens and taste the autumn fruit of the cloudberry baking over low peat fires. The two men clasped forearms and this time, Kearan watched cautiously, not intruding on their greeting.

Stepping back a few paces, Derick addressed the Longhunter. "I am Derick Davidson, youngest son of the former Clan Dhai Chieftain and brother to the present Chief, Duncan of Ross-shire. Our lands are in the eastern highlands, near unto the highland burgh of Dingwall and some near Cromarty."

Suddenly, the stranger began to tremble and tears rose in his clear blue eyes, spilling over and running into his beard. "Am I dreaming, lad?" the hunter asked.

Derick placed a hand on the man's shoulder, waiting for an explanation. The hunter spoke again.

"I am Donald Davidson of the Black Watch, 42nd Highland Regiment of Foot, now disbanded, and brother to Duncan, Chieftain of our clan in Ross-shire." The two men stared at each other, the enormity of this disclosure almost too much to comprehend.

"Ye are Duncan's own lad?" the stranger asked. "Are ye Duncan's son? Can it be? Does my brother yet live?"

The questions came so fast that Derick could only nod in affirmation.

"You were but a bairn when I left Scotland for the last time, as were your wee brothers."

The Longhunter began to weep unashamedly and clasped Derick to his breast in a strong embrace. He shook his head with the wonder of his discovery, wiping the tears with the back of his hand.

"Does my brother live?" the Longhunter repeated. His eyes were searching, intense, questioning.

"Nay," Derick answered quietly. "He is dead."

"He is dead?" queried the Longhunter. He shook his head slowly, tears still coursing down his cheeks and onto his beard. "What happened to me brother, to Chief Duncan?"

"His wounds were grievous sore and troubled him for many long years," Derick answered quietly. "He passed from the land of our fathers eight years ago when I was but twenty, and glad to go, he was. He suffered much. I witnessed his pain most of me life, and it drove me to commit unlawful acts of revenge on those who had so brutally afflicted him. I am glad me father no longer suffers. He is buried with the clan fathers in our ancestral burying ground."

The Longhunter felt the hurt behind his nephew's words, like open wounds, unhealed, and raw. Kearan felt Derick's anguish too and wondered at his confession, his declaration of unlawful acts and deeds. What could he mean? Had he fled Scotland as a murderer, an assassin, a criminal? Surely not! He must be speaking of war and all was fair in war.

"Is your oldest brother the present chief?" asked the Longhunter.

"Aye, Duncan, our father's namesake and the eldest son is now the Chief of Clan Davidson," Derick confirmed.

"Aye," said the Longhunter, "and that's as it should be. He will be a strong chief to his people, if he is like his father and grandfather before him."

"And ye—ye are truly me blood kin, me own Uncle Donald?" Derick asked. "The clan thought ye were killed many years ago during an ambush near Fort Duquesne. Somehow, I felt ye were yet alive. I thought one day to find ye."

A dominate characteristic of Clan Davidson was their magnetic blue eyes and the Longhunter's eyes were no exception. Despite the silver-black beard and fur cap, the singular features of the hunter bore a strong resemblance to Derick's father and to his father's people.

Kearan stood a little apart, watching the two men while her heart swelled with pleasure. She was happy to be a witness to this unusual reunion, but at the same time, she felt troubled at Derick's admission of unlawful deeds.

"We heard you were missing and presumed dead," Derick explained to his uncle. "Hundreds of the Highlanders never returned from battle, and many stayed in the Colonies after they were disbanded. Did ye not attempt to contact our people?"

Donald Davidson looked uncomfortable with the question, feeling a measure of regret over his inability to contact his people in Scotland.

"Aye, I wrote once a year after I left the Watch and sent a personal missive with Major Campbell who was last with me at Bushy Run. I heard only last year that he died on the sea voyage. Nearly ten years ago now. I check the post when I come from a hunt, but I find no answer to me letters. Any message sent to me homeland seems to vanish. Who can say why? I hear this from others who send letters to their kin. Perhaps," he added sorrowfully, "It be me fault. I am away so often." Derick nodded.

"I had no wife, no bairns, and no reason to return, so I stayed in the Colonies after the wars and joined the longhunters in their solitary life. It suits me, lad. I am a free man here." He laid one strong hand on Derick's shoulder. His voice grew husky, almost a whisper.

"Many a time, lad, me heart longed for the misty land o' me fathers, to hear the sweet voice of me own people. Believe me, lad, believe me. But after Culloden Moor where your Da' was wounded, me heart was crushed. 'Twas near gone out of me. When the 42nd dispersed after the wars, I stayed in this wild, free land and claimed this bonny country as me home."

Derick felt empathy for his uncle, understanding well his reluctance to return to his clan in Scotland. How could he fault him? Hadn't he done the same thing? He had children, a home, and land, and still he had chosen a life of exile like so many of his countrymen.

What would his uncle think of him when he discovered he still had children living in Scotland? Would he be disappointed to learn that he fled from the King's men and was suspected of treasonous activities in the Highlands? After all, his uncle had served with the Royal Highlanders in service to the Crown.

And what of the wide-eyed young Kearan Mackenzie, his inquisitive young pupil who trusted him, who wanted to learn to defend herself with the sword, a lass who may never understand the cause for this terrible impasse in his life?

Perhaps, Derick thought with a heavy sigh, only Daniel Morgan, the self-proclaimed American, would understand.

Chapter 8

Complexities of Love

Many waters cannot quench love,
Neither can the floods drown it

Numbered among the longhunters of the Virginia wilderness was Donald Davidson, former soldier of the Highland Regiment of the Black Watch, a regiment of Scots enlisted by the English crown. The Royal Highland Regiments assigned to the war campaigns in the American Colonies disbanded after the French and Indian War, but a great many of the soldiers remained in the American Colonies. Intrigued with the Colonial life and the adventurous spirit of the longhunters, Donald Davidson, formerly of the Black Watch, joined these freedom-loving frontier hunters.

The extended hunts so loved by the longhunters were lonely and dangerous ventures. Living in the wilderness during the winter months and in his cabin on Cedar Creek during the summer time, suited Donald Davidson's solitary way of life. He enjoyed the seclusion and rest from the ravages of war and gained a measure of prosperity from the lucrative fur trading business.

For several days following his arrival at Soldier's Rest, the Longhunter, as he was called by those who knew him, remained at the Morgan farm, visiting with his newly discovered nephew and exchanging news with the friends and neighbors of Daniel Morgan. It was a pleasant time and provided much-needed respite for the packhorses after their long and arduous trek through the wilderness. The Longhunter most often trapped and hunted along the small streams flowing into the Ohio and Kanawha Rivers, but this season he had explored the outlying hunting grounds, far from any white settlement.

During the late February evenings, neighbors and friends gathered around Daniel Morgan's fireside to discuss the latest happenings in the Colonies. The conversation inevitably turned to animated rehearsals of the early British engagements: the Forbes Expedition, Braddock's Defeat, Bushy Run, and Pontiac's War. Morgan and Donald Davidson had participated in those early blood-soaked battles.

The looming threat of possible encounters with the British and Indians was discussed at length with no resolution in sight. With the French driven from the northwest Colonies, the Patriots now faced a more formidable foe—the same red-jacketed soldiers they had fought alongside during the earlier campaigns of the fledgling nation.

It was voiced among the network of longhunters who frequently traded with the Indians, that the Indian contingents would join with the British as they had the French, with one goal in mind—to stop the westward advance of the Colonial settlers into Indian territory. The American Patriots would be facing not only an alarming number of British military forces, but also the collective tribes of Indian nations who, in reality, were defending their hunting grounds and domestic territories.

At mid-morning, the third day after his return to Frederick County, the Longhunter took leave of the Morgan's hospitality, thanking Abigail for her kindness and generosity. He presented her with a beautiful beaver pelt to make a fur cape. Derick joined his uncle in the dooryard as the elder Davidson prepared to leave.

"Come with me, lad," the Longhunter said to Derick. He was loading the packhorses, making ready for the trek into town. "Sure to be an adventure, an education in fur trade, and ye can help me gather up me supplies for the next season. Have ye been to town yet?"

"Nay, only been to Boston for a few hours. Morgan and meself left in a wee bit of a hurry," Derick said, recalling his and Morgan's hasty departure from that unfriendly town. "We didn't see but a tavern, a mighty ramshackle one at that. I've been here since then, laying low, keeping me head on me shoulders."

His uncle laughed. "A guid plan for the dead o' the year, but come with me to Winchester. I'll show ye around, and ye can see where I abide in the warmer months." He paused, a twinkle in his blue eyes. "It's not like our home in the Heilan', lad, but 'tis home to me. Perchance ye might stay a fortnight or so—if ye can bear to part from the lass that is."

Derick felt his face grow warm, and something like anger rose in his breast. His uncle was speaking in jest, he presumed, but the statement did not set well. They were standing in the exact spot where he instructed Kearan in the art of parrying effectively with her sword, breaking the thrusts and slashes of her opponent.

"I have no attachment to the lass, Uncle," Derick said. "She is only a child, a mere lass who wants to use the sword, 'tis all, and not as ye are implying. Me heart is..." He broke off and looked away, feeling the familiar sadness creep over him, blocking out the luster of the otherwise pleasant day and leaving him somewhat frustrated.

"Forgive me, lad," the Longhunter said apologetically, "I failed to remember—ye are recently bereaved of your bonny wife and your bairnies too. I missed much of me kinsman's life, so long have I been away from me home in bonny Scotland." The Longhunter looked contrite and returned to his thoughts but from another perspective.

"Aye, ye speak from your sorrowing heart, lad, this I can see, and ye may well have no intentions toward the young lass, but her eyes speak of other things, and they're a telling me that her heart is turned toward ye, laddie."

"Nay, Uncle, ye are misguided by the light ye chanced to see. For love of the sword, ye see a sparkle dancing in her eyes, and it's not for love of a man. I be like her kin, a brother, a tutor perchance, but 'tis all. Not as ye are a thinkin', Uncle."

Donald Davidson shrugged his broad shoulders, raised one eyebrow, and nodded his head, saying no more on the subject. He could see the suggestion disturbed his nephew, so he kept further thoughts on the matter to himself.

The door to the farmhouse opened, and Kearan and Morgan came down the dooryard path, now fringed with a few sprigs of new green grass, the harbingers of spring. Derick turned to his uncle. "Perhaps I will come with ye after all, to see where ye abide. I can stay a fortnight or so, to be sure. Drilling the riflemen is Morgan's main objective, and he doesn't need me hanging about for that. Here he comes now to bid ye farewell, Uncle, so I'll ask the old wagoner to give me leave. I'm not officially with the militia although Morgan doesn't seem to understand this."

"What's all this?" Daniel Morgan said, slapping Donald Davidson none too gently on the back. "Looks like you're a fixin' to make tracks for Winchester. You've a mighty nice catch here, Davidson." Morgan ran his hand over an especially plush beaver pelt.

"Aye, that I do, Cap'n Morgan. I'll be trading me furs on the morrow in Winchester. I've a mind to take me nephew with me, maybe have him stay a spell at me cabin on Cedar Creek. Can your lads do without him for a fortnight or two?"

"A fortnight? Why, sure thing. I think we can spare him for a while. Be good for Derick to meet some town folk, get to know the lay of the land around Virginny. All he's seen of the Colonies is Boston and that by the seat of his britches. My place, of course, and the neighbors hereabouts. By all means, Davidson, take him with you."

The Longhunter fastened his gaze on Derick with a look of ultimate satisfaction. "There ye be, nephew," the Longhunter said cheerfully. "Gather your trappings, and we be off."

Kearan had been standing quietly by, listening to the men make their plans. She handed Donald Davidson a lunch she had wrapped in brown paper and then placed her hands on her hips, staring at the three men with a look of dismay on her upturned face. She turned to Derick.

"What about my lessons, Mr. Davidson?"

"Practice what I've taught ye thus far, and the rest will keep until I return. I'm sure one of Morgan's lads will be happy to be relieved of his drill duty to practice with ye, isn't that true, Daniel?"

"No doubt of that," laughed Morgan heartily. "They'll be standin' in line, just a waitin' to cross swords with our pretty little gal, especially Thomas Aubrey, eh, Kearan?" A warm flush colored Kearan's cheeks and a fire kindled in her brown eyes.

"He is only a friend," Kearan said defensively, "and just to set the record straight, Daniel Morgan, if he has other intentions, I'm not interested, not in the least." Morgan loved to tease Kearan and did so at every opportunity.

Derick turned to Morgan and said, "The lady doth protest too much, methinks." He was quoting the familiar old line from Shakespeare. "Hamlet, act three, scene two," he added reciting the location of the memorable old quote. The literature lesson over, Derick loaded the last bundle of fur pelts onto the packhorses.

"Well, Mr. Shakespearian quoter, Mr. Edinburgh University scholar, Mr. Sword Master," said Kearan, half-mocking, half-serious, "I have one for you! 'It is not in the stars to hold our destiny, but in ourselves!' I believe this verse will fit nicely here."

The Longhunter's eyes widened with amusement, and he peered at Kearan over the back of the packhorse. His thoughts on the subject were now confirmed in his mind. The lass cared for his nephew.

"Touché," said Derick with a final tug to the harness. "Ye don't believe in Divine Providence, then? If we can chart our own destinies, then what need we of God?"

"Surely, you jest, Mr. Davidson," Kearan said, surprise and disbelief clouding her face.

"Aye, I do, but the quote is not clearly stated. I see ye study the works of Shakespeare yourself, Miss Mackenzie and now I must confess, I am vanquished by the lady."

"Indeed you are, sir. Contrary to what you have heard or may believe, we are not all mindless barbarians out here on the frontier. Some of us are quite familiar with the poets and the playwrights." Derick slapped the horse on the rump and turned to face her.

"I do not presume to vex ye, Miss Mackenzie, but I did notice young Aubrey's attentions toward ye. Quite naturally, me mind traveled in that direction."

She calmed herself, her indignation fading away at the mention of Thomas Aubrey.

"We will resume your lessons when I return in a fortnight, aye?" Derick asked, ignoring her apparent confusion. "And never did I think ye were a mindless barbarian," he added with a slight smile. "The barbarians inhabit the Highlands of Scotland."

Kearan felt confused and reassured at the same time, but the fire left her eyes. "Aye," she said adopting his brogue. "In a fortnight then. I shall be waiting and practicing with me sword." She laid her hand on the hilt of the sword still strapped to her side.

Derick regarded the young girl standing in the pale winter sunlight. Her moods rose and fell like the turbulent tides of the North Sea, but she was young, impetuous, reckless, and full of spirit and life. In time, he thought, she would soften into mature womanhood, and for one brief instant, he felt sad, like something would be lost in the passing.

"Be wary of the blade, lass," Derick warned. "It can harm ye if ye are careless." He still marveled at Kearan's natural ability with the sword, a fact he never mentioned to her, fearing she would become overconfident and reckless. In his brief time of instruction, she had mastered some difficult techniques with graceful ease. Her timing was extraordinary, precise, and coupled with her natural dexterity of movement, she wielded the weapon with amazing accuracy.

"I will gather me things and saddle me horse, Uncle," said Derick without further discussion. He left the little company standing in the dooryard, and in a short time returned with Warrior, who was stomping his feet, eager to be off for a run. The Longhunter was already mounted, the reins of the two additional packhorses tethered behind.

Derick secured a leather satchel with his personal effects to the saddle and then swung onto his mount. Daniel Morgan reached his hand to Derick and the two men clasped forearms, their eyes meeting in understanding and mutual friendship.

"Take care, my friend," Morgan said, "and we'll see you back at the field in a fortnight. If you stay longer, send word or we'll think you were hanged by the British." Morgan backed away a few paces, leaving Kearan standing next to Warrior, her hand gliding along the smooth flank of the horse.

"Aye, in a fortnight then," said Derick.

Wanting to say farewell, Kearan lingered next to Warrior's side, hoping the Scotsman wasn't annoyed at her brashness.

Kearan was almost boyish in appearance, not fully a woman, but neither a child. Her dark hair blew loose about her face as she turned to Derick, an appealing look crossing her features.

The same odd sense of protectiveness washed over Derick again, like waves of the sea, and he wanted to ask Morgan to watch over the vulnerable young girl, to keep her safe, but he knew he could not. She had a father and a brother to protect her, but neither seemed concerned for her safety. The thought nagged at his mind, and he felt reluctant to leave. There had been too many farewells in his life, he reasoned, and good-byes affected him unnaturally. He must put this parting out of his mind.

"Farewell, lass," he said simply. "I will return when the first spring flowers brighten the dooryard."

"Farewell, Mr. Davidson," Kearan said reaching a small hand to him. "God go with you and keep you from harm. I shall remember you in my prayers."

Derick took her hand, pressed it for a brief moment, and then withdrew. She smiled at him and then backed away a few steps.

"Thank ye, lass," Derick said and reined his horse through the open gate to follow the Longhunter who was already moving along the road to Winchester.

Kearan and Morgan watched the departing figures as they rode away. A hint of spring was in the air, and a small flock of robins lighted on the nearby fence, chirping loudly and inspecting the food supply in the farmyard. The migrations had begun, announcing the approach of spring in the Shenandoah valley. The earth was warming, painting the grasslands along the rivers a lush green and bathing the fertile fields in warm sunshine.

Morgan turned to face Kearan, a worried look wrinkling the scar on his amicable features. "Kearan, gal, I can see you are taken with the Scotsman," he began abruptly, "and I wish to heaven you weren't. He' packin' a heavy load on his back and it wouldn't be a good idea for you to be tangled up with him. I've been like a second Pa to you and I don't like seein' you yearnin' for what shouldn't be. Stick to our frontier lads, our Virginny men, the young riflemen who are just standin' in line to court ya. Why, some of them young bucks would give their eyeteeth if you'd just give 'em a chance."

Kearan felt chagrined. Was she so transparent in her feelings? Obviously, Daniel Morgan had thought so. She didn't feel she was yearning for the Scotsman—or was she? She decided to challenge this assumption.

"Uncle Daniel," Kearan said, using her pet name for him, "I don't know what makes you think I am 'taken' with the Scotsman. Have I acted in a way that seems inappropriate to you?"

"Confound the female folk of this world!" Morgan said with annoyance. He shook his head in wonderment. "Why can't you just answer me plainly, gal? You dance around the Maypole like a giddy young'un. I'd be a blind man not to see you're lookin' at Davidson—and no, you haven't acted improper, if that's what you're a meanin'. You don't have to act any particular way. It's written on your face, in your eyes."

Kearan was taken aback at this statement. "It is?" she asked, somewhat embarrassed.

"Gal, I've known you since you wore nappies," Morgan said, "and I guess I can read you plain as day."

Kearan felt rebuked and ashamed. A warm blush crept over her face and tears rose in her brown eyes. She searched Morgan's sober face for confirmation of his surprising declaration. She read the truth plainly in his eyes. Daniel Morgan would not tease her about the Scotsman if he weren't truly concerned for her welfare.

Suddenly, she laid her head against his shoulder and began to weep. A pitiful little groan escaped her lips and Morgan closed a strong arm around her shoulders in a comforting manner, but his words were gruff.

"Stop that infernal bawlin', gal. Won't help a lick and makes a man feel completely useless and lower than a snake's belly."

"But—what should I do?" Kearan wailed against him. "Does he know how I feel? I am so foolish, so stupid. Have I disgraced myself in front of him and everyone else?"

"No, gal, I reckon not. Just folks who know you as I do, those who can read your thoughts, that's all, so stop your bawlin'. I simply can't abide it. Weepin' women folk are an awful bother to a man. Frankly, I'd say Davidson is caught up in his own personal grief and doesn't take much notice of what's goin' on around him. Of course, I could be wrong, but it appears that he's occupied with his own wagonload of baggage to sort through, so best leave him be."

"Then why are you so worried if he doesn't notice me?"

"Well, he sees you as a child now, Kearan, but that can change in time. The Scotsman rides a crooked trail, and our frontier lads are far less complicated. Mind me now, Kearan. I'm just lookin' out for your tender young heart, that's all. I'd do the same for my own gals."

Kearan pulled away from Morgan and wiped her eyes on the back of her sleeve. She searched in her pocket, pulled out a lace-edged handkerchief, and blew her nose.

"Why do you think Mr. Davidson has an insurmountable past?" Kearan asked, wiping her eyes. "I know he left Scotland for personal reasons and lost a sweetheart, a wife, I believe. Do you think he is a bad person?"

"Well, of course not! Did I say he was a bad person? Quite the contrary. Davidson's an excellent soldier, a strong, honorable man, a true friend to me, but he's snowed under with personal issues, things you don't need to bother your little head about. He'll work through his troubles in time, I reckon, but just the same, he's too serious, too old for a young gal like yourself, and his ways are too thorny to untangle right now."

"But, Uncle Daniel, aren't you considerable older than Abigail?" Kearan queried, her question posing a slight challenge.

Daniel Morgan cleared his throat roughly and gave Kearan a look of annoyance. Morgan's intention was to spare the trusting young girl, spare her from being involved in a relationship far too complex for an inexperienced frontier girl to muddle through. Morgan respected Derick Davidson and valued his friendship, but he wished to spare Kearan of any entanglement that could lead to unhappiness and hurt.

"That's entirely different," Morgan said with a finality forbidding any further discussion on the matter, but Kearan was not to be put off so easily.

"Daniel Morgan," Kearan said, a plaintive note in her voice, "answer me truly and I will try to understand. Please answer me this—can a person help whom they might love in this life? Is there some way to stop the feelings stealing over your heart when you find yourself near that particular someone, even though you might wish not to care, not to love?"

Daniel Morgan considered young Kearan Mackenzie for an extended moment and then looked away from the intense perplexity in her dark eyes. He gazed across the barren winter fields lying fallow beneath a scattering of feathery clouds and thought of his own land, Soldier's Rest, a name he had given the farm after returning from Pontiac's War. At this particular moment, it seemed anything but restful.

Love and hate still ruled the world and was still the driving force that bound the world together or set it spinning out of control, turning men against men, nation against nation, or binding together the defenseless, the helpless, the innocent, those who dared to love in perilous times.

For once, Daniel Morgan had no words. How could he answer honestly? The only measure he had was his own experience, the knowledge of a love so strong, it compelled him to travel many treacherous miles just to be with Abby, the woman he desired more than any woman in the world, but why? Only heaven knew why. Was love predictable, something he had power over, a passion he could either embrace or refuse? He had not given the question much thought before.

Later, propped against the pillows in the big four-poster bed he shared with Abigail, Daniel Morgan turned to his wife who sat beside him on the bed, braiding her long honey-gold hair in the flickering light of the bedside candle.

"Abigail," Morgan said turning to face her. Immediately, Abigail stopped braiding her hair to look quizzically at her husband. Daniel Morgan only addressed her as "Abigail" when something was troubling his mind, or when a serious discussion was forthcoming.

"What is it, Daniel?" she asked with some apprehension. A little shiver of fear ran down her spine, and she unconsciously set the hairbrush aside. Had war been declared by the Patriots? Had there been an Indian attack?

"It's Kearan, Abby. I fear she's lookin' at Derick, and I'm sure he's not lookin' back, not in his present state of mind. If he were a lookin', wouldn't be any sense to it anyway."

"Is that all you're worried about, Daniel? I thought it was something serious. You scared me."

"It *is* serious, Abby. I feel responsible. I brought the Scotsman here, and now this happens."

"What's happened, Daniel? He is only teaching her to use the sword for pity's sake. He is a perfect gentlemen and I like him. Is there something else I don't know about?"

"Yes, Abby, and I might as well tell you—Davidson fled Scotland because he feared he would be arrested for," Morgan paused, his words coming with difficulty, "for murder."

Abby paled and clutched her husband's arm. "Oh, Daniel, surely not. I can't believe he is a murderer. Not Derick. Why would he murder anyone?"

"In revenge—because they murdered his wife."

A little gasp escaped from Abby's throat, and she clasped her hands to her breast. "Who are 'they', and how did it happen, Daniel?"

"Well, he told me his story in bits and pieces, whenever something happened to stir his memory. I could see he was grievin' somethin' awful when I met him in Boston, so I brought him to Virginny. I liked the man immediately, the minute I met him." He sighed. "I didn't think the story worth repeatin', so I kept it to myself. Derick wanted me to know his situation, just in case there was trouble down the road."

"Tell me, Daniel. I want to know."

"Well, seems like Derick's been plagued by sorrowful events most of his young life, Abby. His Ma was raped and killed by Cumberland's men when he was only a babe." He felt Abby clutch his arm before he continued.

"His father was badly wounded in '46 at the battle with the English at Culloden Moor. You know how the British love to flaunt this victory in our face, just to keep us from tryin' it ourselves. Anyway, Derick's father never recovered his health. When his sons were old enough, the brothers roamed the Highlands in disguise, looking for English encampments and garrisons. When they found soldiers camped on clan lands, they would attack, burn the garrisons, and send the soldiers packin' back to England."

"Oh, Daniel, they were sure to be discovered. What could Derick have been thinking to exact such revenge? Go on, dear."

"His Pa sent the brothers to Edinburgh to be educated since they had money, considerable land, and titles. Derick met a gal there and, as fate would have it, they fell in love. Abby, men are fools where love is concerned. That's a fact." Abby smiled but said nothing.

"Well, Derick brought the gal to his Highland home, married her, and they had a family."

"Derick has children?" interrupted Abigail incredulously. "Where are they, Daniel? Are they still in Scotland?"

"They are with his brother, Duncan, and his wife, Margaret. They have no children and love Derick's babes like their own. He also has a twin sister somewhere in Scotland. Their father died several years ago so Derick's brother is the present chief of their clan."

"And what of his wife, Daniel?"

Slowly, Daniel Morgan shook his head. "After he married, they lived peaceable for some time on his place in Cromarty, wherever the devil that is, somewhere in the north of Scotland. The English suspected the Davidson brothers of the attacks on the garrisons, but could never prove it. They couldn't arrest the entire clan, so they hatched a plan to trap Derick Davidson." Morgan rubbed the scar along his cheek.

"Soldiers went to his house while Derick was away hunting," Morgan continued, "and waited for him to return. They had some trumped up charges but nothing legitimate. When Derick rode up to the gate, his wife, Meagan, he called her, ran to warn him, and...and the soldiers shot her dead, Abby, right in front of Derick. Meagan had their babe in her arms, but the babe was unharmed." Abigail began to weep softly and hid her face against Morgan's chest as though to hide from the terrible scene he recounted.

"It was an awful bloody business, Abby. Derick fought his way through the soldiers and escaped. He quickly organized his clansmen and they found the soldiers before they could reach

England. Derick took them out with brutal revenge, burning their bodies and leaving them in the road."

"Oh God, have mercy," Abigail cried piteously. "Won't they arrest his brothers, his family?"

"Derick made certain his brothers had credible alibis before the blood feud took place. The safety of the entire clan depended on their innocence. They couldn't prove Derick committed the deed, since he and his clansmen were in disguise, but who else would exact such revenge, Abby? The English knew he did it and would have arrested him eventually. There was no way out. They would have hunted him down, so he just disappeared."

"Oh Daniel, how terrible! What do you think? What would you have done in such a case?"

"They murdered his wife, Abigail, shot her down in cold blood without a cause. Derick took justice into his own hands. He knew there would be no justice from the English. I expect it goes agin your religion, Abby, but he felt he had no choice. It was his wife—the woman he loved." Unconsciously, Daniel Morgan pulled his own wife closer to him.

"I don't understand, Daniel, oh I don't understand."

"I know you don't, gal, and I don't expect you ever will. It's just the way a man thinks. Who understands it? Who even tries? Just the way of it, the way a man is, that's all."

"What happened next, Daniel?"

"He left his children with his family and came here, simply disappeared from Scotland." Morgan sighed. "I couldn't tell Kearan all that business, Abby. My stars, it's an awful commentary."

"Of course, you couldn't tell such an innocent as Kearan the horror of such a terrible tragedy, Daniel."

"I don't know what's gotten into the gal's head anyhow," Morgan exclaimed. "Moonstruck, I guess. All the frontier lads are wild after her, and she goes and looks at one she oughtn't to look at." He ran a brawny hand through his sandy hair. "Have Silas and Lily Jayne mentioned anything, Abby?"

"No, Daniel, they haven't. I don't think the possibility that Kearan might be interested in Derick has occurred to them—Kearan yearning for Derick would seem remote. They are pleased he is giving her lessons with the sword, but then, they like to indulge Kearan. You know they do, Daniel." Abigail unconsciously wound a strand of hair around her finger, thinking of the horrific events Daniel had just related.

"Daniel, did Kearan tell you she cared for Derick? Perhaps she is just infatuated. You know how it is with a stranger, someone different from the boys she grew up with, someone with an education and genteel ways and, well, Daniel, I must admit—he is an attractive man."

Morgan looked at his wife with surprise, and she smiled demurely.

"Not to worry, Daniel Morgan, the Scotsman holds no attraction for me and definitely has issues that seem quite overwhelming. Unless God is his helper, he will certainly be...well, without help."

Daniel Morgan looked solemn as he held Abby close to his heart. "Kearan didn't say she cared for him," Morgan explained, "not exactly, but she does, Abby. I can see it. She asked some hard questions today, questions I couldn't answer."

"Such as?"

"Such as; can a person help whom they love, and, can you stop the feelings of your heart even if you don't want to love someone?"

Abigail looked uncertain. "Why didn't you answer her questions, Daniel?"

"Because," he paused and picked up the golden braid laying across Abigail's shoulder, "because I know the confounded answer, Abby. I couldn't tell Kearan how it is, so I didn't say a thing. Just sent her home, blast it all anyway."

"And what do you know to be true, Daniel Morgan?"

Morgan dropped her braid and pulled back the coverlet as if he were too warm. The intimate conversation made him uncomfortable, and he looked like he might leap from the bed. Morgan was not given to sentiment, but when it concerned his wife, Kearan, or his own girls, his manner turned soft, and he couldn't quite understand why, nor did he like the way it affected him. He took a deep breath and said in a husky voice, "I know…you can't help lovin' someone, cant stop the feelin's, even when the trail's not marked on your map."

Abigail smiled at his unique description and reached for her husband's hand.

"Well said, my love, and you're so right. The trail is not always clearly marked, but the unexpected stops along the way are by far the most beautiful, the most rewarding. I have found it to be so. Don't worry, Daniel. Kearan will find her way and so must Derick. We must leave them in God's hands. Poor Derick. The events of his past are far too difficult for mere mortals to untangle."

"Abby," Morgan said settling himself against the pillows, "just talkin' about this here love business makes me nervous. It's too all-fired complicated, and it makes my head hurt. Put out the candle, will ya, Abby gal?"

Chapter 9

Cabin on Cedar Creek

*Two never kindled a fire
But what it lit between them*

After arriving in Winchester, the seat and business hub of Frederick County, Donald Davidson took his catch of animal pelts to the fur trader who was doing a brisk business. The Virginia longhunters were slowly returning from the hunting and trapping season of 1774, and they were eager to hear any news of conflicts between the Patriots and Loyalists. For the most part, the longhunters were solidly behind the Patriot cause.

The town of Winchester was a brawling, cursing, boisterous settlement, a town of rough and hearty frontiersmen, land speculators, and hopeful settlers. Clapboard and log structures lined Main Street where mud-spattered buildings housed a variety of diverse businesses, two dry goods stores, and several taverns. Horse droppings and refuse of every imaginable kind fouled the muddy streets. The only stone structures in the town were the Anglican Church and the Frederick County jail, both of which did a prodigious business.

As the two Davidson men walked down the boardwalks of the muddy main street to the town center, they heard lively conversations drifting through the open doors of Winchester's taverns and public houses. Men recently returned from winter hunts were spending their wages and catching up on the latest happenings in the Colonies.

Located in the center of town, Fort Loudoun dominated the heart of the settlement. During the French and Indian War, Colonel George Washington had directed the construction of the fort in 1756. Derick walked around the parameter of the fort, examining the four bastions built of earth, wood, and stone, not unlike fortifications used in Scotland. British soldiers still maintained the fortification, but the garrison had fallen into disuse as a military command center.

During the earlier campaigns, the fort had served as a British headquarters. Watching the English soldiers milling about the town was too much like the on-going occupation of Scotland; the British presence sent a disquieting message to the frontier community.

Settlers of the Quaker persuasion walked about the town in their austere clothing, selling crusty brown pies made from dried wild apples. The Shenandoah Valley was fertile ground for the apple and fruit orchards growing in profusion on the gentle slopes of the valley, and the local Quakers gathered the apples by the cartload to bake into pies, which they sold to the townspeople. The Longhunter bought several fruit pies and a bag of dried apples to take to his cabin on Cedar Creek.

The Virginia Colony was not a Quaker community like the neighboring Pennsylvania Colony. It was predominately an Anglican parish. The Quakers, walking about the streets of Winchester, handed small leaflets to passersby, denouncing any aggressive action by the Patriots. Derick was surprised at the unusual amount of dissenting faiths. Many of the settlers appeared to have the liberty to choose their own spiritual path, but the frontier people, although deeply religious, did not ascribe to any particular church affiliation, choosing instead to worship God according to the dictates of their hearts, attending religious meetings when convenient.

Frequently, religious meetings were held in neighborhood barns or brush arbors. Because political or public debates denouncing and objecting to Loyalist views were not permitted, the gatherings often turned into political opportunities to air one's views. Derick found this practice to be quite unusual and wondered if his uncle ever attended these religious meetings or worshiped with such a strange mixture of professed Christians.

Abigail Morgan was a confessed Christian and Daniel Morgan professed belief in the Almighty God, but religion wasn't a personal thing with Morgan, and he did not have much tolerance for the organized religious activity of the frontier people. After his return from Boston, he permitted Abigail to say a blessing at mealtime and to attend church meetings with Nancy and Betsy, but these concessions were the extent of his acceptance.

Clan Davidson, along with many of the Scottish clans, adhered to the highly structured and organized religion of their motherland. Derick found the Colonial manner of worship amazingly liberal and unceremonious.

Quakers from Pennsylvania had moved into the Fredrick County community, hoping their pacifist views would attract the local folk and avert further talk of a coming revolution. But the Colonials and Patriots of the county were not adverse to taking up arms when necessary and were themselves militant about asserting their independence from the British Crown, although armed resistance was not mentioned when the British presence was in Fort Loudoun.

The Longhunter bought a store of food supplies, repair parts for his traps, and additional equipment for the next long hunt. He prepared to leave for his log cabin located near a small stream southwest of Winchester.

Derick had thoroughly enjoyed the experience of fur trading and buying trapping equipment. He listened intently to the bargaining process and discovered that his uncle was a clever trader, leaving with far more than he had bargained for. The trade goods were loaded onto the pack animals, and the two men headed south on the wagon road to the Longhunter's cabin.

Before leaving Winchester, Donald Davidson posted a letter to his family in Scotland, telling them of happenings in the Colonies and of his unexpected reunion with his nephew. Knowing interception of the communication was probable, he made no mention of names or their whereabouts. If the letter was received, the clan would understand the significance of his account and his allusion to his nephew. The British would be watching the post in Scotland, looking for some word from dissenters. They must be careful.

Pleased that Derick was with him, the Longhunter was in high spirits as he and Derick rode leisurely along the wagon road. Perhaps, he thought to himself, they could spend the summer together, and Derick might even accompany him on his next long hunt.

"Why did ye choose the life of a longhunter, Uncle?" Derick asked as they rode abreast along the uneven dirt road. Deep ruts slowed their progress, and wishing only to run, Warrior snorted and blew through flaring nostrils at the slow, plodding movement.

"Many reasons, lad," answered his uncle. "Most longhunters earn enough money trading furs to last more than a year, if there be a good season. Me trade for just this season amounted to two thousand dollars or better. More than a farmer earns in several years of hard labor. Well, lad, I reckon longhunters find fur trading more profitable and considerable less wearisome than pushing a plow." He turned in his saddle and grinned at Derick. "Maybe we're just lazy."

"Nay, Uncle, ye are not that!" Derick chuckled. "Hunting and trapping are considerable work, to be sure, but far more agreeable for a man. I be keen to hunt meself, the red stag in the highland bens. For a hunting man, 'tis a pleasurable challenge."

Donald Davidson nodded, remembering the thrill of trailing the red deer, king of the Highland hunt. "Of course, the trapping and hunting life isn't for everyone," admitted the Longhunter. "Family men are best suited to farming, but solitary men like meself, well, we can wander where we please. Of course, there's danger a plenty—hostile Indians, bears, blizzards, sickness, not to mention the thieving renegades and lying crooked men. And, lad, some men don't take to that kind of danger, but, by and large, this kinda life suits me well. I be a solitary man, lad."

Moments passed before Derick spoke again. "And if there be a war, if the Colonies revolt completely and seek independence, will ye join the Patriot's, Uncle? Ye were a soldier once."

Looking toward the range of mountains in the distance, the Longhunter thought for a long moment. The Blue Ridge loomed in sight, shimmering blue and purple in the afternoon light, like the misty crags of Ben Wyvis in the Highlands.

"I was a soldier many years ago, lad, when I had no choice in the matter, when the Black Watch fought for the English Crown, for the British cause. I did me time. I fought and killed until the ground was soaked in blood. During the heat of battle, I fought

French, Indians, and whoever got in me way. Then...I walked away, and glad I've been ever since."

"Ye won't fight again, Uncle?" As Derick waited for his uncle's reply, the horses' hoofs beat a predictable rhythm on the steadily rising incline of the road.

"I have no more reason to fight, no desire to fight. If I take down me claymore again and go to war, I would fight with the Patriots—for independence. But think ye, lad, what will it mean—what be the cost? Like as not, I be fighting agin me own countrymen, me own people. The British will enlist our lads again, to be sure. The English understand their worth and know the Heilan lads can fight better than their own British soldiers." The Longhunter paused in his thoughts, a melancholy tenor lowering his voice to a husky note.

"I have grown to love me freedom...freedom from tyranny...and I love this bonny land wi' wide open spaces. This be me home now, lad. There be a land to settle and a wilderness to tame." The Longhunter clucked to the packhorses now lagging behind and then turned to Derick, a serious look in his intense blue eyes.

"Most of all, lad, I find meself unaccustomed to the yoke. Ye know how it was. I must be free." Again, he paused, a deep grief evident in his voice. "It would grieve me sore, lad, to fight agin me own people, me clansmen, pointing a rifle at me own clan across a strange and terrible battlefield—what would I do?" The Longhunter sighed. "Perhaps I will go to the Ohio country where no white man lives."

"Live with the Indians?" Derick asked incredulously.

"Aye, perhaps. They be a free people." He smiled wryly, knowing his nephew was quite dubious about his living among the Indians.

Derick could not believe his uncle was serious, but the Longhunter offered no further explanation. The subject brought a dark cloud, a premonition of dread that hovered over Derick like a dark specter of doom. He did not pursue further discussion on the matter. There was no resolution to the perplexing dilemma of war, no way to join the Patriot's cause without fighting against the Highlanders whom the British would surely press into service for the coming conflict.

Just as the moon rose over the shadowy range of the Blue Ridge Mountains, the two Davidsons arrived at the Longhunter's cabin on Cedar Creek. The cabin itself was constructed from seasoned oak logs, notched and fitted at the corners and chinked between the gaps. The entire structure consisted of one large main room with a stone fireplace opposite the door. A bed was built into the wall and covered with an ancient woolen plaid. In the peak of the high-pitched roof, a loft was fitted and used for storage and an extra sleeping room.

The log house was welcoming, and Derick liked it at once. Books from Scotland, England, and some printed in the Colonies lined oak shelves built into the walls on either side of the fireplace. It was an impressive library for a man of the frontier. Several chairs made from barrels and padded with wool and beaver skins gave the room a comfortable, tranquil feeling. A trestle table and two long benches stood in the middle of the room, and an oil lamp with a glass globe set in the center of the table.

The Longhunter kindled a fire and lit the lamp, and the room soon warmed. He hung a large iron kettle from a hook and swung it over the flames. In a short time, a pot of venison stew was simmering over the hot coals.

After a simple meal of stew and bread, the two men fed and groomed the horses and brought the supplies from the log barn into the house to sort and store.

"On the morrow," said the Longhunter as he put the last of the supplies away, "I can show ye around me property. Cedar Creek empties into the Shenandoah River and, aye, but it's a bonny trail."

Derick nodded his agreement and rose from his chair to remove a broadsword from the wall where it hung above a wooden chest. "This be your sword, Uncle?"

Leaning back in the rocking chair he had constructed from wild cherry wood, the Longhunter nodded assent. "Killed many a man with me claymore," he commented. "Carried it through all the battles I fought for the British during me time with the Black Watch. Served me well, lad."

Derick examined the basket-hilted broadsword and ran his fingers along the double-edged blade. The sword was still sharp and ready for use.

The Longhunter smiled. "I keep it ready, just out of long habit, I reckon." He rose from his chair and opened the wooden chest. On top of the military issued Black Watch uniform, a Highland pistol, dirk, and battleaxe, were kept oiled and ready. The red uniform jacket was marked on the sleeves with the epaulet of a Lieutenant and appeared to be well cared for. The Longhunter lifted the pistol from the leather belt.

"This pistol was made from the highest grade steel in the armories of Stirlingshire. I brought it with me when I came across many years ago," the Longhunter said. "Your brothers were wee lads then, and ye hadn't made your appearance. I never cared much for the pistol. If I depended on me pistol to save me, I be a dead man more than once." He lifted the dirk from the chest. "Sgian dearg," the Longhunter said and smiled.

"The red knife," Derick translated from Gaelic. "Aye, Uncle, more dependable—always ready." Derick lifted the battleaxe and the remainder of his uncle's war memorials from the wooden chest, examining each article with keen interest.

The Longhunter returned to his place before the fire and talked of his days with the Black Watch. He spoke of his decision to stay in the Colonies after his regiment disbanded and of his many adventures as a longhunter. When the fire on the hearth burned low, he added more logs to the hot coals.

"I have another sword I wish for ye to see, lad, a weapon I find far more useful." He took a small, worn book from his pack and handed it to his nephew. The volume smelled of the Longhunter, of smoke, drying venison, and the wild earthy odors of animal skins.

Derick opened the small leather-bound book, a puzzled look on his face. "The Kirke's Bible?" Derick questioned. He spoke of an Irish Gaelic translation used by many in Scotland, a well known but difficult to obtain volume, a Bible not owned by the common people. The Davidsons of Ross-shire owned this translation, but found the Irish Gaelic to be too arduous to translate into their own Scottish Gaelic and, therefore, not truly beneficial.

"Nay, lad. A testament translated into Scottish Gaelic, the very first translation to be printed. James Stuart of Killin, and his assistant, Dugal Buchanan of Rannoch, published this testament in Edinburgh seven years ago in '67, from the original Greek and Hebrew. I bought this copy from a Quaker woman. She found it in a sea chest of some passenger who died on the voyage across the water. She couldn't read it, but she drove a hard bargain nonetheless."

Derick thumbed through the pages, some marked with slips of paper. "Did ye not learn Greek and Latin, Uncle?"

"Your Da' and your Uncle David went south to Edinburgh to study, but I enlisted in the King's service to represent our family and the clan. Your Da' would be chief someday, and David was the youngest, so it fell my lot to go, and I went willingly, aye, that I did. The Crown, George II in those days, was pressing every noble and titled family in Scotland for enlistment."

"Couldn't the clansmen have represented the family?" Derick asked.

"Well, the King had his own motives for requesting the landowners' sons to serve in the military. That was his way of repressing any rebellion from influential families in the Highlands. The King feared the large landholders with so many clansmen and crofters. Me service in the Black Watch granted favors to our clan, and at the same time, a measure of cooperation from the Scottish nobles. 'Twas a tricky, dirty business, lad."

The Longhunter stared into the fire, his mind recalling another time and another place. "Nay, laddie, I never attended the University. I can read English, of course, but having the testament in me own Gaelic has comforted me greatly."

"Is this the sword you are speaking of, Uncle?"

"Aye, but I never knew it be a sword until I read about it in me testament. Did ye know this book is also a sword?"

Derick shook his head in negation and handed the book to his uncle who opened the testament to a well-worn page and began to read. "*And take the helmet of salvation, and the sword of the Spirit, which is the word of God.* So, there it be, lad. This wee book is a sword, aye, and the sword of our Lord. What think ye of that?"

"It's not a killing sword, Uncle. How can we defend ourselves with a wee bit of paper and leather?"

"I canna tell ye how this spirit sword works, lad, but it's bigger and sharper than any claymore I ever slung across me back. Been trying it out for some time now, and it be an able weapon, 'that's certain. Listen to the words in a missive of Hebrew letters." He thumbed through the book until he found the passage. "*For the word of God is quick, and powerful, and sharper than any two-edged sword, piercing even to the dividing asunder of soul and spirit, and of the joints and marrow, and is a discerner of the thoughts and intents of the heart.* Think of that, lad! This sword will cut into our thoughts, find secret motives, and discover our very heart."

Derick was silent. Visions of his beautiful wife, Meagan, broken and bleeding on the hard cobblestones, and of dead British soldiers, their bodies burning in the road, raising a black, putrid odor that reached unto heaven, played over in his mind. The sword of the Longhunter had gone there, cutting into his troubled thoughts. He must tell his uncle. He must tell him now—tonight.

"Uncle," Derick began, "I have used another sword, a sword red with blood, and I must tell ye. It is right ye should know." He sucked in a deep ragged breath and went on. "Me wife, Meagan...I did not tell ye how she died."

The Longhunter settled back in his chair and nodded, the testament still clasped in his hand. He listened in uninterrupted silence as Derick poured out the details of the horrific night that set him on a path he had not chosen, to a land far from his children and home. He held nothing back, and when he had finished, he was trembling with emotion.

During the appalling narrative, the Longhunter said nothing, but his eyes brimmed with unshed tears. He laid a calloused hand on Derick's knee, pressing it ever so gently. There was something in his touch, in the manly, kindly gesture that spoke volumes to Derick. No words were necessary, for the simple press of his hand conveyed compassion and understanding. Derick felt his uncle's concern over his heartbreaking loss and knew he would not condemn, would not accuse.

"I'm sorry as I can be, lad," the Longhunter said softly. He drew a long breath, placed the testament in his pocket, and settled into his chair. After a few moments, he spoke again. "Some grief is so deep down, so powerful, the telling of it won't fit into words we can speak."

Derick nodded and propped his elbows on his knees, cradling his head in his large brawny hands. Despite his efforts to staunch his grief, the tears came, hot and bitter, slipping through his fingers and dropping onto the rough wooden planks of the cabin floor. Outside, an owl hooted in the nearby forest, and Cedar Creek babbled on in a continuous cadence over the rocks.

The Longhunter said no more, and allowed his nephew to weep, not reproving his lack of control, knowing it was far better for his sorrow to be spent. At length, Derick raised his head and spoke.

"I have dishonored me family, Uncle, me clan as well. Sorrow for Meagan and hate for her murderers drove me to take justice in me own hands. An English court would never allow justice for Meagan's murder—nay, never. I hunted those men down, passed sentence on their crimes, Uncle, and then executed them meself." He leaned forward, clasping his hands together between his knees.

"Are ye sorry that ye killed those men, lad?" asked the Longhunter.

Derick did not need long to answer. "Nay, Uncle, I canna say I am sorry. Me sorrow is for Meagan, for me clan, me bairns, but I am not sorry I avenged Meagan."

The Longhunter gazed into the fire dancing on the hearth. "What of your brothers, Duncan and Daniel? Won't the lads be questioned?"

"Me brothers are innocent, Uncle. I made certain they had an alibi, one that would stand in an English court, should they be questioned. I planned it well. Me brothers were entertaining several English officers that dreadful night. Of course, they knew what I was doing, and would have joined me, but I couldn't allow it. Far too dangerous. Duncan has me bairns." At the mention of his children, tears began to course down his face. "It was me own private battle, Uncle, and no cause to involve me brothers. Me clansmen were with me."

"Haven't ye killed men before?" asked the Longhunter. His voice was gentle, kind, sensing the tragedy in his sorrowing young nephew.

"Never...never in all me life have I killed any man in cold blood. Aye, I have killed in defense of me clan and family and in battle, but never have I slain the wounded or those who surrendered their arms. Ye know, Uncle, it has been the way of our clan, a matter of honor with our people for generations. Aye, I have driven men from me lands, burned their camps, and stopped them from molesting me crofters, but never—never have I raised the sword recklessly or in vengeance and hatred—until now."

The fire on the stone hearth popped and crackled as it ate into a vein of pitch pine, hurling colorful sparks up the stone chimney and lighting the room and sending shadows dancing across the walls.

Donald Davidson rose from his chair and hung a kettle of water over the flames for tea. He said no more until he placed a mug of fragrant steaming tea into Derick's hands and seated himself again, his mug cradled in his hands. Then he spoke.

"The killing of a fellow human being anytime, under any circumstance, is never easy, lad," the Longhunter said, sipping his tea, "and I've killed many a man in me life, but only in war time, and 'twas enough of killing, but we Scots, we are fierce with those who are fierce. It's perplexing to a man—to understand the right or wrong of it. I've pondered those troubling thoughts many a times meself."

"You don't fault me then?" Derick asked. His blue eyes pleaded, beseeching his uncle to understand the reason for his brutal retribution, a personal justice meted out by his own hand for the murder of his beloved wife. Derick wrapped his long fingers around the hot mug, warming his hands, but inside, his heart felt cold, implacable.

"The law of a country and of the Crown in particular," the Longhunter offered, "well, 'tis not always equal, lad. Nay, neither does man's opinions necessarily agree with the laws of nature, as ye well know. A man ought to be guided by his own good judgment, and if he be not a reprobate, by his own conscience and the established principles of God, by what he knows to be right. I canna say ye are evil because ye exacted revenge on the executors of Meagan's murder. I canna say at all. Justice does not triumph in every case. It's a known fact. Aye, it is shamefully so. The laws of a land, they be for the natural man, lad, but there is a higher law. The testament says, hate and vengeance, they are never justified. Nay, and never satisfied either."

Looking into the perceptive eyes of Donald Davidson, Derick sighed deeply. "Ye do fault me, then."

"Nay, I do not fault ye, but there be a higher court, a judge ye must take your case before—one who brandishes an honorable sword, who tries the hearts of men, and then judges rightly and honorably."

Uncertainty settled over Derick's countenance, and weariness settled over his spirit like gathering gloom. The hour was late, and the fire smoldered into glowing red coals. Donald Davidson rose from his chair and banked the hot coals with ashes, signaling the end of day. He would not stir up the fire again. Pressing Derick's knee again, the Longhunter said in his low, mellow voice. "We'll talk of this another day, lad, when time has healed your sore heart, and the pain no longer pierces so sharply."

"And when will that be, Uncle? I think never. A year has passed, and still the wound festers, bleeds. The scene plays before me mind like a relentless, demonic plague. I fear it will never end. I fear it will drive me mad."

"But ye are here now, lad, and 'tis a good place to find the path again, to find strength, a place to bury the ancient times with all its sorrow. Perhaps," said the Longhunter with a twinkle in his eye, "that's why I stayed meself. 'Tis a bonny land for a man to lay his past to rest, to forget that his sword runs red with blood. Aye, lad, you will see."

"Have ye a past, Uncle? Derick asked with a lift of his shoulders. He wanted desperately to take courage in the words of his uncle.

"All men have a past, lad, because all men are born broken. 'Tis why we need a Savior—to put us together again and to bury our sins in the sea."

Derick did not understand his uncle's thought, but he didn't feel like pursuing the idea. Instead, he said, "I cannot think ye had a past to regret, Uncle, nothing in the long ago so unpleasant ye wished to forget it. Did ye ever love a lass?"

A slow smile touched the Longhunter's lips and his eyes gazed into some distant place. "Aye, I did…long ago it was. The truth is, lad, I never wed because I loved her so…but she could never be mine, so I joined the Black Watch. I went away."

"Such a sad tale, Uncle," Derick mused.

The Longhunter turned in his chair and looked straight into Derick's eyes. "Aye, lad, but 'twas best, 'twas best. Memories of her dear face be sweet to me." He nodded his head. "Her memory has been enough. I never loved another—only her. She is gone now…these many years." Then he smiled a whimsical little smile and rose from his chair, lit a candle, and handed it to Derick to carry to the loft.

The following weeks at the cabin on Cedar Creek proved therapeutic and healing for the troubled mind of Derick Davidson. He sent word to Morgan, informing him that he would remain with his uncle until May. The tragic events prompting his flight from Scotland were never mentioned again. The two men spent hours exploring the forested trails in search of wild herbs, which the Longhunter hung to dry from hooks in the cabin loft.

In April, they dug the fragrant sassafras root, brewing the herb into a strong spring tonic and diffusing the liquid into an astringent for cuts and wounds. Donald Davidson's knowledge of the medicinal and culinary use of herbs and plants fascinated Derick and he learned the names and uses of the various plants springing up on the hillsides and along the banks of the nearby streams. A warm southerly wind blew across the Blue Ridge, warming the cold earth and bringing a renewal of energy and life to the Shenandoah Valley.

With the onset of spring in 1774, a sparse but steady migration of settlers passed through the Shenandoah Valley. They pushed beyond the Appalachian Mountains, despite the treaties forbidding settlement beyond this boundary. Many of these would-be settlers were Virginians and Pennsylvanians.

Hostilities and threats from the Indians mounted with the increasing encroachment into their territory and finally culminated in May when a group of white settlers led by Jacob Greathouse and Colonel Thomas Cresap, committed a hideous act by killing the family of Tah-gah-jute, Chief Logan of the Mingo tribe. Once again, Logan took to the warpath, seeking vengeance for the senseless murders of the innocent women and children of his family.

Word of the murders reached Winchester and the cabin on Cedar Creek. The Indian uprisings would only bring more tension and strain to the already fragile relations between the Virginians and surrounding Indian tribes. Lord Dunmore, governor of Virginia and stanch Loyalist, talked of forming a counter-offensive and set about to raise a military force to quell the unruly Indians.

"Will ye join Dunmore if he calls up the militia?" Derick asked his uncle. They were sitting on the workbench in the yard near the cabin door. The Longhunter was making a green bow from pinewood, stripping the bark away in long smooth strokes. Working quickly, he notched and strung the bow before the sap could dry and make the bow too rigid for good flex. He rubbed the surface of the bow until it was smooth and then handed it to Derick.

"Nay, not unless I'm pressed into service, lad. Seems like a private quarrel to me. His Lordship, Dunmore himself that is, dinna need an entire militia unless his greed for land sees this uprising as a chance to grab land in the Ohio territory, or maybe to beat the Pennsylvanian settlers to the choice land."

"Do ye ever trade with Indians, Uncle?" Derick pulled back on the bow, testing the flex and strength of the arc.

"Aye, at times. Logan's been friendly to whites. He's a Mingo, part of the Iroquois confederation. Met him once, on the Virginny side of the river. Quite friendly and hospitable. This recent uproar appears like a blood feud to me, like the clans in the land of mist and tears," he said smiling, "certainly no grounds to call up an entire military. Whites murdered Logan's family—Logan seeks revenge." The Longhunter paused then turned to Derick. "What do ye say, lad?"

Derick colored, a warm flush creeping up his neck. What could he say? The manner in which his uncle had related Chief Logan's objective sounded too much like his own experience, the reverberating echo of an ancient tale, a story winding its way down through the centuries to this present day, even to his own doorstep. The simple question disturbed his thoughts, but he could not answer.

He handed the bow back to his uncle and said, "It's a good bow, Uncle, strong enough to bring down a large deer, aye."

The sun was setting in the west, casting a crimson and gold glow on the two figures sitting in front of the cabin. Derick decided it was time to change the subject. "Me heart is thankful, just knowing me kinsman, me own family, have found a place to dwell peaceably in this new country. Aye, and a bonny land it is, too."

"Aye, lad, and for me, it is guid to hear the ancient tongue of me fathers spoken once again, especially by me own nephew—Duncan's own lad. The old ways cling to ye yet, lad, like thistle sticks to your plaid when ye walk through the glen, like grains of sand sticking to your feet when ye walk along the sandy shores of Moray Firth. Ye are part of it all, still...still."

"Just so, Uncle," Derick replied quietly. "No doubt, twill always be so, for 'tis who I am." He felt a warm affection for the Longhunter, his father's own brother, a man who had so miraculously appeared in his life.

"Tomorrow, I will return to Morgan's farm," Derick said, "to work with the militia lads. I've a feeling the lads will be called up soon, especially with the recent Indian unrest and talk of revolution blowing in the wind. Morgan is anxious to drill the militia again. But…I am sorry to leave this quiet place, indeed I am."

"Aye, and it is a quiet place and it be a bonny place for a solitary man like meself, a home of me own with papers to prove it."

The elder Davidson had shown Derick a fireproof stone safe built into the chimney, a place where he kept the deed to his land and a considerable amount of money he had saved over the years. He wanted his nephew to know where he kept important things, should anything unforeseen ever happen. "And," continued the Longhunter, "the lass will be a waitin'—for her lessons," he hastily added.

Derick caught the slight allusion in his uncle's tone, and his eyes fell on the newly strung green bow. His uncle's words reminded him of the brown-eyed girl waiting for his return, waiting to continue instructions in the art of sword fighting. She was like the green bow, young and malleable, winsome and beautiful, a vulnerable reed to be molded into a woman. Many of his recent memories were difficult to think on, poignant with tragedy and remorse, yet—this particular memory was not one of them.

Chapter 10

Call to Arms

*Kings will find armies
And armies will find men*

Derick Davidson returned to his comfortable quarters at Soldier's Rest and continued his regime of training with Morgan's riflemen. Although a swordsman by tradition and choice, he was growing fond of the long barreled Pennsylvania rifle and knew that one day, his beloved claymore would hang above a mantel, replaced by more modern and precise military weapons.

The riflemen spent hours devising possible battle scenarios they might encounter in an actual skirmish. These military exercises were quite similar to those used by Derick's own clansmen. Watching the methods of Captain Daniel Morgan as he trained the militia was an education in covert ranging and warfare, not unlike the techniques employed by his countrymen.

Derick's own expertise in guerilla warfare made him a formidable opponent in close combat, and Morgan's men found the Scotsman to be a challenge in his physical abilities and his mental acuity. His knack for escaping a trap or laying an ambush fit well into Morgan's frontier style of warfare. No one dared cross swords with Davidson and expect to win the contest. No man could outrun him, could match his ability to escape a trap, or discover his hiding places.

Twice a week, Derick and Kearan crossed blades in the dooryard of Morgan's farm. She had progressed to the place where all she needed was consistent practice and a willing opponent to help her practice honing her skills. Not truly believing she could actually win the contest, sometimes the young riflemen of the militia took Derick's place as her opponent. The riflemen came away sweating and frustrated, vowing to stick to the long rifle and leave the swordplay to Kearan.

In June of '74, Mingo Chief Logan killed eight settlers and took two captive during a raid near the Monongahela River. The following month, he attacked settlements along the bordering regions of Pennsylvania and Virginia, killing at least thirty civilians. Logan's retaliation for the murders of his family was purposeful and bloody. What had started as a personal vendetta against the white perpetrators of the senseless slaughter had turned into a full-scale retaliation by the governor of Virginia, Lord Dunmore.

In late June of 1774, Dunmore, whose given name was John Murray, the man appointed to the Virginia governorship by King George of England, called up Daniel Morgan's Colonial riflemen for service. The King encouraged the governor to rid the borders of Virginia and Pennsylvania of the Indian war parties that were harassing and killing the frontier settlers. Lord Dunmore hoped to raise a military force of 2,000 men to pursue the Indians and destroy their villages and encampments across the Ohio River. Such a vigorous campaign raised questions about the Crown's motive. Was the King trying to distract and divert the settlers in order to gain time and additional support for the revolution?

After receiving the summons from Dunmore, Morgan and sixty of his riflemen prepared to leave for the Kanawha and

Ohio River valleys. They were to meet at the tiny settlement of Wheeling situated on the southeastern banks of the Ohio River. There Morgan would join forces with Major Angus McDonald and Colonel William Crawford in a two-pronged effort to subdue Indian hostilities.

On hearing rumors of this, Kei-tugh-gua, Cornstalk, chief of the Shawnees, a leader who had formerly held out for peace negotiations, gathered a confederation of Shawnee, Delaware, Wyandot, Mingo, Miami, Ottawa and Illinois, to drive out the white invaders. Captain Daniel Morgan prepared his Virginia riflemen to face their dreadful rival for control of the northwest frontier. Both sides of this continuous struggle were contending for power, for position, and for land.

"Last chance to officially join up, Davidson," Morgan said to Derick.

The two men were in Morgan's kitchen where Abigail and the servants were busily packing supplies for the journey up the Kanawha. Nancy and Betsy Morgan were relegated to stools by the hearth and warned to keep out of the way of the ongoing preparations.

The little girls watched their father with large, sad eyes, knowing he would soon be leaving on a dangerous mission. Dressed in pink calico dresses with white pinafores, they sat in silence, sensing the seriousness of the occasion.

"Ye know I won't lift me sword to aid the British cause, especially for that greedy governor of yours." Derick made a beckoning motion to Nancy and Betsy who ran to him at once and scrambled eagerly onto his knees. Derick had grown fond of the girls. He missed his own children immeasurably, and playing with the little Morgan girls helped to fill this empty place in his life.

"Don't call him my governor, Davidson," Morgan stormed. "He's from your country after all. I won't claim him for Virginny either, no sir, not on your own sweet life. Those fat old parliamentary bigheads appoint whoever suits their fancy, or whoever will carry out the King's wishes. There's Major McDonald from our own county, and he's a Scot and a Patriot. He'll be leadin' our part of the campaign, so what's your miserable excuse now, Davidson?"

"Hold a wee, Morgan. For one thing, I don't know McDonald. After centuries of fighting the bloody English, some Scots joined up with the Crown simply because there was no other way to live peacefully on the same island. But—I'm not one of them. If I join ye now, the Crown loving Murrays will eventually find me out and I be hanged in a crack as a traitor in exchange for favors, titles, lands. Aye, Morgan, it be true. Clan Murray is a powerful clan in Scotland, supporters of the Crown."

"Well, the Patriots are in the same position," declared Morgan. "I was hoping to have parted company with fat old King George by now, but here we are, still chewin' the fat alongside the redcoats again. Makes my blood boil. Perhaps this campaign agin those rowdy Shawnees will move things along, although I can't see how. Here's hopin' it might spark Dunmore into action against the Patriots. Maybe he'll get war fever. This could be just a diversion though." He rubbed his chin.

"Well, at any rate, this campaign will be good practice for my riflemen. They can get some genuine fightin' in before we face the real war yet to come."

Morgan smiled crookedly, showing his missing teeth. The old scar was growing pink against his cheek as he spoke. "Do you still have a hankerin' to go with your uncle on the winter hunt?"

"Aye, I'm ready to go, me friend. Warrior is saddled up and pawing the ground. I'm heading for Cedar Creek after I bid the riflemen farewell." Morgan was lacing up his moccasins and leather leggings.

"You could stay on here—watch the farm for me—take care of things."

"Nay, friend, ye have hands enough to care for the farm, and it might be disquieting for Abigail—me being here while ye are away." He spoke in a low voice so Abigail would not hear.

Morgan nodded, knowing the Scotsman and his inherent sense of propriety, but not understanding the necessity of such precautions in times of war. If there were any man he completely trusted, it was Derick Davidson.

"Come over here, Betsy—Nancy," Morgan said with pretended gruffness, "and kiss your Pa goodbye." The two little girls ran to their father, hugged and kissed him, while tears ran down their plump little cheeks.

Despite Morgan's attempt to offset the emotional distress of parting with a brusque attitude, unwelcome tears welled up in his own eyes. Morgan's daughters meant the world to him. They were his pride and joy, the bright spot at the end of his turbulent, busy days. He kissed them repeatedly and then kissed Abigail who clung to him.

"Oh Daniel, Daniel, come back to me. It has been so long since you've left on such a long and dangerous mission. I cannot bear this," said Abigail weeping. "I fear you will not return."

"Now, Abby, turn me loose, gal! I gotta go. You know I do, so quit your frettin' and fussin' over me. And don't worry, I'll be back home before Christmas, sure as I'm a standin' here." Morgan kissed her again, turned on his heel, and abruptly left the kitchen with Derick, not daring to look back at his weeping family.

It was July, and the morning was already warm. Morgan and Derick rode their horses to the training field where the riflemen were busy loading the packhorses. The sturdy animals would carry their food supplies, ammunition, gear, and tents over the many treacherous miles ahead. The riflemen had camped in Morgan's field overnight, hoping for an early departure to the Ohio country. Families living near the Morgan farm lingered about the field, saying their last farewells to the company of riflemen who seemed eager and ready to be off to join Dunmore's campaign.

The younger riflemen were in high spirits, like men who were going to a picnic, calling and joking with one another and discussing possible skirmishes with the Indians. They speculated on who was the fiercest of the Indian chiefs or who of their number might get close enough to slay the proud Sachems of the Indian Confederation and bring back a scalp on his belt.

Many of the younger riflemen had little or no experience in actual border clashes with the natives, nor had they participated in close combat encounters, so they boasted and bragged of victory and conquest, of glory and honor, and of their triumphant return with the colors of the Virginia Riflemen flying aloft in the breeze.

Morgan had taught them well, and this training was in their favor. They were disciplined and regimented riflemen, the best sharpshooters in the Colonies, but even these accomplishments were no guarantee against the wily and cunning Indian counterparts who were also proficient in guerilla warfare.

The warm day began with a vivid blue sky and a scattering of fleecy white clouds stretching across the Blue Ridge in a continuous band of wispy, feathery white. A soft balmy breeze blew from the south, and the colors of the Virginia militia waved gently in the breeze. Mothers and fathers were saying goodbye to their sons; sweethearts were bidding tearful farewells as the men loaded their packs and shouldered their rifles. Morgan and Derick rode by on their horses, and the families of the riflemen knew it would not be long before the company headed down the road to the Ohio River and to an uncertain future.

Among the riflemen of the Virginia militia who were going to the Ohio with Dunmore's campaign, was Morgan's right hand, Silas Mackenzie, and his son, Alfred. Both Mackenzies were avid hunters, skilled woodsmen, and crack shots with the Pennsylvania rifle and both had trained with the militia and volunteered to accompany Morgan and his men on this military operation.

Lily Jayne and Kearan accompanied the men to the field, determined to see their men off, but they dreaded this hour of exodus. The oversight of the never-ending farm work would settle on the shoulders of the frontier women while their men folk were away.

Kearan kissed her brother fondly on the cheek while Lily Jayne clung tearfully to Silas. Thomas Aubrey, a long time friend of the family, found Kearan among the well-wishers and drew her aside, requesting a private moment with her. They stood near the newly constructed dry stone fence running the length of Morgan's hay field, a little apart from the rest of the noisy throng of Virginia riflemen.

"Kearan," Thomas began in an unusually solemn tone, "I reckon you'll be prayin' for my safe return."

Kearan smiled at the tall young man in buckskin hunting jerkin and leather breeches. She had known Thomas Aubrey since they were children, and it was no secret the young frontiersman was fond of her and wished to court her.

"Of course I will pray for you and for all the riflemen, Thomas," Kearan said, "for every father, son, and brother who goes into battle. But, don't worry, Thomas, you will be home before Christmas, and all this awful conflict will be over."

Thomas looked fondly at Kearan, the only girl he had ever cared for, the girl he wanted for his wife. He was a strong and strapping young man, with sandy brown hair and honest hazel eyes. His family owned a farm in Frederick County, and Thomas was a hopeful young blacksmith with a growing business. He operated his smithy on the outskirts of Battletown, a village east of Winchester. He did quite well for himself and was a good manager. It would not be long before he saved enough money to begin construction on a home of his own.

"I know," Thomas said nervously, "this isn't exactly the finest place to speak to you about...well, about what's been on my mind, Kearan. It's been some time now and...I've wanted to tell you... to ask you..."

"Please, Thomas, don't say it," interrupted Kearan. The young man jerked slightly, as though she had struck him. He shifted his weight from one foot to the other and then gathered his courage again. He would not be discouraged by her apparent rebuff. Thomas forged ahead, determined to have his say.

"How can you know what I'm a goin' to say, Kearan? You haven't heard me out, and it's only fair to hear what's on a fella's mind."

"Thomas Aubrey, we have grown up together on this frontier, in this valley. I know you very well, almost as well as I know my own brother, Alfred. I think I can safely assume what you wish to say to me. The men in this field today are leaving for battle; they want to bear their hearts, to say now what they might not have opportunity to say again. This is an emotional time for everyone, Thomas, and it is a familiar parting scene."

Thomas appeared somewhat chagrined at her words, but she must hear what was on his heart. "I'm not your brother, Kearan Mackenzie. I...I love you," he said in a rush.

"There, I reckon I've said it now," Thomas said with a measure of relief, "and I've wanted to say it for a long time, maybe for years, Kearan, since you were ten years old. You must know how I care for you. Please say you'll wait for me, say there is hope. Why, Kearan, we're meant for each other—have been since we were young'uns. I want you to wait for me—wait until I get things fixed enough to have a proper courtship."

Kearan glanced around at the riflemen, at the families gathered about the field awaiting the call to march. The noisy chatter of children and the whoops and shouts of the men resounded in her ears, blocking out Thomas Aubrey's words and disturbing her thoughts. She did not want to hurt Thomas, nor did she want to give him any false hope.

This young man pleading with her now she thought to herself, was the kind of man Morgan spoke about—one of her own kind, a man who would work hard for a home, care for her needs, raise a family, and at the end of his life, die in his bedstead at a ripe old age. It would be a good life, albeit predictable and ordinary. Kearan caught Morgan's eye as he sat astride his horse, scanning the field of eager riflemen. He smiled at her, showing the dark gap where his teeth were missing. Derick followed Morgan's gaze and his eyes met Kearan's.

For one brief moment, their eyes locked, and then Derick glanced away. What had she seen in his gaze? For the briefest moment, she thought she read more than casual interest, but she could be imagining, even wishing for, more than was truly there.

An amused smile curved Derick's lips, and when he caught her eyes again, Kearan could read the message in his blue eyes all too well—he was laughing at her, teasing her. Oh, if it weren't for this troublesome Scotsman! What was the matter with her anyway, and why did she feel this sudden quickening of her heart? Derick Davidson disconcerted her, made her feel like she was ten years old, and at the same time, he caused the blood to run hot in her veins. Something about this man challenged her, captivated her, and drew her mind away as no other man could. Perhaps he was drawing her heart away! He didn't know what she was thinking, and she was glad.

"Kearan?" A voice sounded in her ears, interrupting her reverie. It was Thomas Aubrey. She nearly forgot he was there! He was pleading, earnest, beseeching her to consider him. She turned to him again, bringing her thoughts back to the present moment, away from the Scotsman, the man who tore at her tender young heart and for the life of her, she couldn't understand why. She laid her hand on Thomas' arm in a sisterly gesture.

"You are a dear friend, Thomas, like a brother to me, and I do care a great deal for you, like a sister would, but I cannot pretend it is more. I believe you are a fine man, and I believe you will find a woman who will love you as you deserve to be loved, but please, Thomas, don't speak to me of love—please. It will spoil our friendship to know...to hear those words spoken again."

Thomas had not missed Kearan's glance in the direction of the Scotsman, and he had noticed the sudden light springing into her eyes when she saw him ride up on his horse like a conquering knight. He had suspected for some time that Kearan was infatuated with this handsome stranger. He knew she spent time with him at the Morgans' farm, learning to use her grandfather's sword, but he knew the sword lessons were not all that interested Kearan Mackenzie. Without further thought, he decided to broach the subject.

"It's Davidson, isn't it, Kearan?"

She looked taken aback at his words and bit her lower lip.

"I've seen you watching him when you think he's not a lookin'," continued Thomas, "but I can tell you this—he's not interested in you—nor any of the frontier gals around these parts. He's not your kind, Kearan. Some say he fled Scotland because of a secret past, because of some dark deeds, and he is..."

"Stop it, Thomas, stop it!" Kearan interrupted. "How can you repeat what is only speculation? It grieves me to know you would stoop to such callous gossip."

The young rifleman dropped his head and then raised it again, a fire burning in his hazel eyes and a stubborn look setting his jaw.

"I like Davidson as a man, as a friend—all the riflemen do, but it doesn't change the fact he's not your kind of fella, Kearan. He's a foreigner, for pity's sake, a son of a Scottish chieftain, not a man who would ever care for a plain frontier girl. He would never understand your ways, Kearan, not as I would."

At the mention of her plain ways, the color drained from Kearan's face. Thomas saw it and sighed, shaking his head in frustration.

"Kearan, I'm sorry. I didn't mean that you are just any plain old frontier gal. Was the wrong way to put it, to say it."

Kearan only stared at him, and Thomas shook again his head in frustration.

"This is not how I wanted to bid you farewell, Kearan. I apologize for sayin' too much, for sayin' it the wrong way. I was outta line, but you're right about one thing—this is an emotional time. I want you to know before I leave...I do love you, always have, always will. If true love holds value for you, Kearan, be sure I've stored up plenty in my heart...for you."

"Please, Thomas, say no more, I beg you. It distresses me so. I wish to part as friends. Your words are a torment to me. I'm sorry you said them, even more sorry that I heard them. I cannot help how you feel, no more than I can help how I feel. When you return, we will both have changed. This is your first campaign, and you may feel differently when you return, and perhaps, I will too. Papa says war changes people, and they are never the same."

"I will not change, Kearan."

"You cannot be certain of that, Thomas. The frontier women can't go to war, but what happens on the battlefront touches us, changes our lives. I value our friendship and don't want it to change, Thomas. Let us stay as we are and leave the future to God's choosing."

"I may change in some ways, Kearan, I'll give you that, but I will not change in my feelings for you, I promise you that." He looked into her brown troubled eyes. "Farewell, then." He tried to muster a smile. "We'll be back before the snow flies."

Kearan nodded mutely, and gave him a brief, sisterly hug. "Farewell, Thomas, and God go with you." She turned away from him with a heavy heart. She knew how much he cared for her, and it grieved her to know she could not return his love, but she could not, at least not now.

Chapter 11

Measure of a Man

The best apple is on the highest bough

The men managing the sturdy packhorses that carried the army's supplies lined up at the rear of the procession. The riflemen took their places at the head of the convoy, waving their last farewells and adjusting their backpacks for the long trek to the Ohio Valley. Some of the men were mounted, but most were on foot. They were dressed in the common frontier uniform of the riflemen: a hunting shirt, buckskin breeches, leggings lacing to the thighs, and Indian style moccasins. Attached to their hats were a buck's tail and wild turkey feathers, which waved jauntily in the morning breeze.

Morgan rode briskly up to the stone fence where Lily Jayne and Kearan stood watching the departing company of riflemen and waving their last goodbyes to Silas and Alfred.

"You women folk stick together till we return," Morgan ordered in his most somber tone. He was all business now and the usual mocking banter was absent from his voice. "You'll need to watch out for Abby and the girls, Kearan, but be careful of yourself and don't go ridin' about the countryside alone or after dark and stay inside at night. Lock your doors and keep your rifle loaded and handy. There are some no good drifters who know you women are at home without your men. I wish Davidson were stayin' on.

Confound the stubborn Scots! I'd feel a heap better about leavin' if he were stayin' on, but the man is a stickler for appearances. If you need help for any reason, send for him on Cedar Creek. He'll be with the Longhunter 'til huntin' begins."

At his words, Lily Jayne threw her apron over her head and began to weep. Kearan slipped an arm around her mother, lifted her chin, and looked up at Morgan.

"We'll be fine, Uncle Daniel. Please don't worry. I will check on Abigail and the girls regularly. We have the servants to help us. We will manage. Just do your job and come back to us safe."

"I know I can count on you, gal," Morgan said with confidence. "I left Abby in the house a cryin'. She can't bear to watch us leave. Too hard for her, you know."

"I will stay with her for a while, Daniel," Lily Jayne volunteered, happy for the chance to do something useful. "Be careful of my son, Daniel Morgan, and do come home soon and make sure you bring Alfred back to me."

"I'll stick to him like a tick on a hound dog," Morgan said and touched his hat in farewell. Lily Jayne clasped his hand briefly and then walked to the house where she found Abby lying on her bed weeping her heart out.

From the ranks of riflemen moving along the dusty road, an occasional Indian war hoop erupted. "Farewell, Kearan, gal," Morgan said. "Take care of yourself and stay safe until we return."

"Godspeed, Uncle Daniel—until we meet again." She blew him a kiss.

Derick Davidson rode up on Warrior and reined his horse next to Morgan who sat astride Samson. They shared a moment of silent understanding as they clasped hands in a wordless farewell.

"There's one thing I wanna say, Davidson," said Morgan in a serious tone. "In Virginny, a man's worth and abilities are measured by his present status, not by his past. I should know."

Without further comment, Morgan abruptly turned his horse around and galloped off toward the men at the front of the procession, now disappearing down the road to an uncertain future.

Standing by the dry stone fence, Kearan and Derick watched the families and friends drift apart, leaving the field for their homes, some still weeping, others smiling confidently. They stood alone by the fence while the last of the Virginia riflemen vanished around the bend, a dust cloud rising behind them and drifting slowly away.

Kearan bit her lip to keep it from trembling. The best of the Virginia frontier, including her father and brother, were going away. What if they never returned and what if they were killed in battle? She looked up at the Scotsman who sat like an Arthurian knight on Warrior's back.

Derick continued to watch the riflemen as they marched away, wishing he could somehow join them. The militia was required to swear allegiance and loyalty to King George, albeit they did so with their fingers crossed behind their backs, waiting for the day the Patriots could rise up for the cause of independence. However, that was not an option for Derick; it was something he could never do. He looked down from his horse at the slight form trembling from the emotion of this parting moment and from the troubling words of Thomas Aubrey.

Without a word, Derick stretched his hand down to her and Kearan grasped his strong arm without any hesitation. He swung her up effortlessly onto the back of the horse, saying nothing. Turning his horse around, he rode away from the field, away from the riflemen who were now only an obscure dot in the distance.

No words had passed between them, but when their eyes met for that one brief instant, he had read the thoughts of her heart, had understood her sorrow. How desperately she wished for someone stronger this very moment, someone to take the pain of the difficult parting, someone to share the heaviness of the charge Morgan had given her.

She had understood the meaning of Derick's silent gesture—his strong arm reaching for her, lifting her from the earth with one smooth motion. She knew instinctively he would swing her onto the back of his horse—beside him.

As they rode toward Morgan's farm, burning tears stung Kearan's eyes when she remembered what Thomas Aubrey had said only a short time before; *he is not your kind, Kearan.* She held firmly to the rim of his saddle, feeling his nearness and the strength of his person. She could smell the masculine scent of horse and leather and buckskin.

Oh God, she prayed silently, *if he is not my kind, take this feeling from my heart. I don't want to care for him if this is truly not in your plan. But how does he know me so well? How did he know what was in my heart if I am not his kind?*

They reached the dooryard of the Morgan farm, and still, they had not spoken. Derick reined up his horse in front of the stable and turned slightly in the saddle to assist Kearan, reaching around so she could grasp his arm and slide down from Warrior's back.

"Must you go?" Kearan asked softly.

"Aye, I must."

Kearan nodded mechanically, took his arm, and slid from the horse. She turned to look at him. "Why...why did you bring me... bring me on your horse, I mean."

He looked puzzled seeing the tears still glistening in her eyes.

"Because your mount is in the stable, lass. Have ye forgotten?"

"Is there another reason?" she queried.

Derick looked perturbed. He dismounted and threw Warrior's reins across the saddle. Then he looked away, across the fields to where the distant ridge of purple mountains rose in the blue morning mist. An uncomfortable and strangely sad silence hung between them.

"Don't weep, lass," Derick finally said, but he did not look at her. The lines of agitation had left his face, and his tone was gentle, tender. He looked at her then. "The lads will come home soon. I don't think this campaign will last long. This skirmish is not a regular war."

"But you didn't answer my question."

He looked away again and the perturbed look returned to his face. "Your mount is stabled here, lass, and ye needed a ride."

Kearan sighed. Morgan might be right about the Scotsman. He was a difficult man to understand.

"Mr. Davidson," Kearan began, "why didn't you go with the militia?" She had wanted to ask this question a hundred times before and now the moment seemed right. They were alone with nothing to hinder a private conversation.

At her persistent question, a glimmer of mischief shone in Derick's eyes. "I could have been shot, perhaps even scalped, or possibly taken prisoner, or even burned at the stake." He was hoping to lighten this awkward moment. The conversation had grown far too personal, and he wished for it to end.

"You are not truthful, Derick Davidson. You have not given me an honest answer. Indeed, I don't believe you have answered any of my questions honestly. Why didn't you join the militia, go with the riflemen?"

Now he appeared serious. "Because I am neither a frontiersman nor a militia rifleman, and God knows—I am not a British soldier. Aye, lass, 'tis reason enough."

"But what does it matter when you can fight and shoot as well as any of the riflemen? You can at least defend the frontier from the hostile Indians, can't you? Can't you think in terms of our safety? Suppose the Indian raiding parties come up the Kanawha into the Shenandoah—then what? I know Morgan wanted you to join the militia."

Fire rose like a blue flame in Derick's smoldering eyes, and Kearan felt certain she had crossed some invisible line, a line she had promised herself never to cross again. The flame died away, and he seemed to gather his thoughts.

"I have personal reasons, lass. I am not a coward...if ye are thinking so. I do not fear the battle, nor do I fear death."

"Oh, Derick—Mr. Davidson, I mean. I truly know you are not a coward, but is it really true—what they are saying—you have done something so very terrible? Is this why you left Scotland? I need to know. I want to hear it from your own lips, to know the truth. Someone told me you left your homeland because, well, because..."

"I left," Derick said interrupting her words. "I left because it was best for everyone concerned—for me clan, me family, aye, and for meself as well. It is that simple, lass." Derick sighed heavily and then continued.

"Aye, it is true what ye heard. I committed an unlawful act of vengeance, an act for which I felt wholly justified and still do. However, the Crown did not see things as I did, and they have the final say in me homeland, even though Scotland is a separate country with a different culture and a people very unlike the English."

Derick paused and looked toward the distant mountains. An icy veil appeared to descend between the Scotsman and his young student. When he spoke again, his words were fierce and cold, without warmth or life.

"Now ye know, and ye can stop wondering and speculatin'. It is not a pleasant story, and one I will not repeat to a young lass. I don't expect ye to understand, nor do I care if ye do not. I hope this will end your inquiry into me affairs. Ye have no right to question me, to question any man."

Kearan felt as though he had slapped her. She could feel his anger, a slow, hot anger radiating from somewhere deep within. The intensity of his pain and hurt spewed from him, making her shy away, recoiling from the fire that burned in his eyes. For a brief instant, she even feared him, feared the power of the storm raging inside him.

Kearan visibly withdrew, cowering from the impact of his harsh words. She looked so pitiful standing there, so wretched. He had shaken her faith in him, and now she seemed unsure of his reaction. He had been too careless in his attitude toward the innocent girl standing in the morning sunlight, her brown eyes brimming with unshed tears and her dark curls tumbling about her face.

Derick shook his head, frustrated with himself, disturbed at the awkwardness of this moment and at his inability to lessen the reality of his own situation. He had frightened her—but she had wanted to know.

Kearan struggled to maintain her composure. Her delicately curved lips trembled slightly, and her brown eyes still held tears. Derick knew that he had shamed and embarrassed her. He was the cause of her trembling lips.

After a long silent moment, Derick opened his strong arms, reaching them toward the trembling girl and without hesitation, she went to him, resting her dark head against his chest while hot salty tears spilled from her eyes.

Understanding her distress all too well, Derick allowed her to weep, wetting his hunting shirt with her tears. After all, he was once married to a gentle lass with tender eyes and soft womanly ways. He held her trembling form, saying nothing, only letting her know everything would be all right, he was there for her, like a caring older brother and she need not fear him.

"You scare me sometimes, Derick Davidson," Kearan sobbed, "and now, my father and brother are going away, and almost all the men I know—those I grew up with. They are all gone. Now you are leaving us too. Oh, Derick, I want you to stay, even if you frighten me with your harsh words!" Her momentary fear of him had fled like the rising morning mist.

"Forgive me, lass. I spoke out of me own troubled heart. I meant no harm. I cannot stay, Kearan, nay, I cannot. I am sorry ye were frightened of me. Twas all me own fault. Best for ye to remember this, lass—I am a man with a broken heart and it speaks in most unpredictable ways. Ye should know by now. Do not weep. Ye are a strong lass, a woman warrior, and ye must bear up and abide until the men return."

The Scotsman's words were comforting, reassuring. Kearan dabbed at her tears, and Derick continued. "Ye are sorrowful because ye know I am...an exile, a castaway, and because the lads are leaving, but this trouble will pass and ye will adjust to the absence of the riflemen. Ye must be brave, lass, and dry your tears. I cannot stay here while Morgan is absent, but if ye ever need me, I will be with the Longhunter on Cedar Creek and ye can send for me."

"But I feel safer when you are here at Soldier's Rest," she said looking up at him.

A fleeting shadow passed over his countenance. "My presence will not assure your safety, even though I stay," he said bitterly. "I am only one man, lass." Kearan caught his tone and felt the sting in his words.

Derick dropped his arms and lifted Warrior's reins. He swung into the saddle and looked down at Kearan, so pitiable and young. "Godspeed, lass, I must go." Suddenly, he felt a strong urge to stay even though he had made up his mind to leave. He hesitated, the old protective feeling creeping over him again.

"Must you really go?" Kearan asked laying her hand against Warrior's flank.

Still he hesitated, not understanding why he felt restrained. Was this strange foreboding an ominous sign of danger, or was he only thinking of his own painful past when he had left his own home unguarded and vulnerable to an enemy. Scenes of that awful day came rushing to his mind. He saw his young wife running up the cobblestones to warn him. Through the stillness, he could hear the shots ring out, see Meagan's crumpled body lying in the road. Derick shook his head, driving out the tortuous scenes from his mind.

"Aye," Derick said at last, "I must leave now. I know Morgan and your father have given ye good instructions for safe keeping. Mind them now, lass."

"Good-bye then," Kearan said sorrowfully. She could see his mind was set to leave and she could not persuade him otherwise. "Please greet the Longhunter for me."

"I will do it, lass."

"Will you stop by Soldier's Rest on your way to the winter hunt?"

"Aye, to be sure. For Morgan's sake, I will make certain everything is well with Abigail and the bairns—and with ye and your mother of course."

Derick looked into Kearan's dark troubled eyes before turning away without another word. He vanished from sight around the bend in the dusty roadway just as the company of riflemen had disappeared from view.

Kearan lingered for several moments, watching the retreating figure of the Scotsman and his horse then squared her shoulders, and lifted her chin. She brushed the last of her tears away and strode toward the house where the women of Frederick County had gathered.

Derick arrived at the cabin on Cedar Creek near dusk, when the purple shadows stretched long across the Shenandoah valley like silent specters, when the last rays of shimmering sunlight streamed through the tall trees like golden pillars. The Longhunter sat at his workbench in front of his cabin, shelling brown beans by the waning light.

"Hello, Uncle," Derick called as he neared the cabin.

The Longhunter had observed his approach warily, his rifle at the ready. When Derick shouted a hello, his uncle recognized his nephew and joyously returned the greeting. He laid aside the basket and rose from the bench where he had been shelling beans.

"Well, it's happy I am to see ye on this fine summer evenin', lad. Ye look just like your Da' when he was a coming through the gloaming from Glen Feshie after a hunt. Oh, how it wrings the withers of me heart, laddie." A sad smile crossed his features, and his blue eyes grew misty at the memory of his brother.

Derick dismounted and embraced his uncle warmly. "Tis happy I am to see ye too, Uncle."

"Well, have ye changed your mind then—about joining me on the winter hunt?" queried the Longhunter hopefully.

"Aye, that I have, Uncle. Morgan's riflemen were called up and are going against the Indians near the Ohio. Ye know how I might feel about crossing swords alongside me old enemies."

A light danced in Donald Davidson's blue eyes, and he nodded knowingly. "I can imagine it well enough," said the Longhunter, "but this is a different time and a different country."

"Aye, Uncle, so it is."

"When I was in Winchester last, I heard about Lord Dunmore a calling up the troops. They say his High and Mightiness, John Murray himself, wants to raise 2000 men from Virginia. I'm ashamed to call him a Scot, but that he is, and in bed with King George. Auch, lad! Can ye imagine? Calling for militia right near harvest time? Only a bunch of blathering idiots would go agin the Shawnees over a blood feud with the Mingo Chief. Me-thinks Dunmore, misguided Scot that he is, has more to gain than just picking a quarrel. Well, enough talk for now. Put your horse in the barn, lad, and make yourself to home. We can talk news later. Aye, son, Ye'r a sicht fir sair een, indeed ye are.

Chapter 12

March to the Ohio

Fear is worse than fighting

The migration of the pioneers into the wilderness areas west of the Appalachian Mountains indeed incited resentment in the Indian inhabitants of the area. Most of the white families settling in the unprotected backwoods country were seeking free land, a home, a place to raise a family unmolested by the King or their Indian neighbors. The majority of these white settlers were the hearty stock of Scot, Irish, and German emigrants.

Among those joining the movement toward the northwest Ohio country, were explorers, surveyors, and seekers after land. Many of the surveys were made under authority of the proclamation of 1763 that granted land to those who had served in the French and Indian War or to men who had purchased the rights of the war veterans. All were vying for choice land in this vast virgin territory. Of these shrewd land speculators, Governor Dunmore himself was more than just casually interested in obtaining prime land.

As Morgan marched his riflemen over 200 miles of backwoods country, he contemplated the governor's motivation for such an extensive military campaign. Dunmore had decided to divide the army into two separate forces. This action made Morgan unusually apprehensive. General Andrew Lewis would command the southern division of the army while Dunmore himself would later join Lewis at the point of rendezvous after he broke camp at the mouth of the Hockhocking River. In Captain Daniel Morgan's estimation, this plan seemed sketchy and unpredictable at best.

There were too many unknown factors concerning the recent activities of the Indian tribes, and the governor of Virginia paid scat attention. Lord Dunmore had little experience with Indian warfare and dividing the army would only serve to weaken its defenses should an attack be launched against one portion of the divided army.

The governor had called for the strongest and ablest of the frontier scouts, sharpshooters, seasoned Indian fighters, and militia riflemen to support the effort to end the Indian hostilities. The more Daniel Morgan thought on Dunmore's campaign, the more concerned he became over the lack of protection for the families on the home front. Anything might happen while the most capable of the frontiersmen were away from home.

As they proceeded toward the Ohio through the dense forests of maple, oak, and cherry, Morgan decided to ask his militia riflemen to take a *pledge of honor*, a pledge not to allow Dunmore's campaign to distract or divert them from the Patriot's cause, which could explode at any moment. Even now, the finest of the frontier men were marching away from a possible altercation with the British to the east. This critical detail exasperated Morgan and caused him to become distrustful of Dunmore's motives. He felt an urgency to complete this mission as quickly as possible and return the militia to their post in Frederick County.

In addition to Morgan's riflemen, various other companies of Virginians were also marching to the rendezvous point to join Lewis in the southern prong of the army. Some had been with

Washington at the surrender of Fort Necessity. Others had fought with Braddock at the Monongahela, and still others with Forbes at the capture of Fort Duquesne. Some had fought with Bouquet at Bushy Run and in the Ohio Wilderness. These rugged men of the frontier had been engaged in border warfare with Indians and white renegades for most of their lives. They were familiar with both the English and Colonial military strategies, understood the wily methods of Indian fighting, and often employed the same battle techniques, even to the taking of scalps as trophies.

These typical backwoods frontiersmen included officers of rank in addition to the regular militia of Virginia and Pennsylvania. Volunteers, hunters, and trappers came along for the sheer joy of the contest. They wore the fringed and beaded buckskin hunting shirts common to the border country. Their shot bags were ornamented and their powder horns hung from heavy leather belts. Their feet were clad in tough leather moccasins with leggings that laced halfway to the thigh. Each man carried a tinderbox and his own personal arsenal, which included his flintlock, tomahawk, war club, and several sharp knives, and always, a scalping knife.

The officers were equipped in like manner, except most militia officers carried a long sword. Since many of the officers were Scots, they wore the traditional claymore broadsword sheathed at their sides or across their backs. In battle, their manner resembled the warlike highlander, and they proved to be a ruthless and formidable opponent.

The safe transport of supplies through the rough wilderness of western Virginia was the chief difficulty for the army as they marched along the westward trail. Packhorses carried the supplies for the army since a wagon convoy would have been impossible to bring over the rough, uneven ground. The dense undergrowth had to be repeatedly cleared away before the animals could proceed.

As a means of supplying the army with food, beef cattle were driven over the treacherous trails while the packhorses were led over the difficult areas by pulling them along with stout leather harnesses. Navigating the streams and marshes proved to be a challenge for the entire expedition. Except for the longhunters and Indian traders, few white men had ever traveled the entire length of the Kanawha Valley.

The route mapped out for the trek covered nearly 200 miles of trackless forest rising over rugged and mountainous terrain. Whenever possible, the marchers followed Indian hunting trails and buffalo trails circling the base of the hills rather than negotiating the steep riverbanks. The army skirted around creeks, lakes, and ravines in an attempt to prevent a difficult passage for the drovers and those who led the packhorses.

As the army approached the Alleghany Mountains, frequent rain showers impeded their progress through the slippery mountain passes. The Gauley River, a troublesome tributary to the Kanawha, had to be crossed, and it proved a strenuous undertaking for man and beast alike. The banks of the river had been washed out by the recurrent rains and supplies and animals were lost when the packhorses slipped and rolled into the white foaming waters. The riverbed was a mass of stones and uneven pools with rapidly flowing and swirling eddies of water. Ropes were attached to trees on the opposite bank and used to aid both men and beasts in crossing safely to the western banks of the river.

Cornstalk, the proud leader of the Shawnees and the Indian war confederation, watched the army's progress from the western slopes of the thickly treed mountains. He felt a mounting offense for his nation, for his people. It was a breach of honor that could only be answered through bloodshed. His warriors were angry and ready for war.

In earlier times, Cornstalk had chosen the warpath to resolve territorial rights, but now, he knew the white man would never stop coming. They would come until the Indian nation would be pushed from his land, his home. Always, there would be more. Perhaps this would be the last battle for the redman.

Cornstalk had fought some of these same men at Bushy Run and at Fort Duquesne. He remembered well the kilted wild men from across the great water, men more ferocious than his own fierce warriors. Reluctantly, he had agreed to lead the combined Indian tribes, but he had secretly hoped for a peaceful resolution. The tribal leaders had called for vengeance on the white invaders, and the pressure from his tribesmen had forced his hand. He must fight.

In late summer, the weary company of Virginia riflemen led by Captain Daniel Morgan arrived at the rendezvous point on the western side of the mountains. The worst of the march had been accomplished. Various other companies from Pennsylvania and Virginia were also arriving and the camp was promptly named, Camp Union. The site was a hubbub of activity. A crude fort and a shelter for ammunition and supplies was hastily erected.

Under the able command of Major Angus McDonald of Frederick County, Virginia, Morgan and his riflemen were persuaded to accompany McDonald on an advance mission to cross the Ohio River and proceed into the hostile Indian Territory. Dunmore's orders were to burn and destroy Indian villages along the march in an effort to harass and terrorize the Indian inhabitants. After their departure, General Andrew Lewis arrived at Camp Union to take command of the southern division of the army. He waited patiently in camp for instructions from Dunmore who was camped somewhere to the north.

When Major McDonald and the riflemen had advanced to within six miles of Wakatomica, the Shawnee town on the Muskingum River, they halted in a small clearing in the forest to rest. The guide for the expedition into this hostile territory was Jonathan Zane, a well-known guide who had spent many years exploring the frontier and was well acquainted with Indian strategies. Zane seemed somewhat anxious as they halted in the clearing and notified Major McDonald that he would scout ahead for possible Indian sign.

Morgan felt ill at ease. He stood at attention, instructing his men to keep a sharp eye. "I don't like this place, McDonald," said Morgan to his commanding officer. Morgan and McDonald were old friends, both hailing from Frederick County. They disregarded the usual protocol of officers and worked the trail as old friends. "Too quiet," Morgan noted. "Not even a bird song in the forest. If you know the ways of those sneaking Indians, I'd say they're out there watchin' us this very minute."

Angus McDonald's keen eyes strained to see beyond the trees at the edge of the small clearing where his troops had stopped to rest. "Aye, does seem kinda quiet like," McDonald agreed. "Sometimes I think Dunmore sent us out here to be killed off by these irate Indians. Can't help thinking it, Morgan. I don't trust this whole campaign. Makes me nervous as a chicken on butchering day, but we're bound to follow orders, like 'em or not."

"And what does Dunmore know about frontier fightin' anyhow, I'd like to know," Morgan said sardonically.

"Aye, 'tis a question for the records, to be sure. His Lordship leaves orders for General Lewis to remain in camp while the northern army lollygags somewhere north of us with the governor's hand picked army of relatives and friends. Now tell me, Morgan, does this make sense?"

"You're askin' me?" Daniel Morgan fairly spat out the words. His eyes continued to sweep over the clearing, his rifle held at the ready. "If you just happened to observe, Major, the cream of the Virginia frontier is with General Lewis in camp. If there is an attack on Lewis' army before Dunmore arrives, how can the army withstand a large contingent of war-crazed Indians? What the devil is Dunmore thinkin' anyhow?"

"He's not thinking, and that's a fact," McDonald said with disgust, "or maybe he is—only it's not the same way we're a thinking. The river has long been the boundary for our two cultures, many a year now, and is written in the treaties as well, but the King of England wants the Indian nations completely vanquished, 'tis true enough." McDonald offered a rueful smile. "Sort of like the Scots at Culloden Moor, same thing."

He paused to scan the parameter of the clearing. "Old King George thinks we can accomplish peace by using terror tactics and treaties. It will never happen, Morgan, not until one or the other of us is completely broken—in body and spirit." He sighed. "That's the way of it. Always has been with the English King."

Morgan reached into his pocket for his tobacco pouch, bit off a plug of prime Virginia tobacco, and handed it to McDonald. "Well, think of this," Morgan continued. "Lewis has the finest and ablest body of frontiersmen ever gathered together and all in one place. You take out those men, and the Patriot's cause is weakened as well, not to mention, we lose some of the finest bordermen and frontiersmen to boot. Now, Major, don't think I haven't considered that. Dunmore is a devout loyalist, a King kisser, and an in-law to Old King George in the bargain." Morgan spat a stream of brown tobacco juice into the tall grass at the edge of the clearing.

"Just before crossing the Ohio," Morgan continued, "I talked with John Cutright, the Bear Hunter, from up on the west fork of the Monongahela. He and his brother, the Indian Scout, named a number of noted riflemen and frontiersmen who are with Lewis and some with Dunmore. The Wetzels, Zanes, Carmichaels, Cutrights, Earlywines, Simon Kenton, Michael Stoner, and Boone, just to name a few. The Bear Hunter is scouting for the army, and he's considerable alarmed about this whole affair. Says he saw Dunmore himself consulting with the Indian leaders at Fort Pitt."

"Well, if they're on such good terms, what is all this uproar about?" stormed McDonald. He laid his huge hand on the sword sheathed at his side. "I didn't march all this way through this howling wilderness just to burn Indian villages!"

"And what's all this ruckus about John Connolly?" Morgan queried. "He's Dunmore's man in the border country, and accordin' to the Bear Hunter, he's been holdin' regular parlays with several of the notable Chiefs. If they're chewin' the fat and smokin' pipes over the council fires, then what in the devil are we doin' a burnin' up their home turf? Does this make sense?"

McDonald shook his head and shrugged his broad shoulders. "Beats me, Cap'n." He glanced around the clearing and shouldered his rifle. "Let's get outta here. This place gives me the itch. Besides, we've rested long enough." He silently signaled to Captain James Woods to take the lead and move out.

Woods led his men in the advance position up the trail. They passed through a dense, swampy area several hundred yards long. Suddenly, Zane came crashing through the woods on a dead run, waving his arms and yelling, but before the company could organize, a barrage of gunshot accompanied by wild yelping broke through the dense coverage of the forest. Four riflemen fell to the ground. Immediately, the other highly trained riflemen sprang into action, ducking behind trees and fallen timber, leveling their rifles, loosening their shot bags and powder horns, and unsheathing their knives and battleaxes. Morgan hurried his troop along the tangle of swamp grass, impatient to assist McDonald and Woods, shouting orders as he sprinted fearlessly toward the fray. His men followed in hot pursuit.

Several riflemen lay wounded amid the chaos and confusion of gunfire, and two more of the militia lay still, apparently dead from bullet wounds. The remainder of the company remained sheltered behind trees, firing at the hordes of painted Indians with brutal accuracy, every rifle ball finding its mark.

When Morgan arrived on the scene, a heated exchange of gunfire quickly followed. For thirty minutes, the riflemen defended their position at the edge of the swamp against the wildly screaming Shawnee Indians. A continuous volley of gunfire blazed from the guns of the riflemen.

After a particularly intense exchange, the Indians charged with a flourish of tomahawks and war clubs, hoping the riflemen would not have time to reload their weapons, but Morgan's men were adept at reloading their flintlocks quickly. The fierce return of fire from the sharpshooters and their own Virginia battle cries deflected the Indian's forward charge, causing them to retreat from the skirmish and from the vigorous counterattack.

The Shawnees slunk away with all haste, carrying their dead and leaving a chaotic scene in the small clearing. Resentment and anger for the white invaders had spurred them into action, and they had hidden unobserved in the forest, waiting for the ideal moment for an ambush. They disappeared into the dense, murky swamp to return to the safety of their own villages.

When the last of the Indians had vanished into the marshy woods, Morgan heard the unearthly war cry of the Scottish Highlander ringing through the forest in bold defiance of the Indians who were now quitting the field of battle in obvious defeat. This time, however, the hoarse Gaelic war cry piercing the dense, smoke-filled air came from Angus McDonald, who stood like a nemesis at the edge of the forest, his claymore held over his head in one hand, his rifle in the other, while blood trickled down his raised arm where a rifle ball had sliced open his flesh.

McDonald bellowed his victory cry in English so all might hear: *"Beware of MacDonell! Beware of his wrath! He knoweth no bounds to his love or his hate!"* In these strange and peculiar moments when men triumphed in battle, they became like the men of ancient times, fierce and wild, unlike their civilized selves.

Years later, Morgan was to hear another eerie cry that would send chills along the spine of the strongest Indian Warrior. Lewis Wetzel, the Deathwind, blowing through the forests of Virginia and Ohio, had perfected his fearful and mysterious battle cry by listening to the feudal wail of the Highlanders.

Jonathan Zane, his buckskin tunic ripped open from his run through the forest to warn the militia, slowly shook his head while Morgan shuddered at the dreadful bellow of victory and promised revenge on the head of the enemy. In some respects, it reminded

Morgan of the bugling call of the bull elk, daring his opponent to enter his territory. Morgan turned away from the terrible sight of Angus McDonald as he challenged the Indian assailants while blood and sweat dripped from his face and arms. It was a terrible sight—watching this strange battle ritual and the blood-spattered man whose ancestors were steeped in the highland traditions of combat.

Morgan could not help thinking of Derick Davidson, who even now was on the trail west with the Longhunter, heading for the Ohio and the long winter hunt. Derick Davidson, however, was far different in bearing and manner than Angus McDonald. McDonald was an American soldier, frontiersmen like himself, but still holding fast to the traditions of his Scottish ancestry.

The blood of the Scottish Chieftains ran in Derick Davidson's veins, and it was apparent in his commanding presence, a personal magnetism that could lead and direct men. He would have triumphed in battle, most certainly, but minus the verbose and hostile threatenings so expressed in the Highland battle doggerel. His noble blood would not allow him to roar and boast—or so Morgan thought.

When Zane had ascertained that the Indians had left the immediate area of battle, Morgan and McDonald walked through the company of riflemen, assessing the damage of battle and attending to the wounded. Two soldiers had died during the initial ambush. The belongings of the fallen men were placed in a knapsack to be given to their families. Graves were dug and the bodies buried beside a large oak tree near the edge of the forest. The riflemen covered the graves with rocks and disguised the site with bushes dug from the swamp and transplanted near the base of the tree. All evidence of freshly dug graves was obliterated.

One of the sharpshooters, also a preacher from Augusta County, Virginia, said a solemn prayer over their fallen companions. This was part of war; a sad but necessary rite for those who died in battle. The fallen must be buried, and most often, the bodies were hidden from the enemy, buried in a lonely and unmarked gravesite in unfamiliar land.

"Heavenly Father," the preacher began, "this here company of men are compassed about on every side. We are in a time of great danger. You are our only hope, our only protection in this here unfriendly land. Our days are numbered, written in your book, but we know not when our appointment with death shall come. Might we all be ready for that great day." The riflemen shifted uneasily under the branches of the oak tree, hats held reverently in their hands, respectful of the prayer.

"These here fallen men," the preacher continued, "whose bodies we commit back to the dust, have come to their appointed time which no man can change. We trust, Almighty God, they made peace with their Redeemer before they were so cruelly cut off from this present life. May we each consider the certainty of death and the judgment to come." A few dry coughs and clearing of throats resonated from the group of riflemen. There was a general feeling of uneasiness from the men standing at the graveside.

"Lord," the preacher said in conclusion, "we would ask your protection for the remainder of this here mission and for victory in the battle before us. We ask you to prepare and comfort the hearts of the kinfolk of these, our fallen brothers." The preacher paused and looked intently at the group of silent men. "This we ask in the name of Jesus, our Savior, and our Lord forever. Amen."

The assembly of sober riflemen murmured amen, but whether in agreement with the prayer or simply from relief that the prayer was over—no one could tell. The mourners dispersed, and the casualties of the battle were duly listed in the logbook.

Among the wounded was young Thomas Aubrey and Silas Mackenzie's son, Alfred. Lily Jayne's words echoed in Morgan's ears. *Be careful of my son, Daniel Morgan, and make sure you bring Alfred back to me.* Morgan was glad Lily Jayne was not here to see Alfred just now. The young man suffered a leg wound, not too serious, and if infection didn't set in, he would likely recover. Infection was often more deadly than the wound itself, and many a soldier died from the ravages of infection and blood poisoning rather than bodily damage from a rifle ball.

For the first time in his life, Daniel Morgan felt the need of someone more powerful than himself. The words of the preacher struck a chord that long ago had been silenced. Morgan was not a God fearing man, but he realized his command over the riflemen could not keep them safe, nor could he manage the outcome of the battle by his own brute strength. He was only a man, a man who needed something more in his life. What this *something more* was, he was not certain.

As he knelt by the suffering Alfred Mackenzie, Morgan looked around for the preacher, someone who could speak words of reassurance to the wounded soldiers. What could he say to his men to inspire hope and faith? His ways were rough and crude, and he was acutely aware of his inability to articulate his true feelings. Morgan felt compassion and warmth for his riflemen, but he was unable to express either. He was a cursing, brawling, fighting frontiersman with a tongue made of hardened leather. The only soft things in his life were Abigail and his little girls.

His mind went to Derick Davidson, the Scotsman whose words fell like a soothing balm on his ears. The two men were vastly dissimilar, yet at this moment, Morgan longed to hear the deep base burr of the Scotsman, to feel the strong grip of his hand. Derick Davidson's very presence conveyed strength and inspired Morgan to reflect on his own rough ways.

Thoughts of Abigail came to mind, and Morgan knew she was praying for him and for all the riflemen. It seemed he could hear her soft voice in the whisper of the wind, and he wished he were at Soldier's Rest with her and his little girls, safe and secure. He banished the intrusive thoughts from his mind, chastening himself for such unsoldierly sentiment at this critical time. He must be getting old and soft. He was thirty-eight years old with still plenty of battles to fight. There was a mission to complete in the Ohio country, and he must stay focused, stay the course.

Morgan lightly squeezed Alfred Mackenzie's shoulder and moved along the row of wounded men to kneel beside Thomas Aubrey who lay on a movable gurney. "How's it a goin', Thomas?" Morgan asked. This was a ridiculous question, but one expected from your commanding officer. The young man's wounds were serious. A ball had shattered a rib and lodged deep beneath the splintered bone. Blood pooled at the site of entry, and the boy was weak. Because the ball had entered from the side, his rib had deflected the lead ball so no vital organ had been penetrated.

The doctor's aides had endeavored to stop the bleeding, but they were unable to remove the rifle ball. Thomas needed a surgeon.

As fate would have it, one of the men killed during the ambush was the only surgeon on this particular mission.

"I'm not doin' well, Cap'n," Thomas said weakly. He groaned with pain and then spoke again. "Can ya do somethin' for me, Cap'n?"

"What is it, son?"

"It's Kearan, Cap'n. Can ya tell her for me..." Thomas paused, drawing a ragged breath. "Tell her...tell her I'm sorry. She'll know what I mean. She'll understand."

"I'll tell her, Thomas, but you can tell her yourself when we get back to Frederick County."

Thomas managed a weak smile. One more thing...Cap'n." Pain crossed his features and he had to wait a moment before he could speak again. "Tell Davidson for me...tell him I'm sorry. He's a good man, Cap'n. I was wrong to be jealous...to fault him." Another long pause. "I meant no harm."

Morgan raised his eyebrows but did not comment on the man's request. "I'll tell him, Thomas, but now, you need to rest, need to be quiet. I'm leavin' the wounded here with a guard. We'll pick our men up day after tomorrow. Then we're returnin' to camp across the river. We'll get you to the doc. He will take the nasty ball outta your side, young man. We'll have you to home before the snow flies."

At first light the next morning, McDonald advanced the company to the village of Wakatomica some six miles away. The plan ordered by Dunmore was to terrorize the inhabitants, destroy the village, and then return to the army camp on the other side of the Ohio River.

After the ambush that left two of his men dead and several wounded, McDonald was uneasy with Dunmore's orders for this mission, but he reluctantly complied. He felt he was needlessly endangering his troops just to burn a few Indian villages. He sent an express with a runner to Lord Dunmore, informing him of his movements, and then marched his troops to Wakatomica.

When they reached the village, they found it evacuated. The Indians had removed their families and goods to villages farther away in preparation for the real battle soon to come when Dunmore and Lewis united their forces. The riflemen torched the fields of standing crops, the bushels of corn and produce, razed the entire village, and returned to camp, picked up their wounded, and immediately marched to the Ohio River and the protection of the larger army. However, another devious plan was unfolding at this very moment, a plan to bring the Colonial army to complete and total destruction.

Chapter 13

Battle at Point Pleasant

It is not with the first stroke that the tree falls

The slight but steady vibration of the cold earth next to Derick's ear awakened him from sleep. He lay perfectly still, listening. He could hear nothing, but when he placed his hand on the bare ground, he could feel, ever so faintly, the recurring throbbing that said something was moving. He sat up slowly and looked around. The Longhunter was still sleeping. A thin gray line was showing along the horizon in the east. Dawn was approaching. The forest was quiet, not a sound. Derick waited, listening intently before crawling from his bed role and strapping on his sword. He picked up his rifle and quietly crept up the eastern slope of the hillside until he reached the summit. He was standing on the last range of rocky hills before reaching the Ohio River and the Indian Territory. For protection from possible Indian raiding parties, the Longhunter had chosen to camp on the eastern slope, avoiding anyone who might be traveling the Ohio River valley.

It was still too dark to see anything clearly in the valley below. Again, Derick put his ear to the ground. The vibrating seemed stronger. He climbed on top of a large boulder and lay flat, waiting, listening. First light began to filter through the mist-laden trees, but the valley below lay in darkness. Was it a herd of buffalo?

Derick had never seen buffalo, but the Longhunter said they moved through the flat lands, along the river valleys.

After listening for some time, the low guttural sounds of men's voices drifted up the hillside. Derick strained to see through the brush and tangled vines. The forest was unusually quiet. Only the faintest peeping of the morning dove could be heard in the distance. Light penetrated the darkness, and Derick slipped the spyglass from his pack and held it to his eye. Moving stealthy along the valley floor was a large body of Indians painted for war. He watched from his perch on the boulder for several moments and then quietly retraced his steps until he reached camp on the opposite side of the hill. The Longhunter was up and waiting, a sober look on his face. He handed Derick a plate of griddlecakes and honey with some venison steak and gravy. Coffee boiled in the camp kettle.

"What did ye find, lad?" the Longhunter queried.

"A large contingent of Indians," Derick answered. He began to devour the breakfast. "They be creeping along the glen, next to the burn, just the other side of the ben." Derick was enjoying the warm food and the aroma of the fragrant coffee.

"You mean they're creeping along the valley next to the river on the other side of the mountain?"

"Aye, that's what I said."

"War paint?"

"Aye. Carrying many weapons."

"The army must be camped nearby," the Longhunter said with some alarm. "It's an ambush, sure as I be a standing here. Well, we gotta warn the army, lad. We can head south on this side of the range for a wee, then cross over the summit to see what's afoot. Let's hope we can find the army camp before the Indians do."

"What about the packhorses?" Derick asked as he finished the last of his breakfast and gulped down some coffee.

"We'll tether them and leave the beasts here," the Longhunter replied. He looked around at the camp that was sheltered from view in a natural hollow. "Tis a safe place for now, lad. We'll leave our gear in camp. Gotta travel light. Just take our guns, powder, and shot. Let's pack things away and be off."

They tethered the horses to a long rope and stashed some parched corn and venison jerky in their packs, filled their canteens with fresh water and set off on a brisk run. After a half mile of vigorous running along the eastern slope of the range of low rocky hills, they crossed over the summit. Halting at the top, they climbed onto a large outcropping of rock that enabled them to see over the trees. The Longhunter retrieved the spyglass and peered into the valley below. In the distance, he could see the army camped at the mouth of the Kanawha River. The sun was just about to rise in the east. Suddenly, a simultaneous blast of gunfire and the noise of wild screaming exploded near the army encampment. The Longhunter groaned and shook his head in frustration.

"Auch, lad, we're too late! The Indians be upon them this very minute," he said with an anguished moan."

From the army camp on the Kanawha, a bugle sounded the call to arms, and the drums followed in quick succession. Gunfire shattered the early morning stillness, piercing war cries echoed and bounced along the valley. The appalling sounds of deadly battle drifted up the hillside to the ears of the two men watching from above the camp.

"The lads be organizing," Derick said looking through the spyglass and studying the movements of the army as they prepared for battle. "Must be, the lads had some kind of warning. There's an advance guard a wee distance from the main camp, trying to hold the enemy's forward approach."

"How many Indians do ye calculate?" the Longhunter asked. He was disconcerted over his failure to warn the army in time.

Without a word, Derick handed the spyglass to his uncle. The Longhunter held the scope to his eye. Another groan soon followed. "There be a thousand or more warriors coming through the valley, moving toward the army encampment with their chiefs in the lead. It's a confederation of tribes, to be sure."

"Aye, it appears so," Derick commented. "I didn't see Morgan or the riflemen in camp, but we can't see everything from up here. Should we go down and join the Colonials, Uncle?"

The Longhunter put down the spyglass and looked long and hard at his nephew. "Are ye a spoiling for a fight?"

"Nay, but I don't like the odds, Uncle. The Virginians are me friends, and I'd venture to say they'll be needing some help."

The Longhunter put the glass to his eye again. "Well, looks like Dunmore's not in camp—far as I can see. Peers he hasn't arrived on the scene. Ye be right, lad, the odds be agin the Colonial army."

"Who else can ye see, Uncle?"

"Look down there on the right. That's General Lewis and his men making a stand. There's Charles Lewis, too. That be his brother. If I were a betting man, I'd say there's a sight more Indians than there be Colonials in this fight."

"Uncle," Derick said in a serious tone, "when I crossed the water, I said that me fighting days were over, but I feel something a stirring in me blood, something that makes me want to help the Virginians."

"Auch, lad, I understand," the Longhunter said to his nephew. "After centuries of bleedin' the land red with the blood of our countrymen, you're bound to feel a challenge rising in your soul."

"I'm growing to love this land, Uncle. The Patriots—they still have heart, they still believe in freedom. Somewhere along the way, I lost me purpose, me reason to fight on, but I see it in the strength of the Patriots. Aye, Uncle, I want to live free." Derick had finally voiced what he had known for months—that he would join the Patriots in their magnificent cause.

"If ye truly intend to abide in this new homeland, then ye must choose your burden, lad: to fight or not to fight. Either choice bears a troublesome load. If ye fight, ye might be killed, and if ye don't, ye might be enslaved—or bear the torment of doing nothing. If ye want the blessings of freedom, then ye must share the weariness of supporting the Patriot cause, maybe with your life."

The Longhunter's words were like an arrow to Derick's heart. He must choose, regardless of the outcome. His uncle would not judge him. "Will *ye* fight, Uncle?" Derick asked.

Donald Davidson, former Lieutenant of the Black Watch, Scottish warrior of many battles, hesitated briefly, and then spoke. "Aye, I'll fight with the Colonials until Dunmore arrives," the Longhunter said solemnly. "Enough talk, lad, let's find a fighting place."

Sprinting down the western slope of the mountain, the two men stayed under the cover of the trees. As they drew closer to the camp, they crept unobserved to another outcropping of rock where they wedged themselves between the boulders for the fight. They arranged their ammunition for fast reloading and set their canteens close by.

"We'll be a using our trusty rifles from this vantage point," the Longhunter said. "I guess it's maybe 130 yards to the skirmish. Indians sneaking all along this southern flank. We'll have no trouble finding a target, that's certain." He lifted the spyglass to his eye and studied the battle in progress.

"I see Cornstalk and Logan leading the Indians: Shawnee, Mingo, Delaware, and Wyandot—all there. There'll be the devil to pay before this day is over. Looka there! Those Indians sneaking around the flanks are after the officers. Some officers down already. Don't see Captain Morgan or his men anywhere. What a shame. The sharpshooters need to be here for this fight. Guess we'll have to help 'em out."

Fire belched from Derick's rifle, and a tall Indian fell to the ground without a sound. The Longhunter put his spyglass away and rested his rifle on top of the flat rock surface. A slow smile spread across his bearded face. "This be a bonny rock for the long shot, lad."

A deadly exchange of gunfire between the Colonials and the Indian allies continued for the next four hours without any sign of respite or relief for the army. Dunmore's troops did not appear, and the Colonials were suffering heavy losses, many of whom were officers. The blasts of the rifles and the wild yelping of the Indians reverberated though the valley of the Kanawha, and the two lone men targeting the Indians from their hiding place among the rocks were running low on ammunition.

"I think some of those Wyandot Indians creeping along the army's lower flank have spotted us a shooting at 'em," the Longhunter observed. "See 'em a looking up this way? We done well to fool 'em for this long, but methinks our game is up, lad. We better make tracks over this mountain or get some more shot and powder from the army's supply shed." The Longhunter pointed to a knot of warriors who were pointing back at them. "Well, lad, we be discovered. Here come four of those red devils."

"I'll take out the one on the left," Derick said taking aim. "You take the right."

"Then what?" the Longhunter asked with a twinkle in his eye. "There's still one apiece, and I doubt if there's time to reload before they be on us."

"Aye, you're right, so ye best be quick, Uncle." Derick did not fear for himself, but he wasn't sure the Longhunter was in the mood for hand-to-hand confrontations. "It's the great sword, I expect, so be ready," Derick warned. Once again, fire flashed from Derick's Pennsylvania rifle, and the Longhunter fired in quick succession. Two Indians fell twenty yards from where Derick and the Longhunter were hidden. The two remaining Indians ducked behind trees and took aim with their muskets, straining to see their rivals hidden among the rocks. The muskets the Indians received in trade from the French and British were often faulty and not as accurate as the Pennsylvania long rifles. Fortunately, for the American Patriots, the Indians were also poor shots.

Derick stood up in an attempt to draw fire from the two Indians and then quickly ducked down to safety. The ruse worked and both Indians fired, emptying their muskets. Derick leapt from cover and charged the Indians with his claymore drawn and the Longhunter on his heels. The Indians were desperately trying to reload, but seeing the huge Scotsman charging toward them with his deadly sword raised, the nearest warrior took aim with his tomahawk and the weapon sailed through the air with deadly accuracy. Derick dodged swiftly to the right and the tomahawk flew by his head and buried itself in the Longhunter's shoulder with a sickening thud, knocking him to the ground.

With a bellow of rage, Derick fell upon the Indian with his claymore, dispatching him in an instant. The remaining Indian had dropped his musket and was running from the scene, back to his companions and the ongoing battle below.

The Longhunter lay in a pool of blood where he had fallen, the tomahawk embedded deep in his flesh. Derick knelt at his side and quickly pulled the weapon from the Longhunter's shoulder opening the wound. A fresh surge of blood spurted from the gash and the Longhunter moaned in pain. Desperately, Derick opened his pack and removed the cloth bandages he carried for emergencies. He pressed the cloth to the wound and held it firmly in place for several minutes. Then he tied another bandage securely around his uncle's chest.

"Nay, lad," the Longhunter said breathing heavily. "I'm thinking it's me time and...and I might just slip away. I—"

"Don't' talk, Uncle. Ye will *not* slip away. Nay, ye will not," Derick said and felt a knot twisting in the pit of his stomach. If he had not dodged the Indian's tomahawk, his uncle would have been unharmed. The weapon was meant for him, not for the Longhunter. "We'll fix ye up, Uncle, but I must get ye away from here. The Indians will be back. Tis a bad bleed ye have, that's all. No organs cut, just muscle and bone." Derick was not truly certain of his conclusion, but he felt better for saying so.

"I'm a feeling so...so weak, lad. Bad bleed...will kill a man," the Longhunter said between gasps.

Without further delay, Derick sheathed his sword, picked up the Longhunter, and carried him from the site where he had fallen. He laid him gently on the ground near the place where they had relentlessly fired on the Indians. Next, he gathered their gear, reloaded, and shouldered the rifles. Picking his uncle up with care, he cradled him in his strong arms, fearing at any moment that his uncle would continue to bleed away his life. Then he began the arduous trek back to the camp on the eastern slope of the range, avoiding areas that would leave an obvious trail.

Derick reached camp almost two hours later, exhausted, but greatly relieved to have escaped the battle scene on the river, and hopefully, without pursuit. He didn't believe the Indians would follow him this far, not when a battle of such significance was still in progress on the other side of the mountain.

He made a comfortable bed of spruce boughs for the Longhunter and kindled a fire before retrieving the camp kettle to boil some water. Finding their extra clothing and the medicine pack, he gently removed the Longhunter's shirt, cutting it away and removing the compress to expose the gaping wound. The tomahawk had slashed deep and clean, cutting flesh and muscle to the bone, which was splintered and partially severed. When Derick removed the cloth compress, blood poured from the site. The Longhunter appeared to be growing weaker. He must stop the bleeding, or his uncle would surely die.

After the water had boiled, he worked quickly, washing out the deep cut with an infusion made from dried yarrow leaves steeped in the boiling water. After the bone fragments were washed from the wound, Derick basted the area with a thick yarrow salve the Longhunter had made during the late spring. The salve had a beeswax base mixed with crushed, dried yarrow leaves and flowers. Lastly, he packed the wound with clean cloth and wrapped it tight around his uncle's chest. To Derick's great relief, the bandage did not saturate from profuse bleeding.

According to the watch he fished from his uncle's hunting shirt, it was four in the afternoon. It was October 10, 1774, and the fierce battle at the mouth of the Kanawha had steadily escalated. Derick wondered why Dunmore had not made an appearance, and where in the world were the Virginians from Frederick County? They had all but disappeared.

The Longhunter moaned, and Derick went to his side. Kneeling next to him, he asked, "Can ye drink some coffee, Uncle?"

"Aye…a wee. Ye did good on me wound, lad. I'm feeling a wee stronger."

"Ye need a doctor, Uncle. The wound needs sewn shut. Moving about might start the bleeding again. I'm strongly thinking of going back to the army camp and fetching a doctor for ye."

"Are ye daft, lad?" The Longhunter seemed to rally at his nephew's statement. "The army is barely holding on…officers down…the doctors busy."

"If ye thought ye would be tolerable for a few hours," Derick said ignoring his uncle's words. "I'd like to slip into the army camp and see the lay of the land. I can make it by meself in an hour or so. Be back before dark. I know me way."

"I'll be fair enough, lad," the Longhunter answered weakly. "Just lay me rifle by me side…and me testament. I'll be here…when ye return."

Derick brought water and food and placed the rifle by the side of the Longhunter. He seriously doubted if his uncle could manage to fire it should an occasion arise. Locating the Longhunter's Gaelic testament, he placed it next to him on his bed of spruce boughs, then added wood to the fire, and cared for the horses.

"Be back in three hours," Derick said and shouldered his rifle. He knelt by his uncle and laid one strong hand on his uncle's shoulder. The Longhunter grimaced. The grayish pallor of death was on his countenance. Derick fully intended to bring a doctor back to care for his uncle, even if he had to hold a gun to his head.

In little over an hour, Derick was at the outcropping of rock where he and the Longhunter had shot a score of Indians before their discovery. The bodies of the three Indians had been removed, but there was no sign of Indians in the immediate area. The intensity of the battle seemed to be waning as evening approached. With little difficulty, Derick slipped into the camp of the Colonials and immediately met with a Sergeant who looked at him with curiosity.

"Where in the world did you come from, and who are you?" asked the Sergeant in amazement.

"Derick Davidson from Frederick County. Camping with the Longhunter on the other side of the mountain. We heard the battle and decided to join in. Been up in those rocks all day—"

"Oh," the Sergeant said with a light in his eyes, "so you're the ones firing from those rocks and picking off the redskins on our southern flank. We were trying to see what was going on but didn't have a spare minute to investigate."

"Aye, it was the Longhunter and meself, but he has been seriously wounded by a tomahawk. Can ye spare one of your doctors? The Longhunter is in bad shape, Sergeant."

"Listen, Davidson," the Sergeant said sympathetically, "I appreciate your help today, and I'm sorry your friend was wounded, but all our doctors are either dead or down for the duration. It's a bad piece of luck for the army, but it's true nevertheless. We had three surgeons and every one of 'em is down. Can't even take care of our own wounded. Blast that Dunmore anyhow. Sorry, Davidson, wish I could help."

Derick felt physically sick. "Where is Captain Morgan and the Virginians from Frederick County?" Derick asked somewhat impatiently.

"Morgan is across the river with his men and Colonel Crawford, stirring up another hornet's nest I suppose. He and McDonald were in a skirmish with the Shawnees earlier, and Morgan brought his wounded riflemen back to camp."

"Then where is Dunmore and his northern army?" Derick questioned.

The Sergeant let fly an oath. "Ha! Now that's a good question. Peers he missed the battle altogether. I gotta go, Davidson. Sorry I can't help you."

Disappointment and frustration rose in Derick's heart like a burning fire. What could he do now? "Before ye go, Sergeant, can ye tell me where Morgan left his wounded men?"

"Yup, that I can do. Third row of tents, halfway up. That's the army infirmary. A blast of gunfire ended the conversation and the sergeant hurried off.

Derick sprinted off in the direction the sergeant had indicated. He found Morgan's men in the tent where their Captain had left them in care of the army doctors, only now, the doctors were among the casualties. Alfred McKenzie was lying on a blanket, sweat covering his brow. Thomas Aubrey seemed barely alive. The rest of the wounded needed medical attention, but no one was caring for the wounded men. Some were crying out for water and relief from pain. Derick located the water bucket and dipper and gave each man a long drink.

The riflemen were overjoyed to see Derick Davidson in camp. Those who were able plied him with question about Morgan and the ongoing battle. Where in heaven's name were the doctors, they wanted to know. Derick spoke with them briefly and said he would return to the camp after he cared for the Longhunter's wounds.

Since no doctor was to be found, Derick left the chaos of battle, slipping along the edge of the encampment until he gained the cover of the forest. He saw General Lewis directing the battle, his stern face, blackened with gunpowder, his courage unyielding. The Colonials were slowly advancing on the field, pressing the Indians back. Derick felt a surge of hope rise in his breast. He wanted to stay and help, but he couldn't leave the Longhunter alone.

Just as darkness fell over the eastern slope of the mountain, Derick reached camp. From all indications, the Longhunter appeared to be sleeping. God forbid that he had died in his absence. Derick knelt by his side and gently touched him. The fire had burned to glowing embers and the moon was beginning to rise. "I'm back, Uncle. How are ye feeling?" The Longhunter opened his eyes. Thank God, he was still alive!

"Rough, lad, rough. I be glad ye are back."

"I thought to bring a doctor with me, Uncle, but they all be down, everyone of them. The battle lasted all day, but it seems the Colonials might be gaining ground. Lewis is a true leader—saw him, black from powder and unforgiving in battle. Morgan is across the river and Dunmore never showed up. It's a pitiful sight, Uncle. I saw Morgan's men in the infirmary tent. Wounded, with no help."

"Auch, lad. Ye should have...stayed. They need ye...and I'm but one man."

Exhaustion and disappointment seemed to collide around Derick Davidson's senses, like the crashing sounds of battle. From the depths of his being, a groan escaped, ending in a dry sob of frustration. "Don't say it, Uncle. Ye are me own blood, all that I have in this land and I canna leave ye. I am only one man, too. Do not fault me, Uncle." Derick felt a shaky hand rest on his shoulder.

"Aye, lad, and so ye are, so ye are. We…ye and me…we'll fight this battle together. And lad…I do not fault ye."

Even in his weakened state, the Longhunter sensed that his nephew was reliving his past, his frustration over not being there to save Meagan, the loss of his home and family. Loss itself, loss of any kind rekindled the pain. He must live. His nephew could not bear another loss. God being his strength, he would live.

Derick's hands trembled with fatigue. Thoughts of Kearan Mackenzie drifted unbidden into his mind like a soothing balm. He had told her that she must disregard emotion in a critical situation, and yet, the full gamut of emotions was storming against his own soul. He pictured the dark haired lass with her grandfather's sword at her side, riding her horse through the fields like a female warrior. Somehow, the image was comforting.

"Dinna fash yourself," the Longhunter said using the familiar old Gaelic expression. He was watching Derick, his eyes bright with pain. Death was always one sword thrust, one well-placed shot away. For a man with a weapon, death lurked in the shadows of every battle. It was a risk every soldier understood. "Nay," the Longhunter repeated faintly, "Dinna fash yourself…not for me, lad."

"I won't fret meself, Uncle, but I canna help but think, ye would not be suffering now, had I not jumped aside."

"Nay, 'tis me own fault." He sighed wearily. "I thought...me fighting days were over...not raise me sword again...but I just couldn't...couldn't help meself." Using his good arm, the Longhunter felt for his testament. Derick placed it in his hand and the Longhunter laid it across his chest. "This be me sword...remember?"

"Aye, I remember, but me claymore is me trusted friend for this battle, Uncle."

"There is another friend...one that sticks to ye...like a thistle..." His words died away, drifting into silence. He turned his face toward the east and lay still, very still.

The sounds of battle had died away hours ago, and the thickly forested hills were quiet. In the shadows, an owl hooted and an answering call echoed in the distance. Gentle rain fell like tears in the camp of the Longhunter and Derick erected a canvas shelter over his uncle as he lay sleeping.

Fatigue dragged at Derick's body like a lead weight, and his mind swam in a pool of unsettling thoughts. What if his uncle died on this rocky hillside? If he didn't, how could he get him back to Winchester where a doctor could see to his wound? It had taken several weeks over difficult trails to get this far. And where in heaven's name were Morgan and the Virginia riflemen?

The owl hooted again; this time it was closer. Derick raised himself from where he sat by his uncle and stood next to the fire, feeling strangely uneasy. Just as he laid his hand on the hilt of his claymore, a rush of moccasin feet slipped through the stillness and he swung around, but it was too late. A heavy object hit the side of his head, and he plunged into darkness.

When he awoke, it was near dawn. Light was creeping along the eastern horizon in a thin white line. Derick tried to move but his hands and feet were bound with tight buckskin thongs, and blood oozed from a gash on his head, which throbbed dreadfully.

Glancing around the camp, he saw six Indians, all painted for war. They were breaking camp, loading the packhorses with all their supplies for the winter hunt. The Longhunter had been moved from his place by the fire, and Derick saw that his eyes were open and sunken with pain. Indignation rose in Derick's breast and he strained at his bonds with all his might, but hope of freeing himself from his restraints seemed futile. He caught his uncle's eye just before a tall lanky Indian noticed that he was awake. The Indian stepped lightly to where Derick lay on the hard ground and knelt beside him.

"You kill...many warriors." The eyes of the red man were dark and intense, and to Derick's astonishment, they were not accusatory, but held admiration and respect. Derick answered nothing.

"We take," the Indian said pointing to the packhorses and supplies.

At the edge of the clearing, two Indians were deftly constructing a gurney, which they fastened to one of the packhorses. When this was completed, they lifted the Longhunter onto the gurney.

"No!" Derick shouted at the tall Indian who appeared to be their leader. "His wound will bleed. He cannot travel."

The tall Indian's black eyes blazed, and he stood over Derick's powerless form like a towering demon. Derick lay helpless, bound hand and foot, and unable to help either himself or his uncle. The Indian pulled out his hunting knife, the blade glinting in the pale morning light. Before he could plunge the weapon into Derick's chest, the Scotsman rolled over and thrust his bound feet forward with all his strength, landing a heavy blow to the Indian's mid section. The tall Indian doubled over, groaning in pain. To Derick's amazement, his Indian companions laughed and called to their fallen comrade, obviously enjoying the incident.

When the tall Indian recovered himself, he once again approached Derick, only this time, he had two of his companions restrain the big Scotsman while he cut away the leather thongs on his feet. Then Derick understood. The Indian was cutting away his bonds so they could travel. Derick sighed with relief.

A leather thong was fastened around his neck as a lead and his hands remained bound securely behind him. Before the war party left camp, the tall Indian pulled Derick by the leather lead to where the Longhunter lay pale and helpless on the gurney. Pulling up his hunting shirt, the Indian pointed to the Longhunter's shoulder. The ugly wound had been neatly sewn shut and a yellowish oily salve was painted over the gash.

With a slight nod of his head, the Longhunter signaled Derick to cooperate with the Indian war party. What choice did he have? If he didn't comply, the leather thong around his neck would be pulled back, choking the breath from him and bruising his throat. He had to obey. There was no other option.

The Indians left camp quietly, marching north for some time before turning west toward the Ohio River. At the point where the Ohio joined a tributary called the Hockhocking, the Indians joined a larger contingent of tribesmen who carried canoes for navigating the river. Derick breathed a sigh of relief when they placed his uncle into the bottom of a canoe that would glide smoothly over the water instead of bouncing along unevenly after the packhorse.

The Indians were leaving Virginia and crossing into the heart of the Indian Territory. Derick knew beyond any shadow of doubt that he and his uncle were bound for the stronghold of the Indian

Nations of Ohio where he would most probably meet his death—a gruesome and hideous death at a burning fiery stake.

Chapter 14

The Captives

No door ever closed, but another opened

"Abigail, oh Abigail," Kearan called running up the steps of the kitchen entrance to the Morgan farmhouse. Her cheeks were pink with cold, and the icy blast of wind caused her eyes to sting and tear. She knocked firmly on the locked door with her mittened hand. The bolt slid from the latch and the door swung open. Abigail Morgan looked surprised, but her two daughters smiled a warm welcome.

"Come in here right now, Kearan, before you catch your death of cold," Abigail said pulling her inside the warm kitchen. "What on earth are you doing out on such a freezing cold day as this?"

"I have news, Abigail, news from the men," Kearan said pulling off her mittens. "The riflemen—they are coming home. The first—those who are strong and able, have begun to arrive home already."

Abigail's hand flew to her throat. "Is Daniel with them?"

"No, not yet. You know very well, Abby, that he won't come back until the last of the militia has left for home. He wouldn't consider leaving someone behind."

"You're right, of course," said Abigail. "I am just so eager to see him again, to know that everything is all right." She hung the kettle over the fire to make tea and brought pewter mugs from the cupboard. The women sat at the table, and the two little girls, eager and expectant, crowded close beside them, knowing this conversation held some great significance.

"And how are my two best girls?" Kearan asked placing an arm around each child and hugging them both at once.

"I am doing quite well, thank you—ma'am," answered Betsey using her very best manners, "but Nancy cries for Papa all the time and won't do her lessons. She told Mama she wouldn't do her sums again until Papa comes home. Mama says she is sulking."

"Well," Kearan said with a smile, "you can stop your crying, Nancy, because your papa will be coming home very soon."

"Will he really?" Nancy asked looking at Kearan with hopeful blue eyes.

"Absolutely. Really and truly," Kearan assured her. "He is probably on his way right this minute." The two little girls clapped their hands joyously and began to skip around the kitchen. Abigail laughed with delight.

"Now that you two little lassies know about your papa coming home," Kearan said, "run along and play unless you have lessons to finish. Your Mama and I want to have a private little chat."

Nancy and Betsey looked hopefully at each other and then at their mother for approval of this plan. When Kearan came to visit Mama, the girls knew that lessons would wait. Abigail nodded her consent and the girls squealed with delight. Without further prompting, the children skipped to their room to find their dolls.

The kettle sang over the fire, and Abigail brought the tea and poured the fragrant liquid into the pewter mugs. From the warmer next to the fireplace oven, she placed several slices of freshly baked bread on a blue plate accompanied by a dish of wild berry jam.

"Now, Kearan," said Abby, "tell me your news...and please hurry before the girls weary of their play and return to the kitchen." She sipped the tea, her hands trembling slightly with anticipation.

"Benjamin Barnett came by early this morning on his way to Battletown," Kearan said in a rush of words. "He looked for all the world like he would drop in his tracks. We let him borrow a horse, and he was ever so grateful. He had been walking for almost two hundred miles, Abby. I told him that since he had the horse to ride home, he must stay awhile and tell us all the news. We fed him a huge breakfast, and he told us all he could remember about the riflemen and what happened on the river in October." She paused, taking a sip of hot tea and spreading jam on a slice of bread.

"Oh, please hurry, Kearan," Abby said nervously, "I can't stand the suspense a minute longer. There is such unreliable news, and who knows if what we hear is accurate."

"Well, the battle with the Indians at the Kanawha in October was a long hard fight, and that part of the report is accurate. Of course, we knew that already. The Colonials won the day in the end, but with heavy losses on both sides. When the Indians attacked the southern army camp, Daniel and most of the militia riflemen were with Colonel Crawford across the Ohio, deep into Indian territory so they missed the battle on the river. I suppose that was a blessing." Kearan sighed then continued. "Ben says that so many officers were lost, Abby, including Charles Lewis, the brother of General Andrew Lewis, the commander."

"How dreadful," Abby said with genuine empathy. "It must have been an awful struggle. Please go on, Kearan."

"Well, it seems that Captain Morgan had met some hostile Indians earlier in September when he and Major McDonald were on an advance mission in the Ohio territory. Two riflemen were killed outright and..." Kearan paused, drawing a deep breath. "...and Alfred and several others were wounded, some very seriously. After the mission was complete, the wounded were taken back to camp on the other side of the Ohio, and...and...oh Abby, it is too terrible, too awful!" Kearan covered her face with her hands and began to weep.

"Tell me, Kearan," Abby said placing a hand on her arm, "I want to know. Don't keep anything from me."

"Thomas Aubrey...he died in camp, several days after the battle," Kearan sobbed. "He had been severely wounded in the advance mission and all the army surgeons were down or killed. Oh, Abby, just think—I sent him away to battle—just to die with a broken heart. He loved me, Abby, wanted to marry me, wanted me to wait for him, but I couldn't, I just couldn't, and now, he is dead—dead, Abby!" She laid her head on her folded arms and continued to sob.

After a moment, Abigail spoke. "Don't, Kearan, please don't weep. If you didn't care for Thomas, how could you promise to wait for him? Don't blame yourself for something you can't help. You didn't love him, and you were honest about your feelings. That's what matters. When our men leave for battle, we have no promise that they will return." Abby patted Kearan's shoulder and felt tears in her own eyes. "Thomas was a good young man, and he knew the danger and consequence of war. He understood that, Kearan. Just the same, it is always hard to lose our young men. This will be especially hard on his folks—their only son."

Kearan raised her head and dabbed at her tears with her handkerchief. "We must go visit them, Abby. Thomas was their pride and joy and we've known each other since we were children. He was such a strong and strapping young blacksmith. Who would have thought..." Kearan's voice trailed off.

"Do you know the details of the battle, Kearan?"

"Only as a man relates details," she said smiling through her tears. "They were ambushed from what I understand, Abby, taken unaware, and Ben says that Lord Dunmore was not even present for the battle."

"What? Wasn't even present? Dear Lord, help us! What about your family, Kearan—Alfred and Silas?"

"Papa is bringing Alfred with him. He has a leg wound, but Ben says it is improving every day and that Alfred should recover fully. Papa and Alfred should be home in a few more days. Ben also mentioned that the Longhunter and Derick were somehow involved in the battle on the Kanawha, but nobody knows exactly how this came about."

"The Longhunter hasn't been in a skirmish on the border since he quit soldiering many years ago," Abigail said, "so it is strange that they would be fighting in that battle."

"That's so, Abby, and Derick refused to join the militia, but at the same time, he and the Longhunter were on their way to their winter hunting camp. The riflemen said Derick came to the army camp looking for a doctor, said that the Longhunter was seriously wounded in a struggle with the Indians. Nobody seems to know much. They haven't seen the Longhunter or Derick since he came into camp. It appears he wouldn't have gone far with the Longhunter wounded. They have simply disappeared."

"If they were involved in the battle, it seems odd that they would not report to the army after the battle was over," Abigail reasoned. She shook her head in consternation. "Maybe Daniel can tell us more when he returns. Perhaps even now he is searching for them. I know it would be hard for Daniel to leave if he knew they were out there somewhere and needed help."

"Benjamin says that Captain Morgan would be the last to leave someone behind and unaccounted for. I know that's true, Abby. Uncle Daniel will figure this out. He was with Lord Dunmore's company when the peace treaty was signed deep in the Ohio country and wasn't present at the battle. Ben says signing the treaty was a big production and totally controlled by Dunmore himself. General Lewis was fit to be tied, said Lord Dunmore didn't show up at the battle with the other half of the army on purpose, that the army had to fight without Dunmore's men or the militia riflemen. After all that, Dunmore tried to keep General Lewis away from the treaty negotiations. I understand that General Lewis disobeyed direct orders from Lord Dunmore and—oh, Abigail, who knows what will happen next!"

"It's an unsettling situation, Kearan. General Lewis could be accused of starting a rebellion against the King's authority. The British will hang him for treason if that is the case. I'm sure Daniel will support General Lewis. He doesn't have much confidence in Governor Dunmore, that's a fact. Lewis' actions could have far-reaching consequences, Kearan."

"I just want our men to come home, Abby. If only the King would leave us alone, allow us to make our own decisions, to be an independent nation."

"Well, I'm just glad Daniel is safe and will be home soon." Abigail shook her head sadly.

"I know a war is coming, Kearan, and I know Daniel will fight with the Patriots. I'm afraid it will be a long and bloody battle. We women of the frontier must be strong. We must keep the home fires burning bright for our men and for independence."

"But what do you think of Derick, Abby? Where could he have gone, especially with the Longhunter wounded? He must have set up camp somewhere nearby to wait out the winter and care for the Longhunter until he recovers. We must pray for them every day, Abby, pray that God will keep them safe from all that might befall them." Tears brimmed in Kearan's eyes. "We live in such dreadful times, Abby, such dreadful and perilous times. But you are right—we must be brave, we must be strong, even when we feel weary with the effort."

Abigail laid a sympathetic hand on Kearan's small one. "Daniel says you are a very strong young woman, Kearan, but he worries. He believes your heart is turned toward the Scotsman. Is he right, Kearan?"

A warm flush crept to Kearan's cheeks, and she turned her face away but not before Abigail saw what was written there. "Uncle Daniel says he is not my kind, Abigail," Kearan said in a soft voice, "that I should stick with the frontier boys, those I grew up with." She sighed and plucked at some imaginary lint on her wool dress.

"I asked him if a person could help loving someone, but he wouldn't answer me. Oh Abby, I will confess to you. My heart is so tortured! I have loved Derick from the first time I saw him on your wedding day. He was standing at the fireside, and our eyes met and I...I..." She dropped her head, pausing to gaze into her mug of tea.

"I know he doesn't care for me," Kearan continued, "but I simply can't help caring for him, Abby. Sometimes, I think I see something stirring when I am with him, something in his eyes that tells me he cares a little, but then, the next time I see him, it is gone, vanished without a trace. I don't know what to think."

"You must know, Kearan, Derick Davidson is a complicated man to say the least. He is very unlike our frontier boys. Our lads are simple, hard working, honest men—not to say Derick is not an honorable and decent person—just different, that's all."

"I know he is different, Abby, and that is what is so compelling about him. He is *not* our ordinary frontier boy. There is something very noble and at the same time, so pathetic about him. That very quality endears him to me. Nevertheless, every day that I wake, I pray God will take the caring from my heart, but so far, it's still there. Why is this so difficult to understand, Abby?" She looked at Abigail Morgan with troubled brown eyes.

"Because people are different, I suppose. Derick has a history, Kearan, and it has shaped the way he thinks, and his past life in Scotland consumes his mind. If you and Derick are meant to be together, and it is God's will, then sometime in the future, God will bring it about—in His own time. And, if God has someone else in mind, well, don't close the door. Meanwhile, dear girl, you must learn to wait and not allow your feelings to get in the way of common sense. Stay open to other relationships, Kearan. God has a plan for you. There is much to consider, much to pray about."

During the early weeks of December, the militia riflemen of Frederick County trickled home. They came on foot over the treacherous miles of raging rivers and mountain passes with a Shenandoah winter breathing down their necks. Those who were fortunate enough to cross over their own doorsteps sound and whole returned to their homes as different men.

The horrific battle at Point Pleasant on the Kanawha and Ohio had changed them forever. Boys had become men, and the careless and indifferent returned with a new seriousness of mind and heart.

All romantic notions of fame and glory had vanished, and only the realities of war with its brutality and death remained. The riflemen had tasted the coming revolution and fully understood the cost, considering well their part in this unfolding drama. Life was precious, but freedom to exercise one's own free will was more precious, more valued than life itself. The Patriots would sacrifice, they would pay the price.

It was late December when Daniel Morgan and the remaining militia riflemen returned to Frederick County. Harvest was over, but the continual need for wood, the care of the animals, and hunting wild game for food kept the men of the households active and busy. For the women, the work never ceased. Caring for the children, cooking, cleaning, and washing and mending clothes consumed their days. In good weather, the frontier families headed for the nearest village for necessary supplies. The latest news of the Colonies and the persistent rumors of war were continually rehashed about the villages.

Daniel Morgan had been home only a few days when the Mackenzies came to call. Alfred Mackenzie was not present since he was still nursing his leg wound, but Kearan and Lily Jayne accompanied Silas for an afternoon of "catching up."

In the home of Daniel Morgan and the Virginians, fires burned bright during the long winter months of 1775-76 and the men of the county anxiously waited for spring and news of the success or failure of the first Continental Congress which convened in Philadelphia in September, 1774.

The Colonial delegates met to consider their options in response to the Intolerable Acts, which sparked outrage and resistance among the Colonists. The King had issued a series of measures to curtail the growing rebellion in the Colonies, the latest of which the King named the Boston Tea Party.

The English crown was duly notified by the Continental Congress that the Colonists would boycott all British trade goods if their list of rights and grievances were not duly considered. If the Intolerable Acts were not rescinded speedily, another Continental Congress would convene in the spring to organize the defense of the Colonies and the onset of what would become the War for Independence.

Abigail set a lunch of pork pie and sweet potatoes on the table and the two neighboring families spoke of the tragic death of Thomas Aubrey and other neighbors who had lost family members in the battle. After much discussion, the talk around the fireside turned to matters that were more personal.

"Uncle Daniel, where do you think the Longhunter and Mr. Davidson have camped for the winter?" Kearan asked during a lull in the conversation. Silas and Daniel exchanged worried glances.

"Well, Kearan gal, you already know I was last to leave the Kanawha Valley for home, so me and the riflemen, we nosed around the area looking for their camp."

"Did you find it?" Kearan asked trying not to sound overly interested.

"Yep, we found it all right."

"Well?"

"Nobody home."

"What do you mean, Uncle Daniel?"

"Their camp was deserted," Morgan said with finality. He had hoped the conversation would not turn this direction during their first afternoon visit. Only he and Silas were aware of the startling evidence discovered at the camp of the Longhunter.

"You might as well tell the women folk, Dan'l," Silas suggested. "They'll be finding out sooner or later. Best be hearing it from your own mouth I say."

The women looked at each other in alarm. "What did you find, Daniel?" Abigail asked.

"Well, we found their camp all right, on the other side of the mountain not far from the Kanawha and Ohio. I reckon the Longhunter had no idea the army was camped on the other side of that range. His camp was well hidden, nestled among the trees in a hollow where nobody a traveling through the river valley could find him, just for safety, I reckon."

"How did they come to fight in the battle?" Kearan asked. Her hands clenched in her lap and she bit her bottom lip.

"Well, they must a heard the shooting or maybe saw the army just scoutin' around. Anyway, somethin' decided them to join the fight. They took up positions in the rocks on the western slope, firing down on the Indians most of the day accordin' to the army. You could see the black powder and shot all around them rocks. The Indians must a finally seen 'em, cause there was sign of some hand-to-hand fightin' a going on. Blood all around and evidence of a tussle twenty-five yards or so from them rocks. I followed their trail from the rocks and found their camp."

"But why weren't they in camp and where would they go after the battle, Daniel?" Abigail asked. "If the Longhunter were wounded, they couldn't have gone far. Surely you would have found them."

"We didn't find them, Abigail," Morgan said with finality, "so don't be lookin' like that." Abigail's face had drained of color and her hand grasped Daniel's arm.

"Perhaps it wasn't their camp at all," Lily Jayne suggested. "Lots of hunters pass through the Kanawha Valley and who's to say it was their camp."

"It was their camp, all right," Morgan said confidently. "I found positive evidence." He went to his pack where it hung on a peg by the kitchen door and fished out a package wrapped in a scrap of what appeared to be a torn buckskin shirt. Unfolding the material, he laid a well-used Gaelic testament on the table. Opening the cover, he read, *"This testament belongs to Donald Davidson of Ross-shire, now of Frederick County Virginia. This is his sword, the Sword of the Wild Rose."* Morgan paused, not wanting to say what he felt to be true.

"I don't think he would have left his Bible in camp," Morgan concluded.

"What are you saying, Daniel?" Abigail persisted. "Tell us plainly. It seems they left in a hurry and failed to bring the Bible along."

"No, Abby, I don't think so. The camp had Indian sign everywhere. We followed the trail to the river. The Longhunter was on a gurney pulled by his own packhorses. Derick was on foot. They were taken across the Ohio by the Hurons. We saw their sign."

"As captives, you mean? Oh no, not that!" wailed Abigail. "That is worse than being killed outright, worse than death in battle. How terrible, how awful. Oh, I cannot bear the thought!"

"Now, Abby, if anyone can get outta that mess, Derick Davidson can. With the Longhunter wounded, he couldn't do much and I reckon he wouldn't leave him. I'd a gone after him myself, but the trail was cold. Too many days had passed and they'd be deep in Indian Territory by the time we caught up. Besides, our men were worn to a frazzle and lookin' to home."

Kearan had gone pale, and her eyes were bright with tears. She reached for the testament and held it against her breast as though to hold the owner close to her heart. "Will the Indians torture them, Uncle Daniel?"

"Far as I know, when the Hurons take a captive, it's usually death at the stake, but I'm wonderin' if there's not something more to this here capture. For one thing, the Indians went outta their way to find their camp. Rarely do they mess with a wounded man. They just kill 'em. Why, they fixed up a gurney just to drag the Longhunter to the river, so they were wantin' him alive. That's a good sign, but we'll never know—probably never know what happened."

"Now, Lily Jayne," Silas said seeing her tears. "Derick Davidson is a smart man. Maybe he'll figure some way outta this mess. If'n he was on his own, he might manage to escape, but he won't leave his uncle, no by gum."

"The treaty that Dunmore and the Indian confederation signed in the Ohio country," Morgan acknowledged, "says that all prisoners are to be released, but then, who knows if they'll honor it. I don't even know if the Hurons signed it. The Mingos didn't. Chief Logan just sent a missive along with his personal grievance." The little company fell silent. There was nothing more to say.

Turning to Morgan, Kearan asked. "Will you keep Mr. Davidson's horse here at the farm until he returns? I have cared for Warrior ever since the men left Cedar Creek last autumn. He is used to me and trusts me. When I came over to the farm to check on things, I would take him out for a run and groom him too."

Daniel Morgan looked at his young neighbor with genuine sympathy. The long months of absence had not lessened her interest in the Scotsman, and despite his warnings and Derick's apparent lack of interest, she still thought about him, still cared for him. Morgan knew Kearan was trying valiantly to hold onto hope, to believe that the two men were still alive and would return one day. If she could care for the Scotsman's horse, then she could keep him alive in her heart.

"I know he left Warrior in your care, Uncle Daniel, but I would be happy to look after him until Derick returns."

"The stable hands can tend the horses, Kearan, but if'n it makes you happy, I don't mind you carin' for Warrior. Some usual kind of work is a pure distraction in these troublesome times. Heaven knows, we are scratchin' like an old hen for something to keep our minds thinkin' right. After all, Davidson left the stallion here at the farm since he's used to bein' here."

When their neighbors had left and the house was quiet, Daniel and Abigail sat by the fire listening to the rising wind of a winter storm. "Good to be home on a night like this, Abby, gal," Morgan said absently. He rested his head in his large hands, his elbows on his knees. His broad shoulders sagged. The long months of constant tension had been physically demanding and emotionally draining.

Abigail rose from her chair and went to him, seating herself on the bearskin rug by his side. She laid her head against his knee, saying nothing. Feeling her presence, he stroked her hair with his large hand, trailing one finger across her cheek. After a moment, he spoke. "What, Abby?"

"I'm so sorry, Daniel," she said taking his hand. "Derick was your friend—a close friend, I know. I wish it were not so...so clear-cut, so definite."

"The capture was definite, Abby, the outcome—well, that's still uncertain. I only hope Derick can escape before they torture him." A low growl came from deep in his chest.

"The whole affair makes me sick, Abby. The campaign itself was only a diversion from the real issues. Everything about it was terrible; the rugged country, the climate, the enemy—and to beat it all; we're not sure who's on what side."

"You are home now, Daniel. Try to think on other things. A man can only do so much."

"And it's never enough, Abby, never enough. War is comin' soon, and the British promise to smash our resistance into the very dust. The Colonies and the Patriots are hangin' on a meager thread spun from guts and passion. I only hope, Abby gal, that the thread doesn't snap." He sighed deeply, pulled his wife closer, and fervently wished for spring.

Chapter 15

Sachem of the Wyandots

The chief's house has a slippery doorstep

The stocky Indian in the front of the canoe lifted his paddle from the water, slowing their pace to allow the opposing current to carry them toward the riverbank. Derick sat in the middle of the canoe, his hands and feet bound. The Longhunter lay in the bottom with his good arm across his eyes, blocking out the glare of the sun. The day was clear and cold with a hint of wood smoke wafting in the breeze.

Derick studied the tall, stocky Indian, noting the well-formed muscles and his long straight torso that broadened into wide shoulder muscles that could paddle the canoe almost effortlessly. His black hair was straight and pulled into a scalp lock. Now and then, the Indians black eyes met Derick's blue eyes, and he could read a deep hatred in their shining depths.

After crossing the Ohio River, the war party had separated. Three of the Indians set out on foot leading the packhorses with the Longhunter's supply of food and traps for the winter hunt. The remainder of the party paddled up the Ohio to the mouth of a small river they called Hockhocking. From that point, the Indians paddled strenuously against the current, eager to return to their strongholds, away from any possible retaliation.

They had been traveling for several days, paddling against the current of this crooked little stream whose banks were edged with sprawling trees and a dense growth of tangled brush and tall grass. In some places, the stream was so shallow that the canoes had to be carried upstream until the river deepened again and the canoes could be returned to their watery track.

The Indians were less cautious as they proceeded upstream, and Derick sensed they were nearing their destination. When the party camped at night, Derick's bonds were removed and he remained under guard while they slept.

Traveling up the river, Derick devised a hundred different plans of escape, and at one point, an occasion had presented itself, but he refused to act on the opportunity. What would happen to the Longhunter if he left him alone with his captors?

Derick felt certain he could find his way back to the Ohio and east to Frederick County, but he could not abandon his uncle. Whatever fate awaited them at the Indian camp, they would meet it together.

At last, they reached their destination. The Indian warriors jumped into the water and dragged the canoes to a sandy bank, and then assisted the two prisoners to shore. A well-trodden path led from the river to a wide valley where tall stalks of corn stood barren and lifeless after the harvest. The soil beneath their feet was rich and dark, abundant with growing things. Dogs barked and children laughed, just as they did in the villages of the Colonials.

Pumpkin, squash, and a variety of gourds were stacked near the edge of the fields, waiting to be sorted and stored for the winter. Outside the wigwams, animal hides were stretched over long poles, drying in the late autumn sun. Derick could see the women bending over low fires, their cooking pots emitting odors of meat and vegetables that wetted his appetite.

An imposing company of Indians—men, women, and children, looked toward the party of returning Indians, all beginning to whoop and gabble in excited tones, and then running down the trail to meet them, black eyes shining with curiosity.

They had obviously arrived at a prominent Indian village, a stronghold deep in the heart of the Ohio country, a territory forbidden by treaty to the white man.

Each day on the journey west, one of the Indian braves had carefully tended to the Longhunter's wounds and Donald Davidson was gradually regaining a measure of strength. He was still very weak from loss of blood and could offer little resistance to his captors. The Indians understood that his chance of escape in his present condition would be very unlikely.

When still bound in the canoes, Derick tried to communicate with his uncle, but was soundly kicked when he spoke aloud to the Longhunter. The two men devised a silent code of eye movement and nods to communicate during the long passage to the Indian village. From every indication, it seemed that the Longhunter felt the time to escape was not yet.

Derick had been greatly relieved when his uncle began to slowly improve from his near death condition, but now, he questioned his pleasure in desiring his recovery. His uncle might meet a more horrendous death at the hands of the merciless Indians.

As they walked up the trail to the main part of the village, mangy mixed breed dogs nipped at their heels and children holding pointed sticks screamed and whooped, jabbing at the prisoners with pretentious bravery. The two captives were separated, and Derick was taken to a large bark-covered wigwam and shoved through the low opening. Once inside, his hands and feet were bound with buckskin cords and a guard was posted at the entrance.

He leaned against the poles supporting the bark structure, wondering what would happen next. The wigwam itself appeared solidly built, offering no easy escape. He looked around the crude dwelling with curiosity. In the center of the wigwam, a fire burned in a small circle of stones. A hole in the roof allowed the smoke to escape. Animal furs and various articles of clothing were folded neatly around the outer edges of the bark hut. Dried herbs hung from the curved poles and a cooking pot and stack of firewood stood by the entrance.

Loud voices penetrated the rough bark exterior of the wigwam; quarreling sounds, loud and insistent. In an hour or so, a guard entered the wigwam and jerked Derick to his feet. "Come," he said in English.

Derick followed the Indian to a long lodge style wigwam in the very center of the village. Inside the wigwam, a group of Indians all dressed in intricately beaded deerskin costumes sat around the fire. They appeared to be waiting for him. The Longhunter was not present.

Derick recognized the tall lanky Indian he had kicked in the stomach at the Longhunter's camp on the other side of the Ohio. The Indian had disappeared after the encounter, and Derick had not seen him again until now. Their eyes met and a slight nod from the Indian told Derick he was recognized.

The Indian wore the symbols of a Chief and his bearing was dignified and ceremonial for this occasion. Raising one hand, the chief signaled for silence. All turned to listen. He addressed Derick, speaking in halting English.

"I am Tarhe, the Crane, Chief of the mighty Wyandot people, Warrior of the Hurons Nation. Many winters, I live. I see much, I fight much. Tarhe's war club—red with white man's blood. Murder no good. I fight for Logan, my friend."

The chieftain paused, looking around at his comrades and then pointed to Derick. "You," he said pointing a long finger at Derick's chest, "you kill many warriors. My braves want death, want revenge for white enemy who murders."

Derick understood that Tarhe referred to the murder of Logan's family and knew the incident was a great offense to the entire Indian confederation. A blood feud had begun, and for some reason, he was being accused of the same base actions. Life or death hung in the balance, and this matter would be decided in this very council meeting. He must be extremely wise and cautious.

From the not so distant past, his own bloody revenge for Meagan's murder loomed up before him to taunt his conscience. If death was the outcome of this meeting, he would be getting no more than he had meted out by his own hand, his own personal blood feud. He drew in a deep breath.

"I am a warrior like yourself," Derick began. "Because I kill many in battle, you want to kill me?" He looked directly into the intense dark eyes of the chief. "Your reasoning is faulty. Great honor is given to the greatest warrior—not death and dishonor."

"You are not a soldier," Tarhe said flatly. "You come with the hunter. You kill from rocks. Your talk is from across the water. You are not a soldier."

"I fought with the soldiers on the Ohio that day. I do not murder your warriors without cause, only in battle."

The chief turned to the council gathered around the fire. "Does this man speak true?" He looked from one to the other.

"No soldier," said an Indian in halting English. "Shoot from rocks, kills many braves. Kill Standing Elk with long knife—long gun." The rest of the war council grunted in agreement, nodding their heads and talking in their native tongue in low guttural tones.

Derick recognized his accuser as the Indian who ran from the fight during the skirmish among the rocks. He turned to Tarhe and spoke. "Only during battle do I kill, not to murder," he affirmed. "Your Warriors came to kill us. I killed first." Then Derick spoke directly to his accuser. "You are no Warrior—you ran away from battle."

The outraged Indian rose to his feet and grabbed Derick by the shirt. He raised his tomahawk to strike a blow, and immediately two guards restrained their irate comrade. He shook them off, the intense hatred for the captive unmistakable. He seated himself on the hard-packed earthen floor, breathing heavily.

Tarhe spoke to the Warrior for several minutes in the Wyandot tongue, obviously displeased with his uncontrolled behavior. The dark piercing eyes of the Chief turned to Derick, boring into the face of the captive as though to read the countenance of the huge Scotsman.

"Bring the hunter," Tarhe said to a guard.

In a few moments, the Indian guard escorted the Longhunter into the wigwam. He was supported on either side by a young brave who seated him opposite Derick around the council fire. Tarhe raised his hand for silence.

"Hunter—friend of Tarhe, friend of Logan."

The Longhunter nodded his head and met Derick's eyes across the dancing flames. Although weak in body, he emulated peace and tranquility. A slight nod of his head signaled his confidence in the positive outcome of their plight.

"He kill," Tarhe said pointing to Derick. "He murder many braves from rocks. Murder Standing Elk with long knife, brother to Beaver Tail whose mother is Yellow Moon. Beaver Tail want death of white man for murder of Standing Elk. Hunter speak."

"Many years I hunt beside me brothers, the Indian people," said the Longhunter. "Never have I raised me hand against me Indian brothers—except in battle. Me nephew, me own blood kin, we fight for army—alone in rocks. All day we fight, and me wound is from the one ye call Standing Elk." He pulled up his shirt to show his wound. "This man," he said pointing to Derick, "kills Standing Elk in battle. No murder."

"You speak with crooked tongue, Hunter!" Beaver Tail raged. "Do not believe white man," he said turning to the council. "He murders Standing Elk. No cause, murders like Greathouse! Take head from Standing Elk. He cannot rest."

Outrage and indignation burst from the council like a crackling brush fire, and Tarhe raised his hand for silence. He addressed Derick. "You take head?"

"I did not, nor do I ever take any body part of those fallen in battle, not even a scalp as your people do."

Derick's eyes met those of his uncle. Both men knew he had deftly dispatched the Indian with his sword, but he had left the battle scene immediately, paying little attention to the fallen Indians. Removing the head from the body was a great offense to the Indian nation and not easily overlooked, even in a fair battle.

"Chief Tarhe," Derick said addressing the chief in deference to his authority, "is there one among your people who speaks the tongue of the white man and the tongue of the Wyandot? I would like to speak to the council so all may understand my words."

Tarhe thought for a moment and then motioned to a guard. He spoke to him briefly, and a few minutes later, the guard returned with a handsome dark-haired youth in his late teens. Although he wore the same buckskin clothing as the other warriors in the village, he was obviously a white man. His dark eyes shone with intelligence and he seemed confident and majestic in his bearing.

"Adopted son—White Eagle," Tarhe said with a measure of pride. "He speak. Come."

With his hands still bound, Derick left the council lodge and followed the guard and White Eagle to the same wigwam he had left earlier. The guard stepped outside the entrance, and Derick was left alone with the white Eagle.

The features of the white youth were strong and manly, but he bore little resemblance to his Indian father. White Eagle motioned for them to sit by the fire on a bearskin rug.

"Who are ye?" Derick finally asked, "and can ye translate from English to the Wyandot tongue?"

"Yes, I can translate," White Eagle answered in perfect English. "My name is Isaac Zane, son of the Zanes of Virginia, brother to Ebenezer, Silas, and Jonathan. The Wyandots captured me when I was nine years old while returning from school to my home near the south branch of the Potomac River. I have lived among the Wyandots for most of that time. Now and then, I manage to escape, but my Indian father, Tarhe, who has a great fondness for me, always brings me back. I am treated well and am not unhappy, but I miss my family in Virginia."

The young man spoke rapidly, glad for this opportunity to speak to another white man. He abruptly changed the subject. "Who are you and what have you done that your life is in danger?"

Derick drew a ragged breath. "I am Derick Davidson, recently from Frederick County. The Longhunter and meself were camping near the Ohio, preparing for the winter hunt. By mere chance, we came upon the battle at the river. The army needed help so we hid among the rocks overlooking the camp and shot our rifles from there. A small party of Indians confronted us in a bloody skirmish. One they call Standing Elk threw his tomahawk striking the Longhunter. I killed Standing Elk in self-defense and the others in active battle. One warrior ran away. He is me accuser. Says I murdered Standing Elk without cause. This is not true. I do not believe they understand. Can you help me?"

The youth looked doubtful. "The warriors with Beaver Tail were his brothers. He seeks revenge. I do not respect him for his cowardice. All the warriors who were at the battle seek vengeance. They wish to strike back for their defeat on the river. There is much talk about the white prisoners. They are happy for a captive to kill, to give a voice to their anger.

"They captured us after the battle, at our camp, so I don't consider us prisoners of war. We were kidnapped from our hunting camp."

White Eagle shrugged his shoulders. "That makes little difference to the Indians. They consider all white men to be trespassing on their lands. I will explain to them, but it is doubtful they will listen. My Indian father, Tarhe, will try to trade or maybe ask for ransom, but the warriors want to kill. Many braves were lost at the river. I believe sir, you must prepare for the worst."

Derick's mind reeled, wondering what "the worst" might be. Would his life end in a fiery death and seeming dishonor? Perhaps it was God's justice. After all, he had exacted vengeance on those who murdered Meagan. Why should he expect less from Beaver Tail? He would reap what he had sown.

"Will they kill the Longhunter too?" Derick asked.

The youth shook his head. "No, they will keep him. He will help them hunt—trap, like the white man. Our hunters have watched him for many years, and he is a friend to the Indian. He brings good luck, good hunting, and many skins."

Such welcome news caused Derick much relief. The Longhunter would be spared. "If I am to die, can you get a message across the river?"

"Perhaps, but it will take time, maybe years. I thought you might be exchanged, but after hearing your story, I doubt it."

"If ye ever return to your people again, lad, find Daniel Morgan of Frederick County. Tell him what happened here. Say Derick Davidson died here and..." The words seemed to stick in his throat. "...ask him to get word to me family in Scotland. Tell Morgan. He was me true friend."

The youth nodded. "I will tell him, Mr. Davidson. I have a long memory—I will not forget. I will do all I can to save your life."

"If you are free to go, why do you stay?" Derick asked.

"My Indian father, Tarhe, has no son, and he loves me fervently. He knows my heart is sad at times, so he watches me closely. I have escaped before and lived with my white family, the Zanes. When I miss my Indian family, I come back to the Wyandots." The White Eagle shook his head in perplexity. "It is not easy to belong to both worlds."

White Eagle rose to his feet signaling an end to their talk.

"Shall I speak to the council?" Derick asked.

"I believe I should speak in your behalf, Mr. Davidson. Although I am young, I have influence because of my father and my white heritage." He smiled. "I will try to stop the warriors from spilling more blood. Your presence will only anger them. They will not listen to reason when angry. If they want vengeance, they will not listen to Tarhe, my Indian father. I will try, Mr. Davidson, but it does not look good for you. Even now, they are gathering wood for the fire." He paused at the door flap of the wigwam. "I will return after I speak with the council."

The guard posted at the entry returned and Derick's feet were bound together tightly with buckskin cords. He was shoved against the far side of the bark hut, and the guard gave him a solid kick for good measure.

In the council lodge of the Wyandots, Isaac Zane, adopted son of Chief Tarhe, pleaded for the life of the white prisoner.

Several hours later, White Eagle returned. His expression was grim and he shook his head as he ducked through the low door. "I'm sorry," he said to Derick, "but I did all I could. The warriors are crazy. They want a reason to satisfy their anger and you are here. That is good reason. My father feels Beaver Tail is not telling the truth, but the other warriors support his claim. They witnessed against you. Tarhe is trying to persuade the warriors to ask for ransom. He says you are an important man; kill many men in battle, a brave warrior." The White Eagle looked hopeful. "Will the British pay?"

Derick's heart sank. This was too unbelievable, too incredible. The British would not only refuse to pay ransom—they would help the Indians kill him! King George's men would be gathering wood with the rest of the tribe. His flight from Scotland doubtless left the British authorities wondering over his disappearance and notifying the British army of his whereabouts would only serve as an opportunity for the Crown to arrest him if the Indians didn't execute him first.

"Nay, lad, the British will not raise a ransom. I am not officially in the British army. I...I am," he paused, the words coming from a conviction deep inside him, "...a Patriot. I will not fight with the British. I came to this land to be free from English tyranny. Why would I fight for them?"

"But you did fight with the British army at the river."

"I fought with the Patriots—the frontiersmen, the settlers, the riflemen. Those are the Patriots. The British army with Lord Dunmore did not fight. They didn't even show up for the battle. I fight to live free, White Eagle—for liberty."

A slow smile spread across White Eagle's handsome features, and he spoke with Indian-like candor, "Freedom? All who live seek freedom. The Great Spirit made every brother and sister, white, red, or black to live as free people. We resist and revolt when men or rulers seize our liberty." He shook his head solemnly.

"Contrary to what you might think, the Wyandots want to live in peace with the whites, but they wish to exist as they always have, on their own lands. So, we fight to save our lands, our way of life. We fight for our freedom as you do."

The fire burned low in the circle of stones and Derick's heart felt like a lead weight. His feet began to tingle from the tightness of his bonds and he strained at the cords in an effort to stretch them. He turned to White Eagle.

"Ye are a smart lad, Isaac Zane. Ye see on both sides of the castle wall. I came to this land to find a home, not to gain wealth and lands, but to live as I choose. The people who settled this land came for the same reason—to be free. There must be some way to find this freedom." He sighed heavily and then looked questioningly at White Eagle. "For me, the quest will soon be over."

Isaac Zane could hear the hopelessness and despair in Derick's voice. "Do not give up hope, sir. The one you call Longhunter is speaking with the council now. They have known him as a friend and seem to respect his words."

White Eagle left the wigwam, and Derick was alone again inside the bark hut with two guards posted at the entrance. He worked feverishly at loosening his bonds, but the leather was impossible to stretch loose enough to work his hands free. Now that he knew the Longhunter would not be killed, he would take his chances and try to escape if the opportunity came.

In late afternoon, an Indian woman brought some water in a gourd and held it to Derick's lips. He drank greedily having had no water since morning. She added more wood to the fire and left the wigwam. He could smell food cooking on the open fires outside the neighboring wigwams and his stomach growled impatiently.

From the direction of the council lodge, an outbreak of loud voices and whooping echoed through the village. Perhaps, Derick thought, his fate had been decided.

In a few minutes, Chief Tarhe, Isaac Zane, and the Longhunter entered the wigwam. They helped Derick to his feet and he could tell from his uncle's countenance that the council meeting had not gone in his favor. Chief Tarhe spoke first.

"Many warriors say you speak with crooked tongue, you kill Standing Elk and his brothers. Say you not soldier fighting at the Kanawha. You take head of Standing Elk. Say you must die in fire."

Derick looked straight into the dark eyes of the chief. "What do ye say, Chief Tarhe? Do ye think I murdered Standing Elk and took his head?"

The Chief stood erect, crossing his arms over his chest. He was a tall man, at least six feet and four inches, and his muscles were sinewy and strong. He towered above the rest of the warriors, but looked eye to eye with Derick Davidson. He considered the question, careful in his response.

"Many times, Tarhe speaks. His council listens; they follow wisdom of their chief. No more do they listen. Anger flames like fire inside them. For Standing Elk, for Logan, for what is coming to our people, they hate. Defeat—more treaties. How long?" Tarhe's eyes held an infinite sadness. He studied the face of his captive before speaking again.

"White men break treaties. Tarhe not stop the anger of his people. He not stop the white man's feet. He comes again. Always, he comes. Tarhe wants peace. No peace. He fights for his home until hair is white like snow. Tarhe has sorrow." After a long moment of silence, he said, "Tarhe has no more words. His heart is run away."

From the sadness evidenced in Tarhe's eloquent speech, Derick understood that the warriors demanded his death. He was falsely accused, but the tide of insurrection had swept away any hope of justice. Their own chief could not persuade them otherwise.

The Longhunter's countenance was pale and his wound throbbed from sitting long hours around the council fire. White

Eagle helped him to sit down by the fire in the circle of stones. Weak and sick at heart, the Longhunter began to speak to Derick.

"Did what we could, lad, but this incident has turned into a blood feud of the worst kind. They say you took Standing Elk's head so he is doomed in the after-life to wander about with no head. I testified that this was not true, but they want a death sentence. It's a set up I'm a thinkin'." He shook his head incredulously.

"Tarhe can overrule the council's decision, but if he does, he'll have a grand rebellion on his hands, especially if he takes me word over five of his warriors. But take courage, lad, I have another sword."

Isaac Zane spoke next, addressing Derick. "My father persuaded the council to wait three days before the death sentence is carried out. By then, their anger will cool some and perhaps we can offer the council another plan. It would take too long to get outside help. Let's hope some other means will arise."

Despite long hours around the council fire, Chief Tarhe of the Wyandots looked regal in his blackened buckskin tunic and leggings. Symbols of the porcupine clan and the Wyandot tribe were painted on the exterior of his tunic and his dress moccasins were intricately beaded and fringed with dyed quillwork. A beaded and embroidered pouch hung from his left shoulder, fashioned from the highest quality of deer hide. As he turned to leave he said to Derick, genuine sincerity in his voice, "I am Ne-at-a-rugh—your friend."

When Tarhe neared the exit, Derick called after him. "Wait, Ne-at-a-rugh—Chief Tarhe, if I must die in three days, allow Longhunter to stay with me in me wigwam."

White Eagle quickly translated for Chief Tarhe who already understood the white man's request. He nodded solemnly. "Blue Eyes keep. Hunter stay."

Tarhe and White Eagle left the wigwam, speaking instructions to the guards as they passed out into the cold winter evening. The stars glittered in the heavens high above the earth and the fires burned low in the wigwams of the Wyandot village. The moon rose over a huge rock formation the Wyandots called Standing Stone, and the moonbeams shimmered on the Hockhocking River, making a golden path on the water.

The guards entered the wigwam and removed Derick's bonds leaving him free to move about the interior of the bark hut. After he made a bed on the bearskin rugs for the Longhunter, his uncle fell instantly asleep. The Longhunter was completely exhausted after the long ordeal at the Indian council.

Derick rubbed his swollen feet and wrists and began to examine the wigwam for some way of escape, fearing the guards would soon return to fasten his restraints. Chief Tarhe's words came to mind, I am Ne-at-a-rugh, your friend. His words sent a silent message of hope, perhaps an opportunity for escape before the three days expired. He must be patient, but he must be ready.

The cooking pot and utensils had been removed from the wigwam. Derick saw nothing he could use to dig or cut. All his weapons had been taken from him He had no gun, knife, or sword, and he saw nothing in the wigwam that would serve as a possible weapon. He might try to remove one of the supporting poles, but if he attempted to dismantle the wigwam, the guards would hear him.

Every so often, one of the guards looked in to make certain the captive was not improvising a means to escape. In addition, four stalwart Indian guards were placed around the circumference of the wigwam to insure that no one entered or left without their knowledge.

After hours of mulling over possible escape plans, Derick lay down on the hard-packed earthen floor of the wigwam. The fire was warm, and the small room was amazingly comfortable for a cold winter night. He was grateful that the guard had not returned to bind his hands and feet. Perhaps he had forgotten. If he were to escape, he must be free from those miserable buckskin thongs.

Derick reached in his pocket and felt for the locket that held a likeness of Meagan, the wife he had loved and lost. The Indians had missed the keepsake while searching his person for weapons. He opened the tiny gold locket with the fine gold chain and held it close to the firelight. His life with Meagan had been more than simply a man with a lass. They had known love; unfeigned, undisguised, and true. Meagan was gone now and he longed to move past this unrelenting hurt, but how?

The years he had shared with his wife seemed so long ago, in another lifetime, another world. Two years had passed since he had boarded the ship in Scotland to sail across the ocean and find a new home in the American Colonies.

William, his babe, would be nearly three years, and his other children, Kate, Duncan, and Alasdair, would be learning to read and write letters. He wondered if they thought about their father, maybe longed to see him again. He wondered if Doran told them stories of their exploits as children growing up in the Highlands, of Clan Davidson and their home by the sea, the land where fog rolls in from the North Seas to mix with the mist and tears of his people.

He sighed deeply, knowing this unbidden introspection came from the knowledge that if he didn't find a way to escape from the Wyandots, he would never see his bairns again; never find the freedom he longed for.

Despite his plan to stay awake, he began to drift off from sheer exhaustion and the extreme tension of the day. As he hovered between wakefulness and sleep, another face floated from the mist, drifting waif-like before him. It was Kearan, her dark hair falling about her face as she spun circles in the snow on a moonlit winter night.

CHAPTER 16

Man Without a Sword

Lofty is the deer's head
On the top of the mountain

Derick felt a hand shaking his shoulder, instantly awakening him from sleep. He instinctively reached for his dirk, but it was not there. The same hand covered his mouth, and a man's voice breathed a warning, "Quiet, lad, it's your uncle."

Derick relaxed again, sucking in a ragged breath. The fog clouding his mind cleared, and he remembered—he was a captive in the Wyandot village, a prisoner awaiting a horrible death at the fiery stake. The reality of his situation assaulted his consciousness, apprising him of the present and oppressing his mind with the absolute certainty of his impossible predicament.

"Talk," the Longhunter whispered, "before the village stirs about. I be rested, feeling stronger, lad. Are ye with me now?"

"Aye."

All was quiet outside the wigwam while the village slept. Only the occasional barking of a dog could be heard in the distance. Perhaps the guards were sleeping too. The fire in the circle of stones was reduced to hot coals that glowed red and gold, reflecting off the walls of the wigwam. Inside the hut, the air had grown chilly and damp. The Longhunter was sitting up, propped against a lodge pole. Derick sat up, shaking the last remnants of sleep from his weary mind. He moved close to the Longhunter.

"I've a wee suggestion," the Longhunter said in a whisper.

"Aye, let's hear it," Derick answered. He put his finger to his lips, crawled to the door of the wigwam, and listened intently. He heard nothing, crawled back to the Longhunter, and nodded. "Say on, Uncle."

"Ye canna wait long to leave this fine lodging. They be watching closely, expecting ye to break out the night before your execution." The Longhunter grimaced at his own words. "So ye must disappear before they be expecting it."

"Tonight?" Derick whispered.

"Nay, too late. It's near dawn."

"Aye, but remember, Uncle, they be tired from the journey up the river, the long council yesterday."

"True, but there's no time. Ye need meat—water."

"I am a Highlander, Uncle. I will survive."

"What will ye do?" queried the Longhunter.

"Use what I have. Will ye help me?"

The Longhunter smiled in the dimness of the wigwam. "Aye, lad, ye needn't ask."

Derick picked up a good-sized rock from the circle of stones. "This be a bonny weapon," he said in a whisper. "I'm thinking Indians don't count rocks. The Scots are the bonniest rock throwers they be. Have ye forgotten, Uncle?"

"Nay, I've not forgotten, but it's many a year since I threw a rock at a man, but I can use one as a wee club."

"I don't want them to know you're a helping me, Uncle.

"I'm nary a threat to the Indians, lad. Beaver Tail is a holding a grudge agin ye. I be in no real danger."

"Aye, and I don't want ye to be. If only I had me sword, Uncle, then perhaps me escape plan would work."

In muffled tones, Derick described his strategy with the Longhunter who added his approval and input. After all, Derick thought, he had nothing to lose if he were going to die anyway. Even if he were killed in the attempt, it would be far more merciful to die from a bullet or a blow from a tomahawk than a slow death by fire. Maybe, just maybe he would survive.

A faint light began to streak the eastern sky with pale pinkish smudges that spread across the treetops of the nearby forest. Songbirds twittered and flew among the branches, announcing the approach of another day. Outside the wigwam where the white captives awaited the outcome of their plight, the night guards were replaced with fresh sentinels who spoke eagerly in the low melodic language of the Wyandot people.

Derick heaved a sigh of disappointment. "Too late this night, Uncle," he murmured softly, "The village is stirring, but if the occasion arises even now—be ready." The Longhunter nodded, and Derick replaced the stones in the circle, hoping no one would discover his intention to use them. He was proficient at throwing rocks with deadly accuracy, as were most Highlanders. The Crown had made it unlawful for the Scots to bear arms of any kind or to own weapons, so they devised their own natural weaponry from the land. They became skilled in using slingshots, rocks, and poles as deadly missiles in their own unique covert warfare.

Well after the sun was up, the guards escorted an Indian woman into the wigwam. Her face was flat and expressionless, and she did not speak. She handed Derick and the Longhunter a dish of venison stew and a gourd of water and then added wood to the fire. After she left the wigwam, Derick quickly removed two pieces of wood from the fire and hid them under the bearskin rug. Both men ate and drank all the food and water the woman left for them. In the days to come, they would need their strength.

"Why do ye suppose they haven't replaced our bonds, Uncle? Doesn't seem logical," Derick pointed out. "Not that I wish to be bound," he grinned.

"Me guess is that Tarhe fixed it up. Prisoners are usually bound and gagged, with only enough food and water to keep them alive until they be executed." He lifted his hunting shirt to expose his wound, then asked. "How does it look today, lad?"

"Better," Derick replied, "and ye seem stronger in your spirit, Uncle."

"I be that, lad." He touched the wounded area on his shoulder and said, "It beats all—they patch me up after nigh killing me."

"Because ye are profitable to them. I recollect ye saying ye might want to live among the Indians, aye?"

"Aye, so I did say, but on me own terms, lad. I be blessed it be Tarhe kidnapped me, not some bloodthirsty Shawnee or Mohawk. I hear talk among the trappers. They say Tarhe is a just man, doesn't abide mindless torture. Ye are the exception, of course." The Longhunter smiled wryly and Derick grunted.

"That makes me feel real guid, Uncle," Derick said.

"His white son, Isaac Zane, the White Eagle of the Wyandots, has influence with Tarhe, that's certain," the Longhunter added, "so that's in you're favor. Tarhe's wife died several years ago and she was always agin torturing prisoners. A white French woman she was. I hear tell from the trappers that she was some kind of nobility, very bonny, they say. She and Tarhe had a daughter, Myeerah, and Tarhe adores the lass. Some say the lass and White Eagle will marry."

The flap of the wigwam was thrown back and Tarhe and White Eagle entered, their faces expressionless and void of emotion. Tarhe's eyes quickly surveyed the room, and he and White Eagle sat down by the fire next to the two captives. After several moments of silence, Tarhe spoke. "Dinyehta," he said in his native tongue. "Snow. Come soon. Many snows. Hunter well. Strong. Trap, hunt."

Derick and the Longhunter nodded, and then Tarhe pointed to White Eagle, signaling him to speak.

"My father, Chief Tarhe, wants the hunter to know that we admire his ability in the hunt. We mean no harm to the Hunter. You have Tarhe's word. We wish for him to go with our warriors on the winter hunt. Game is growing scarce as white men trespass upon our hunting ground. We must become more skillful to get enough meat to feed our people. We trade skins for blankets and the things we need. Hunter has traps with big teeth. Tarhe wishes to know if you will hunt with the Wyandots and not run away."

The Longhunter rubbed his beard thoughtfully, his blue eyes fastening on the handsome face of White Eagle. He saw no treachery on his countenance and felt he was speaking the truth. The Longhunter turned to Chief Tarhe.

"Ye hold me nephew captive. Ye will kill him in the fire in two days. How can I hunt with warriors who would murder me kin?"

White Eagle rapidly translated the Longhunter's words to his father.

"Blue Eyes—great warrior," Tarhe said. "He not die in fire."

Derick exhaled a lungful of air in a burst of impatience. "I mean no disrespect, Chief Tarhe, but ye speak in riddles. I do not understand your speech." For the first time, Derick saw a flicker of humor rising in the Chief's eyes.

Tarhe was not an old warrior, but rather young for a chief, a handsome man with pale skin and black eyes. He was tall and lean with a very masculine presence. White Eagle could have been his brother instead of a son. However, Tarhe had no son and White Eagle was his choice, what he considered honorable in a son of a Wyandot chief.

"Blue Eyes free," Tarhe said to Derick. "You go. Hunter happy. Make long hunt."

"How can I go?" Derick asked. "I am continually under guard, and the warriors will kill me if I try to escape."

Tarhe shrugged his shoulders indifferently and turned to White Eagle, waiting for him to speak his thoughts in English.

"My father knows you will find a way," White Eagle explained. "Last night, the moon rose over the Hockhocking to shine upon the face of Standing Stone. Your face returned to him from the surface of the stone. You are a brother, a warrior from the great tribe who came across the water many lifetimes before the white man became our enemy."

"I have never been your enemy, nor have me people," Derick said in defense. "Explain what ye mean."

White Eagle translated, and Tarhe indicated that his adopted son should speak for him.

"Long ago," White Eagle began in the resonate voice of the storyteller, "our grandfathers lived north of the O-Hi-O in the land of long winters. A ship filled with mighty warriors with very pale skin arrived from across the great water, and we welcomed the strangers. Our hearts knitted together with these warriors. Some had eyes like the sky on a clear day. They called themselves Viking. We lived together in peace and harmony for many years, sharing all that we had." White Eagle hesitated, but his father urged him to go on with the legend.

"The Viking warriors married our young maidens, and our skin became pale. After many winters, the Viking warriors went away, and for two lifetimes, no man came from across the water. Later, others came who were not like the Viking. They had a King who wanted our land. They brought the spotted disease and death to our people. Some brought strange gods and told us we must worship the queen of heaven or burn in the fires of the afterlife. They call themselves Jesuit. It was a sad time for the Wyandot who the French call Huron." White Eagle pointed to the bearskin rug he was sitting on.

"They took our hunting grounds so the Wyandot left the land of long winters and came to the O-Hi-O where we are to this day. Our grandfathers never forgot the Viking warriors and told us not to forget. They said our blood ran together, and our hearts were as one."

"Stand, brother!" Tarhe said to Derick. A rare smile lit up the Chief's face as though he had revealed a great secret.

Derick stood, hoping Tarhe would escort him out of the village to safety, despite the opposition of his own warriors who demanded his blood. The two men were exactly the same height and Tarhe looked directly into the eyes of the tall Scotsman, one his equal.

"I am Ne-at-a-rugh—friend. Come," Tarhe said to Derick.

Tarhe and White Eagle left the wigwam without further explanation and Derick obediently followed. They walked to another long wigwam at the center of the village that was larger than most of the other dwellings. Tarhe threw back the deerskin flap to the entrance and motioned for Derick to follow. For one brief moment, Derick thought this might be a trap. He hesitated, trying to peer into the dim interior of the wigwam.

Isaac Zane, White Eagle spoke. "Enter in peace, Mr. Davidson, and do not fear. This is my father's longhouse."

Derick entered the bark house that was similar in structure to other wigwams in the village. This dwelling was longer and more spacious as suited the house of a chief. Clothing and deer hides hung from the lodge poles and intricate beadwork and wampum belts decorated the walls. Fur rugs and blankets were scattered on the hard-packed earthen floor. Various weapons, cooking utensils, and a small wooden chest completed the furnishings of the first room. A wall of woven reeds served to divide the dwelling into two separate rooms with fires burning in the center of each room.

A young girl of about sixteen came around the partition and startled in alarm at the appearance of this strange white man in her home. Tarhe spoke to the young woman in rapid Wyandot and she glanced furtively at White Eagle for confirmation. White Eagle nodded, then spoke.

"This is Myeerah, Walk-in-the-Water, Chief Tarhe's daughter, and his only child." Isaac Zane smiled broadly. "So that is why he needed a son. He found me to his liking and brought me to the Wyandot village. I am deeply honored that he chose me, but it is not the best way to get a son."

Derick could not help smiling. "Why didn't your family pay ransom for you?"

"They tried many times, but Tarhe wouldn't give me up. My brother, Jonathan was ransomed. We were captured at the same time."

Tarhe understood most of what the White Eagle had said and laid his hand affectionately on White Eagle's shoulder. "Son, great chief, Homayuwaneh."

The young girl listening attentively by the fire in the circle of stones had creamy white skin and deep green eyes. Her thick brown hair hung to her waist in long braids. She was tall, regal in her bearing, and beautiful to look upon. She was definitely Tarhe's daughter although her white ancestry dominated her noble features.

Derick offered his hand to the young maiden. Myeerah glanced at White Eagle and he nodded his approval. She stepped forward and took Derick's hand and he bent over the slender fingers and kissed them. Myeerah's eyes opened wide in astonishment and she blushed to the roots of her hair, not certain what to do next. White Eagle laughed heartily and Tarhe smiled.

"I am pleased to meet ye, Myeerah," Derick said in a gentle voice. "I only wish our meeting could have been under different circumstances."

The White Eagle laughed again and translated the Scotsman's words to Myeerah and Tarhe. Myeerah dropped her eyes, awed at meeting a white man from another culture.

"My father wished for you to meet his daughter," Isaac Zane said. "Her mother was French nobility, and she and Tarhe fell in love when he was visiting Detroit. They married at a young age—perhaps sixteen. Myeerah's mother died several years ago, and he feels a great sadness in his heart for the woman he loved. He sees the same sadness in the Blue Eyes."

Derick was stunned. He did not know how to respond to this unusual insight from the Wyandot chief. How did this Indian know he shared the same sorrow? His eyes met Tarhe's in mutual empathy. "I truly understand the magnitude of your loss. Tis a great sorrow to bear."

After White Eagle translated, Tarhe nodded his understanding and then spoke a few words to Myeerah. The three men left the longhouse, returning the captive to the wigwam used to hold the prisoners.

Giving the guards a cursory glance, Derick entered the wigwam alone and seated himself by the fire, shaking his head in frustration. "I don't know what to make of all this, Uncle. Tarhe takes me to meet his daughter like we're on a social call and then tells me I be free to go. What on God's green earth is he a sayin', and how am I supposed to, 'just go'? How can I leave this wretched wigwam with four guards waiting outside to tomahawk me if I try? Ye be telling me that, Uncle."

"I know ye were hoping Tarhe would make it easy on ye, lad, but it looks like ye will be needing the rocks after all. Reckon he wanted ye to meet his daughter because he's not expecting ye to stay around." A smile curved the lips of the Longhunter.

"I believe Tarhe is leaving ye to your own devices. He's left ye unbound. That's about the best he can do, but he's not about to give ye a bloomin' escort to the river. Ye are on your own, lad."

That night, the cooking fires blazed brightly outside the wigwams, and the Indian village abounded with excitement. Special foods sizzled and popped over the fires, and the women chattered and laughed as they prepared the feast for the next day. A ceremonial dance would take place to honor the brave warriors who fell at the battle on the Kanawha. The bodies would be escorted to the ancient burial ground where Chief Tarhe would speak to the families and the tribe.

The same Indian woman brought food and water and after she left, Derick turned to the Longhunter and said quietly. "It might be best to make an escape when the tribe is mourning the dead at the burial grounds. What do ye think?"

"I think they'll tie us up during the ceremonies tomorrow so they won't need to bother with watching us. They'll be wanting to enjoy the feasting or whatever they do," the Longhunter pointed out. "Ye best be a high tailing it out tonight, lad. The warriors be all wound up tomorrow and looking forward to when they can put ye in the fire. I say don't wait. Go late tonight, lad, after they're tired from all this here ruckus."

After the village had settled into sleep, Derick and the Longhunter waited for the guards to grow sleepy. "What if they blame ye, Uncle?" Derick asked. "Ye might end up the worse for it."

"Don't ye worry about me, lad. I'll blame ye, of course," he said smiling. "You're the one they'll see before a rock hits them in the head."

Derick held a large stone in one hand and the stick of firewood in the other. In his pockets, he carried the remnants of food he had managed to save from their meals. He was ready for the escape. With his heart pounding, he approached the exit. If he failed, the guards might tomahawk him on the spot. The Longhunter nodded and threw back the deerskin flap for Derick. The two guards posted at the entrance were bobbing their heads, weary from the activity of the day.

Before the first Indian could raise his head, the stone crashed against his temple and he crumpled silently to the ground. The guard on the other side of the door jerked awake just in time to see the club poised above his head and then he crashed to the ground in a senseless heap.

Derick grabbed up a knife and tomahawk and sprinted through the village toward the river but not before the rear guards came from the back of the wigwam, alerted by the sound of the falling Indian. They gazed at their prostrate comrades in disbelief and darted into the wigwam.

The Longhunter lay on his bed, rising up to peer at the guards as though being awakened from sleep. The Indians hastily exited the wigwam to alert the village. Dogs were barking and several warriors emerged in a lethargic manner from their wigwams. Within a few minutes, a party of warriors formed a search party and ran toward the Hockhocking, knowing the river would offer the fastest means of escape.

On the banks of the Hockhocking River, Derick slammed a rock into the bottom of the overturned canoes and shoved all but one into the river. He leapt into the remaining canoe and paddled swiftly away, glad for the cover of night and the water current moving in the same direction as he paddled downstream. He heard the barking of dogs and paddled to the far side of the river where he would be less visible. Rounding the first bend in the river, Derick heard the wild yelping of the Indians as they searched frantically for their canoes, dragging several from the frigid water. He hoped he had smashed the canoes hard enough to make them leak and slow the progress of the search party.

Several Indians had set out on foot, hoping to overtake the white captive before he could get too far down river. A path stretched parallel to the riverbank in close proximity to the village. Angry warriors dashed along this well-traveled footpath, yelping their war cries and peering toward the river. The sky remained overcast, obscuring the moon from view, and making it difficult to see through the semi-darkness. The river was the best road for traveling at night. Only one canoe was undamaged by the heavy thrust of the Scotsman's stone.

When the trail along the river ended, the warriors would have to clear a path through the brush and thick woods to keep up with the canoe. If they could not catch the Scotsman before the trail ran out, the runners would have to turn back.

Three Indians following in the canoe were gaining on Derick. They were making quick time with the additional paddlers. Derick glanced over his shoulder to see the canoe of Indians rounding the bend not far behind him. His strong arms dipped the paddle in and out of the water in quick succession, but the three irate warriors were still coming. Finally, one fired a musket, but the shot fell short, splashing in the water a good ten yards from Derick's canoe. It would have been pure luck if the shot found its mark: he was barely visible in the darkness, and the Indians were poor shots.

At a series of bends and twists in the river, Derick saw a thick clump of brush growing near the water. He paddled to shore and quickly pulled the canoe into the dense thicket.

He ran quickly along the river just as the first faint light of dawn began to penetrate the eastern horizon spreading a gray mist across the river. A large sandstone rock formation jutted across the river and he scrambled on top and lay flat on his stomach. From this vantage point, he could see the river below, but there was no access to the rock face from the riverside. The progress of the Indians had slowed since they were now bailing water from the canoe with their hands. Derick stood, watching for the perfect moment, and then hurled the first rock toward the canoe of Indians. It hit with a thud against the side of the leader's head, and he slumped forward.

The remaining two Indians looked nervously toward the riverbank and finally spotted Derick just as he hurled another jagged rock. The projectile flew with amazing force through the rising mist on the river and hit the Indian in the throat. Blood spurted from the wound like a pulsating geyser. Wild yelping ensued and the remaining Indian paddled rapidly toward the bank as the canoe sank lower in the water.

Derick climbed from the rock and began to run inland. He ran swiftly, glancing over his shoulder to see if the Indian was pursing him. He ran for miles, pacing himself at a manageable speed, a habitual practice of endurance when running from the King's men in the Highlands. He topped the crest of a hill and stopped short. A party of five Indians were advancing in his direction.

A young buck was hanging from a pole supported on the shoulders of two warriors. They halted in mute surprise, not certain what to think of this lone white man in the wilderness. They dropped the buck to the ground and reached for their weapons. Derick pulled the knife and a tomahawk from his belt and waited.

One of the warriors gave three short yelps and charged, his tomahawk raised. Derick stayed rooted to the spot until the last possible moment, and then dodged, grabbing the warrior by his scalp lock. Derick Davidson was powerfully built, and at six feet four inches, he dwarfed the smaller Indian.

Before Derick could dispatch the flailing Indian, a wild whoop erupted from one of the warriors who held up his hand in the sign of peace, speaking rapidly in the Wyandot tongue. To Derick's surprise, they all lowered their weapons, and raised their hands for peace.

Derick dropped the Indian to the ground, and the warrior rolled away from the large hulk of a man. Peace was a good option since he was outnumbered one to five. The Indian spoke to his companions, and a lively debate followed. The Indian suing for peace laid down his weapons and came to stand before Derick.

"Me, The-nain-ton-to—the Red Fox."

Derick studied the young Indian brave who looked vaguely familiar. He searched his memory for some clue.

The Indian held up his hand. "Many moons. We fight. Long knife say, 'no kill'. Blue eyes speak. I go." The Indian held up his arm before Derick's eyes. There was a large knot where the bone had been broken at the wrist.

Suddenly, Derick remembered. He and Morgan had encountered this same Red Fox in an ambush on the way to Virginia. Morgan would have killed the Indian except for his intervention. After the battle, when the Indian had returned to consciousness, Morgan suggested that he kill the prisoner with a thrust of his claymore, but he had refused. He would not kill a wounded man. Morgan, disgusted at his refusal, had simply pointed the Indian to the forest and said, "Go!"

"Me go. me live," Red Fox said smiling at Derick. "Long knife go." Red Fox pointed to the forest. "Red Fox, Ne-at-a-rugh—friend. No forget Blue Eyes."

Derick nodded and then clasped Red Fox by the forearm in a gesture of alliance and friendship. "Ne-at-a-rugh—friend," Derick repeated. The rest of the hunting party did not seem as forgiving. He was trespassing on their hunting grounds and he was a white man, the foe of the red man. Derick knew the hunting party could overpower Red Fox and take control of the situation. Red Fox, however, seemed to hold some authority with the party and was perhaps the leader.

They were obviously unaware of what had transpired at the Wyandot village. One of the Indians was looking curiously at the tomahawk Derick had returned to his belt. He still held the knife in one hand. Immediately, anger flashed in the warrior's dark eyes and a loud protest burst from his lips. He pointed at the tomahawk, his face twisting in anger.

A hot dispute developed between Red Fox and the contending warrior who raised his musket toward Derick's chest. Before he could fire, Red Fox knocked the weapon from his hand with his own tomahawk. Grabbing the warrior around the neck, he held the blade against his throat and spoke through clenched teeth.

"Yun-ye-noh!" Red Fox said with fury in his voice. "Yun-ye-noh!" He loosed his grip on the warrior and shoved him away. Pointing to the north, he said to the hunting party, "Go." There was no further debate. The disgruntled warriors picked up the dead buck that was lying on the ground and headed toward the river. Alone with the tall Scotsman, Red Fox watched his companions depart from the top of the rise.

"Long Knife—go," Red Fox said emphatically.

The words were a welcome relief to Derick's ears, but he was not certain which way the Ohio lay. "I want to find Ohio River, Red Fox. Warriors on Hockhocking kill Long Knife. Go to Virginia."

Red Fox shook his head, but he seemed to understand what the white man was asking of him. "Come," Red Fox said and beckoned Derick to follow him. He turned south but did not travel toward the Hockhocking. He avoided the river and any possible confrontations with Indians traveling by canoe.

They followed an animal trail through the woods, across small streams and rugged hills. All day, the white man and the Indian ran at an easy lope that covered miles without tiring the runners. Derick was weary from a night with no sleep, but he kept pace easily with Red Fox. When the sun began to sink over the hills, Red Fox stopped to make camp, leaving Derick to build a fire. Red Fox left the trail to hunt and returned with a wild turkey, skinned and ready to cook. Derick roasted the young turkey over the fire while Red Fox built a shelter of bark.

After they had eaten the succulent roasted turkey cooked to perfection, Red Fox said, "Din-yeh-ta. Snow come. Much snow. Red Fox go Cayuga, Tal-gah-yee-tah's village."

"Tal-gah-yee-tah?" queried Derick.

Red Fox nodded. "Cayuga...Logan."

"Chief Logan?"

Red Fox smiled. "Red Fox...Cayuga ya winoh—woman."

A smile spread across Derick's face. He lifted his eyebrows at Red Fox, and the warrior laughed.

"Red Fox married?" Derick queried. He wished fervently that he could speak to Red Fox in a personal way. There was so much he needed to know. Could Red Fox be taking him to the camp of the Cayuga? That would certainly be a mistake. Chief Logan was no longer on friendly terms with the Colonials.

Shaking his head, Red Fox pointed to himself. "Red Fox—Huron. Ya-winoh, Cayuga. Logan no," he searched for words, "no happy. Red Fox want ya-winoh." He clasped his two hands together to make one.

Derick understood. Red Fox loved a Cayuga woman from Logan's village, but Logan was not happy with the arrangement. Perhaps she was a relative and he did not want her to go away to another village. Red Fox must do something to gain approval for the marriage.

The young warrior moved into the bark shelter. "Red Fox be Cayuga. Logan happy." Leaning on one elbow, he looked at Derick, a question in his dark eyes.

"Blue Eyes, ya-winoh? Woman?"

Derick could tell from the intonation in his voice that he was asking a question, wanting to know if he had a woman. He sighed, looked into the fire, and shook his head in negation. "No," he said, but in his mind's eye he saw Meagan running down the cobblestones to meet him. "No, Red Fox, no ya-winoh."

"Red Fox find ya-winoh. Blue Eyes happy." He unrolled the deer hide he carried over one shoulder and wrapped it around him like a cocoon. He motioned for Derick to come into the shelter.

Derick complied. He had no blanket, but the fire was warm, and he was not uncomfortable. He wished for his woolen plaid, the warmest garment a man could own. No doubt, the Indians would come to appreciate it on a cold winter night. At least he was still alive, and he was grateful for the heavy buckskin hunting jacket he had worn for the winter hunt.

He lay down on the cold ground to sleep. Although he was exhausted, sleep evaded him. When he closed his eyes, his mind replayed the events of the day in vivid color. He speculated on his future in this vast howling wilderness and marveled at how he came to such an impasse in his journey. His life in Scotland seemed far removed, like a dream lost in the mist, so vast was the gulf that separated his past from the events of this present day.

He remembered his broadsword, his constant companion, and knew the Wyandots had the claymore in their possession. Of all that he had lost in the American Colonies, his sword seemed the greatest of all losses. The Scottish broadsword defined who he was, all that he had ever been, the battles fought, and won, and lost. It was the pride of his country and the honor of the ancient days, and now, he was a man without a sword.

Chapter 17

Stranger in the Stable

The little fire that warms
Is better than the big fire that burns

Soon after the first Continental Congress met in September of 1774 and the bloody battle at Point Pleasant was fought during Dunmore's campaign in October of that same year, hostilities between the British crown and the Patriots escalated dramatically. Morgan's company of militia riflemen returned from Dunmore's War in January of 1775. The year opened with the knowledge that war with Great Britain was now inevitable. Loyalist and Patriot sympathies were sharply noticeable throughout the thirteen Colonies, and lines were drawn between the two, dividing family and friends.

The Battles of Lexington and Concord on April 19, 1775, marked the first military engagement of the war for independence, and from the onset of the revolution, the prospects for a Patriot victory looked dim in terms of munitions and veteran soldiers. In addition to the frontiersmen in the rural communities and border areas, the Colonial militia consisted of farmers and shopkeepers, all of whom were passionate for the cause of liberty but were unskilled in professional soldiery. What they lacked in tactical knowledge and traditional battle strategies, however, they made up for in zeal and dogged determination.

In Massachusetts, the Patriot militia allegedly hid military supplies in and around Concord and Lexington. Lieutenant Colonel Francis Smith and about 700 British regulars received secret orders to capture and destroy all the supplies in order to reduce the Patriots already scanty supplies of shot and powder, thereby weakening the revolt.

Through the efforts of Patriot spies, the British plan was uncovered weeks before the actual expedition took place, and the Patriots moved the supplies to undisclosed locations. The night before the battle, Paul Revere and William Dawes rode their horses throughout the countryside, warning the Patriots of the advance of the British troops. The Patriots prepared for battle.

Shortly after sunup, the battle began with the Patriot militia vastly outnumbered. At Concord's North Bridge, several hundred minutemen fought valiantly and defeated three companies of British regulars who withdrew in their attempt to cross the bridge. They had not expected such stiff resistance from the Patriots.

On the road to Boston, British reinforcements arrived to make a combined force of 1,700 British regulars. Despite the superior number of British soldiers, the minutemen harassed the British army until they arrived at Boston where they took refuge. The Patriot army blockaded the land access to Boston and Charlestown, resulting in the siege of Boston which lasted for ten months.

George Washington was acting as commander of the Patriot military effort, and the minutemen and Patriot militia made up the fledgling Continental army. They were largely disorganized at the time and Washington would have his hands full organizing an army that could withstand the assaults of the greatest fighting force in the world.

To build an effectual and skilled army with farmers and shopkeepers was an awesome undertaking, but liberty and independence were causes Washington believed in, causes that to him were morally justified.

In Frederick County, Daniel Morgan enlisted in the Continental army as Captain of the Virginia riflemen. The men trained under his strict command were men who had defended the frontier for years and fought with bravery and proficiency in Lord Dunmore's war. They were in every sense of the word, veteran fighters, if not veteran soldiers.

It was May 1775, and the second Continental Congress convened in Philadelphia. After days of debate and indecision, George Washington was elected as Commander in Chief of the entire Continental army. John Hancock coveted the position, but he lacked the military experience of Washington, a Virginian and a veteran soldier.

The sun was low over the training field on Daniel Morgan's farm that spring, and after a day of rigorous training, he sent his riflemen home.

Abigail had ridden her horse to the field, and together they walked their mounts leisurely toward the house, talking quietly as they strolled along the well-worn footpath. A figure approached in the distance, and seeing the couple walking their horses, raised a hand in greeting.

"Who in the world is that coming from the woods, Daniel?" Abigail asked somewhat alarmed. "He looks scary, like an Indian."

"Dunno," Morgan replied and strained his eyes to see through the humid haze of the late afternoon. "Looks like an Indian from here, sure enough. Dressed like one anyway." Morgan lifted his rifle to the ready and pushed Abigail behind him. "Can't be an Indian though," he said thoughtfully, "he has a beard." The figure continued coming toward them. "Well...by jiggers, if that don't beat all, Abby, I think it's Davidson!"

"Really, Daniel?" Abigail queried in astonishment.

"Well, as I live and breathe," Morgan exclaimed excitedly, watching closely as the figure came into clear view. "It's the Scotsman for certain."

Abigail came from behind Morgan, looking intently toward the tall figure approaching rapidly from the trees. Derick Davidson stopped ten feet from where the Morgans stood gaping at him in wonder.

"Aye! It's me, friends," Derick said, his lips curving into a smile. "I guess ye weren't exactly expecting company for supper."

He had been on the trail for weeks and his buckskin clothing fashioned after the Indian pattern was ragged and muddy. His beard had grown and his hair was tangled and unkempt.

For a moment, the couple on the footpath was speechless, and then Morgan began to bellow a genial welcome. "Why—come over here, you stinkin' trail rat. You're a bloomin' sight for sore eyes, and that's a fact! We gave you up for a dead man, so we all been a grievin' and a wailin' for the lost Scotsman. And here you turn up six months later, lookin' like you crawled through King George's garbage heap."

Morgan grabbed Derick in a bear hug, laughing with obvious delight over the return of the captive. Derick returned his greeting in kind.

"You're just in time for the action, Davidson," Morgan said. "Yes, indeed, you are a welcome sight. C'mon to the house, and we'll get some supper in you and find out what's happened. Well, Abby, don't just stand there with your tongue tied up in knots—say somethin'."

"Derick," Abby said with tears in her voice, "how pleased I am to see you alive and well, albeit, you look the worse for wear." She held out her hand to Derick, and, despite his rough appearance, he bowed over her hand and kissed it.

"It's a great comfort to this old 'trail rat' to see ye again, Mrs. Morgan," he said with genuine pleasure. "Ye grow bonnier as the days go by. I trust ye and the wee lassies are well."

"If that don't beat all I ever seen," Morgan said slapping Derick on the back. "I can count on my friend to act like a prince at what time he smells like a pauper. Well, I know you've a good yarn to spin, so let's get on up to the house. You look half-starved. Here, Davidson, get up here on Samson and I'll ride with Abby."

When they arrived at the dooryard, Derick dismounted and said to Morgan, "I'll stable the horses and greet me old friend, Warrior. Oh, how I've missed me horse, Morgan. Then I'll clean up a wee bit and come in for supper. I can't do anything until I get out of these clothes and have a bath."

"You still have some clothes in the stable room, Derick," Abby said. "I'll have some fresh water and soap sent out for your bath. Do you need a comb?" Abigail laughed at her own question. "Of course you do! I'll send some necessary items as well. Supper will be in an hour or so. I can't wait to hear your story. Should I send for the Mackenzies, the neighbors? I know they will want to hear about your adventure."

"Nay, Abigail. I am too weary and not feeling up to a social time tonight. I hope ye understand."

"Of course. There's a picnic planned for tomorrow so you can just rest up tonight, and we can hear about your experience later. It is not necessary that we hear the entire account tonight. We are all just thrilled that you are alive and well. Save the particulars for later."

"Thank ye, Mrs. Morgan."

Derick put the horses in their stalls and walked to the end of the stable where Warrior was kept when at the Morgan farm. The stallion was gone. Warrior's saddle and bridle were missing from the tack bin as well. Derick checked every stall, but Warrior was not in the stable. Surely, Morgan would not have sold the steed thinking he might not return. Morgan had said nothing to that effect when he left him only moments ago.

Hoof beats pounded through the dooryard gate and Derick opened the stable door a crack and peered out. He did not want anyone to see him in his present state. To his amazement, his own stallion entered the dooryard with Kearan Mackenzie riding the big steed. Her long dark hair was flying loose, and her grandfather's sword was sheathed at her side. She laughed aloud and reached down to pat the horse. Swinging from the saddle, she brushed herself off and adjusted her sword. What had she named her sword—Liberty?

Derick stepped back into the shadows where the extra harness was kept, hiding behind some horse blankets hanging from wooden pegs. Kearan would probably stable the horse and be on her way. She would not notice him in the shadows since the light in the stable was quite dim.

Kearan entered the stable and lit an oil lamp, then unsaddled the sweating horse. "There you are, you big baby. Didn't that nice run to the spring make you feel better? I think I'm spoiling you." She began rubbing the horse down with a towel, talking softly as she worked. "You have spring fever, don't you, Warrior?" The stallion whinnied affectionately and nuzzled at Kearan's pockets.

She produced a small apple, and Warrior chomped it appreciatively. "Now, I'll just get the combs and give you a good grooming. I know you'll like that."

Suddenly, the big stallion lifted his head and his nostrils flared. His ears moved forward, listening intently. Tossing his head, Warrior pawed at the floor, whinnying loudly. Kearan looked around the stable, wondering what had disturbed the stallion. She was quite comfortable with the horse, having worked the stallion diligently for the past nine months, hoping that one day his owner would return to find him in excellent condition.

After a cursory glance around the stable, Kearan saw nothing amiss and began brushing Warrior with the practiced hands of an expert groom. The horse seemed to settle down with the pleasant sensation of the currycomb stroking his tired muscles. As she worked, Kearan talked soothingly to the horse, trying to ease his nervousness before leading him to his stall for the night.

"Well, Warrior," Kearan said gently, "when your master returns, you will be all ready for him to ride off to war, and I'm sure by then, he will realize how much the Patriots need him. As for you, big fellow, you can stay here with me. Exercise, and the hands of a gentle lady to soothe your muscles—what more could a Warrior-horse ask for?"

Derick Davidson was only ten feet away from the sweet voice of the young woman. Her words were like gentle rain falling on parched soil and in some way; it touched him to know she had cared for his mount in his absence. She had no way of knowing if he was alive or dead, but she was counting on his return, believing that someday he would come back to Frederick County and claim his horse.

A strange muffled sound came from the girl, and she began to weep softly as she continued her grooming. "Don't worry, big fellow," she soothed quietly. "Even if your master is away for a very long time, I'll take care of ye."

When she pronounced the word 'ye' just as the Scotsman would have said it, her voice broke. Laying her head against the warm body of the horse, she wept bitterly. Her sobs were piteous, and she wept as though her heart would break. "If only I knew, Warrior, if he were alive or dead...then maybe I could bear it. Oh, how I miss him."

Again, the horse tossed his head and whinnied, stomping his feet with impatience. Kearan ceased her weeping and backed away, looking about the stable suspiciously. She dried her tears on her handkerchief and drew her sword, and then walked to the far end of the stable. She peered into every stall, her sword at the ready.

Derick heard her footfalls coming in his direction and prayed he would not be discovered. Kearan drew near the open bin where the extra harness and horse blankets were stored. At first, everything seemed in order, but then she looked down and saw a pair of Indian moccasins protruding from beneath the horse blankets.

Kearan froze on the spot, her heart skipping a beat as she stared down at the moccasined feet. The form of a large man was hidden behind the folds of the saddle blankets. What should she do? He was obviously up to no good! Should she run to the house for help? Morgan would be there by now since the riflemen had gone home for the day. Her mind made up, she lifted her chin and raised her sword.

"By the great sword Liberty," Kearan said in a commanding tone, "come out from behind those blankets at once, sir—Indian, scoundrel, whoever you are or I will cut you to pieces with my sword, do you hear me?" For emphasis to her threat, she pushed the blade against the blankets and the sharp tip easily penetrated the woolen cloth, finding the hard belly of the person concealed behind the coverings.

"Lass," cried a voice in the familiar Scottish brogue that she had come to love, "pull back your weapon! Ye are drawing blood."

Kearan recognized the voice at once and pulled her sword away. She tore away the blankets, throwing them aside in a rush. She gasped in shock at the man standing before her in ragged clothes, unkempt and filthy, with a trickle of blood oozing from a small slash in the front of his shirt. His beard had grown, nearly covering his face. Kearan's hand flew to her mouth, and her eyes widened in astonishment.

"Derick, oh, Derick, is that really you? Why in the name of good sense are you hiding in the stable? Where did you come from anyway?" Her questions tumbled out one after another.

"Hello, lass," Derick said wearily. He should have known better than to try and hide from this spirited girl, he thought.

"You look dreadful, and I think I cut you," Kearan said anxiously. "If you had not spoken first, I wouldn't have recognized you. Let me see that cut!" She stepped forward to examine the wound, but he raised a hand to restrain her.

"Only a wee scratch, but ye could have done me worse, lass. I was praying ye wouldn't happen on me hiding place. When I saw ye coming through the gate, I hid meself. Needed to clean up a wee before I made me grand entrance into civilization again."

Kearan gaped at him doubtfully, trying to decide if this was real, or she was only dreaming.

"Aye, 'tis me own self, lass. Back home, and it's glad I am to be here, that's certain." He looked down at the flesh wound on his stomach, tearing open the filthy shirt to inspect the slash. "Just needs a guid cleaning up, that's all."

Warrior heard his master's voice from the grooming station and trotted up to greet Derick with several slobbery nuzzles. The horse pushed his head against Derick and rubbed vigorously. The horse whinnied repeatedly, blowing through his nostrils until his master acknowledged his presence with some meaningful slaps and caresses. Derick forgot his disheveled appearance and the cut on his stomach, chuckling with pleasure over seeing his horse.

"I missed ye, old friend," Derick said to the stallion. "I be home again old fellow, and I can see ye are looking well, thanks to ye, lass," he said turning to Kearan with inquiring blue eyes.

She stood with sword in hand, a fiery light dancing in the depths of her brown eyes. "Well, I see you've missed your horse!" From somewhere deep inside her, a little laugh escaped. "And, you have assumed correctly—Warrior and I have become good friends. I've been taking care of him until you should return. Uncle Daniel said it was a good idea." She shook her head in bewilderment and asked, "Have you been with the Indians and managed to escape, and do the Morgans know you are here?"

"Aye, lass, the Morgans know I'm here. I saw them in the field, and nay, I didn't exactly escape from the Indians, but I was with them." He paused, embarrassed. "Ye can see what an intolerable condition I'm in at the moment, so if ye will excuse me, I wish to bathe meself. I am not presentable, lass. I will come to the house later and explain me story."

Kearan sheathed her sword and said, a note of disappointment in her voice, "No need to explain. I will leave you then. Shall I attend your wound first?" She waited for an answer, but Derick only shook his head in the negative, saying nothing. He continued to stroke Warrior's neck and run his hands over his sleek muscled body.

"Well," Kearan said, "is there anything else you wish to say to me...I mean...well, I suppose you heard me...talking to Warrior that is...when you were hiding from me." A warm flush rose to her cheeks.

The words she had spoken to the horse in the privacy of the stable played over in her mind. Warrior would keep her secret, and the beast demonstrated almost human-like empathy for her tears, but her words had not been in secret!

Derick could not lie to the girl. He had heard her weeping, heard the distress in her voice, her expression of concern over his long unexplained absence. Disappointment was written on her features, but he was not sure why. From her words, he assumed that she was looking forward to his return, but now, the lass seemed vexed. She stood motionless in the shadows of the lamplight, waiting for him to speak.

"Aye, lass, I heard ye."

"Well, I was...I was...very concerned, of course...as we all were. I wanted to believe that you...well, that you would come back. Naturally, I had no idea anyone was in the stable and overheard me...talking to the horse, that is." Once again, she felt like a babbling fool.

Kearan could not count the times she had felt utterly ridiculous in the presence of this man. It was an extremely disconcerting and humiliating fact. Truth be told, she felt almost certain that Derick Davidson did not even remember her name. After all, he had only spoken her given name twice before. What he truly loved and cared about was his horse, and that was indisputable.

Derick continued to caress his mount with obvious affection, not attempting to speak again. Kearan moved aside and walked toward the stable door. When she reached the exit, she turned and said, "Actually, I don't know why I even cared if you came back. I was speaking my heart to Warrior because in reality, I'm tired to death of caring for your horse. I was only weeping from pure frustration. Caring for your horse is a great bother, you know." Her words stung, biting through his blind indifference.

Wrinkling his brow, he looked at her in mild confusion. "Aye, lass, dinna fash yourself, Kearan, don't be grieved with me. Surely, ye jest and canna be speaking truthfully. I am distressed to hear that me horse was so troublesome for ye. I didn't expect ye to... to..." He stopped in mid sentence, studying her beautiful child-like face as though he saw her for the first time. Her dark curls clung to her damp cheeks and her eyes shone with some unspeakable pain. He could not finish his thought. Somehow, he must have missed something along the way. He felt at a complete loss.

"You are totally missing my meaning, as usual, Derick Davidson, but never mind; it wouldn't do any good to explain myself. However, there are two redeeming aspects of this ludicrous interlude—your return to Frederick County and the knowledge that you do remember my name. That is some comfort. Good-night."

Kearan slipped outside into the cool spring evening, closing the door quietly behind her. She leaned against the heavy oak frame, taking slow deep breaths, and then she walked to the orchard where her horse was tethered. Pink and white blossoms covered the trees in a profusion of soft spring color, blending their hues with the spreading gold and purple clouds as the sun sank low across the western skyline.

Kearan mounted her horse and rode home in the gathering twilight, vowing never to talk aloud to a horse again. Before she arrived home, she leaned over the saddle and spoke to Duchess, her own beloved mount, and then realized that she had already broken her vow.

Derick bathed, shaved, and washed his hair, and then put on his first set of clean clothes in almost four months. He felt like a new man. He was grateful that he had left some clean clothes in his room at the Morgan farm. The bath had invigorated him, making him feel as though he had left the long trek back to Virginia and the months of weariness behind him.

At supper, Derick ate heartily, savoring every morsel of food and declaring it was the best meal he had ever eaten in his entire life. When asked about his capture and release, he recounted a minimum of information, saving the details for another time. He would sleep long tonight and wake in the morning when he felt fully rested.

Tomorrow was the Lord's Day, and Abigail had invited the community for a spring picnic and farewell party on the lawn. The militia would be leaving soon, and the gathering served as a final farewell to the riflemen who would be leaving with Daniel Morgan when his orders arrived.

Before retiring for the night, Derick asked Morgan about the Longhunter and learned that he had not returned in the spring, as was his usual habit. Word had spread among the trappers along the Ohio and Kanawha that the Longhunter had been spotted with a Wyandot hunting party, so there was evidence that he was still alive. No one had spoken with Donald Davidson since his capture, and it was assumed that his nephew, Derick Davidson, had been killed or was held captive by another tribe of Indians somewhere in the Ohio country.

Morgan told Derick about the Battles of Lexington and Concord and the escalation of the Patriot cause in the Colonies.

After news of the battle at Lexington, many Virginians had enlisted in the militia. Morgan suggested that Derick might want to rethink his noncommittal position concerning the war for independence.

That evening, Morgan, puffing on a pipe of top grade Virginia tobacco and sending clouds of gray smoke into the mellow spring night, walked with Derick to his quarters at the end of the stable. He talked leisurely, but his mood was solemn and grave. Morgan spoke of Dunmore's nighttime raid on Virginia's stockpile of gunpowder stored in the magazine at Williamsburg, and then hiding the powder aboard a war ship on the James River. He expressed his concern for his family and for the safety of the Virginia frontier when the riflemen left on their campaigns.

At the door to his room, Derick said to Morgan, "Kearan Mackenzie rode up on Warrior when I was putting the horses in the stable. She saw me at me worst, although I tried to hide meself but she found me and held me at sword point, not certain who I was."

Morgan chuckled softly. "That sounds like the gal. Kearan's feisty, all right. She's been a taking your horse out, but I don't keep track of her comings and goings. Her Pa lets her do as she pleases, and Kearan loves takin' care of horses. She has free rein of the place around here. Why are you tellin' me this?"

"She seemed vexed with me and I feel beholdin'. She was taking care of Warrior, and it seemed like a great deal of trouble for her. What should I do?"

"Why, Kearan Mackenzie loves horses better than she loves any man, Davidson. Rare trait in a gal. Takin' care of your mount was no trouble to her. I think you're readin' this wrong." A dubious look crossed Morgan's features as he studied his friend thoughtfully.

"In fact, I know you are. No need to feel beholdin', but you outta wake up and look around."

"What are ye a meanin'?"

Shaking his head in wonder and puffing vigorously on his pipe, Morgan said, "Never mind, Davidson. Some subjects are just too confounded complicated for the ordinary man. Just rest up tonight. We'll talk more about the war effort tomorrow when you're feelin' more like yourself."

Morgan smiled roguishly, showing the gaping space where his teeth were missing. "Glad you found your way back to Virginny in one piece, Davidson. I knew if anyone could make it back alive, it would be you." Rubbing the scar along his cheek, he met Derick's eyes with his own and said, "Goodnight, my friend, and rest well."

Derick extended his hand to clasp Morgan's and then abruptly changed his mind. This hot-tempered, cursing, and often-crude man had been his friend, a true friend in every sense of the word, a man he could count on in any situation. He grabbed Morgan in a huge bear hug and said, "You're more than a brother, Morgan, and it's happy I am to know that ye are me friend."

Morgan coughed, embarrassed by Derick's unexpected show of affection. He cleared his throat, and said in a husky voice, "Same here, Davidson, same here."

The two men separated for the night, each man so vastly different from the other, yet each having the same core values, those things that truly mattered. Both men understood the value of having a true friend in perilous times.

Chapter 18

"Take it back!"

A wave will rise on quiet water

Despite his plan to sleep late, Derick awoke with a start, trying desperately to remember where he was and how he came to be there. He sat up in bed, breathing heavily, and then surveyed his surroundings. He relaxed, falling back against the pillows with a dull thud. He had finally arrived at Daniel Morgan's farm last evening, he remembered. Dressing quickly, he went to the kitchen of the familiar farmhouse and after exchanging morning greetings, he joined Daniel Morgan at the breakfast table. Abigail handed him a strong cup of coffee and placed a plate of ham, eggs, biscuits, and jam in front of him. He breathed in the heady aroma of good home cooked food with exaggerated appreciation. Morgan laughed to see his enjoyment of their simple fare.

The morning had dawned bright and promising, and Abigail had persuaded Daniel to accompany her and the girls to the Sunday worship service in Winchester. It seemed as though the entire county had turned out to hear the sermon. The pastor, a Patriot, encouraged the county folk to be courageous and fight for the cause of freedom without a second thought of guilt or shame. Wartime brought the colonists to their knees in a renewed commitment to their faith and to their country.

Sunday afternoon was a hubbub of activity at the Morgan farm. Tables were set up on the lawn, and the women scurried about, placing food on tables and shooing the children away from poking their fingers into the pies. The men sat under a grove of maple trees on the east side of the lawn and talked of the possibility of taking the city of Quebec, a British stronghold in the Canadian north.

Morgan was optimistic about this plan. If the campaign to Quebec was approved, his riflemen would be one of the two companies of militia from Virginia to engage the British. With Washington busily cementing the plans for the venture, all Morgan needed was orders to depart for Cambridge where the proposed campaign would commence. He was hoping they could complete the venture with a victory before winter set in and they had to endure the harsh weather of a Canadian winter.

That Sunday morning, Derick took Warrior for a long run. After returning his horse to the stable, he joined the men who were in a heated political discussion under the shade trees. They sat on wide board benches supported by tree stumps and overturned wooden buckets. Derick sat down on a half barrel and exchanged hearty greetings with the men of the community. All were eager to hear of his activity among the Indians and of his recent return to Frederick County. A flask of hard cider had been circulating among the group and Silas Mackenzie handed the flask to Derick. He shook his head.

"Haven't ye gentlemen heard what Shakespeare had to say about strong drink?" Derick asked, a glint of humor in his blue eyes.

"No—we haven't heard, and who in the wide world is Shakespeare anyhow? Do we know him?" John Weaver asked. "I don't recall ever hearin' that name 'round these parts."

A low rumble of laughter erupted from the group of men. Derick slapped John on the knee. "He was a writer of plays and a wee bit of a philosopher, I have no doubt. Shakespeare said, *O God, that men should put an enemy in their mouths to steal away their brains!* There ye have it, friends. As for me, I need me brains in good working order, that's certain."

"Well, by thunder, ya sure must a had yer brains about ya last October at the battle on the Kanawha," Silas Mackenzie declared enthusiastically. "We heard all about it, yes, indeed. Heard it was you and the Longhunter shootin' from those rocks up yonder on the hillside. Now, by cracky, we gotta hear how on this earth ya got away, and where ya been whilst the Patriots were stirrin' the pot in Frederick County! So, let's hear it, Davidson."

Everyone voiced agreement so Derick graciously complied with the request. He felt uncomfortable in recalling his exploits in the face of such an eager audience, so he related the story with less drama than it would be re-told in the years to come. The listeners were fascinated by stories of survival in captivity, but Derick played down his role in the frontier drama, turning the attention to the plight of the Longhunter and his wintering with Chief Logan in the Indian village.

The women called for the gathering of neighbors to come for the meal, interrupting the final phase of the tale. Derick promised to finish his story after they had all eaten. Prayers were offered for the riflemen who would soon be leaving and for the bounty of food prepared by the women. After the meal, some folk took their leave, but many stayed to visit and to hear the end of Derick's story. The group of listeners gathered under the trees, some sitting on blankets on the grass, and some on the board benches.

Derick looked around the group self-consciously and said, "Well, friends, just before that fine meal, I was relating my adventure at the point where I was moving inland, away from the river to escape the warriors traveling on the Hockhocking. In the forest, I suddenly came upon a hunting party of five Hurons. We startled each other in surprise. and we all went for our weapons. I had only a tomahawk and a knife with me." Derick noticed that Kearan had joined the group of young people seated on the grass to listen. She smiled timidly and waited for him to continue.

"Actually," Derick said feeling more conspicuous than ever, "there's not much more to the story. One of the Indians in the hunting party recognized me from an earlier skirmish with your host, Daniel Morgan, and meself, as we journeyed from Boston to Virginia. During that incident, I persuaded Mr. Morgan to allow the wounded warrior to go free, so we sent him away after a fierce fight with his comrades."

Daniel Morgan harrumphed in disgust. "That Red Fox well nigh killed me! I was rolling around and a chokin' and eatin' the dirt and grass right along with that stinkin' varmint. I had to knock the scoundrel senseless with my bare hands. Then after he wakes up, Davidson wants to turn him loose. Well," Morgan reasoned, "I reckon it turned out all right seein' as the rascal returned the favor."

Derick laughed softly. "He never forgot me kindness in saving his life, so it was a fair exchange. Some of the warriors saw me tomahawk and knew it came from the Wyandots, so they wanted to kill me on the spot, figuring I'd killed off some Indians to get the weapon, but Red Fox wouldn't let them harm me."

"And did you kill some Indians, Mr. Davidson?" one of the young boys asked, his eyes bright with curiosity.

"Well, lad, I must admit, I killed a few. There was no other way around it. Now, to shorten me tale a wee, Red Fox took me to the village of the Cayuga, called *Mingo*. The village is on the western side of the Ohio River not too far from Fort Pitt. *Tah-gah-jute*, Logan, is their chief. I spent the winter in the village."

"Wasn't this Red Fox a Wyandot, part of the Huron nation?" Silas Mackenzie asked, scratching his head.

"Aye, he is a Huron, but Red Fox loves a maiden in the Mingo village. Logan won't let her leave, so Red Fox felt the lass was worth changing his location."

"I suppose Logan is still harassing the settlers along the border country in revenge for slaughtering his family," Morgan speculated. "That's what started that whole stinkin' war anyhow, plus the fact that Dunmore had a hankerin' for more land across the Ohio. Was a good opportunity for him, not to mention that little war would serve as a diversion for the Patriots."

"I think Logan is over his blood feud," Derick said. "Chief Logan was very gracious to me, and we had many interesting conversations during the long winter. He speaks English well. When he knew me heart was longing for Virginia, he allowed Red Fox to take me to the Ohio River and point the way home. I've been traveling home for several weeks. Aye, and it's glad I am to be here, too."

Sensing that Derick Davidson would not reveal anymore about his experience in the Mingo village at this particular time, the neighbors began to gather their families and leave for their own homes. Some were tearful as they parted, knowing they might not see their friends and neighbors again for many long months, perhaps never. War would separate them, and who could say who would return? The community prayed earnestly that the fighting would not come to their own county, to their own doorsteps.

Abigail, Lily Jayne, and Kearan, helped the servants carry the food and dishes into the house while Morgan, Silas, and Alfred Mackenzie, now recovered from his leg wound, carried the benches away. Then the men went to the shooting range to fire the new rifles which had just arrived last week. The rifles were part of the munitions for the upcoming campaign, and the men were eager to test the long rifles from Pennsylvania.

Derick lingered under the grove of trees, still bone weary from his long trek to Frederick County. Although he was eager to try out the new rifles, he bade the men go without him to the field, pleading weariness. Kearan came from the house clutching a parcel in her hand. She seated herself on a colorful quilt at Derick's feet and then handed him the parcel wrapped in brown paper.

"What's this, lass?" Derick asked curiously.

"I want you to tell me," Kearan said smiling. "Perhaps you will recognize it."

Derick unwrapped the small parcel to reveal the Longhunter's Gaelic testament. A look of wonder crossed his features. "Where did ye find this?" he asked incredulously. "I thought the Wyandots took everything—our hunting supplies, our personal effects...."

"Uncle Daniel found this little book at your camp site near the Ohio River. After the battle at the point, he was determined to find you. He was able to track you from the rocks to your camp on the other side of the mountain. The soldiers who were recovering from their wounds in the army camp said you had stopped in to see them and tried to find a doctor for the Longhunter. That was the last time anyone saw you alive." Her voice trembled a little at the memory. "I imagine the testament was overlooked when the Indians captured you, or perhaps it was simply of no value to them."

"The wee Bible is written in Gaelic," Derick said, "so it's not much use to anyone except the Longhunter and meself. He kept it on a log, close enough to reach it if he wished to read. Ye are right though, the Indians had no use for the wee book."

"Well, that is a blessing," Kearan said. "The Longhunter will be pleased to know his Bible was preserved."

As Derick thumbed through the pages of the testament, he felt an unaccustomed mist rising to his eyes. The ordeal of the last nine months settled on his shoulders like a lead weight, and he felt a tragic sense of loss when he thought of his uncle. His weariness, coupled with the knowledge of the Longhunter's unwilling captivity, seemed to overpower him at this weak moment. He knew how precious the testament was to his uncle, and it saddened him to know he was in hostile Indian country without this source of comfort.

"I didn't have time to fight them off," Derick said absently. "The Indians were on me before I could draw me sword—to defend meself and me wounded uncle. Those warriors tracked us to the camp t'other side of the hill, just as Morgan did. Didn't think they would try to find us after the battle, but I figure we made them plenty angry, shooting from the rocks as we did. That was a costly lesson to learn about the ways of the Wyandots: they seek revenge." His mind drifted to another time, a time when he planned the same kind of vengeance, and for a moment, he forgot about the girl sitting at his feet on the grass until he felt a small hand gently touch his own.

"I'm so very sorry about the Longhunter," Kearan said sympathetically, "but he will come back to us. I feel certain of it. He is brave and wise and knows the ways of the frontier very well. Besides, you said they want him to trap and hunt, so it's very doubtful they would harm him."

Turning to the young girl, Derick realized with a new awareness that she was now a woman grown, no more a child. Her words were careful and discreet, unusual and wise for all her eighteen years. He was suddenly conscious of her nearness, of her gentle hand on his, a gesture clearly meant to comfort and reassure him.

Only yesterday, that same hand had thrust a sword to his belly, demanding that he surrender. He marveled at her unpredictable and capricious temperament. But then, this was her nature, her Scottish blood, the high-spirited ways of Clan Mackenzie—her ancestry.

Now, her dark eyes were soft and misty, filled with compassion, and Derick saw adoration in their depths, a sentiment he did not wish to see. For the first time in nearly two years, he understood that Kearan Mackenzie loved him, loved him as a woman loves a man, not as a teacher and his pupil, not as a friend, but a love born of some providential arrangement, something ethereal and beyond human choice. She had grown into a woman in his absence, but he had not been fully conscious of this change—until now.

The reality of this revelation shook him profoundly. At the same time, her tender caring touched his unresponsive heart, a heart he had closed to any thought of love or even the remotest possibility of a relationship with another woman.

Kearan had sensed the depth of his heartbreak; she had understood the thoughts of his sorrowing heart. She had followed the crooked path to find him where he was, in his solitary and lonely way. She wanted to comfort him, to be there for him, and without words, she was offering her love. It was visible in the light shining in her eyes, in the soft touch of her hand, and in the mellow tone of her voice.

"Indeed, lass," Derick said huskily, "I...I trust ye are right... about me uncle, I mean."

He remembered that they were speaking of the Longhunter, but his mind had drifted to the liquid brown eyes of the young woman sitting on the handmade quilt on the vivid green grass, her lips trembling with womanly passion.

Derick's eyes studied her face, the soft curve of her lips. He saw the cluster of dark curls tied with a scarlet ribbon, falling across one of her shoulders. Some strong emotion, like that of an incoming tide sweeping to the shore, rolled swiftly over him. It seemed to knock him down, to fill him with a powerful and indescribable love. He wanted to touch Kearan's soft curls, to kiss the trembling lips as he had once kissed Meagan's. With a great effort, he tore his mind away from the tormenting thoughts. "Oh Meagan, Meagan," he groaned inwardly, but in an audible voice, he whispered, "I'm sorry, so sorry."

From her seat on the quilt, Kearan studied the Scotsman, puzzled at his words, watching the changing emotions cross his features like dark clouds hurrying across a stormy sky. With a gentle voice, she prompted him back to the present, knowing he was lost somewhere in his dark past, struggling with some nameless enemy.

"The Longhunter—you were saying..." Kearan encouraged.

Derick shook his head, endeavoring to rid his mind of his somber reflections. He gathered his random thoughts and said with assurance. "The Longhunter is an honorable soldier, a noble man, unlike meself, lass. The spirit of me clan rests on the Longhunter in a strong way. Aye, he is much like me own father who died some years ago. Me father...he was wounded at Culloden and never fully recovered his health."

"But why do you say, 'unlike meself', Derick Davidson? Why don't you leave your past and any dishonor behind where it belongs and live up to your noble heritage? Bury the ancient times and all those ghostly torments."

"You don't know what ye are sayin', lass. Ye have no thought of the injustice suffered by the highlanders and that of me own people. I have plotted revenge in me heart, just as Chief Logan did, and carried it out without a backward look—until...until now. Aye, lass, ye have no thought of what I have done in me past."

"Perhaps not. Perhaps I do not fully understand, but I know you came to this country to find freedom, to leave your life and your troubles behind." Pausing, she looked at him thoughtfully, "but actually, you do not understand true freedom, the freedom that liberates a man from his past."

He smiled quizzically, his eyebrows lifting at her comment. "Ye are such a bairnie lass to be speaking such blather. I can never be liberated from me past. It follows me, even to this country."

"Well, Mr. Davidson, you are wrong about that."

"Am I now?" A look of disgust crossed his features. "For generations, the clans and me family have fought and died for independence, the right to live by the dictates of our own free will, and ye say...I do not understand freedom." Derick gazed at the ground beneath his feet, seeing something else soaking into the grass. "Our blood cries out from that bonny land of mist and tears—cries for justice, for liberty and freedom, for simple human decency."

"Yes, that might be so. The Patriots long for the same liberty, but I speak of another liberty, a freedom that cannot be won with swords and guns."

"Aye, I've heard of it. Ye speak of the liberty spoken of in the wee testament, a liberty won by another sword. Aye, me uncle speaks of it, but this is no time for paper swords. This is a time for sharp swords, for rifles and guns and war clubs. If this is not so, then why does Morgan urge me to fight with the Patriots? Shall I fight with the testament in me hand, or shall I use me claymore?"

Kearan's body tensed at his words. She appeared to be searching for some way to explain and did not answer right away. She looked toward the east to watch a flight of birds migrating north from some winter respite.

Derick opened the testament. "Me uncle says the testament is a sword," he continued, "a sword he needs and uses—most of the time. He has spoken of this often enough, but I can't say I understand his reasoning. He fought at the Kanawha, although it was with reluctance. He was a fierce soldier once with the Black Watch."

"Perhaps he had seen enough of war and bloodshed," Kearan answered, "but there are times…" she paused in her thought, "that you must fight. I am persuaded that you need both—a claymore at your side and a Bible in your hunting shirt. And…if God had his will in all of this, no one would fight and kill, but he doesn't, and that is the sad reality of our time."

"Aye, and there you have it, lass. Exactly so, but don't misunderstand me. I believe in a sovereign God, but at times, I wish He would step down from His throne in the bonny blue and help us out a wee bit."

A smile curved Kearan's lips and she pulled her knees up under her skirt, hugging them close and resting her chin against them. The Scotsman truly did not understand the concept of a personal salvation. This man was a mystery to her, perhaps even to himself, but he was honest and straightforward, and despite the dark deeds of his past, he possessed a noble quality of character she could not explain. She decided not to pursue the present subject. It was far too weighty for a Sunday afternoon.

"There is something very mysterious in the strange inscription written in the Longhunter's Bible, penned by his own hand," Kearan noted. "Tell me, Derick Davidson, what does it mean? What is the Sword of the Wild Rose?"

Derick opened the Bible to the first blank page and handed it to Kearan, pointing to the inscription written there. She read the words aloud, *"This testament belongs to Donald Davidson of Ross-shire, recently of Frederick County Virginia. This is his sword, the Sword of the Wild Rose."*

"You see, lass," Derick explained with the patience he used to address a child, "many of me clan refer to themselves as the 'wild rose' because the Scots would not be ruled by the English King—and for good reason. The English fought among themselves for power, for the crown of England. The house of Lancaster was the red rose and the house of York, the white rose, but we Scots, aye, we were the 'wild rose'. For generations, we had our own country, our own way of life, and our own King. We declared our independence in 1320 and promised to stand by the pledge stated in the Declaration of Arbroath."

Since the Scotsman was addressing Kearan like a student, she decided to play the part. She held up her hand and smiled, signaling for him to wait. "What does the declaration say and what did you pledge?" she asked in her student voice.

He smiled at her childish remarks, recognizing his patronizing blunder and appreciating her good-natured response. He looked away, seeing something in the distance, a place she could not go, could not possibly understand. He spoke the words almost reverently. "As long as but a hundred of us remain alive, never will we, under any condition, be brought under English domination. It is not for glory, nor for riches, nor for honor that we fight, but only and alone for freedom, which no good man surrenders...but with his life."

A heavy stillness followed the words of the ancient declaration as Kearan digested the significance of the ancient pledge. Derick offered no justification, no clarification, for the statement stood on its own merit, needing no literary exposition.

Finally, Kearan broke the silence. "Why, Derick," she said gently, "it is beautiful, so noble, so self-sacrificing and right. It expresses what the Patriots are endeavoring to achieve at this very moment, the very same thought, with the same passion and purpose. We no longer can abide a King from another country to rule over our own lands and over our lives. We must live free or die trying."

His laugh was almost bitter. "Aye, and so we fought too, but the outcome remains unchanged. We could not stand by our own declaration, lass. Me countrymen, they died by the thousands, but the English soldiers kept coming, they just kept coming until they took our freedom, our lands, and finally, even our hearts. The ruling government is tearing apart the ancient clan system with its ancestral roots. Now," he said in a weary voice, "we are subject to the laws of another nation, aye, even after we swore allegiance to die to the last man for our freedom, for our country."

Kearan touched his hand lightly, her eyes misting with compassion. "I'm truly sorry, Derick, for all that you have lost through the years, for all you have suffered, but here arises another opportunity, another chance to find freedom." Her eyes softened, and her voice grew gentle. "I know...I know about your wife...about your great trouble, but you are here in America, a place where you can put the past and all its sorrow to rest. Let the Patriot cause be your Declaration of Arbroath. Do you remember the inscription written on my grandfather's sword—wrong cannot rest, nor ill deed stand?"

The passion in her words and the fire in her eyes stirred an old sadness, and he said, "I have no heart left. Nay, lass, I do not...and the Wyandots have me sword."

"You have no heart?" Kearan answered incredulously. "Who took it then?" she demanded. "You would allow an English King to take away your heart? Ha! I say to you, Derick Davidson—take it back!"

Take it back? The words struck him like a blacksmith's hammer, awakening some half-forgotten memory that rang with a strange new life. *"Take it back!"* Slowly, a memory from the past took form, and he recalled the words spoken long ago. It was the last battle cry of Alasdair Mackenzie, son of the Earl of Cromartie, whose family had lived at Castle Leod for as far back as he could remember.

They were neighbors, living in the shadow of Ben Wyvis and fighting alongside Clan Davidson for their lands, for freedom from tyranny. Alasdair was wounded and taken prisoner at Culloden, and as he was dragged away, he cried out in desperation, *"Take it back, Clan Davidson, take the field!"* The story of Alasdair's final words was re-told at every clan gathering, as though his frantic plea could somehow restore what had been lost, but the words had died with the Jacobites at Culloden. Now, those words rang in Derick's ears, like the clanging of some ancient and distant bell.

When he made no response, Kearan raised from the quilt. Observing something unusual, something fearful in Derick's manner, something almost terrifying, she asked with a tremor in her voice, "Are you all right? You look so...so strange."

"Aye, lass," Derick said, rising from the bench and looking down at her, a curious flame burning in his blue eyes, "I am fair enough, fair enough."

Kearan had seen that same frightening look in his eyes once before, when he had spoken to her of his early life in Scotland. She remembered that she had pressed him for answers, only to shrink from the intensity of his gaze and the terrible, frightening reaction it had evoked. That same burning passion blazed in his soul now, and once again, she shrank from his dark, piercing, blue eyes.

Seeing her wariness of him and the uneasiness in her posture, Derick softened his strong manner and softened his voice. "Methinks," he said in a milder tone, "would be well for ye to learn more about your clan—the family in the Highlands ye never knew. Ye, too, have a fire burning in your soul, a fire that cries out for freedom." He wondered at the young lass, a girl who only moments before had challenged him, even mocked him, scorning the very idea that someone would dare to take away his heart.

His eyes fell on the testament lying open on the bench, its well-worn pages fluttering in the warm afternoon breeze. Those few words written in his uncle's hand leaped before his eyes as if they were alive... *Sword of the Wild Rose*. There was something bittersweet, something significant about the phrase. Yes, he was a wild rose, to be certain, as was the Longhunter, but where was his sword? He must find it.

Chapter 19

From the Dust

Though your sins be as scarlet
They shall be white as snow - Isa 1:18

In the valley of the Shenandoah, Daniel Morgan waited for the outcome of the war talks and for the next sweeping tide of dissention to roll down from the north, signaling the onset of actual combat. Morgan's riflemen were ready, yet they were still hopeful that there could be a peaceful resolve. They tended their farms and planted their crops as usual, but by the arrival of summer, the Revolutionary War had begun in earnest.

In June of 1775, at the urging of George Washington, the Continental Congress authorized the raising of ten companies of riflemen, two from each Maryland and Virginia and six from Pennsylvania. Daniel Morgan's riflemen came highly recommended by Horatio Gates under whom Morgan would later serve. He and his expert riflemen were among the chosen recruits from Frederick County.

After Patrick Henry's impassioned speech at Richmond, Virginia, earlier in March of 1775, Loyalist Edmund Burke spoke to the House of Commons pleading for reconciliation with the Patriots. Burke expressed his support for the grievances of the American Colonies under the rule of King George III, urging the King to leave the Americans to govern their own colonies.

"If England and King George and America's freedom cannot be reconciled, which will the Colonies choose? They will cast your sovereignty in your face. No body of men will be argued into slavery," Burke warned.

Now it was apparent that peace was no longer an option. Henry's speech was voiced far and wide, and his poignant statement rallied men by the hundreds to the Patriot cause. Burke had tried unsuccessfully to pursue peace, but it was too late. England was confident of victory over this ragtag rabble of rebels who dared to defy the greatest power in the entire world. Still, the voice of freedom spread through the Colonies, repeating Henry's speech to all who would listen.

"Gentlemen may cry, 'Peace! Peace!' Henry stated, *"but there is no peace. The war is actually begun! The next gale that sweeps from the north will bring to our ears the clash of resounding arms! Our brethren are already in the field! Why stand we here idle? What is it that gentlemen wish? What would they have? Is life so dear, or peace so sweet, as to be purchased at the price of chains and slavery? Forbid it, Almighty God! I know not what course others may take; but as for me, give me liberty, or give me death!"*

The morning after Abigail's farewell picnic, Derick Davidson and Daniel Morgan mounted their horses and rode to the town of Winchester. After the long winter of looking over his shoulder and peering behind every bush, the gentle roll of the horse beneath him and the pleasant ride through the blossoming countryside, alive with the vibrant greens of spring, was quite enjoyable for Derick. It just felt good to be back in friendly country.

In Winchester, the two men tied their horses in front of a weather beaten clapboard building that housed the Winchester Mercantile, a general store that doubled as post office. It also served as a gathering place for county folk who liked to exchange gossip and share the latest news of the Colonies. Morgan was waiting for orders from Washington in the post or by courier, while Derick hoped for some word from his clan in Scotland.

Mr. T. M. Mathias, owner of the Mercantile, handed Derick two letters. Morgan nodded to a group of frontiersmen and locals who were playing cards around a rickety table near the back of the Mercantile. Joining the group, he turned a chair around and pulled a wad of tobacco from his hunting shirt. Derick pointed to the letters and nodded toward the door. Morgan acknowledged his gesture with a wink, and Derick headed for the exit.

Derick walked down the length of the dirt street to the stone edifice of the Anglican Church, the most prestigious building in Winchester. He tried the door and found it unlocked. Slipping inside, he sat on a rough wooden pew at the back of the small sanctuary. Opening the first letter, he saw the bold script of his brother's hand and read the contents, his hands trembling slightly with anticipation.

Dearest brother, your missive was received with great joy, although the post took nearly a year to arrive. Fear not brother—all is well. Your bairns thrive under Margaret's loving care. The babe, William, is a miniature of yourself. Your sister, Doran, is to be wed soon to a nephew of the Earl of Cromartie, Rannoch MacLeod, of Clan Mackenzie, now residing at Castle Leod. Doran is loath to give up your wee William of whom she is so fond, but we comfort ourselves knowing she will be close at Castle Leod. Doran sends her fondest greetings and bids ye not to worry over her—Rannoch is a worthy lad.

At the mention of his youngest son, William, only a wee babe when he left Scotland, and of his twin sister, whom he adored, Derick's eyes misted with hot bitter tears. How he longed to see his children and family! His chest tightened with homesickness and longing, but he had nothing to offer them—no home, no land, and no security or safety in this volatile country of red-men and revolution. His children were safe and tenderly cared for by Duncan and Margaret, who themselves were childless. They bestowed all their love and attention on their nephews and niece.

If Duncan produced no heir, Derick's eldest son, Douglas, would become the next clan Chief if the English tyrants did not completely clear the clans from the Highlands. Thus far, and because of the clan's vast land holdings in the north, which Duncan generously allowed them to "improve," he had favor with the English government, even though he detested the endless tap dancing to stay in the King's favor.

When Derick felt calmer, he resumed reading the letter. *We were amazed to hear of your miraculous encounter with our lost Uncle Donald ye now call, "the Longhunter." Your sons are especially intrigued with the tale. We hear of the terrible unrest in the Colonies and pray for your safety, brother. When these dark days are over, ye can return to your fond homeland and to your bairns. We trust that time has lessened your pain and the many tribulations ye endured in the land of mist and tears. Ye remain in our prayers always.*

Fondest regards, Duncan Davidson IV

The second letter was addressed to the Longhunter. After Derick read Duncan's letter over several more times, he decided to post another note to his brother and then take the letters to the Longhunter's cabin on Cedar Creek and place them in his uncle's moneybox. If anything unexpected happened, the Longhunter would discover the letters when he returned to Virginia. He would return to the Mercantile and post his letter to Duncan.

Entering the store, he found Morgan in a hot debate with several men over their Loyalist sympathies. Ignoring Morgan and his ranting political diatribe, which was not the least bit unusual for Morgan, Derick borrowed a quill from T.M. Mathias and bought some paper to post his letter.

He wrote a hasty note to Duncan telling of his capture and release from the Indians and of the revolution sweeping across the Colonies. He wrote a short personal note to each of his children and begged them to remember their father who loved them always. He prayed the missive would get through before the ports were blockaded and the mail became unpredictable at best.

T. M. Mathias opened the door of the Mercantile wide and ordered Daniel Morgan and the group of dissenters to take themselves and their differences outside his store before a fight broke out. Derick smiled to himself as he handed the letter to Mathias to post. The storekeeper took the letter and shook his head in consternation.

"That Daniel Morgan can't just have a friendly chat about politics," growled Mathias as he placed the letter in the mailbag. "Nope, by gum, he has to put his oar into every mush-headed, meaningless dispute, and then stir the pot 'til it boils over. Known Morgan for years and never in all my born days have I seen a man who loves to fight more'n him." Mathias shook his head again, and Derick nodded his agreement and shrugged his broad shoulders in wonder.

"I been here a long time, Davidson," the storeowner said with conviction. "Morgan was just a young buck when he came to Frederick county back in '53, maybe was sixteen or so. Winchester was just a raw settlement at that time, and that ain't a sayin' much.

'Twas a dirty, sweaty, one horse, one street town, with brawlers who disliked rules and made up their own. I was a young man myself back then. We all figured out how to make a living and settled in for the long haul, right here in the Shenandoah wilderness."

"Well, Mr. Mathias, looks like you've made a fair living here in Winchester," Derick said looking around at the well-stocked shelves.

"Can't complain, Davidson, we all made a life, even Morgan. There was many a time when I threw that rascal outta my store and into the street. Why, he'd just pick up the scrappin' at some tavern in Battletown. Never missed a lick either. Took up the fight right where he left off. Every time that young wagoner took to the road, I used to thank God. He'd often be gone for weeks at a time."

"I've heard some of those stories," Derick said. He looked toward the open door to see Morgan head to head with his contender.

"Morgan used to work for Robert Burwell," Mathias continued, "driving a wagon for his overseer, John Ashby. Now that Ashby was a scrapper himself, much older, and certainly oughtta been far wiser than Morgan was, but he was a brawler to beat all himself. Rode a horse like the devil was on his tail, drank like a fish, and cursed the air blue."

"Doesn't sound like respectable company for an impressionable young lad," Derick said.

"Why, I reckon not!" Mathias agreed emphatically. "Ashby was a poor example for young Morgan. The two of them would come snarlin' into town to drink, start a brawl with whoever was handy, then bite and gouge, kick and punch until they were black and blue and their clothes nigh ripped off their backs. That was Morgan's kinda fun! Now, just go figure that one out."

Derick could not help but laugh at the storekeeper's depiction of Morgan's early life on the wilderness frontier. Thankfully, age had mellowed him some, and of course, there was Abigail and the girls.

"They were well acquainted with the Sheriff, I can guarantee you that," Mathias added with a shake of his head. "Next to Ashby, I'd venture to say Morgan was the foremost frontier brawler in the whole of Frederick County, if not in Virginia itself—well, until Abigail came along." A slow smile spread over the face of T.M. Mathias, and a sparkle of some long ago memory lit up his eyes. He smiled knowingly.

"Well, now, Abigail had a way about her, that's a fact," Mathias said softening somewhat. "Never saw anything like it in my life. She was a beautiful woman—still is for that matter. I reckon we all were kinda smitten with her," he added chuckling. He rubbed his chin thoughtfully.

"Well, she figured out how to tame the wildcat in Morgan. Don't know why she loved that polecat, but she did." Mathias grabbed a dust rag and began to polish the counter vigorously before continuing his narrative.

"What Abigail ever saw in Daniel Morgan was a complete mystery to the whole bewildered town, but none of us minded much except for a few who wanted to court that pretty gal." He sighed.

"Well, by gum, I'll have to admit—her takin' up with Morgan was a real puzzlement to me—to the entire community for that matter, but we finally said a hearty 'Amen' to the match if it would tame Daniel Morgan. At least," the shopkeeper affirmed, "it gave us all some peace and quiet and some well-deserved relief from that scalawag."

"Time has a way of mellowing some lads," Derick suggested.

"Now, don't get me wrong, Davidson, I'm not sayin' Morgan doesn't have some good qualities about him. He's a hard worker, a true Patriot, and if you're on his side of the fence, he's a loyal friend, but God help ya if you're not."

"Well, Mr. Mathias," Derick said with a glint of mischief in his own eyes, "appears like Morgan might have his fill of fighting before the year is over. Aye, more fighting than he cares to see."

"That's a fact now," Mathias said in a less animated tone. "I suppose we need Morgan's kind in the Continental army if the Patriots are to win this campaign. Hard tellin' what's waitin' around the corner for our frontier lads."

Derick nodded solemnly and the conversation ended as other patrons entered the store. Derick purchased some food supplies to take to the cabin, and then left the Mercantile. During the storekeeper's account of Morgan's youthful escapades, Derick could hear the old wagoner debating loudly in front of the Mercantile.

Outside in the dusty street, Morgan stood eye to eye with a known Loyalist sympathizer, one of the few in Frederick County. The day was hot and dry for the month of June. Beads of perspiration stood out on Morgan's forehead, trickling down the scar on his cheek and lip. It was easy to see he was only seconds away from throwing a punch.

"You got some mighty big ideas for such a small head," Morgan was saying to his adversary.

Approaching the two mean, Derick said casually, "C'mon, Morgan, we've some business a calling us, so leave this gentleman to his own opinions."

Before Derick could finish his sentence, a post rider came galloping up the main street, clods of dirt and pebbles flying from the hoofs of his horse and showering the pedestrians along the walkways. The face of the post rider was grimy with dust, and his horse was lathered with sweat. He dismounted quickly, opened his saddlebags, and took out several sheaves of newspaper. A crowd of people soon gathered around, waiting to hear the news from up north.

"The fighting's begun in earnest," panted the sweating rider. "Well, nigh to Boston town. Here is the report, spelled out in black and white."

Wiping his hands on his soiled apron, T.M. Mathias walked from his store, took one of the papers from the messenger, and pushed a copy over a nail on the wall of the Mercantile. This was the usual method of posting important news for the townspeople to read. All who came would find the post since almost everyone frequented the Mercantile of T.M. Mathias.

Those who could not read or write, begged someone to read the account aloud. Derick, who stood head and shoulders above most of the crowd, read the paper in a strong clear voice so all could hear.

"This June, 1775, the British invaders attempted to seized Bunker Hill, some call Breed's Hill, and the Patriots resisted the British tyrants with passion and vigor. The casualties among the British were staggering. The Patriots fought well, but due to lack of munitions, ran out of powder and shot. In the end, the Patriots were fighting hand to hand after the British advanced over the hill on the third attempt. The battle did little to lift the siege of Boston and the Patriots remain unabated in their siege efforts. General George Washington is calling for men to take up arms and fight for America's independence from the tyranny of British rule."

When Derick finished reading the post, silence hung in the air as men looked at each other dry lipped, knowing peace was now impossible. This news sounded the death knell for any peaceful negotiations, and the Colonials must steel themselves for the fight to come. An earsplitting war whoop erupted from Daniel Morgan and seared the silence like a hot knife. Morgan eyed the Loyalist partisan he had been debating and let fly another whoop. Others joined in, and the town of Winchester rang with the Patriot's victory cry.

After posting a letter to General Washington, Morgan mounted his horse and rode to Soldier's Rest with news of the battle at Bunker Hill. Derick left Winchester for the Longhunter's cabin on Cedar Creek where he hoped to spend some time resting and fishing by the stream. He stopped by the home of Doctor Benjamin Rinehart, his uncle's nearest neighbor, telling him of the recent news from Boston and the reason for the Longhunter's long absence.

Doctor Rinehart, a retired military surgeon, gave Derick the set of keys securing his uncle's properties. Any time the Longhunter was off on a hunt, the doctor sent his hired men once a month to the cabin to insure that no squatters had taken up residence and that everything remained in good order.

The doctor himself was a landowner with an impressive home and acres of profitable farmland. Donald Davidson and Benjamin Rinehart were not only neighbors, but they had served together in the Seven Years war before settling the stretch of land along Cedar Creek.

Derick unlocked the padlock on the cabin door and entered the cozy log dwelling. Laying his trappings aside, he built a small fire on the hearth to drive the mustiness from the room. He took the pots and cooking utensils to the creek to wash and then prepared a simple meal. He swung the kettle of fresh water over the fire and added the makings for a dried venison stew.

While the stew simmered slowly over the fire, he unlocked the stable and led Warrior to a stall for the night. He fed his faithful companion and then groomed his sleek coat with long even strokes. The beast swayed drowsily, enjoying the pleasant sensation and feeling full from his supper of oats and hay. Grooming the stallion was always a relaxing and pleasurable task for Derick. How he had missed the noble steed in his long absence. He was deeply grateful that Kearan had lovingly cared for Warrior and taken time to exercise and work the splendid stallion with resolute devotion.

As Derick worked, he thought of Kearan, the beautiful and impetuous young woman who only yesterday had sat at his feet under the shade of the maples. He recalled that soft moonlit night when he had watched her turn circles in the snow while her dark curls tumbled about her head and her eyes were tearful with self-recrimination. How young she had seemed then, how willful and daring!

At the memory, a smile tugged at his lips and his heart stirred in a strange and wonderful way, a way he did not fully understand himself. Surely, he was not falling in love with the sword-wielding girl! The thought seemed so ludicrous, so far removed from reality. He quickly dismissed the notion from his mind, but he could not quite dismiss the lovely picture she made on the lawn yesterday, nor could he forget the tender touch of her hand on his as she tried to comfort him.

He was no longer blind to her youthful worship, nor had he missed the look of adoration when she looked at him from her seat on the quilt. To think that she might love him disconcerted him considerably. Despite his efforts to ignore the winsome lass, she had begun to occupy his thoughts, to appear before his mind at the most unexpected times. What was he to do? Derick could hear her words echoing in his mind, reminding him of her strong and passionate nature. In truth, he loved her high-spirited ways, although he would never have told her so.

In the stillness of the gathering shadows, Kearan's sweet, melodious voice spoke again. *"I say to you, Derick Davidson—take it back!"* It was the cry of her passionate young heart. She had pleaded for him to take heart again, to forget the past with all its heartache and defy all those who dared to take his freedom.

Derick pushed the unsettling thoughts from his mind and returned to the cabin where the odors of the hot bubbling stew cooking over the open flames of the hearth fire caused his mouth to water. In his mind, he could almost smell the pungent and pleasant aroma of his Highland home, of fragrant peat fires and hot buttered oatcakes.

After enjoying the tasty supper, Derick settled into his uncle's rocking chair with a cup of hot coffee, contemplating a quiet evening of relaxation and reading. He had missed this simple pleasure during his captivity in the Indian camp.

He thumbed through several books on the shelves that comprised the Longhunter's library and decided on a volume of poetry by an unfamiliar author. As he leafed through the book, he came upon a yellowed letter next to a well-worn page beside a poem simply titled *Liberty*.

> I sought her on the wind swept moor
> With sword in hand, I called her name,
> Elusive still, she fled away
> Like morning mist along the shore.
>
> I sought her still through battle din
> Amid the cries of death and woe,
> She flew away to mountain glen
> Where angel spirits fear to go.

I sought her still with sword and shield
Regarding neither friend or foe,
Soon I returned with empty hands
A broken shield, a sword, a bow.

I looked inside my searching soul
To one who offered Liberty,
He took my sword, my shield, my bow
Unlocked love's door, and set me free.

How could I then lift sword unless
To honor God, this cause be right,
For I would lay my honor down
And love you more than what is right.

Derick could almost feel the presence of his uncle as he read over the lines again, *soon I returned with empty hands, a broken shield, a sword, a bow.* The words were underlined in ink from a quill pen and brownish stains like teardrops had fallen onto the page. Who was the Longhunter's lost love? Who was the lass he left behind to join the Black Watch and go to war? He had said she could never be his, so he left all that he had, content with her memory. What point of honor was there in that? *I never loved another—only her,* he had once said. If the Longhunter ever returned, he would ask him about the mysterious lass he had loved, but for honor's sake, had given up. He had equated his battle for love with war and loss and honor.

Derick picked up the yellowed letter, hesitated, and then unfolded the tear stained missive. Perhaps the letter held a clue to the mysterious love of Donald Davidson. Derick read:

> My dearest Donald,
> *I received your letter not long after you sailed for America, and I felt constrained to reply to your kind words and best wishes. God only knows if we shall ever meet again in this life, but I pray that my words will be of some comfort as you face your enemies in a strange land.*
>
> *Since we were all bairns, I have loved both you and Duncan. Our lives grew together as the wild mountain heather, and we shared all that we had. I never realized in those early days, dearest Donald, that you loved me as a sweetheart, but it was your brother I loved always. Duncan was so distraught to think you joined the Black Watch, not for yourself, but for us... for him...and for me because you felt our future happiness would be made difficult by your presence. It pains me deeply to hurt your noble heart for you are an honorable man and...*

Derick could read no farther. He folded the letter with trembling hands. This was a letter from his own mother, Derick thought, the mother he had really never known. The Longhunter had loved her too, but she had loved his father, Duncan.

Love and honor had compelled Donald Davidson to leave his highland home and join the Black Watch so his own brother might marry the lass they both loved. Derick's mother was Donald Davidson's mysterious lost love!

He recalled that the Longhunter had once said that the lass he loved had been gone many years now. No marvel his uncle had wept when he first saw his nephew in Morgan's dooryard. Derick was the son of the woman he loved and Derick marveled at such selfless love.

Laying the book aside, he opened the wooden chest with the Longhunter's weapons and ran his hand over the rough wool of the distinguished uniform of the Black Watch. He took the Gaelic Bible from his hunting shirt and placed it reverently on top of the red woolen jacket that bore the insignia of first Lieutenant, 42nd Regiment of Foot. When his uncle opened the chest, the Bible would be there, waiting for him.

From the breast pocket of his hunting shirt, he retrieved the gold locket with Meagan's likeness and carefully placed it beside the Bible. He could not go on living with his dead wife. He would cherish her memory, the mother of his children, but he must move past this crushing sorrow. His eyes misted with tears and he longed for some way to move past this part of his life.

From somewhere in the shadows of his memory, the words of his uncle came to him like an audible voice. *For the word of God is quick, and powerful, and sharper than any two-edged sword, piercing even to the dividing asunder of soul and spirit, and of the joints and marrow, and is a discerner of the thoughts and intents of the heart.* "Think of that, lad! This sword will cut into our thoughts, find secret motives, and discover our very heart."

For some time, Derick reviewed his life, trying to justify the secret motives that had driven him to this secret place of loneliness and despair. Try as he may, he could not seem to validate his actions, nor could he excuse the premeditated acts of vengeance he had perpetrated on those who had murdered Meagan. The lines of the poem echoed in his mind, *How could I then lift sword unless To honor God, this cause be right...*

Anger swelled in his chest until it became a physical pain. But why was he angry? He had glutted his vengeance, had evened the score, but somehow, punishing his adversaries didn't seem to satisfy his consuming hatred.

Perhaps for the first time since his flight from Scotland, he realized the depth of his anger, the final result of his rage, and where it had taken him. Hatred had driven him to murder and driven him from his homeland, from his children, and from God Himself. He was a prodigal, a castaway, with no hope of a future.

He buried his head in his hands and began to speak aloud, pouring out his bitterness to God. Then he lifted his head and challenged this invisible God, not in the form of rote doggerel or memorized prayers, but as he would have addressed another man his equal, a brother, or perhaps, if he could have remembered her, even his own mother.

"If you are God and can see the very thoughts of me painful heart, the secret motives of hate and revenge, aye, even the bitter resentment I feel for ye, why do ye still seek me out?" Derick fumed and raged at God, his voice rising with a myriad of unanswered questions. "Why would ye care? Ye dog me steps and plague me mind. I canna fight ye. Ye have taken away all that I have and left me a broken beggar with no comfort, no hope. Aye, I could have conquered me hate, but I dinna want to. Do ye hear me, God? I wanted to hate, to strike, and to kill for Meagan's sake. For that, ye fault me, plague me!"

Once again, he heard the voice of the Longhunter as if it were God speaking. "Nay, I do not fault ye, but there be a higher court, a judge ye must take your case before—one who brandishes an honorable sword, who tries the hearts of men, then judges rightly and honorably."

"Me sins are too many and there is no way back," Derick breathed in a despairing tone, "and me past is a tangled web of regret. It is too hard to make a new start in this strange troubled land." He groaned in anguish, and again, he heard the Longhunter speaking to his conscience.

"All men have a past, lad, because all men are born broken. 'Tis why we need a Savior—to put us together again, to bury our sins in the sea."

Derick sighed wearily, picturing the heart of a broken man, a man like himself, strong in body, but so very poor in his spirit. He knew if anyone in this world ever felt broken, it was he. If anyone needed forgiveness, he would be the man.

As he waited in the stillness, light and understanding began to penetrate the darkness of Derick's troubled mind, and a sweet and peaceful presence seemed to fill the room.

God was speaking to him now, and though he feared no man, Derick feared the one sovereign God who had allowed the difficult circumstances of life to chasten him simply because... because He loved him.

God saw far beyond Derick's sins, beyond the passion that had driven him to commit murder, and God was seeking him still, enveloping him in a powerful love that spoke of forgiveness and assurance. The sweet Spirit of God, was pursing Derick Davidson. He wanted to lift him from the murky quagmire where he had languished since Meagan's death.

Everything in Derick's life had pointed to this very moment, to this very place. God had been there all along, in the shadows of his life, moving among men and orchestrating everything that concerned him. Surely, this supernatural love had guided him to Morgan, had caused the Longhunter to cross his path in a vast wilderness country. He was a fugitive, and God was seeking him alone, the longed after son who didn't deserve pardon, yet God offered it now.

Derick heard Kearan's voice penetrate the thick blanket of love surrounding him, *"I say, take it back."* He would *take it back*, all that he had lost in his quest for vengeance, the peace and security he had forfeited in order to vent his rage. The cost had been far greater than the gain and he was tired of fighting. He would give up his long battle with God.

While the hickory logs burned to glowing red embers on the stone hearth, Derick Davidson, a man who came boldly before his Creator with his unanswered questions, a man who had lived his own way, finally made peace with the Almighty and with himself. There was no question now. He knew beyond any shadow of doubt that God had heard him in the dark night of his despair.

And in spite of his human weakness, God loved him still and had sent his Son to redeem him, to forgive him. Even when he had turned away in anger, God had come after him, sought him across the vast ocean, and brought him to the end of his long and perilous journey. In the Longhunter's cabin on Cedar Creek, Derick Davidson renounced his stubborn will and gave his life and his future days to the Sovereign God who had searched for him through the mist and tears of his life.

The fire on the hearth had turned to ash when Derick rose from his knees with a remarkable sense of lightness and an incredible freedom; the heavy burden he had carried for many long years was lifted off his shoulders. He did not quite comprehend this kind of liberty, and for a moment, the feeling almost unsettled him. Until now, he had only dreamed of freedom. Even this new land of endless opportunity had not brought the freedom he had longed for, neither was he freed from those invisible cords of oppression and sin. No matter how diligently he had pursued liberty, he had remained bound—until now.

A unique and marvelous liberty filled his being. Silver or gold could not purchase this spiritual freedom, nor could it be won by conquest or obtained through an impressionable title or vast estates. Neither King nor country could offer this liberty.

With a sense of awe and wonder, Derick reveled in the joy of divine liberty and forgiveness. He was truly a free man now, free from all that had bound him, free to follow his heart. He looked around the cabin as though seeing it for the first time. Noting the claymore broadsword hanging on the cabin wall, he retrieved it with a flourish.

With trembling hands, Derick ran his fingers over the smooth blade and then held it aloft, sweeping it in a wide circle above his head. "By the help of the Almighty God," he said in a quavering voice, "we will—we will take it back—all of it, but we will take it with honor."

Derick lifted the dirk and the Gaelic Bible from the Longhunter's chest of war memorials and opening the Bible to the book of Psalms, he read in the 71st chapter, verses 20 and 21:

You have allowed me to suffer much hardship and pain, but you will restore me to life again and lift me up from the dust of the earth. You will restore me to even greater honor and comfort me once again.

Chapter 20

Celebration and Separation

A man may do without a brother
But not without a neighbor

"Abigail, turn me loose and get into that carriage," Daniel Morgan said rather gruffly as he grabbed the pummel of his saddle and prepared to mount Samson for the ride to Winchester. His new rifle purchased from Fielding Lewis, George Washington's brother-in-law, was sheathed to his horse as was his saber and personal belongings.

"Oh, Daniel, I can't, I can't," Abigail cried.

Hating the sight of a weeping woman, Morgan ignored her tears. "You won't come to Winchester with me, then?" he queried. "We'll be a meetin' at the Golden Buck tomorrow mornin', leaving from there, you know. Thought we had this all settled," he added with a sigh. "Reverend Thruston's wife has kindly offered for you to stay over." He looked at Peter who sat patiently waiting while sitting on the driver's seat of the carriage. "The carriage is ready, Abby. Will be our last night together for many a long month, gal," he said hopefully. "Better come along."

Morgan managed to free himself from Abigail's grasp and mounted Samson. He looked down at her pitiful tear-streaked face, and his heart wrenched with a sudden longing to stay.

Abigail was barely thirty years old, and to Morgan, she seemed as young and vulnerable as that long ago day when he carried her away to live with him. How thoughtless and foolish and demanding he had been! Abigail was barely sixteen then, still a child in many ways. He was ten years her senior and had already lived a hard and worldly existence.

Something about Abigail Curry's youthful innocence and compassionate heart had attracted Morgan to her. She was unlike any woman he had ever known and she touched some part of him that yearned and longed for something entirely opposite of himself. It was that simple. She had captivated him, was the other half that made him whole, the melodious chord in his otherwise discordant life. From his earliest memories, Daniel Morgan could not recall any tenderness or compassion in his early life.

Now, as he looked down at his wife, he recalled the feathery soft touch of her hand on his, her gentle voice that spoke to him of love and concern. Morgan realized how very much he needed her tenderness, and her caring spirit. By her own subtle influence, Abigail had curtailed his impulsive and willful outbursts and polished his crude and unskillful ways.

In truth, Abigail had enhanced every positive thing in his life. She kept him balanced, always appealing to the better side of his rough nature. She taught him to read and write, to educate himself and to improve upon every aspect of his life. Everything good in his present situation, he owed to Abigail.

With thoughts of Abigail lingering in his mind, Morgan dismounted and went to her side. Lifting her chin in his big brawny hand, he said in his deep gravelly voice, "Abigail?"

She winced a little, knowing that when he said, "Abigail," in that tone, something stern was about to come forth. No doubt, she reasoned, he was displeased with her tears, but how could she help it? She promised herself that this time, she would not cry, but when the time came for Morgan to leave, she had reneged on her promise and broken down. She couldn't bear the thought of life without Daniel Morgan by her side. The very thought that he might be killed was unbearable. Of course, she wanted freedom for the Colonies, but that meant some of the county men would not come home again. She turned her head away and refused to look at her husband.

"Abigail," Morgan repeated sternly, "look at me, gal." She turned her eyes to him then and Morgan softened when he saw the pain in her green-blue eyes and her grief-stricken face. He dropped his hand and said, "Abby, oh Abby, please don't weep. You make it hard on a man. I'll do my best to stay alive—to come home again. I don't want you to fret over me, do you understand? It's hard enough to leave, even when I know for certain that it's right."

She nodded benignly but said nothing. Her eyes had dulled, losing that inner light that for her was Daniel Morgan. She laid a soft hand against his cheek, tracing his scar with one finger.

"And Abby, I want you to remember this—" Morgan paused and took a deep breath. He removed her hand from his face to clutch it tightly in his own. "I'm glad we said our weddin' vows before the preacher—like you wanted. I feel better knowin' things are fixed proper like. If I don't come back, our little gals can hold their heads up high. I would do it again too…for you, Abby."

At his words, she flung herself on him, clinging to his burley frame as though she were drowning. "I don't want to make it hard for you, Daniel, truly I don't. I just don't want to lose you to the war. I know I'm selfish. So many wives have already lost their husbands, and I am so afraid."

"Don't be a feared, Abby. God himself has ordained this revolution. You know I'm not a religious man, but I do believe in your prayers, woman. Just pray for the riflemen, especially for me while we're away at the war. Will you do that?"

Abigail was somewhat comforted and wiped her tears with her handkerchief. "I will, Daniel, and I will pray for even more...I will ask..."

"Fine, Abby," he interrupted, not wanting to hear specifics about the nature of her prayers for him. "Now, get into the carriage, and we'll spend the night with the good Reverend in Winchester."

An hour later that same morning, Kearan and Alfred Mackenzie rode their horses along the wagon road to Winchester to meet Silas and Lily Jayne who had driven their carriage to town the day before. The family would spend the day and evening with Lily Jayne's sister, Maude, and husband, Marcus MacKay. Saying farewell to the men of Frederick County who were going to war would be difficult, but the family was determined to see Alfred and the rest of the riflemen off early the following morning.

Today, however, the town of Winchester would celebrate its patriotism. There would be parades, bands, and a general celebration for the Patriot cause, for the soon departing riflemen and their families. The Reverend Thruston himself had used parish funds to purchase needed supplies for the long march to Boston. Spirits were high, and the men were eager to prove to King George III that they'd had enough and were ready to claim independence from British rule, no matter what the cost.

At an unmarked crossroads, a rider approached from the southern fork. It was Derick Davidson. Brother and sister halted along the roadside and eagerly greeted their friend.

"Well, Davidson," Alfred said with a broad grin, "are you finally going to join up with the riflemen? You'll miss the time of your life if you don't come along."

Derick removed his hat and smiled indulgently at Alfred and nodded politely to Kearan, then turned to Alfred again. "Not this time, Alfred, but I'll join the riflemen after this present campaign. Right now, I'm on a mission to find me uncle, the Longhunter. It's July, and he should be home by now."

Looking thoughtful, Alfred removed his cap and scratched his head. "You're right about that. But sometimes, he comes in from a hunt and we don't see him for weeks, sometimes all summer."

"I've been at his cabin on Cedar Creek and he's not been there this spring. Dr. Rinehart, his nearest neighbor, hasn't seen hide nor hair of him either so I'm thinking he's still held captive by the Wyandots."

"Maybe he doesn't want to come home," Kearan suggested. "He might like that kind of primitive life. After all, he's kind of like an Indian himself and doesn't answer to anyone." She smiled at Derick, feeling her heart quicken as she gazed into his deep blue eyes. He held her gaze and she felt her cheeks grow warm. She had not seen him since he left Soldier's Rest for the Longhunter's cabin. Kearan's horse pranced and nickered loudly, eager to be off again.

"Well, are we just gonna stay here in the middle of the road jawin', or are we a ridin' to Winchester?" Alfred asked as he held his horse in place."

"Go ahead, Alfred," Derick said. "I'll escort your sister safely to town. There is something I wish to show her."

Kearan's eyes widened. In her heart, she longed to be alone with the Scotsman, but then again, she wondered at the appropriateness of riding alone with this man. Her eyes held a question, but she said nothing.

"Fine with me," Alfred said with relief. He was obviously not interested in propriety at this particular moment, and wished only to be on his way to town. "I get teased enough about my sword-carrying sister hangin' around my neck like the proverbial millstone," Alfred complained. "Just take care of her, Davidson, or Pa will have my hide. See ya in town then."

Alfred gave his horse a substantial kick and was off at a gallop, executing a victory yell as he disappeared down the road to Winchester.

"And just what do you wish to show me, Mr. Davidson?" Kearan asked with a lift of one eyebrow. "Something to do with that new sword I see strapped to your side?"

"Nay, lass. This is the Longhunter's sword, but I want to tell ye about it. The Wyandots have me sword as I told ye before. Will ye come with me?" Derick was glad for this chance encounter with Kearan and Alfred. He had meant to ride back to Soldier's Rest to visit, but the days had passed all too quickly and now the riflemen were ready to leave for Boston.

"Well, it appears I have no choice but to accompany you unless I proceed to town alone," Kearan confessed.

"Aye, I doubt ye should try and catch Alfred since he's riding like the devil is after him, so methinks ye have no choice but to come with me." He smiled, turned his horse around, and signaled for her to follow him. He proceeded in the direction from which he had just come. When Kearan pulled her horse abreast of him, a look of concern crossed his features and he said, "Not long ago, ye said I frightened ye. Do not fear me, lass. I wouldn't harm ye for the world."

"I know that," Kearan answered simply.

He smiled then and his smile seemed contagious. Kearan returned his smile, and for one brief instant, his eyes lit up with some strange new emotion that lay hidden just beneath the surface. Kearan sensed that something unusual had happened to Derick Davidson, but what could it be?

"Derick Davidson," she said as they rode along the tree-lined road, "you have indeed frightened me at times. I never feared you would harm me, but I feared your uncontrolled passion, the violence I felt coming from deep inside you. I feared it might be unleashed and I dreaded the consequence. That kind of obsessive force...it was...was frightening. You appeared so strong, so...so wild."

He laughed softly. "Ye think I am a savage straight from the wild and untamed Highlands? Aye, I've been accused of such betimes."

The couple was riding abreast, making their way along the narrow road toward the Longhunter's cabin. The morning sun streamed through the mist like beams of shimmering gold, bathing the two riders in diffused sunshine. Patches of pink primrose dotted the fields, and wild blackberries grew in a tangled profusion by the roadside.

"I didn't mean you were actually wild and uncivilized," Kearan replied. "I know you are a gentleman by birth—in every sense of the word, but there is something impregnable, something unconquerable inside you, a part that could be wild...if you allowed it to surface."

He considered her words for a long moment then said, "Aye, ye have aptly discerned the way o' me...the way I was," he hastened to add.

Kearan caught the innuendo in his comment, but she offered no further opinion on the subject. They rode on in silence, savoring the peace of the quiet misty morning. The clomping of the horses' hoofs and the chirping of birdsong was the only sound to disturb the stillness of the pristine forest and green pastures of the Shenandoah Valley.

Like a lady casting aside her cloak, the mist suddenly parted, giving way to brilliant sunshine, lighting the valley with shades of green and gold and russet. Derick quickened his pace, following the single bridle path to Cedar Creek. He halted, waiting for Kearan to rein up beside him.

"Are you taking me to the Longhunter's cabin?" Kearan asked smiling up at him. "I have never been there, though I have often wanted to go, but Papa said it wasn't proper for a lass to visit another man even though the Longhunter is old enough to be my own papa." Kearan's mare pranced, unfamiliar with the path. She turned her around again, her cheeks blushing pink, realizing that accompanying Derick to the Longhunter's cabin was not so very proper either.

She hastened to change the subject. "This is a beautiful area of the valley, Derick," she said endeavoring to dismiss her embarrassment. "No marvel the Longhunter chose this part of the valley to live. Is his cabin far from here?" she queried nervously.

"Not far now, lass. Just follow me. The trail grows narrow, and then opens into a valley." Soon the woods gave way to a beautiful clearing of about 60 acres that bordered Cedar Creek on one side, and fields and trees on the opposite side. The Blue Ridge rose majestically in the distance, painting the skyline with blues and purples.

Kearan drew in her breath. "It is magnificent," she said taking in the visible expanse of the Longhunter's holdings. Derick nodded in agreement. They dismounted and Derick removed the padlock from the cabin door. Then he opened it and motioned for Kearan to precede him.

"I'll put the horses in the stables for a wee rest and give them a bite to eat before we leave for Winchester," Derick called over his shoulder. Then he turned away and led the horses toward the stables.

"Well, Kearan Mackenzie," she said to herself as she looked around the comfortable cabin, "you've gotten yourself into another part of the swamp. All I need is for someone to come along and find me and Derick alone in this cabin. Oh, why didn't I stay with Alfred!"

Pulling her riding gloves from her hands, Kearan looked around at the Longhunter's home. It was like him, comfortable and pleasant, with books to read and a cozy fireplace to warm the cold nights. When she turned around again, Derick's large frame loomed before her, blocking the entire doorway. She startled involuntarily, stepping backward. He came to her side at once, a puzzled look on his face.

"Sorry," she said.

"What ails ye, lass?"

"I...uh...well, seeing you there just startled me, that's all."

"Are ye thinking we shouldn't be here...alone I mean?"

"Probably not a good idea."

"Then we'll leave. I just wanted to show ye...well, never mind. We needn't stay."

"What did you want to show me, Derick. I came all this way, so I guess I can stay a few more minutes."

"Sit here in the rocking chair, lass, and I'll fetch the stool for meself." Kearan did as he bid, and Derick brought the wooden chest containing the Longhunter's war memorabilia, his Gaelic Bible, and his personal effects. He opened the chest and looked at Kearan from his seat on the stool.

"I want ye to know where these things are stored, lass, just in case the Longhunter or I never return to this county. Someone should know." He paused, seeing the frightened look in her eyes. "Are ye still afraid of me, lass?" Derick asked gently.

Kearan felt tears welling up in her velvety brown eyes. She looked away, not wanting him to see her tears. This man was a mystery to her and in spite of his inscrutable ways, she loved him, loved him so much that her heart ached with longing to be with him. She had prayed, even begged for God to take the feelings from her heart, but He had not. She had this moment with him now, *this one moment*.

All too soon, he would join the riflemen and go to war, and for God only knows how long. What if he was killed in battle, buried in some unmarked grave far from home? Should she tell him her heart before it was too late? This was her only opportunity. He might laugh at her, say she was a foolish child, a mere bairn, but she could bear his ridicule because she loved him!

Kearan's mind turned to poor Thomas Aubrey, the young man who had loved her and dared to tell her so. She had rebuffed him, but still he had tried to win her. Now he was dead, his young life snuffed out during his first campaign. This very thought strengthened her resolve. She would share her heart with Derick. He was speaking, and she brought her mind back to the present.

"Are ye all right, lass? Ye dinna answer me. Look at me, Kearan." She turned her face to look at him.

Derick misread the tears shining in her eyes. "Oh, lass, I would not hurt ye...do not fear me. It pains me to think ye believe...I dinna bring ye here to...to..." He could not finish his words. He stood to his full height and reached out his hand, signaling her that they would go.

"No, Derick, please stay a moment longer. I have something to say to you." She tugged at his hand and he resumed his seat on the stool near the rocking chair. She could see far into the clear blue eyes of this man she so desperately loved. His eyes were troubled now, turbulent, and questioning, all the while searching her face.

"Derick," she began tremulously, "do you remember the first time we met—at Morgan's, house—Daniel and Abigail's wedding day? You were standing by the mantel, and I had just arrived with my family. It was snowing as I recall, a gentle snow that clung to the trees and made the world look like a fairyland. Do you remember?"

"Aye, lass, I remember."

"Well...when I saw you standing there by the mantel like some noble stranger and I...I caught your eyes for that brief, transcending moment, I...I fell in love with you right then, not knowing anything about you, not knowing if you were married, or if you were a philanderer, a murderer, or a thief. I only knew that my heart went out to you and that you were the man for me...and I loved you, that is all."

His face tensed and he opened his mouth to speak, but she gently laid her fingers against his lips, stopping his words.

"No, Derick, do not speak. You must hear me out. This may be the only time I have to speak my heart, and I intend to do so." She removed her fingers from his lips, and he remained silent, waiting, breathing a little heavier, and still searching her face.

"I did not want to love you, Derick Davidson. I tried very hard not to care for you, but now I feel I must confess. Everyone said you were not my kind, that I should stick with our frontier lads, but they didn't interest me, never did. I even tried to love Thomas Aubrey—I did, but it would have been a farce, and he deserved the love of a true wife. Now he is dead..." Her voice trailed off.

Pity and remorse were mirrored in her eyes and her voice wavered. "Oh, Derick, if I had only tried harder to love Thomas, he might still be alive! I sent him away with no hope at all. He had no desire to live because I gave him no reason to hope."

Derick looked incredulous. "Ye blame yourself, lass? War takes the good and the bad, the best and worst of men. Only God himself knows the outcome of such conflicts. It is hard to think on, but for some, it is just their time to go. Don't fault yourself, Kearan. It is foolish to take on such misplaced guilt."

"Perhaps I do feel guilty about Thomas, Derick, but haven't you felt the same thing? Haven't you blamed yourself—even when circumstances were out of your control?"

When he did not answer, she lifted her head to look into his blue eyes, now shadowing with memories of the long ago. "Now you know, Derick Davidson. You know my heart. I am ashamed to be telling you so, but I may never see you again, and I don't want you to leave without knowing that someone desperately loves you—loves you as much—as much as your own lost Meagan."

Derick winced at the mention of Meagan, but he knew Kearan spoke the truth. The lass loved him, and he marveled at the thought.

He ran his fingers through the tangle of his dark hair and said, his voice almost a whisper, "Ye are right, lass. I have regrets, and I have blamed meself, blamed God, blamed everyone and everything, but that is over now. Regret is a thoroughly useless penance."

Gently, he took her hand and stood, pulling her from the rocking chair. A frown wrinkled his brow, and Kearan felt her declaration of love had annoyed him. Would there ever be a time when she wouldn't make a fool of herself in his presence? Tears sprang to her eyes, and she turned her face away.

Derick lay his hand against her soft cheek, feeling the hot tears slide across his fingers. He pulled her closer, into the circle of his arms, and she laid her head against his broad chest, knotted her fists into the folds of his hunting shirt, and sobbed out her shame.

"There, lass, don't weep," he soothed. He comforted her, as he would have his own bairns, smoothing her dark curls away from her damp face and speaking to her in comforting tones.

When she finally grew still, she did not move away, but remained quiet, not wanting to leave his warmth, reveling in his nearness.

He leaned down, moving his lips close to her ear. The blue fabric of her muslin skirts clung to his rough buckskin leggings. She felt like a child in his arms, small and insignificant.

"Kearan?" he whispered.

She nodded her head, listening to the steady rhythmic thump of his heart. This moment in time would be worth whatever he was going to say to her. Even if he shamed her for her unconventional boldness, even if he chided her for daring to speak of such personal matters, this one moment, with her head lying next to his heart, would be worth remembering forever.

"Ye said ye loved me from the first time ye saw me standing by the fireside at the Morgans?"

She nodded an affirmative. Here it comes, she thought, the lecture on love and infatuation, on like kinds marrying like kinds, on youth and impetuousness, on the recent trend in female boldness, and on and on...

"I, too, remember that day at Morgans...when first I saw ye. Something passed between us, 'tis true, but I never knew until I returned from the Indian camp, when we sat under the tree and I saw love in your eyes, I knew then that ye loved me...as a woman loves a man. And it was then I knew meself...I loved ye too. Me grieving for Meagan was long enough—was over, 'twas time to move on."

Kearan thought she must be dreaming. Had he really spoken those words—words she had longed to hear but never believed she would?

She gave herself a little shake and said, "I'm sorry, but what were you saying?"

He chuckled. "That I love ye, too, lass."

"You...you love me?" Her eyes widened and she twisted away from him, looking into his face for confirmation of his words. "Would you mind repeating what you just said?"

He smiled and shook his head and lifted one dark curl with his finger. His eyes lit up with joy and wonder. "Will ye listen carefully now? For the third time...I love ye, Kearan Mackenzie and...I am glad ye spoke of your love, that ye opened your heart to me, willing to shame yourself because ye love me so. That is why I love ye, bairnie lass. Ye are so honest, as pure and true as any lass I have ever known in all me life."

She loosened her grip on his shirt and began to shake her head in disbelief, astonishment written on her face.

"Until I came to the Longhunter's cabin," Derick said, "I never knew how much I cared for ye, but I canna deny it any longer. Even knowing I cared, I made up me mind to leave without ever telling ye. It would be less painful should I never return."

"Oh Derick, you can't leave me now, not now. You just came back a month ago from that wretched Indian camp, gone for almost a year. Please don't leave me again!" Her arms wrapped around his neck, and she clung to him with all her strength as though she could keep him from leaving by sheer strength. Derick laughed, and pulled her arms from around his neck. "Ye are a choking me, lass. Come, let's go outside and sit on the Longhunter's workbench."

They sat on the rough wooden bench, and Derick told her all that had happened when he returned to Cedar Creek. He shared his heart, something he never dreamed possible—not with another woman. But Kearan Mackenzie was not just any woman. He knew she would understand why he had challenged God, shaken his fist at Him, demanded to speak to Him, and then, how God had came so convincingly, came with peace and comfort.

"I feel restored, lass," Derick said, "and I have peace with God." The muscles of his jaw tensed. "There is something I want to say to ye. Living with the nightmare of me past nearly broke me, ruined me. When I buried Meagan, I should have buried all me anger and hatred with her as well, but I didn't. Now, the torments of me past are buried at last—with Meagan. Can ye understand me, lass?"

Kearan laid a gentle hand on his and bit her lower lip, her heart melting at his words. "Aye, Derick, I understand, and I am glad for ye." She smiled up at him, her eyes filling with tears. "It's time to move on with your life. God has brought you to this place of surrender. It is not so difficult, is it?"

"On the contrary. 'Tis a great weight off me shoulders."

Then Derick told Kearan of his life with Meagan. The bitter tone was gone now, replaced by the memory of their shared life. That was all that seemed important now. For the first time in years, Derick spoke of Meagan without the burning anger rising in his breast. Kearan asked about his family and he described each of his three children, his eyes lighting up with pleasure when he talked of them. He held nothing back.

During his narrative, Kearan was quiet, listening carefully to all that he said, noting at times his trembling voice when he spoke of his home in the Highlands, of the mother he never knew, and of the father who was a true warrior and wise chief of their clan. At times during his narrative, Kearan's heart swelled with pity and sadness for all that he had lost, but also with thankfulness and love, knowing God had answered her prayers. She was overwhelmed with gratitude.

Derick looked toward the Blue Ridge, a question weighing on his mind. "Do ye still love me now lass, after all that I have told ye?"

"Aye, my love, even more."

"I be considerable older than ye."

"I'm just a wee lass. Does it really matter?"

"Nay. How old are ye now?"

"Almost nineteen."

"Auch, such a bonnie wee lass are ye. I am thirty summers now."

She paused, looking perplexed. "But what was it that you wanted to show me?"

"Come inside for a wee. I thought we best be sitting outside the cabin in case some neighbor stopped by. Could ruin your reputation, ye know. This will only take a moment. I wish to show ye the Longhunter's war memorials so ye can take care of them until he returns to Frederick County, understand?"

Kearan's heart lurched, and she nodded solemnly, not wanting to think that he may never return.

They went inside the cabin and Derick opened the wooden chest and handed Kearan the Longhunter's Gaelic Bible. "When me uncle returns, if he does, make certain he gets his Bible. I have placed it on top of his things." Derick explained the significance of the other items in the chest and told her of the Longhunter's involvement in the earlier wars. Then he explained how to find the exact place in the chimney where the moneybox was hidden. Derick had added his own stash of gold to the box and should neither of them return, she would know about the Longhunter's important papers. He opened the box and lifted out the letters from Duncan, his brother.

"If anything happens to me or me uncle, Kearan, promise me that ye will try and contact me brother, Duncan. He has me own bairns and may need this money, though I doubt it. All that is in this box will belong to Duncan should I or the Longhunter never return."

"Don't, Derick, oh please don't speak of this anymore. I can't bear it. I have just learned that you care about me—love me, and I don't want to think of death and legacies and...and..."

Seeing her distress, Derick carefully replaced the box, and then gathered her in his arms, holding her close. For so long now, he had resisted this charming lass, ignored her sweet impetuous ways, turned from her wooing of him, and reproached her fiery outburst, but now, he felt free to open his heart to her, to love again. The very thought was heady, exhilarating.

Derick brushed her hair aside with his lips and said, "Nay, lass, nay. I know it grieves ye, but I must make plans, for me own bairns' sake, but deep in me soul, I feel God will bring me back to ye."

"But how can you promise that you will ever return?"

"I canna promise, but I feel in me heart that I will return. I will not go on this first campaign, but I will fight with the Patriots. I need to find me uncle first. At least, I must know if he is well. Perhaps he is dead from his wound by now. Do ye understand? After I know about me uncle, I will take me place with the riflemen. I will 'take it back', as ye have said. I will take back all the English have stolen from me, and especially..." He paused to look into her eyes, "...especially me heart."

She smiled softly, remembering her words to him. "Can I go with you then?"

"Go with me?" He sounded incredulous. She grasped the hilt of her grandfather's sword and lifted her chin in a proud, defiant gesture. Derick could not help smiling. Kearan Mackenzie was the most unpredictable lass he had ever known, and he loved that about her. Life with Kearan would be an exciting adventure, and for a moment, he was intrigued with the idea of taking her with him.

"I have no doubt that ye could survive in this howling wilderness," he agreed. "God help the Indians or any Loyalist who might capture ye, but nay, ye cannot come. I want ye here at home...safe, waiting for me."

"Well then," she said, the fire going out of her eyes, "will you marry me before you leave to find the Longhunter—before you go to the war?"

He could only stare at her for a moment, unbelieving. He laughed. It came from deep inside, a laugh such as he had not experienced in years. He paused long enough to see the fire rising in her eyes again, but before he could speak, the loud crash of a heavy boot burst the door wide open, and the would-be intruder ducked quickly aside, stepping behind the doorframe to shield himself from the possibility of flying bullets. In mere seconds, Derick drew his sword and shoved Kearan behind him, but just as quickly, Kearan drew her own sword and assumed the on guard position, ready for whatever might come through the door.

"Come outta there, you stinkin' nesters, you good fer nothin' squatters, you lazy trespassers! Show your ugly faces afore I blow your bloomin' heads off." The voice coming from outside the door sounded familiar.

Kearan and Derick with their swords at the ready looked at each other in astonishment and began to laugh. There was no mistaking the deep and distinctive voice of Captain Daniel Morgan, Virginia riflemen.

Hearing Derick's low chuckle and Kearan's giggle coming from inside the cabin, Morgan poked his head carefully around the edge of the doorway. He was quite taken aback when he saw Derick and Kearan Mackenzie, swords in hand, ready to do battle.

"Well, hush my mouth," Morgan huffed as he came from around the doorframe and sauntered leisurely into the room. "I wouldn't have figured you two for squatter folk!"

Chapter 21

Long Road to Independence

Wrong cannot rest
Nor ill deed stand

The Patriot committee of Frederick County was comprised of the Reverend Charles Thruston, the Zanes, Angus McDonald, and three other ardent Patriots from the surrounding villages in the county. The men had enthusiastically endorsed Morgan's company of ninety-six riflemen to represent Frederick County with the best sharpshooters the colony of Virginia had to offer.

Despite Morgan's urging, Derick Davidson could not be persuaded to join the group of riflemen, who eagerly awaited orders for their first campaign with the Continental army. However, Derick readily agreed to join the company after he located his uncle. He feared the Wyandot Indians were holding the Longhunter against his will.

Finding the Longhunter was imperative to Derick, and although Morgan had gone to Cedar Creek with the express purpose of enlisting his friend for the military campaign, his pleading was to no avail. Derick made it clear—he would not leave Frederick County for what might be a long military engagement, not without first discovering the whereabouts of his uncle. He remained firm in his resolution.

In early July, 1775, Morgan's company was called to active duty. Their orders were to serve as sharpshooters and snipers to harass the British throughout the ongoing siege of Boston, and to garrison there until plans were in place for the campaign against the British-held city of Quebec. This arduous campaign would be a two-pronged offensive under the leadership of Benedict Arnold, a thirty-four-year old Connecticut merchant, who was also a strong-headed zealot of uncanny abilities, and General Richard Montgomery, a seasoned veteran.

The best of the Virginia frontiersmen assembled in Winchester on July 14, 1775, at one of the town's favorite haunts—the Golden Buck Tavern. On seeing so many brawny Virginians grouped together in one place, someone suggested measuring their heights against a support post of the smoky tavern. To add to everyone's pride over Frederick County's company of riflemen, it was discovered that all ninety-six men of Morgan's company of sharpshooters were, without exception, six feet tall or better!

The riflemen marched in parade through the streets of Winchester, past the county courthouse, past the stone edifice of the Anglican Church, and, of course, past the waving patrons gathered in front of the Golden Buck tavern. The riflemen returned their salutes to a crowd of wildly cheering Patriots while hastily assembled bands played, drummers drummed, and nondescript dogs barked by the sides of wildly excited and leaping children.

To the residents of Frederick County, the riflemen were a wonderful sight to behold—all dressed in the typical uniform of the frontier: a long, fringed hunting shirt the color of dry leaves, tough buckskin leggings and moccasins, and a hat with a buck's tail protruding from the wide band. They carried their rifles and tomahawks; many had even brought their scalping knives. Some of the riflemen were as young as sixteen, and a few as old as sixty, but the majority of men headed for battle were somewhere in their twenties. Morgan's company had one common skill—they were all expert marksmen.

Alfred Mackenzie's leg wound had healed sufficiently for him to join the march to Boston. His father, Silas Mackenzie, remained behind with the home guard. The Virginia frontier and border regions would be left defenseless against the threat of Indians who prowled the borders and could easily take advantage of the absentee riflemen. A home guard was necessary so the older riflemen remained behind for this first campaign.

Abigail lingered along the edge of the dusty walkway with Lily Jayne, Kearan, and Silas, all waiting to say a final farewell to Alfred and Morgan before the riflemen began the long march to Boston.

Morgan rode up astride Samson, sending dust flying through the air as he reined his horse in next to Abigail and the Mackenzies. They were watching the crowd that lined the streets of Winchester and had come to pay their respects to the brave men and their sacrificing families.

Most inhabitants of Frederick County had known the riflemen for years and had watched the young boys grow to manhood while defending the frontier. They were valued friends and neighbors, living together since the Shenandoah Valley was a wilderness teeming with hostile Indians and ruthless renegades.

Morgan dismounted. "Here ya go, Kearan," he said tossing Samson's reins to her. "Take good care of him for me, just like you did for Davidson's Warrior when he was away." He grinned mischievously, and Kearan's cheeks grew pink. She glared at her neighbor and close friend, daring him to mention finding her with Derick Davidson at the Longhunter's cabin. Leaning close to her ear, Morgan whispered, "Your secret is safe with me."

"Oh...you are impossible, Daniel Morgan. There is no secret to be kept and you know it. I have nothing to hide after all. Just go away. I hope the British blow your ugly, bloomin' head off."

Morgan laughed. "Now, Kearan, gal, I know you don't mean that! Better not say something you'll regret later. Besides, that's no way to treat your Uncle Dan'l, a man who's offerin' his life on the altar of his country!"

Kearan scowled at him.

"And, gal, you look as pretty as a speckled pup when you're mad, especially with that sword hangin' on your side. I bet my clean socks you'd like to come with us."

Morgan turned from Kearan's scorching look with a laugh and gathered Abigail into his arms. She was making a valiant effort to contain her tears. "We'll be leaving shortly, Abby," he said in a serious tone. He had dreaded this moment for weeks, the moment of parting from Abigail. As he held her close, he caught sight of Derick Davidson in his periphery as he approached from the opposite side of the street. "Just give me a few minutes with Davidson, Abby. I'll be back shortly."

Morgan motioned to Derick and pulled him aside to speak privately. They stepped into a narrow alley intersecting the main road where they still had a full view of the bands parading down Main Street.

"Davidson," Morgan began without preamble, "I understand why you're stayin' back, but I still wish you were comin' with us. I know your worth as a leader, your fearlessness, and you have a way of keepin' those young bucks focused."

"They'll do fine without me, Morgan," Derick interjected.

"Maybe. Can't say I don't worry over those young'uns. That's what they are, ya know. When the Brits get on us like stink on a polecat, they might lose their focus, their direction." He sighed heavily. "Hated losing the Aubrey boy at the Point. Somethin' about how he talked with me after he was shot. He was young, so young. I felt responsible. Guess Aubrey just sticks in my craw. He was fond of Kearan."

Derick laid one large hand on Morgan's shoulder. "It's because of Kearan ye think of Aubrey. In battle, death comes to the young and old alike, Morgan. You're a soldier—ye know that. 'Tis the price of war. Everyone who signed with the rifleman knows it. Don't blame yourself over Aubrey, Morgan." Derick touched his sword, the blade on which the Longhunter had inscribed with the words, *Sword of the Wild Rose*. Morgan's eyes followed the gesture and rested on the sword.

"I've had some time to consider me reasons for not fighting with the Patriots," Derick continued, "and I'm ready to lift me sword to defend this country against tyranny, Morgan, but win or lose, this time I will raise me sword with honor—not for vengeance."

"I'm mighty glad to hear it, Davidson, but why not change your mind? Come with us now."

"First...me uncle."

Morgan shook his head in frustration. "Davidson, do you know how many years the Longhunter has survived in the backwoods wilderness before you came to the Shenandoah? You Scots have a strange passion about clan ties, don't ya?"

Derick smiled. "Aye, that we do."

"Well, long as you're hangin' around, stop and check on Abigail now and then. It's hard on her and the little gals, you know. Abigail, well, she's such a...a tender kinda woman."

Derick nodded. "Aye, she is that I'm a thinkin'. When I'm about the county, I'll stop in and see her, Morgan. Silas Mackenzie will be close at hand too, ye know."

"Yup, he's a good support to the entire community, can be trusted to handle any situation." Morgan looked serious and abruptly changed the subject.

"And what's this about you and Kearan?"

Derick looked surprised and then disgusted. He frowned.

Morgan cleared his throat and spat on the ground. "Now, I know nothing happened at the cabin so just wipe that dog-ugly look off'n your royal face. Know you by now—Kearan too, but things are different, somethin's changed. Before I leave for what might be a long spell, I wanna know."

Derick lowered his eyes and looked somewhat annoyed. "Aye, Morgan, things have changed—*I* have changed. When I was at the Longhunter's cabin, I made me peace with God—peace with me past, that loathsome baggage I carried across the ocean with me. I was bitter as gall, Morgan, and ye knew it. I suppose everyone knew it, including Kearan. The load was a killing me—taking me soul to hell with it." He reached up and adjusted his hat.

"But Morgan, there in the cabin, God delivered me from the hate and bitterness that has dogged me across an entire ocean. It's gone—all over now. I'm ready for whatever comes, for whatever the future holds for me here on this powder keg, the land where we will finally conquer the British. It's time, ye know."

"Well," Morgan said with a sharp intake of breath, "that's the longest speech you ever made, Davidson, and downright touchin'." He paused, his features sobering. "Seriously, I'm happy for you. Pleased as punch you found...uh...peace with God. Yup, I'm happier'n a pig in a peach orchard! It's high time you let them ugly wounds heal up. I'll have to say, you worried me some, but I always thought you'd come through."

Derick raised his eyes to Morgan and looked straight into the questioning blue-gray eyes of his friend. He knew Morgan was weighing his statement, not wanting to challenge his sincerity but at the same time, not quite sure he believed his confession.

In the distance, a rousing march played near the Anglican Church, and the wails of a baby rose above the hum of the crowd. Derick shifted his position, his tall muscular form dominating the narrow alleyway.

"It was divine providence that we met in Boston, Morgan. Ye have been more than a friend—like me own brother I left in Scotland. I'm sorry for grieving ye with that awful gnawing bitterness. Was just something I had to work out meself, Morgan. Only God could lift that kind of burden." He hesitated, and the muscles in his jaws tightened.

"A man's alone when it comes to facing his own self, looking at his own reflection in the mirror and accepting what he sees—even when it ain't' a pretty sight. I finally took a good look at meself and saw how the hate I had for Meagan's murderers, for the British, for all me losses—well, it was disfiguring me on the inside, destroying me. I couldn't go on, couldn't face another day without facing God—man to man." His voice grew husky. "God found me in that state, Morgan, and he didn't leave me there. He lifted me out of it. I'm sorry if I ever let ye down."

"Well, it's over now," Morgan answered, his own voice rough with emotion, "so don't think on it anymore. And you didn't let me down, Davidson. I figured that someday, you'd get over the hurtin'." Morgan motioned toward the frontiersmen grouping together.

"The young riflemen respect you, and so do I. Forget all those despicable scoundrels who did you wrong and help the Patriots to settle the score. I owe 'em one myself. You saw my back. We'll make America a free nation. You can make this your home, the land of true liberty. Like I told you in Boston, *we will win this time*, and when we do, I want you to be there! I don't want anyone who fights for freedom to miss that day."

"Ye know, Morgan, there's two kinds of freedom—the liberty to do what ye please and the liberty to do what ye ought. I believe it's time for the Patriots to do what they ought—aye, *what they must*."

"I couldn't say it better myself, Davidson. We oughtta free the Colonies from British rule and that blood sucking parliament. We will, by gum, if it's the last thing we ever do!"

Suddenly remembering his original question, Morgan said, "You never answered me. What about you and Kearan?"

"Well, Kearan says ye warned her about sticking with her own kind, that she should choose a gentleman from among the frontier lads. I reckon I'm not her kind, in your opinion, and I wouldn't be your choice for the lass."

Morgan looked uneasy, shifted his weight, and then settled a steadfast gaze on Derick. "I'm not much when it comes to knowin' about gentleman and ladies, love and marriage and the like, but there's an old sayin'—court far and wide, but marry next door. Most times, that's what works the best." He paused, seeing the doubt and uncertainty on Derick's features.

"Well," he continued with a note of compassion in his voice, "do you love the gal, Davidson?"

Derick rubbed his chin thoughtfully. "Only recently did I know it, Morgan. When God buried the sins of me past in the seas, then I knew...knew that I could love again, but I believe I have cared for the lass for some time. It was hard to sort out me true feelings with memories of me life with Meagan."

"I understand what you're sayin' but, well, Kearan's always been special to me. I was tryin' to spare her of a future with a stranger who wouldn't understand her ways. She's kinda feisty, ya know. I could see the gal was lookin' your way...from the very first she was. Didn't want to see her cryin' around over what couldn't be—what shouldn't be." Morgan pulled a plug of tobacco from his pocket.

"Besides, all you felt those days was your own misery and nothin' else. Didn't seem to be interested in the gal in that way, so I thought it best to spare her the grief. She's like a daughter to me, you know." He sighed, a resigned look on his rugged face.

"But, since you've dumped all that miserable garbage in a sea somewhere, and God only knows where, then I reckon it might work—if you truly love the gal, that is. I suppose her Pa won't mind. He likes you well enough. Both of you are descended from that same blistering race of stubborn Scots, although Silas seems to forget that part. He's just a plain old frontiersman."

"But do *ye* mind?" Derick asked solemnly.

Morgan smiled. "It doesn't matter what I think, but nope—I don't mind. You should know right off—Kearan's an awful willful gal at times. Why, she just told me she hopes the Brits blow my bloomin' head off. Of course, that's a bunch of blather. She don't mean it, but she talks like that. She's a handful now."

Derick's eyes grew misty, and he opened his large hands toward Morgan, palms upward. "Me hands are empty, Morgan."

There was something so pitiable, so pathetic in the gesture, but Daniel Morgan understood. A broad smile creased his face, wrinkling the scar along his cheek and showing the dark gap of missing teeth. "Those big hands might be empty now, but afore this year is out, they'll be filled with guns and swords. We've a war to fight, Davidson."

"I be thinking of holding something warmer than the cold barrel of me rifle, Morgan."

"Ha! I just bet you do. You mean…a bonny lass by some chance?"

The two men shared a moment of laughter and then grew serious. It was time to part. Who could say if they would ever meet again, and if they did, how changed both might be. They shook hands and then embraced when the handshake didn't seem quite enough for such a leave taking.

"Godspeed, me friend," Derick said huskily, "and I'll see ye at the front line of the next battle."

"The next battle, my friend," Morgan agreed. He was trying not to show the emotion he felt. Morgan's early life held no warm memories of family and kin, no kind words, or fond farewells. Derick Davidson was more than a friend to him, but he could not say why. He only knew their friendship ran deep and true, without pretense or affectation.

"Now, don't go gettin' yourself captured by the Indians while you're a searchin' for your uncle," Morgan warned. "You'd be as worthless to the Continental army as a one-legged man in a kickin' contest."

Derick laughed. "I'll do me best to stay outta the hands of the Indians and keep me scalp on me head. I've heard some of the tribes are celebrating this revolution—happy to see the Americans pitted against the English, hoping they'll kill each other and leave them in peace."

It was Morgan's turn to laugh. "Can't say as I blame 'em, but the Indians will camp on the side that promises the most land, money, or goods. Some tribes don't trust either side, the British or the Americans. They'll stay out of the fight until it's nearly over then side with the winner."

The two men left the alley and walked to where Abigail waited with the Mackenzies.

One last kiss for Abigail, and Morgan joined the riflemen to begin the long march to Boston. Abigail threw herself on Lily Jayne who was already weeping. Alfred Mackenzie took his place with his comrades, blew a kiss to his mother, and then turned away.

Morgan waved his hat to the crowd as he and his company of ninety-six Virginians left the town of Winchester marching down the road in the scorching heat of a July summer to the enthusiastic shouts and whoops of the Patriots of Frederick County.

Twenty-one days later, on August 6, 1775, Captain Daniel Morgan and his company of Frederick County riflemen arrived at Boston ahead of Captain Hugh Stephenson's company from Berkeley County, Virginia. Both companies had competed to be the first to arrive for the campaign. Morgan's riflemen were the first sharpshooters to join the Continental army at the siege of Boston.

Chapter 22

Sword of the Wild Rose

And I will come again, my Love
Though it were ten thousand miles

By mid September, when the treetops of the Shenandoah Valley were radiant with the gold and scarlet of autumn, and the first chilling frost had swept across the fields, Derick had purchased a sturdy packhorse and assembled enough supplies to begin the difficult passage to the Ohio country. He hoped to find his uncle and bring him home to Cedar Creek, or at least, to discover his whereabouts before the year was out.

According to the typical pattern of wilderness hunters, Donald Davidson should have returned home in early spring, but it was now early autumn. Obviously, his uncle had fallen out of favor with the Wyandots, or was too ill to return to his home.

On his way to the Kanawha, Derick stopped by Morgan's farm to visit with Abigail and the little girls. He greeted Nancy and Betsy with a kiss and offered them some red and white peppermint candy that he had purchased from the Mercantile in Winchester. The girls squealed with delight and pleasure then ran off to play and enjoy the special treat.

"Wiping her hands on a dishcloth, Abigail asked, "Any news from town about the siege of Boston...the riflemen?". A flock of brown hens ran toward her, clucking noisily, hoping for some kitchen scraps. Abigail shooed them away. She stood next to Derick in the doorway. "You know, Derick, I haven't heard much news since Daniel's company arrived in Boston last month."

"There's not much to tell ye, Abigail, not this soon. The riflemen are just hunkering down in camp, waiting for orders to leave for the north. From what I hear in Winchester, it appears that Arnold will be heading up the campaign." He paused and looked around at the neatly kept farm with the late summer garden ready to harvest.

"Everything good here, Abigail?"

"Oh...good as can be without Daniel around." Then she brightened. "Yes, Derick, everything is fine," she added smiling.

Derick could see that she was trying to be brave.

"The farm hands are getting ready for winter; chopping wood, laying up feed for the animals, cleaning the barns, the typical harvest work. There will be butchering to do in late autumn and pressing apples for cider, gathering in the rest of the root crops."

Derick nodded.

Abigail looked pensive, her blue-green eyes straying to the fields where the men were piling straw onto a wagon. "It will be a long winter without Daniel around."

"Are ye fearful, Abigail? Do ye feel safe enough?"

Abigail smiled. "Daniel taught me how to shoot long ago, Derick, and two of the farm hands are staying in the rooms by the stable—the room where you bunked. I rather miss you being there, though. I always felt safer when you were here at the farm. You're like family, Derick."

He returned her smile. Taking Abigail's small hand in his, he raised it briefly to his lips, just as he had on their first meeting. "Ye are a great lady, Abigail Morgan, even in your Virginia homespun.

But it matters not what ye are wearing or the dwelling where ye abide that makes ye a great lady, 'tis what's in your heart. I'm happy ye think of me as your kin."

"And you, dear friend, possess the gift of flattery," she replied. They both laughed. "However," Abigail continued, "I must confess, you've brought a new and commendable perspective for our rough frontier men to consider."

The lighthearted moment passed and Abigail's eyes shadowed with concern as she looked at the big Scotsman with genuine compassion. He was going away, and this would not be an easy trip. Like many of those who traveled the lonely journey to the west, he may never return.

"I feel a great deal of compassion for you, Derick Davidson," Abigail sympathized. "Before Daniel left for the war, he told me of your early life in Scotland...of your beloved wife, the tragedy of her death. He told me that you left your children in the care of your brother." She dropped her head and stared at the ground. "I understand how terrible it was for you, Derick, to leave your family." Abigail lifted her head and her eyes filled with knowing tears.

"Aye," Derick agreed without any trace of the old bitterness in his voice, "me journey in the land of mist and tears ended in great sorrow to be sure. Those memories—they do not sting with poison as they once did, and those dreadful days—they must remain in me past." He smiled down at her but his blue eyes held sadness.

"God being me helper, I will build a new life—start over, " he added on a positive note. "I believe I am ready to claim this wild new country as me own, and if God wills...perhaps, He will find another lass for me to love. Aye, Abigail?"

Laughing softly at his honest confession, Abigail guessed at the allusion. "Perhaps He will, Derick. At any rate, I'm glad you are considering such a possibility. Would be a blessing and an answer to my prayers for you. We want you to be happy, Derick."

"I know ye do, Abigail. Thank ye for your kind words. I believe what ye say is true."

"And are you on your way now to find your uncle?" Abigail said changing to a less personal subject. "You seem to have enough supplies to last the winter, and a packhorse too. Are you taking Warrior with you?"

"Nay, I'm leaving Warrior with the Mackenzies. Kearan offered to keep him at their farm while I'm away. Less bother for ye, and Kearan takes to caring for the beast. I haven't seen the lass these many weeks, so I'm hoping the offer is still good." He touched his hat. "I'll be on me way now, Abigail."

Derick mounted Warrior in one smooth motion and turned to Abigail. "Is there anything I can do for ye? Do ye need anything?"

Abigail moved closer to Warrior and looked up at Derick. "No, nothing. I'm fine. I have everything I need." She paused, laying a small hand against his horse. "Just be careful, Derick, and come back to us." Looking into the calm, resolute eyes of Derick Davidson, tears rose unexpectedly to her eyes. Warrior pawed the ground impatiently, eager to leave.

"When you return from the Ohio country, will you join Daniel and the riflemen?" she asked. "You...well, Derick, you're good for Daniel. He is growing older, you know."

"That's me plan at present. I will join the riflemen eventually. But don't underestimate your husband, Abigail. He is still badger tough and strong enough to take on the British." Abigail's hand twisted in Warrior's mane as though she would hold him there. Understanding her reluctance to let him go, Derick gave her hand a comforting squeeze. "Dinna fash yourself, me lady. I believe Daniel will come home to ye again."

Abigail dropped her hand from Warrior's thick mane and smiled at Derick. "I believe Daniel will come back to me, too, and your words are so reassuring, so comforting."

Nudging Warrior with the pressure of his knees, Derick trotted his horse in the direction of the Mackenzie farm, leading the packhorse loaded with supplies. He turned in the saddle to wave to Abigail then disappeared down the road.

While he was still a little distance from the Mackenzie farm, he saw Kearan standing near the orchard next to a fence post she placed there for sword practice. She wore a crimson colored jacket over a deep blue frock trimmed in white lace. Her long dark hair was tied back with a blue ribbon and fell in ringlets to her waist. The pungent smell of ripened apples and drying leaves perfumed the air with the heady odor of another Shenandoah autumn.

Derick had not seen Kearan since that day at the Longhunter's cabin nearly two months ago when he had confessed his love for her. He had purposely stayed away. Seeing her now, his heart swelled with a renewed sense of happiness.

The silver blade of her sword flashed in the morning sunlight as she slashed the badly battered post with the edge of the sword, sending splinters of wood flying in all directions. Derick smiled to himself as he watched her from behind the barn. Arriving from the opposite direction, coupled with the sounds of her sword striking the post, Kearan had not heard him approach.

Dismounting, he tied Warrior and the packhorse to the rails of the cattle pen and then crept stealthily to where the young woman was doing battle with the fence post.

"Spirit of the wild rose," he challenged in his strong masculine voice, "face your opponent and prepare to defend your position."

Kearan whirled, her long dark hair flying from off her shoulders. The swish of her skirts rustled softly as she turned to face him and her eyes met his in absolute surprise. Indignation and embarrassment spread across her features, and she immediately assumed an on guard position, sword held before her at the ready.

"So—it's you, Mr. Derick Davidson," she breathed unsteadily. "I thought you had disappeared from the face of the earth. And here you are, creeping up on unsuspecting women, terrorizing them as you ride about the county in a decidedly underhanded fashion."

He said nothing, scarcely hearing her words, but seeing her with an overwhelming sense of longing, the picture of her outrage burning a lasting image in his mind. Even in her fury, she appeared heart-stoppingly beautiful, winsome and totally beguiling as she waited in the soft glow of the morning sunlight for his reply.

Derick never allowed himself to think of Kearan Mackenzie in a romantic way, but only as a friend or younger sister. He had tried to deceive himself, believing that he would never love again, that this frontier girl was only a child who would outgrow her infatuation with him. Seeing her now, his heart melted, and he allowed the tender feelings to come, welcoming the sweetness, knowing his passion was pure, heaven-sent, an unadulterated and rare emotion.

Finding love twice in a lifetime seemed too good to be true. Yet, here it was, in all its unspeakable joy and sweetness. Why hadn't he come to her before? He knew the answer. He could confront a horde of redcoats or even the wild and merciless Indians, but he did not want to face another parting, another goodbye.

"What a villain!" she stormed while he continued to gaze at her in thoughtful silence. "Face your opponent like a real man, you cowardly beast—declaring your love to a frontier maiden, then slinking away into the shadows!"

Her words penetrated Derick's wandering thoughts, jolting him from his reverie. He cocked his head to one side, considering her words, and then decided to play along with her game. In one instant, he unsheathed the Longhunter's sword.

Before he could assume a defensive position, Kearan charged in, thrusting her sword at his mid section. Only by skillful maneuvering did he manage to parry the thrust. She was nimble and light, quick with her hand. He could see she was not playing swords, but wielding her blade in dead earnest. He would end this ridiculous and dangerous pretense.

He gathered his wits and began to circle, waiting for an opportunity to end this ridiculous sparring match. He would knock the sword from her grasp with one quick stroke of his blade.

In truth, the lass appeared quite hostile. Derick was perplexed at her obviously aggressive attitude. Their eyes met and locked, but Kearan's eyes burned with an unusually brilliant fire.

"There has not been one time in the past two years," she panted between thrusts and parries, "that you have not bested me, humiliated me to my shoelaces, won every verbal dispute, and triumphed at every session of swordplay, not to mention," she added taking a deep breath, "abandoning me. But this time, Mr. Davidson, I refuse to allow you to win! Do you hear me, Derick Davidson? You are going down—that's right, *going down!*"

Derick's blue eyes sparkled, and he laughed uproariously at her daring boast and at the picture she made in her apparent outrage at him. "Going down? Am I now?" He laughed again at her insolent boast.

His sword met her thrusts blow for blow, steel clanging against steel, sending glittering sparks flying into the air. She fought skillfully, and only then did he realize how well he had taught her and how absolutely determined she seemed. He was larger, stronger, but she was amazingly quick and fought with finesse and assurance.

"What in heaven's name ails ye, lass?" he finally said while sidestepping her sword as she slashed dangerously close to his head. "Ye can hurt a man like that, I be thinkin'." He was beginning to weary of this peculiar game but she seemed determined, relentless.

"Aye," she said mocking him, "and ye be thinking right. I plan to cut off your handsome Scottish head so you won't remember me ever again—you won't remember that I—" Suddenly, she stopped the wild slashing of her sword and lowering the weapon to her side, she looked at him questioningly. The smoldering fire had left her eyes, replaced by a soft pool of tears that reflected her unhappiness.

Derick lowered his sword in turn and waited, thoroughly mystified at her peculiar behavior. Then before he could raise his weapon, she dashed in again, slashing at his legs with a wild churning motion. He leapt backward with a quick motion, feeling the blade of her sword slice through his buckskin leggings.

In his effort to get away from her blade, he lost his footing, tripped, and fell full length onto the ground, face upward toward the sky. In an instant, Kearan was at him, the tip of her sword against his throat. He lay very still, but raised both hands in surrender, stunned at her apparent fury.

"I yield, fair damsel," he pleaded somewhat dazed. The tip of the sword was sharp, pressing against his throat, causing a spot of blood to appear where the tip of the sword rested against his flesh. She looked as though she might thrust him through.

"Kearan," he gasped disbelieving, "What are ye doing? Have ye lost your good sense?"

"Yes indeed. I lost my good sense long ago when I met you and I'm not letting you up—not until you promise me something, and I mean it!"

She kept the sword pressed against his throat. He couldn't move, didn't dare move.

"Anything, I'll do anything, lass. Just put your weapon up. If ye don't move that blade, I'll be a dead man. What is it that ye want?"

She hesitated slightly, and then said, "Do you remember when we were at the Longhunter's cabin?" A blush rose in her cheeks. "When I asked you to...to...marry me?" Her eyes misted with shame.

"It's difficult to remember anything when I'm laying on me back with the tip of a sword pressed to me throat."

She ignored his comment. "I said..." One hand went to her brow, but she did not lesson the pressure of the sword. "...marry me before you go away. Do you remember that I said those words?"

"Aye," he answered, amusement in his voice, "I remember." Despite his awkward position on the hard ground, he grinned. "How could I ever forget those words?"

Anger flashed in her eyes, and she spoke in anguished protest. "That's exactly what I'm talking about, Derick Davidson. I want you to—to forget those words. Promise me that you will—that you won't remember anything I said. Never mention that day again. If you agree, then I might let you live, otherwise—you're dead."

Now he understood. She was ashamed of those impulsive words, even if she had meant them. He must forget that she had ever asked him to marry her, ever uttered those hasty words that violated her womanly sense of propriety, respectability, and decorum. In her own mind, she had breached all of them.

Someday, Kearan reasoned; when he remembered her bold and improper marriage proposal, he might tease her, even shame her for such daring. After all, to request a man's hand in marriage was completely unconventional and against her own personal ideals. Therefore, he must be made to forget that she had ever spoken those words.

Derick smiled. He could do this. "Actually, lass," he said swallowing a lump rising in his throat, "I can't quite remember what ye be talking about. Just slipped from me mind—completely vanished. I canna seem to recall what ye might be referring to."

"Really? You forgot everything that happened that day? Everything I said to you in the cabin?" The pressure of the sword eased.

"At the moment, I can't seem to retain much of that particular conversation," he answered. "Seems kind of foggy and appears to be slipping from me memory altogether."

"Promise?"

"I promise ye, lass. I will simply...forget. I can do that."

Reassured, Kearan dropped her sword and sank down beside him, her blue skirts spreading like a fan on the grass. Derick raised himself rather stiffly to a sitting position and fished for his handkerchief. He dabbed at the spot of blood on his throat and then held it against the bloody scratch where his leggings were sliced through.

As Kearan watched him wipe the blood away, her face crumpled in utter distress. With her elbows resting on her knees, she covered her face with her hands. Hot tears slipped from beneath her fingers and her shoulders shook with unrestrained sobs.

With a quiet gentleness, Derick pried her hands away from her face and held them tightly in his own. Kearan turned her face away.

"Hush now, lass. Dinna fash yourself."

"That's easy for you to say, Derick Davidson," she sobbed. Still, she wouldn't look at him. "And I do fret myself for being such a blooming idiot. I told you all my heart, humiliated myself, and you never came to me. I was an idiot—a fool." She stared at the scratch on his leg that was oozing a slow trickle of blood.

"I cut you, even drew blood, and then made you promise to forget, threatening you with my sword. Why did you come now after all this time? You caught me at a bad time, you know, at a vulnerable moment in my life."

"I'm sorry, lass." He released her hands and she plucked at her skirts.

"I have missed you so dreadfully and…and…" she hesitated, then turned to look at him, her eyes searching his. "I didn't know if you really meant what you said…that day at the cabin."

"Kearan, me bonny lass, I meant every word, but I will confess, I am a coward where love is concerned."

"But why didn't you come to me?" she persisted.

He sighed. "Perhaps because I am afraid of losing another love. I fear nothing, but I find meself wondering if this sweet love is real or only a wishful dream. I stayed away, thinking ye were too young, that ye could not love such as me, but here I am, with naught but love to blame, nothing more." His blue eyes misted. "Do ye understand?"

"Yes, but your fears are unproven, unfounded. Can't you see how much I care for you? But you will never understand me either, Derick. How could you? I don't understand myself. I only know that I love you, that's all."

"Aye, but I do understand ye. I know your ways...how ye are feeling about that day at the cabin. T'was true to your own charming ways, to be certain."

Kearan examined the place where her sword had grazed his leg. Dismay was written on her features.

He shook his head with misgiving. "I'm truly sorry, lass. I should have come. I thought it best...that the parting be not so painful... but I was wrong to grieve ye so. Will ye forgive me?"

"Only if you will forgive me for cutting you with my sword," she replied.

"Ye must know that I don't fault ye, Kearan. 'Tis only a wee scratch."

"That was stupid of me, Derick—to fight you," she said remorsefully. "Will I ever stop doing stupid things?"

He smiled, but said nothing.

"Since you've promised to forget about...that day, I won't fight you again, I promise," Kearan said.

"Well, ye might have been a wee bit gentler with the blade, lass. Ye nigh killed me," Derick added with some amusement.

Kearan sighed. She felt drained and exhausted. Noting her weariness, Derick placed a strong arm around her shoulders and drew her close. She felt strength in his nearness and relaxed, laying her head against his chest, her dark hair tumbling across his hunting shirt like a cascading waterfall. For a long moment, they sat in silence. He twisted his fingers in her tresses, lifting one dark curl to his lips.

"Are you going away?" she finally asked raising her head to look at him.

"Aye, I have come to tell ye so. I am leaving for the Ohio country—to find me uncle."

She looked at him with grief stricken eyes. "So you really are leaving? Can I…" She hesitated, biting her lip, not daring to finish her thought, but he knew her too well.

For one brief and foolish moment, he almost yielded to her tempting suggestion. The thought of her traveling by his side was wildly sweet, like Kearan herself, but he knew it was not possible, not sensible. He answered with genuine reluctance. "Nay, lass. I cannot take ye. I told ye before—ye cannot come on such a dangerous journey."

She nodded slowly, lowering her head and looking down again, knowing his mind was set. She offered no further argument.

With one hand, he turned her face to look at him. "When I return from this war, lass, and the Patriots are free from tyranny—" He paused, his eyes searching hers, "will ye marry me,? Will ye wait for me, Kearan Mackenzie?"

"Why, Derick, you mean…you truly want…" Her voice trailed off and she could not finish her thought.

"Who can say how long this war will last," Derick said wistfully. He looked into the distance, to where the blue-gray haze hovered over the mountains of the Shenandoah. "The days will be long and empty for a lass waiting for war to end, waiting for her warrior to return from battle."

"Perhaps the war won't last so long," Kearan suggested.

Derick's face tensed and sorrow filled his eyes. "I have nothing to offer ye now, but upon my sacred honor, I offer ye me love for all time, for as long as God allows me to live. And if I live through this battle for freedom, I will come for ye, though it be ten thousand miles, I will return. With God as me helper, I will make a home for ye—in this land."

Kearan laid her head against his chest, her heart too full to speak. She could hear the strong, steady beat of his heart and felt an assurance in her own soul.

"I will wait for you, Derick Davidson," she whispered softly, "until this dreadful war is over and…and even longer if I must. I believe you will come back to me. God promised me long ago, when I first saw you at Morgan's wedding that He would bring you from the shadows of your dark and troubling past, and when He did, you would come to me."

Then Kearan smiled at him, a secret triumph shining in her brown eyes. She had wooed this mysterious and sober man, had prayed for God to turn his heart to her, the man whom she had loved from the very first moment their eyes had met at Morgan's wedding. The reticent and brooding Scotsman loved her. She had won his heart. Kearan laughed aloud.

Derick raised an eyebrow but he could not resist her joy. With renewed assurance, he kissed her soft and laughing lips. Happiness swept over him like a rising tide, filling his heart and soul with joy, dispelling his doubts and all the dark shadows of the ancient times.

She said at last. "Derick, has anyone ever asked you to marry them? I mean…am I the only one?"

He thought for a moment. "Nay," he answered amused, "no other lass, not that I remember." Laying his cheek against her soft dark curls, he continued. "But not long ago, I dreamed a bonny lass with tresses dark like yours and eyes the color of autumn leaves—I dreamed she would find the courage to ask me to be hers alone, but then, I determined to ask her meself." He lifted her chin and looked into her eyes. "Will ye truly be me wife, lass, and if the day comes when me bairns come to me again, will ye love them?"

Without hesitation she said, "Aye, Derick Davidson, I will be your wife, and I will love your children as my own, I promise."

The tender kiss that followed sealed their pledge of love, a love that would endure the hardships and brutalities of the American Revolution, a war that would forever liberate the American Patriots from British rule.

Derick raised himself from the dust and offered his hand to Kearan, lifting her with one strong arm. She brushed the dust from her skirts, and Derick placed his hands on her shoulders, turning her to face him.

"I will return for ye, lass, I promise. God has not brought me through this perilous journey to forsake me now. I have learned..." He paused, his voice growing husky, "that there are many ways to victory, and me sword is not always the answer, not always the way to conquer. When I return from this war, I will hang me sword over the mantel of our home."

"You will never fight again?" she queried.

"To be sure, lass, I will fight again—when I must, but I have a longing to use the Longhunter's sword, to be skillful in spiritual warfare. The wee Bible is waiting for the Longhunter's return and I must see that he comes home again. I never quite understood his words to me, but now I do. He traded one sword for another and it has served him well. Do ye remember?"

"Aye, me love," she said imitating his brogue, "I remember well. 'Tis written in the wee Bible. Your uncle traded his old claymore for a new and living sword. The wee Bible is the Longhunter's sword, and it shall be ours too. Aye, this is the warrior's blade, the Sword of the Wild Rose."

Epilogue

The cause for American independence smoldered in the thirteen American Colonies for many years prior to the actual conflict. From the time of the French and Indian wars to the various Intolerable acts of English Parliament, the Patriot cause was heating up for revolution. Along with such vocal Patriots as Patrick Henry and his "if this be treason" speech, the Stamp Act and the Quartering Act of 1765 stoked the fires for independence.

The Boston Massacre in 1770 and the Boston Tea Party in 1773 furthered the schism and was positive proof of a spreading rebellion among the Colonial people; a colorful kaleidoscope of cultures and people who loved freedom and dared to face death rather than submit to King George III of England.

The displaced Scot and Irish of whom I write were among those who rallied for freedom with an intense passion, the taste of generations of English oppression still bitter in their bellies. The German emigrants and native-born Americans were interspersed within this amazing combination of men who made up the first Continental army.

The Intolerable Acts of 1774 led to the first Continental Congress, and the American Colonies were armed for war by the next year. The printing of *Common Sense* in 1776 by Patriot, Thomas

Paine, challenged the authority of the British government to rule the Colonies through an overseas monarchy. The simple language in *Common Sense* spoke to the common people, and they rallied behind the cause for independence.

But what of Derick Davidson, Kearan, Daniel Morgan, and his riflemen? Did they survive the ravages of war and live to see the forming of a new nation—the United States of America?

True to his word, Derick Davidson searched for his uncle, Donald Davidson, the beloved Longhunter, and found him living among the Wyandot Indians, hunting and trapping with them. Before joining Morgan and his riflemen at the Battle of Saratoga in 1777, Derick and the Longhunter spent two years in the Ohio country.

After the war, the Longhunter returned to his cabin on Cedar Creek where he lived out his days hunting and trapping in relative peace. He often visited Derick's family in the Ohio country and lived to be a very old man, happy and full of years. Preferring the memory of his one love, Derick's mother, he never married, nor did he ever return to the land of mist and tears. His faith and courage left a lasting legacy in his new home—America.

Near the end of the American Revolution, Daniel Morgan was promoted to Brigadier General for his outstanding service during the war. His sharp shooting riflemen were noted for their courage, skill, and guerilla campaigns. They became legendary and were known as "Morgan's Rangers." It was said that Daniel Morgan was the best field commander of the American Revolution.

After the Battle of Saratoga, Morgan returned to Virginia and began building *Saratoga,* the home he named for the famous battle he helped to win. Equally famous was the Battle at Cowpens, January 17, 1781, in which Morgan's company overwhelmingly defeated their southern nemesis, Col. Banastre Tarleton. This strategic victory turned the tide of the southern campaign for the Patriots, altering the course of the war in the south, and leading to the eventual defeat of Cornwallis.

Daniel was so ill after the Battle at Cowpens, that he could barely sit a saddle. His faithful companion and friend, Derick Davidson, rode by his side, supporting the General as he lay in a wagon heading for Virginia. Derick accompanied him safely to his home and to Abigail. Morgan's year as a prisoner of war in a cold, damp prison cell during the Quebec campaign, had triggered a bout of rheumatism that plagued him for the rest of his life.

In his latter years, Morgan regained a measure of health, and in answer to Abigail's prayers and tender care, he converted to Christianity. He spoke of his faith with the same enthusiasm he had exhibited in his military campaigns and was quoted as saying, "No nation can exist without true religion. Where you have no faith in God, you are sure to have no government, for as religion disappears, anarchy takes place..."

His pastor, William Hill, witnessed the final days of the "old wagoner" and said Daniel Morgan faced death with the same courage he faced the enemy on the battlefield. He spoke these final words: "*I believe in one God, the first and great cause of goodness and in Jesus Christ, the rebirth of the world. I also believe in the Holy Ghost, the comforter. I further believe that all must be saved through the merits of Jesus Christ.*"

Daniel Morgan died in Winchester, VA in 1802 at age sixty-six.

After Cornwallis surrendered at Yorktown, October 19, 1781, Derick Davidson returned to Winchester to marry Kearan Mackenzie, the lass who won his heart. Derick moved his bride to the border regions on the eastern side of the Ohio River, now West Virginia, and raised a family of three stalwart sons and two beautiful daughters. Derick and Kearan's poignant and touching love story is still told over the bonfires at Wildrose to this day.

While participating in an Indian skirmish near the Ohio River just prior to the Treaty of Greenville, 1795, a young man from Scotland joined the bordermen in the fight. To Derick's overwhelming joy, he discovered the youth to be his youngest son, William, who left Scotland in search of his father in America. Their joyful reunion on the banks of the Ohio was an answer to Derick's prayers. His other children by Meagan remained in Scotland, living with their adopted parents, Duncan and Margaret, who maintained the Davidson legacy in Scotland.

After the Treaty of Greenville, signed nearly twenty years after the onset of the Revolutionary War, Derick and William Davidson struck out for the Ohio country and staked their claim in the beautiful Hocking River Valley. They named their new home "Wildrose." Here they built a permanent home for the Davidsons for generations to come, an ongoing legacy in a land abundant with wild game and rich fertile soil.

On the gently rolling hills of the Ohio countryside, the wild roses bloom in profusion, and above the mantel of the old stone fireplace at Wildrose, the *Sword of the Wild Rose* rests from its long and bloody warfare. It serves as a reminder of the struggles and victories of one particular family, the Davidsons, a family whose descendants recount the pathos and joys of their colorful heritage.

But where are the those Scottish Highlanders today? Where are their lands and their ancient clans? The glens are quiet, wreathed in misty silence. The mountain paths are overgrown with grass, and the villages lie in stony ruin. The warrior's cause is forgotten, but for those of his own blood who still hear the song of the pipes echoing in the glen, a mournful tune resonating from the shadows of their stormy past,

The mysterious war cry of the Highlander is heard no more, and his bonny bride waits in vain for his return. His battles are over and his deeds are done. The ancient tale is told in the land of mist and tears. Never again will he boast of his all-conquering arm over the enemy, nor will his heart leap at the cry of the curlew or the whistle of the arrow, for he sleeps in the shade of the glen, beneath the moss and the heather.

Thoughts on Liberty

"Statesmen may plan and speculate for liberty, but it is religion and morality alone, which can establish the principles upon which freedom can securely stand. The only foundation of a free Constitution is pure virtue, and if this cannot be inspired into our people in a greater measure than they have it now, they may change their rulers and the forms of government, but they will not obtain a lasting liberty." *John Adams*

"Neither the wisest constitution nor the wisest laws will secure the liberty and happiness of a people whose manners are universally corrupt. He therefore is the truest friend of the liberty of his country who tries most to promote its virtue, and who, so far as his power and influence extend, will not suffer a man to be chosen onto any office of power and trust who is not a wise and virtuous man." *Samuel Adams*

"Freedom exists only when a nation obeys the dictates of morality and right reason, that of the natural law and righteous judgment. When a government imposes policies contrary to the laws of nature and common sense, confusion and disorder dominate the society. Where wickedness rules, liberty ends." (paraphrased)

Remember...

By understanding our past, those events that have shaped our world, we can gain the knowledge and insight to change the future—sometimes to alter the course of history. *RCE*

"Cuimhnichibh air na daoine bho'n d'thainig sibh"
Remember the people from which you came....

Resources

1. John H. Rhodehamel, *The American Revolution: Writings from the War of Independence* - Library of America; 2nd Printing edition March 29, 2001
2. Don Higginbotham, *Daniel Morgan: Revolutionary Rifleman* - Chapel Hill 1961.
3. John Buchanan, *The Road to Guilford Court House: the American Revolution in the Carolinas.* New York 1997
4. James Graham, *The Life of General Daniel Morgan* - Kessinger Publishing 2007
5. Sons of Liberty Chapter of the SAR, Brief Biography, General Daniel Morgan
6. Livia Simpson-Poffenbarger, *Battle of Point Pleasant* - Mattox Printing 2003
7. Daniel Morgan Journals, Winchester VA Historical Society - Volume 14, 2002 (Floyd Flickinger, Peter G. Mowitt, Don Higginbotham, Adrian O'Connor, Elizabeth C. Engle, Mary Thomason Morris, Robert A. Wolf)
8. John J. Gallagher, *The Battle of Brooklyn 1776* Da Capo Press 1995
9. John F. Ross, *War on the Run: The Epic Story of Robert Rogers and the Conquest of America's First Frontier* - Bantam; First Edition, May 19, 2009
10. Lawrence E. Babits, *A Devil of a Whipping: The Battle of Cowpens* - University of North Carolina Press, 2000
11. Samuel B. Griffith, *The War for American Independence* - University of Illinois Press 2002
12. Jeff Shaara, *The Glorious Cause* - Fawcett 2003

13. Memoirs of Robert Kirk, (Kirkwood) edited by Ian M. McCulloch and Timothy J. Tobish - Purple Mountain Press 2004
14. Collin F. Taylor, *Native American Weapons* - University of OK press 2001
15. Eric Richards, *The Highland Clearances* - Birlinn 2008
16. Arnoldo Mondadori, *The Life and Times of Washington* – Curtis Publishing 1967
17. R.E. Evans, *The American War of Independence* – Lerner Publication Company by permission of Cambridge University Press 1977
18. George C. Neumann and Frank J. Kravic, *Encyclopedia of the American Revolution* – Scurlock Publishing 1975
19. David C. King, *Saratoga* – 21 Century Books, Millbrook Press 1998
20. Robert G. Athearn, *Colonial America Volume 2* – Choice Publishing 1988
21. Readers Digest, *America's Fascinating Indian Heritage* 1978
22. Gregory Evans Dowd, *War Under Heaven: Pontiac, the Indian Nations, and the British Empire* Johns Hopkins University Press - Jan 27, 2004
23. Julian Alvin Carroll Chandler, Travis Butler Thames, *Colonial Virginia*
24. Sandra Pobst, *Voices from Colonial America* Nov 8, 2005
25. Dr. James A. Hanson, *The Longhunter's Sketchbook* – Fur Press 1985
26. Richard Middleton, *Colonial America: A History, 1565 - 1776* - Wiley-Blackwell; 3 edition September 2, 1991
27. David F. Hawke, *Everyday Life in Early America* - Harper Paperbacks January 25, 1989

28. Allan W. Eckert, *The Frontiersman* - Jesse Stuart Foundation, May 1, 2001
29. Carolyn D. Wallin, *Elisha Wallen the Longhunter* - Overmountain Press January 1, 1990
30. Ruth Carmichael Ellinger, *Liberty* - poem ©2009 Ruth Ellinger, all rights reserved

Endorsements for Sword of the Wild Rose

In her latest novel, Sword of the Wild Rose, Ruth Carmichael Ellinger not only tells an endearing story, but also accurately portrays the character and spirit of Daniel Morgan, a real life revolutionary war general who has not always been adequately recognized for his role in America's War of Independence. The folksy powerfully built Morgan, however, is well known in New York State where his rifle corps contributed significantly to the American victory at Saratoga, and where the defeated British General Burgoyne claimed Morgan's regiment to be the finest in the world; in New Jersey where he allegedly was born and also fought; in South Carolina where his brilliant leadership and strategy led to a critical victory at the Cowpens which stopped the British advance in the South; and, finally, in the Winchester/Frederick County area of Virginia where he lived and always returned after his military exploits and where his body lies today in Mount Hebron Cemetery.

—GEORGE R. SCHEMBER is President of the Winchester Frederick County Historical Society and holds an MA in history from the University of Tennessee. He lives with his wife, Jeanne, in the Daniel Morgan House in Winchester where the General died on July 6, 1802.

When you open the pages of Sword of the Wild Rose, be ready for a tale that tugs at your heartstrings and keeps you on the edge of your seat. In a story as fresh and relevant as today's headlines, Ellinger explores the meaning of liberty, courage, honor, and patriotism while weaving a mosaic of history that is colorful, complex, and constantly riveting. With an amazing attention to detail, Ellinger creates a fascinating array of characters who are compelling, passionate, richly crafted and as memorable as your first love.

—CAROLE GIFT PAGE, award-winning author of 48 books including, *Becoming a Woman of Passion* (Fleming Revell) *The House on Honeysuckle Lane* (Thomas Nelson) and *Hawaiian Dreams* (Barbour, Oct. 2010)

Cover Art for Sword of the Wild Rose by Debra Bryant

Debra Bryant is a native of Kentucky, currently residing in Plant City, Florida. Oils are her preferred medium, but she also works with acrylics, pastel, colored pencil, watercolor, and charcoal. Extensive master classes from nationally known portrait artist, Frank Covino, have been the driving influence of her work

I paint because I love the creative process – the road to discovery from inspiration through signature. As frustrating as the process can sometimes be, it is far outweighed by the achievement of a satisfying painting. In my current work, I am always exploring color, challenging pre-conceived notions, and attempting to put a piece of "me" in every painting. Realistic rendering sometimes suits my purpose, but I also love the freedom that a more impressionistic approach gives.

You can find my artwork at: *http://debrabryant.blogspot.com*

About the Author

Award-winning author, RUTH CARMICHAEL ELLINGER, was born and raised in the beautiful Ohio Valley, setting for the Wildrose inspirational series. Ellinger is a member of the Daughters of the American Revolution, Fairfield County OH, Clan Davidson, and Clan Carmichael, USA. The author lives in FL with her husband, a pastor. They have four grown children.

Ruth can be reached via her website:
www.ruthellinger.com